Bullet of Revenge

by

Herbert Grosshans

Published by
Melange Books, LLC
White Bear Lake, MN 55110
www.melange-books.com

Bullet of Revenge, Copyright © 2012-2016 by Herbert Grosshans

ISBN: 978-1-61235-424-8

Cover Art by: Caroline Andrus

Chapter One

Frank Hummer watched the couple coming through the doors into the shopping mall. The man was middle-aged, a little heavier around the middle than he should have been; the woman about ten years younger in appearance, nice figure, her auburn hair falling in gentle waves down to her shoulders, her eyes rimmed with dark eyeliner. She appeared elegant and brimming with confidence. They stopped in front of a shoe store and walked inside. The man came back out a few minutes later and headed for one of the benches in the mall, looking bored. His eyes met Hummer's for a quick moment. He nodded, lifted his hands with a shrug of his shoulders and said, "Women! They can never make up their mind." Then he sat down, crossing his legs, obviously getting ready for a long wait.

Hummer smiled as he sipped his coffee. He wasn't married, but he knew men hated going shopping with their wives at the best of times, and looking for shoes could not classify as one of the most exciting shopping trips.

His attention was brought again to the wide doors when he saw a couple of burly men in white suits and a woman, also in a white uniform, come into the mall. They looked around for a moment then headed straight for the man on the bench.

He looked up as the trio approached him. Hummer wasn't particularly interested in what he saw, but something in the two burly men's behavior kept him watching.

"Can I help you?" the man on the bench asked.

One of the two men in white suits smiled. "Hello, Harry. It's time to go home."

"What?" the man asked, obviously taken by surprise.

"Don't make a fuss, Harry. Let's go!" Both of the white-suited men grabbed the man and pulled him up.

The man struggled in their grip and called out, "Let go of me, you morons. What do you think you're doing?"

"Now, now, Harry," said the woman. "Be a good boy and come without causing a disturbance. You wouldn't want me to stick a needle into you, would you? I know how you hate needles."

"What the hell are you talking about? You must have me confused with someone else. Let go of my arms!"

"Harry, Harry. The same thing happened the last time when you walked away. You remember the last time?" The woman's voice sounded patronizing.

"There was no such thing as the last time," the man shouted. He squirmed and looked about for help. "Somebody call the police. These people are molesting me."

"Shut up!" one of the two orderlies snapped. "We'll have to subdue you if you don't behave and it won't be pleasant."

Hummer noticed a few people stopping and turning heads, but most people seemed to be more annoyed about the commotion than concerned about what was actually happening.

Looks like some lunatic escaped again. He appears quite normal, but appearances can be deceiving. I wonder who that woman is. Maybe they weren't even together. He may have just assumed in his crazy mind she was his wife.

The two men in white dragged the struggling and shouting man toward the doors. They almost reached the doors when the auburn-haired woman came out of the shoe store. She obviously saw the four people but didn't pay any attention, only when the man shouted, "Let go of me!" she stopped walking and turned around.

Then she screamed, "Harry, what's going on?"

"Call the police, Helen!" the man yelled, struggling to get free from the men who held him.

The woman in the white uniform walked up to the auburn-haired

2

woman and said, "I don't know who you are or what your connection to that man is, but take my advice and don't get involved or you'll be sorry." She poked her finger into the woman's chest and then rushed after the three men as they disappeared through the doors.

The auburn-haired woman followed them, struggled with the doors to get outside.

Hummer's interest was aroused and he got up to see where they were taking the man named Harry. When he arrived at the doors, he saw the two burly men pushing Harry into a white van. It looked like a rescue wagon. It had *Happy Acres Sanatorium* written on the back doors.

As I suspected. An escaped lunatic.

He watched the van pull away. The woman the man had called Helen ran after it but gave up the chase when the vehicle left the parking lot and disappeared into the traffic. She stood among the parked cars, her arms hanging on her sides. Then she turned around and headed back toward the mall, stumbling like a drunk. She appeared scared and shaken. When she walked through the door, Hummer could hear her sobbing. He shrugged and went back to his cup of coffee.

Looking around the mall like a lost child, the woman seemed to notice Hummer watching her and rushed up to him. "Do you have a cell phone?" she asked between loud sobs.

"Yes, I do," he said. "Can you tell me what happened?"

"Please, please, phone the police for me. My husband has been abducted."

"That was your husband?"

She nodded, tears streaking her cheeks dark with mascara. "Did you see what happened?"

"Yes, I did. Do you know who those men were?"

"I don't know." She sounded hysterical.

"They were dressed as orderlies from a Sanatorium. They said they were taking him, your husband, back home. Is your husband by any chance a patient in the *Happy Acres Sanatorium*?"

"Of course not. I've never heard of that place. My husband is a professor doing research for *Globe Labs Institute*. He is as sane as anybody and has no reason to even visit a Sanatorium."

"They called him *Harry*."

3

"That's his name. Harry Middler. I'm Helen Middler, his wife." She sobbed again. "Please, call the police."

Hummer reached for his cell phone, hesitating. "You know, it may not be a smart idea to involve the police, not yet anyway. Kidnappers usually call within hours demanding some kind of ransom. They always stress not to get the police involved. I would suggest you wait at least twenty-four hours before going to the police."

She sank into the chair across from him. "How do you know so much about what kidnappers do?" Suddenly she seemed wary.

"Because it is not the first time I've dealt with this kind of problem." He took out his wallet and removed a card, handing it to her. "My name is Frank Hummer. I'm an investigator."

"A detective?"

He nodded. "A private detective."

"I don't have money to hire an investigator. In fact, I have no idea why anyone would want to kidnap my husband for money. We are not rich. We're just a regular couple with a house and a mortgage."

Hummer gave her a reassuring smile. "Don't worry about money, Mrs. Middler. I'm not in this for the money."

"Then why would you help me?"

He shrugged. "Out of curiosity."

She shook her head, not quite sure what to do. She eyed him with suspicion. "Nobody does anything without getting something for it. What are you hoping to get out of this?"

"The satisfaction that I've helped someone in distress. I do this out of boredom, Mrs. Middler. Call it my hobby. You see, I have all the money I'll ever need…and more."

"Let's say I'll ask you to help me, what guarantee do I have you won't give up because you'll get bored with the case? I mean, without asking for money you don't really have an incentive to finish it."

"It's not only boredom motivating me. I have a strong sense of justice and I hate criminals. Once I'm on a trail, I'm like a bloodhound. I never give up until I've brought the guilty to justice."

"Then, please, help me."

Hummer was about to ask her for more information, but before he got the chance a man approached their table and said, "Hey, Rose, I'm glad I caught up with you."

The woman gave him an astonished look. "Pardon me? You must have me confused with someone else. My name isn't Rose."

The man laughed. "Come on, *Hot Thighs*, I'd recognize you and your red hair anywhere. And I'll never forget the night we spent a couple of weeks ago. You certainly delivered, babe." He made cooling motions with his hand. "Wow, you were hot and worth the couple hundred I paid you."

"What are you talking about? I've never seen you before in my life. And one more time…my name is not Rose." She fairly screamed the last few words.

The man lifted his hands as if defending himself and chuckled. "Whoa. That temper of yours. It got you into trouble before. By the way, here is your handbag." He handed her a leather bag.

The woman ripped it from his hands. "Where the hell did you get my handbag from?"

"You forgot it in that shoe store." The man looked at Hummer, as if noticing him for the first time. "You'd better watch her. Don't believe everything she tells you." He grinned. "And hang on to your wallet, buddy. She's a good fuck, though. Earns every penny you spend on her." Tipping his baseball cap, he turned and walked toward the exit.

Hummer watched him until he disappeared through the door, not quite sure what to think. A loud sob made him look at the woman sitting across from him. Her cheeks were streaked dark and her eyes red from crying. Suddenly she didn't look so elegant and classy anymore. "What actually is your name?" he asked.

"My name is Helen Middler, as I told you."

"That man called you Rose. He had your handbag. How did he know it was yours?"

"I don't know." She opened her bag and took out a wallet. "I'll show you my driver's license to prove that I really am who I say." She removed her license and stared at it. Then she pulled more stuff out of her wallet, most of them credit cards by the looks of it, getting more frantic with every card she pulled out. Her eyes were large and frightened when she looked at him. "My name is Helen not Rose," she whispered. "I've never seen that man before." A loud sob escaped her lips. "I am not a whore, Mr. Hummer. I'm a respectable married woman. You must believe me."

"We can clear that up easily," Hummer said. "Just let me see your license."

"This is not my wallet," she said, her voice cracking with emotion.

"Whose purse is it?" Hummer asked gently.

"The handbag is mine but not the wallet." She shoved the wallet and the removed cards across the table with trembling hands. He picked up one of them, and then a couple more. Shaking his head, he said, "I don't know what to believe. According to this your name is Rose Miller. You live at four-sixty-four Cumberland Street. That picture of yours on your driver's license does you justice. There is no mistaking it…it is you."

"No, it isn't. I am not that woman. Maybe this Rose looks like me but I am not her. I don't live at four-sixty-four Cumberland Street." She put her hands over her face. "This is a nightmare. This can't be happening."

"Do you have a cell phone?" he asked.

She nodded. Reaching into her handbag, she removed a phone.

"What's your number?"

She gave it to him and he dialed it. Her phone rang. Unsure what to do, she looked at him. "Answer it," he told her.

When she did, he said, "Okay, now I'm going to call that number again, but this time let your answering service pick it up."

The phone rang like before. After a few rings, a woman's voice said, "Hi, you've reached Rose Miller. I can't come to the phone. Please, leave a message and I'll call you back as soon as I'm free." The voice sounded sexy and throaty, but he recognized the voice as that of the woman sitting across from him.

He handed her his phone and said, "Please, call your cell number and listen to the voice."

After she finished listening, she slumped in her seat. Her eyes looked distressed and frightened, and when she spoke, it came out in a trembling, emotionless voice. "I am Helen Middler. I am thirty-five years old and I am married to Professor Harry Middler. We've been married for five years. We have no children. We live at thirty-seven Pineridge Cove. We've lived there for three years. My husband works for *Globe Labs Institute.* He's been with them for three years...ever since we moved here. I am a student at the *Henry Hopkins University* where I am taking a course in biology."

She seemed to regain her composure and her eyes lost that look of helplessness. "Are you willing to take on my case, Mr. Hummer?"

Hummer nodded thoughtfully. "Now more so than ever. I have nothing to lose but a few hours of my time."

"Good." She rose from her seat. "We can drive to my house and I'll prove to you I am Helen Middler. I'll show you our wedding album, pictures from holidays and other memorabilia we've collected. We can also drive to the University and confirm my identity."

"All right." Hummer shoved the credit cards back into the wallet. "For the time being we'll hang onto this until we find the rightful owner." He looked at his cup of coffee, still half full, but he knew the coffee was cold now. Shrugging, he got up.

"We can take my car if you like," the woman said, as she walked beside him. "I'll drive you back later to pick up yours. My place isn't far from here."

"Sure. I'm okay with that." He wondered fleetingly why she said *my place* instead of *our house* but shelved it away for future pondering, should it become necessary.

"My car is over in the next row," she said, squeezing between two parked cars to get to the other side. "I don't know why they make these parking spots so small," she complained. "I hope nobody parked too close to my car. I bought it only a month ago."

He didn't comment, just watched her as she walked in front of him. She walked easily in her high heels, and he admired the shape of her legs and her slim figure and the way her hips swung.

I'm not a whore, Mr. Hummer.

Her words rang inside his head and he put any thoughts of connecting her even remotely with the kind of woman the man had hinted at out of his mind.

Until I know different, she is Mrs. Helen Middler, a married, decent woman.

She stopped suddenly and looked around.

"What is it?" he asked.

"I could have sworn we parked the car here," she said, her voice near hysteria again. "In fact, this is the spot. I recognize the license plate of the car next to it, because Harry commented on the odd combination of numbers and letters." She smiled faintly. "He notices those things." She stared at the car parked in the spot she indicated. "This is not my car."

"Perhaps they towed it," Hummer suggested. "Why don't we use my car, drive to your house and take it from there, okay?"

Her lips trembled when she looked at him. "Okay."

She leaned against him as they began walking. "Do you mind if I hold on to your arm?" she asked. "My legs are suddenly all wobbly and weak."

"Go ahead. My car is not far."

She clung to him, stumbling beside him. When he opened the car door for her, she literally fell into the seat.

"You said thirty-seven Pineridge Cove, didn't you?" He started the motor and pulled out of the parking spot.

"Just drive north on fifty-seven and make a right turn on Birch until you get to Pineridge." She sat beside him, slumped over, her breath coming in little gasps. Had it not been for the seatbelt she might have hit her head on the dashboard.

"You look pale," he said. "Will you be all right?"

She let out a small, hysterical laugh. "I don't know if I'll ever be all right again. I'm beginning to think I'm going crazy. This can't be happening to me."

"We'll sort everything out," he said soothingly, a bit worried about her state of mind. They needed to get to her home fast. It was important for her to get into familiar surroundings.

It took only about twenty minutes to get to Pineridge Cove. Most of the houses were two-story homes. Number thirty-seven was no exception. He drove up the wide driveway and parked his car alongside the one already standing there.

"Is that your car?" he asked.

She shook her head. "No. I've never seen it before. I have no idea who would be parking on our driveway."

He helped her out of the car and walked with her up the step to the front door. It looked impressive, with sidelights and a fancy handle. The woman took a key from her handbag and tried to put it into the lock with a shaky hand.

"Problems?" Hummer asked when she failed to push it into the slot.

"It doesn't work," she whispered.

"Let me try," he offered. Taking the key from her shaking fingers, he tried it but the key didn't fit. "Do you have another key?" he asked.

"We only have two. Harry has the other one."

"Are you sure this is the right house?"

Her shrill laugh sounded like that of a woman gone mad. "I think I know my own house, my own door, my own handle. We just installed it a couple of weeks ago. It took us most of the winter to find one we both liked. This is my house!" she almost screamed the last words.

Hummer heard the sound of footsteps coming toward the door from inside the house. He watched as the door opened and a blonde woman stuck out her head. "What is going on out here? Can I help you?" she asked, sounding annoyed. "If you're some kind of religion-pushers, we're not interested."

Before Hummer could say something, the woman beside him shouted, "What are you doing in my house?" and pushed open the door, elbowing the blonde woman out of the way.

"Harry…" the blonde woman screamed. "Call the cops. We're being robbed!"

"Hang on there, lady," Hummer said soothingly. "Nobody is robbing you."

"Help, somebody help!" the woman screamed again. "Harry!"

"What the hell is going on here?" a man's voice shouted. Hummer saw a man rushing down the stairs, taking two steps at a time. He was big, wearing a business suit that seemed ready to bust in the seams.

"You tell *me* what is going on!" shouted the auburn-haired woman. "Why are you in my house?"

The man stopped at the bottom of the stairs. "Your house?" His head swung around to face Hummer. "Who are you people and what kind of nonsense is this?"

Hummer lifted both hands. "I apologize for this intrusion. My name is Frank Hummer. I'm a private investigator and this woman is Mrs.

Helen Middler. She is my client. I'm just trying to establish some facts here. She claims she lives in this house."

"Come again?"

"This is my house!" the auburn-haired woman sobbed.

With a shake of his head, the man said quite calmly, "You are wrong, lady. This is our house. We've lived here for three years." His face looked disgusted. "If this is some kind of ruse to blackmail us, you've picked the wrong couple."

"This is my furniture. That coffee table was a present from Harry's uncle Harold Middler. What have you done with my pictures?" She pointed a shaky finger at a picture hanging above the chesterfield. "We had a picture of my family on that wall."

"You are nuts, lady," the blonde woman said. She had calmed down as soon as the man arrived. "What did you say your name was?"

"Helen Middler."

The blonde woman laughed shrilly. "Is this some kind of a joke? *I* am Helen Middler. And this is my husband Harry Middler."

"You are lying!" the auburn-haired woman screamed. Her eyes searched for Hummer. "They are lying. I am Helen Middler not she, and he isn't Harry. What is happening?" She stumbled to a bench near the wall and practically collapsed onto it. "They are lying," she repeated, her body raked by loud sobs.

Hummer looked from her to the man who claimed to be Harry Middler. "We have a problem here. If you don't mind, I'd like to see some identification from you. As I said, I'm an investigator and I'm looking for facts."

"How about *you* showing us some I.D.," the man challenged him. "How do we know you are who you claim to be?"

Hummer reached for his wallet and pulled out his calling card. "Here you are, sir. This is my company name." He smiled as he handed the card to the man. "I know my motto seems a little tacky."

The man took the card and read it out loud for his wife's benefit. "Hummer Investigations. To nail down the facts you need a Hammer." He gave the card back. "You're right, it is tacky. You should change your name to *Hammer*, it would make more sense."

"I know but I like it the way it is. It breaks the ice between me and

10

my prospective client. You keep the card in case you ever need a good investigator."

"I doubt that but I'll keep it anyway." The man put the card into his pocket and pulled out his own wallet. Taking out his driver's license, he held it so Hummer could read it.

"Harry Middler," Hummer read. He looked at the picture. "Yes, that is you."

"Look at the address."

"It says thirty-seven Pineridge Cove. I guess that confirms you are the people living in this house."

"I'm not showing you any identification," the blonde woman said stubbornly.

"There is no need, Mrs. Middler. I believe I have enough information." Hummer looked at the man. "One more question, Mr. Middler. Can you tell me what you do for a living?"

"It's Professor Middler. I work for GLI, which stands for Globe Labs Institute. Satisfied?"

"I am." Hummer walked over to the auburn-haired woman sitting on the bench and touched her gently on the shoulder. "We'd better leave."

"This is my house," she sobbed. Her eyes showed fear and confusion when she looked up at him. "I'm not crazy. This is my house."

He pulled her up and put his arm around her waist. "Come," he said, gently.

Chapter Two

After pulling out of the driveway, Hummer stopped his car and parked it. Glancing at the woman slumped in the seat beside him, looking scared but also angry, he said, "I have to admit, I'm a bit at a loss here. That couple looked legit to me. They claim they've lived in that house for three years and I have no reason to doubt them. There is one more way we can make sure they are telling the truth, or possibly not, we can talk to the neighbors. They can verify their claim or yours."

"It won't help. Both neighbors to the left and right of us are new. We haven't even met them yet. Mrs. Kelvin across the street is over eighty and quite paranoid. She doesn't trust anyone. And the other neighbors..." She shrugged. "Well, you know how it is. People don't talk to each other in the big cities."

"Hmm." Hummer rubbed his chin. "What are the chances? New neighbors and an old lady who doesn't care about anyone. It is strange in a way. Such coincidences."

She sat there, chewing on her lip. "You don't believe me, do you? By now you probably think I'm some kind of nutcase, especially since they took Harry to a sanatorium. By all appearances he is crazy which means there is a good chance I'm also crazy."

"I'm assuming nothing until I have more facts. We haven't exhausted all our options yet. I suggest we drive to the address of this Rose Miller and see what we can find." It wasn't the only option, but checking out the address was the most logical one. So far, things didn't appear to be in this woman's favor, but he had learned a long time ago, never to jump to any conclusions too early in the game. And to be sure, this was just another game, a puzzle that needed to be solved. He had to admit it to himself he was already hooked. His interest had been aroused and he would put the pieces of the puzzle together, not just for the woman's sake but also for his own.

"I agree." She seemed to regain her composure. "I was afraid you might just decide to dump me right here."

"I would never do that, Missis…" he paused, regarding her with a cocked eyebrow. "What should I call you?"

"By my name…Middler." A tiny smile crossed her frayed lips. "I'm Helen. Call me Helen."

"Okay, Helen. As I told you before, once I'm on a case I don't give up until I've solved it. And your case certainly needs solving."

He started his car again and moved away from the curb and into traffic. Heading south on fifty-seven, he took the exit onto fifty-nine and headed east. Cumberland Street was in Old Harbor, not the best part of the city. He was quite familiar with that area and avoided driving there if he could help it. A new, shiny car parked on any of the streets in Old Harbor may end up with a few scratches in its shiny surface, or if not a broken window, for sure with a broken headlamp. Even the cops didn't like leaving their cars unattended. Too many young punks tried to demonstrate to their compatriots they were tough and not afraid of the law.

It was nearly an hour's drive. Hummer put a CD into the player and let the smooth sounds of Henry Sassmund's saxophone calm his mind. He almost never listened to the radio, not caring for what the young people called music these days, and not finding enjoyment in having his eardrums blasted by steel guitars and guys singing in high, flat girlish-sounding voices.

"You like classical music?" he asked the woman beside him. "Or should I turn it off?"

"No, don't turn it off. I don't mind this kind of music, even though I prefer jazz." She smiled sorrowfully. "Harry loves to play the saxophone in his spare time. He's a real jazz fan."

"Perhaps when this is all over you can invite me to your home and he can play for me," Hummer said, wondering if it would be at thirty-seven Pineridge Cove. He had his doubts.

The buildings they passed seemed to change in shape and appearance. It was easy to see this was an old area of the city, suffering from neglect and possibly indifference. Most of the apartment buildings needed a new coat of stucco or paint. Bricks looked weathered and the paint had peeled off window and door frames.

The cars parked on the streets were old and rusty and the people on the boulevard either walked hurriedly if they were alone or stood around in small groups. Most of the groups were youths, displaying tattoos on their bare arms and necks, dressed in sloppy clothes, their jeans ripped, and their sneakers or boots untied. It seemed they wanted to make a statement, proclaiming they didn't care about their appearance and were proud to live in this kind of environment.

Just before Hummer turned into Cumberland Street, he observed three youths beating up another one, while a couple of girls stood watching and cheering. He was tempted to stop and get out, but decided it wasn't his business. This was the way of life in Old Harbor. Twenty-three years had passed since he had to prove every day he was as tough as the rest of the gang he belonged to, and it would still be the way of life in another twenty-three years. Unless some huge developer decided to put the wrecking ball to every building in the neighborhood and establish another industrial area or a housing project only the wealthy could afford.

The people living here would be forced to move into another part of the city where they would create the same conditions they left behind. Every city had its slum areas because there would always be the kind of people who didn't have the ambition, the desire, or the means to make a better life for themselves or their children. It didn't matter how hard city officials and governments tried, they couldn't stamp out poverty or cure all of the sick people who were dependent on Welfare. Neither could they get rid of the criminals, drunks, drug addicts, traffickers, pimps, and prostitutes. There were not enough cops to take them off the streets and not enough jails to hold them all.

He watched a young man getting out of an old but clean-looking car and climb a set of worn steps to a weathered door leading into one of the buildings. Before he disappeared through the door, Hummer didn't fail to notice his manner of dress, a plain but spotless suit, a tie and shiny shoes.

There are still some people living here who want to get out of this environment, even though the odds are against them. There will also always be those. Some will be lucky, the way my family was.

He remembered the day when his parents told him and his brothers they were moving into another part of the city, a better part, a place where they would have a future. He was fifteen at the time, his brothers Derek and Robert thirteen and ten. It was the right time to move, for them and for his parents.

The building with the faded numbers four-sixty-four above the entrance door was exactly what Hummer had expected, old and rundown.

Helen walked beside him like a woman either drunk or on drugs. Her eyes were empty and her expression almost uninterested. "What of kind of place is this?" she asked with an emotionless voice.

"It looks like a rooming house," Hummer said, holding the door open for her.

They stepped into a narrow entrance hall. On one side was a mailbox with nametags above the slots. He went through the names until he found what he was looking for.

"You live in room thirty-four on the third floor," he told her.

"No, I don't. I've never been here before," she said.

"Sorry, I should have said *Rose Miller lives in room thirty-four.*"

There was no elevator and they had to take the stairs to the third floor. The old wooden steps creaked and Hummer worried they might break under his weight.

"It stinks in here," Helen complained. "I could never live in a place like this."

He didn't comment, but was inclined to believe her. She didn't look like the kind of woman who would take up residence in a rundown building that should have been torn down ages ago.

Unless you have no choice. The thoughts came unbidden. There was always doubt. Another lesson learned a long time ago. Never assume anything without having at least some facts.

As they walked across the dirty floor of the dimly lit corridor, a door suddenly opened and a woman with bright, pink hair in red high-heels, wearing a short skirt and a revealing, tight sweater, stepped out. When she saw Hummer and Helen, she stopped and smiled at Helen. "Hi Rose," she said. "Rough night? You look tired." With a look at Hummer she made a small chuckle. "Don't wear her out. She needs a rest. Poor girl. Her probation officer is giving her a hard time."

Helen stared at her. "Who the hell are you?"

The woman laughed and shook her head. "Are you stoned again, Rose? I thought you wanted to get clean. I'm Raquel, your neighbor. I live in room thirty-two, remember?"

"I've never seen you before today and you've never seen me either. I'm not Rose. My name is Helen. Who put you up to this?" Helen almost screamed the last words.

The woman lifted her hands in a defensive gesture. "No need to bite off my head, Sweetheart. I don't know what you've been sniffing or shooting up, but take it easy. Maybe you should forget about your john for tonight and sleep it off. You're pushing too hard, Rose. Can't make a million in a week." Shaking her head, she stalked toward the stairs, her high heels clacking on the cement floor like the rhythmic sounds of an angry woodpecker attacking a tree.

Helen stared after her. "My name is not Rose," she screamed.

Hummer put his arm around her shoulder. "Come on, Helen, calm down. We'll sort this out, okay? Let's find your keys and see if they fit the door lock of room thirty-four."

She leaned against him and sobbed loudly. "My name is not Rose," she repeated again. Pulling a handkerchief from her purse, she wiped her eyes dry and blew her nose. Then she took out her keychain and handed it to Hummer. "You try it. My hands are too shaky."

He picked a key that looked like it would fit. When he pushed it into the slot it slid smoothly into the lock, like it had been oiled only recently. Turning the key, he heard the soft click and then he pulled open the door.

"It fit." He made the obvious statement. He had secretly been hoping it wouldn't.

Helen followed him silently into the room. It was not large. The furnishings looked shabby and neglected. A bed, unmade, the covers crumpled and filthy looking. On one side was a counter with a hotplate on it. The sink was filled with unwashed dishes. He also saw a small

16

fridge and an old, scratched-up wooden table with two plastic chairs.

The door to the closet stood open, revealing a woman's clothing. The floor was littered with underwear, stockings, bras, and other wrinkled garments.

The pictures decorating the walls were prints cut out of calendars.

His hand went up to hold his nose when he inhaled the overpowering scent of cheap air-fresheners glued against a wall in a feeble attempt to mask the stench of human sweat and stale cooking odors. Looking at the torn curtains covering the window, he registered the cracked and filthy glass. He doubted the window had ever been open to let in some fresh air.

"This is a pig's sty," Helen gasped beside him. "How can any descent woman live in a dump like this?" She seemed genuinely shocked.

"That is a valid question." Hummer looked around and mentally photographed the room and its contents, trying to digest what he saw. Then he took his cell phone and took some photos. He would load them into his computer and study them at home. He did find it difficult to connect the room with the immaculately dressed woman beside him. She did not fit into this picture.

In his mind he recalled the woman with the pink hair who claimed to live in the room next to this one. Sure, she had been dressed in a flashy and cheap outfit, but she had not impressed him as someone who lived in an environment like the one he saw here. He would have liked to have a peek into her room.

An object lying on the table caught his attention. It looked like a photo album. When he picked it up and opened it, he stared at the first picture. It showed a man and a woman sitting on a couch. The woman in the picture was without a doubt Helen, a little younger, her hair hanging down to her shoulders, but still the same lovely, auburn color.

He heard a gasp beside him and realized she had followed him to the table. "That is a picture of me from years ago, but I don't recognize the man beside me."

Hummer flicked through the pages. All were filled with pictures showing Helen in various surroundings. There were some with her at parties in the company of different men. There was even one of her as a little girl. On an impulse, he pulled the first picture from its pocket and turned it around. Something was written on the back of the picture.

"What does it say?" Helen asked.

"To my sister Rose to remember better days. Your big brother Henry."

"I don't have a brother named Henry." Her words came out haltingly, sounding almost forced. "Besides, all of these pictures are fakes. I was never in these places and I don't know any of these men."

Hummer noticed some of the pictures had other pictures behind them. When he pulled one out, Helen let out a little shriek. He couldn't blame her. The picture showed her sitting naked on a chair, her legs apart, leaving nothing to the imagination. She ripped it out of his hand and stared at it. "That is not me," she sobbed. "I would never let anyone take pictures like this of me. Never! You must believe me, Mr. Hummer."

Her face was flushed, her makeup in ruins, her cheeks streaked dark from tears. She looked like a zombie raised from the dead, a tormented soul, and he felt sorry for her. Pulling her against him, he held her, stroking her back.

"I believe you," he said softly.

And he did. Something didn't add up. Everything seemed just too tidy, too deliberate. The woman Raquel coming out of room thirty-two at the exact time he and Helen walked down the corridor, the photo album so conveniently on the table with all those revealing and implicating pictures…

"This is not my place," she said, looking up at him. "I don't know what to do. My husband has been abducted. Strangers are living in my house. I'm a woman without a home, with nowhere to go. Even my name has been stolen."

He was about to reply, when he heard someone coming into the room. Turning, he saw a woman, accompanied by two men in uniforms, standing in the doorway.

"We are looking for Rose Miller," the woman said.

"There is nobody here by that name," Hummer told her.

"This is room thirty-four, isn't it?"

"It is, but there is no Rose Miller here."

The woman gave him a sharp look. "Who are you?"

"I'm Frank Hummer. May I inquire who you are?"

"I'm Sarah Dalton. I'm Miss Miller's Probation Officer."

"Then you know Rose Miller?" Hummer had a sudden hope he might finally get some answers.

When Dalton shook her head, he knew his hopes were dashed. "I've never seen her. I got her file only today." She cleared her throat. Her gaze took in Helen. "Do you have a name?"

Helen looked at Hummer before she answered. "Helen Middler. Yes, that's my name."

"I'm curious. What are you two doing in Miss Miller's apartment?"

"I'm a private detective," Hummer said, removing his I.D. from his wallet and holding it up. "Hummer Investigations."

"What is your business with Miss Miller?"

"I can't tell you. It's confidential."

Dalton gave Helen a sharp look. "Are you sure you are not Rose Miller?"

"Quite sure." Her tone was defiant. "My name is Helen Middler. I've never been in this apartment before."

"Do you have any I.D. to prove you are who you say?"

"No, I don't. My handbag with my wallet was stolen." She sounded flustered and upset, giving Dalton a valid reason to become skeptical.

"You are carrying a handbag over your shoulder. Is that not yours?" Dalton was suddenly suspicious. She opened the folder she carried in one hand and leafed through it. Her face was somber when she looked up. "Your resemblance to the picture of Rose Miller in my file is remarkable. If you can't prove your identity I have to assume you are Miss Miller."

Helen let out a sound of despair and lifted her arms and hands into the air to signify her anguish. "I told you, my wallet with all of my I.D.'s was stolen."

Dalton gave one of the officers waiting behind her an order. "Go and check her bag."

The officer walked into the room. Standing in front of Helen, he held out his hand. "Your handbag, please, ma'am."

Helen gave it to him. "Whatever you find in it is not mine. It has been put there by someone else," she said with a low voice.

The officer didn't comment. He walked back to Dalton and handed her the handbag. Dalton opened it and rummaged through it. "It seems you lied about the wallet," she murmured. Pulling out the wallet and then the driver's license, she studied it silently. Looking up, she said, "I have orders to take you into custody, Miss Miller, for violation of your probation. Please, do not resist." She gave the two officers a sign.

Without saying a word, they walked up to Helen and grabbed her arms.

"Hold it one minute," Hummer protested. "You can't just arrest this woman without making certain she is who you believe she is."

"Since she can't provide me with proof she is this other woman, I have to assume she is Rose Miller. The driver's license she carries identifies her as Miss Miller. The picture in my files confirms it. Unless she can prove otherwise, she is Rose Miller and therefore will be taken into custody. I have my orders." Dalton spoke calmly, her gray eyes cool and steadfast as she spoke.

"Who gave you these orders?" Hummer asked.

"That is classified information, sir."

"That may be so, but I will find out," Hummer said, realizing he couldn't stop her from taking Helen into custody. When he looked at Helen and saw the despair in her face and eyes, he didn't know what to say.

"Please, help me," she pleaded. "Don't let them take me away."

"There is nothing I can do at this moment," he told her. "But I promise I will not forsake you." He meant it. He never made empty promises.

Watching her being escorted out of the room, stumbling between the two officers like an intoxicated woman, he knew he had no choice but to find out the truth about her and the man she had been with in the mall.

On an impulse he grabbed the photo album. Maybe it would provide him with some kind of clue. If nothing else, he would keep it from falling into the wrong hands. He assumed there were probably more nude photos of Helen hidden behind other pictures, some of them quite likely more incriminating than the one he saw.

He spent a few more minutes having another look around. There was nothing personal in the closet or the drawers of the only dresser, nothing but second-rate clothing, some of it unwashed and soiled. In one of the drawers he found a wooden box containing jewelry, nothing of any value, only custom jewelry, cheap and flashy.

It seemed someone had gone to great pains to remove everything that could be traced to the person who lived here. The photo album so conveniently lying on the table didn't prove anything.

When he ran his finger across the top of the dresser, it left a dark streak in the dust covering the faded wood. He didn't believe anyone had lived in this room for quite some time. Opening the fridge, he didn't see anything that could be considered fresh. A half-full bottle of cola, a few slices of moldy bread, and a dry piece of cheese was all he found on the shelves. The sausage in the meat-drawer was covered with green mold and the bottle of salad dressing in the door-shelf was empty.

Opening the cupboards above the counter, he saw a few cans of readymade soups and vegetables, a few boxes containing cereal and pasta, and some spices. The dishes and glasses were old and cracked, not meant for doing any fancy entertaining.

Even the bathroom didn't reveal anything usable. Whoever lived in this apartment was someone with little or no personality, low self-esteem, and not much imagination.

The woman who insisted to be Helen Middler was not such a person, he was certain of that.

This whole affair stinks to high heaven and I smell something rotten. I can't put my finger on it, but I don't have a good feeling about it. There is more to this than appears on the surface. Time to start digging.

He closed the door behind him and listened to the sound the lock made as it clicked into place with a certain feeling of sarcasm. It didn't really matter if anyone broke into the apartment. There was nothing in there of value to anyone, nothing worth stealing, anyway.

He stood at the top of the stairs, planning his next move. Hearing someone coming up from below, he waited to see who it was. When he saw an older woman wearing a long, gray coat, he gave her a friendly smile. "Good afternoon, my lady."

The woman stopped and cackled. "You must have me confused with someone else. I ain't no lady." She peered at him from behind her glasses. "What's a fancy-dressed dude like you doing in this flea-bitten establishment? Looking for some action?"

He grinned. "I'm not a dude. I didn't know anyone used that expression anymore. My name is Frank Hummer. I'm a private detective. I'm interested in a young woman who lives in this building."

"Perhaps you haven't noticed, I ain't no young woman either." She cackled again. "I'm only pulling your leg Mister Private Detective, but you asked for it with your fancy talk. Who is this young woman?"

"Her name is Rose Miller."

"Rose? I know her. Poor girl sure had it tough. Haven't seen her in a long time. She seems to have disappeared. Do you have any news of her?"

"I'm looking for her. Tell me, do you know the girl who lives next to her in room thirty-two? She said her name was Raquel. Pink hair, wears red, high-heeled shoes."

The woman shook her head. "Don't know no Raquel. The woman who lives in thirty-two doesn't have pink hair and doesn't wear no high-heeled shoes. She's seventy-five years old and can barely walk. Her name is Martha Biggs. Lived in that same room for twenty years."

"Interesting." Hummer pulled out his wallet and handed the old woman a twenty. "I appreciate you talking to me and I would like you to accept this as thanks for taking the time to do so."

She grabbed the bill and shoved it into her coat pocket. "You can come in here anytime with your fancy clothes and talk, Mister Detective. I don't mind talking to you. Not at all." She gave him a toothless smile. "If I were younger I might even invite you up to my room like in the old days."

"And I probably would have taken you up on it," he joked. "By the way what is your name?"

"My friends used to call me Maria, but now I'm just plain old Mary."

"Well, thanks again, Maria. Maybe I'll run into you again some time." He winked. "One more thing. If anyone asks you about me, you tell them you've never seen me. Okay?" He tipped his cap and climbed down the stair without waiting for an answer.

Chapter Three

Traffic was heavy as Hummer drove home. He hated being caught in the four o'clock rush hour, especially on a Friday.

I guess I should postpone my golf game with Schumann tomorrow morning. On the other hand, he might be able to give me some information.

Schumann was a detective working for the city police department. He and Hummer had been friends since they were teenagers, and he was not above giving Hummer certain information meant only for law enforcement officers. Sometimes Hummer had to twist his arm a little, but Schumann knew Hummer would never divulge his source or use anything against him.

He looked at the clock on the dashboard and decided to take a little detour to his office.

Nicole, his receptionist, answered his call with "It's nearly four-thirty, Mr. Hummer. I'm on my way out. My boyfriend is picking me up in a few minutes. He doesn't like to wait."

He chuckled softly. "Tony may just have to curb his impatience today, Nicole. Invite him in and make him a cup of coffee. I need you there. I also need to speak to Mr. Marconi. Tell him to wait for me. I'll be there in about fifteen minutes." He switched off before she could reply. She was a capable receptionist but could be a little snippy at times. He felt sorry for her boyfriend should he stay with her and marry her. Nicole would not be easy to live with. She wasn't happy unless she had the last word.

When he drove his car into the parking lot behind the building, he saw Tony's car parked in the space reserved for Nicole. Marconi's was also in its spot.

Nicole gave him a displeasing look when he walked into the front office, but he ignored it. Tony sat in one of the plush leather chairs, sipping from a cup of coffee, his feet on the glass table top. "Hi, Mr. Hummer. Nicole tells me she has to work overtime today. Big case?"

Hummer glared at him. "If you break the glass you'll pay for it, Tony. Tables are not meant for resting your big feet."

Tony removed his feet reluctantly. "I get cramps in my legs if I don't put them up, Mr. Hummer."

"Maybe you should walk around more. Might even help you lose some weight."

Tony sighed. "It's my hormones and my constant craving for food. Must be my genes. My father was a big man. And my mother always bought those readymade foods. Maybe it's those foods."

"Don't blame you parents, Tony. Take some responsibility." He looked at Nicole. "Perhaps you should tell him to lose weight before his heart gives out or before he ends up with diabetes. I don't know what you see in this guy. You could do better."

"I like the way he is. I wish you wouldn't always criticize him, Mr. Hummer. Tony is the best thing that's happened to me in a long time. If you'd take the trouble to get to know him you'd find he is a real nice guy." Nicole's dark eyes flashed angrily. "For a detective you sure don't seem to care about the people who admire you. Tony admires you."

Hummer allowed himself a small chuckle. "I'm flattered. Next thing you'll tell me is how he wants to work for me."

Tony coughed delicately. "Funny you should mention that, Mr. Hummer. I was playing around with the idea of becoming a detective." He hesitated. "The company I worked for did some downsizing. I'm kinda between jobs right now and available."

"What was your job?"

"I'm a computer programmer. Computers are my life."

"Tony is the best. He's a genius," Nicole piped in. "He can get into any database he wants to."

Hummer found his interest aroused. "If I would ask you to find out about certain people, could you do that? I'm talking about information that may be…uh…classified, not accessible to regular people."

"Are you asking if I could break into someone else's computer, like the police department, without anyone knowing it?"

"That's what I'm saying. Can you do that?"

Tony laughed. "Piece of cake. I could get information from the IRS and they would never know I was there."

"How about the FBI?"

"Them too. Just tell me what you're looking for."

"Hmm." Hummer thought about it. "If you are serious about wanting to work for me, this may just be your lucky day, Tony. Do you have any plans for tomorrow?"

"Nicole and I were going to take a drive to my parents' cottage. It's supposed to be a sunny weekend."

"Well, if you want this job you'll postpone that trip. Working for me is not a nine-to-five job from Monday to Friday. Sometimes it requires putting in a few extra hours, which means working some weekends. If you perform well there may even be a bonus in it for you. It depends. Are you willing to commit to that?" Hummer wasn't quite sure yet if he wanted Tony to say yes. It wasn't that he disliked him, but he had a problem with people who didn't look after their bodies. If they couldn't find the discipline to curb their eating habits and perform regular exercises how could they be committed enough to a job that demanded discipline and certain sacrifices.

"He'll do it," Nicole said eagerly before Tony could digest the fact he had been offered a job.

Hummer's eyes studied the young man. "I'm asking *you*, Tony, not Nicole."

Tony got up from his leather chair and stepped around the table to stand in front of Hummer. Holding out his hand, he said, "You bet, I'll do it. You won't be sorry, sir. I'll work day and night if necessary."

Hummer had to laugh when he saw the excitement in Tony's round face. "I won't ask you to do that, Tony. Be here tomorrow morning at eleven. Make sure you have your social security number and some other identification. Nicole will need it for our records. I have an appointment to play golf with a friend in the morning. I should be in the office shortly after lunch."

"I'll be here, Mr. Hummer. Thank you so much for giving me this opportunity, sir." Tony was bristling with eagerness and even some pride. "Sometimes dreams come true. I still can't believe it."

Hummer hated to dampen his enthusiasm. "Detective work is not as glamorous as people think it is. It involves many boring hours sorting out facts and lies, interviewing people, begging authorities for information, sometimes going as far as bribing someone."

"Will I have to carry a gun, Mr. Hummer?"

"I'm afraid you'll be stuck behind the computer. There is no need for a gun, unless you want to shoot the computer. I feel like doing that sometimes." Hummer smiled. "Just be here tomorrow morning and see how you like detective work. You might change your mind after the first day." When he heard the sound of a door being opened, he turned around. "Hey, Marconi," he greeted the man walking in. "Sorry for asking you to stay in the office after hours on a Friday."

The tall, narrow-faced man with the small goatee gave Hummer one of his sardonic smiles. With his immaculately combed black hair, his thick eyebrows, and his dark eyes he needed only a couple of short horns sprouting from his forehead to scare little children at Halloween without putting on a costume. The dark business suit he always wore only added to the image.

"What's so important that you keep me from going home to my old man who doesn't care if I ever make it home?" Marconi said with a sour face.

"Let's go into your office and I'll fill you in." He looked at Nicole. "Thanks for staying, Nicole. You're a sweetheart. There is no need to hang around any longer. By the way, where is your car?"

She heaved a loud sigh. "In the repair shop again. What else is new?"

"I'd say it's time you gave some thought to buying a newer car."

"I suppose it is. This one is becoming too expensive to keep." Her pretty face lit up by a bright smile. "I want to thank you for giving Tony a job." She chuckled. "I'll make sure he's here on time tomorrow."

"That's okay. I know I can always count on you. Also make sure he keeps his big feet off my glass table. Now, get on home." Hummer made

26

shooing motions with his free hand. Then he followed Marconi into his office. Taking one of the leather chairs, he fell into it. "What a day," he said as he stretched out his legs.

Marconi went to sit in the chair behind his desk. "Must be something important you've got there," he said, indicating the photo album Hummer was clutching under his arm.

"I hope it is." Hummer shoved the album across the desk. "Here, have a look. There are some pictures hidden in there which you may find interesting. The woman in the photos is supposed to be someone who calls herself Rose Miller. She lives at four-sixty-four Cumberland, Room thirty-four. See what you can find out about her. By the way, I just hired Nicole's boyfriend, Tony. He's apparently a computer genius. Use him. I hope he lives up to his and Nicole's claims. I don't have to tell you to instill in him the need for discretion. Don't let him see all of the photos. You'll know which ones I mean."

He spent the next hour relaying the events of the day to Marconi, but he didn't tell him his own suspicions and conclusions. He didn't want Marconi's mind to be influenced by his own thoughts. It was important to have someone look at everything from a different perspective.

When he left the parking lot, he saw a black car parked on the other side of the street. It started up at the same time as he joined the traffic and seemed to follow him for a while. He wasn't quite sure if he only imagined it, but he had learned to trust his instincts and never to ignore anything.

* * * *

Martin Schumann didn't like discussing work-related topics when playing golf. It interfered with his game, so Hummer didn't say anything about his case until they went for lunch.

"I need to talk to you about something, Martin. It is kind of a bizarre case I've stumbled upon and I don't want to bother you with the details. A client of mine has been taken into custody by her probation officer. Can you find out where they have taken her? Her name is Rose Miller."

"When did this happen?"

"Yesterday afternoon. She was taken from her residence at four-sixty-four Cumberland."

Schumann lifted an eyebrow. "Cumberland? Since when are you taking clients who live in the slums? Business that bad?"

Hummer shrugged. "Like I said, it's a bizarre case. I'm kind of fishing in the dark right now. Don't know yet what to make of it."

Schumann rubbed his shoulder with a beefy hand. "Speaking of fishing, I don't think I'll be able to make it next weekend for the fishing tournament. Must have pulled a muscle last week when I arrested some punk who tried to run away from me. He was a big son-of-a-bitch."

"That's why you played such a lousy game today. I wondered about that. We could have cancelled, you know."

"And miss having you beg me for help in your recent case?" Schumann chuckled good-humoredly.

"I never beg, my friend. I only ask for small favors." Hummer signaled the waitress to bring the bill. "I'm afraid I have to run. I hired a new guy yesterday and I want to be in the office when he starts to work."

"A new guy," Schumann mused. "Anyone I know?"

"I don't think so. He's as green as they come but eager. He'll be doing most of his work on the computer. Actually, he is Nicole's boyfriend. He just lost his job."

Schumann laughed. "I always knew you were a soft touch underneath that bristling exterior. Now you're hiring guys out of the goodness of your heart. Very touching."

"Don't read anything into this, Martin. If anyone knows me it's you, and you know I don't run a charity outfit when it comes to my employees. I do nothing without a good reason. If he isn't any good he'll be in the unemployment line faster than you can say *sorry for that remark*."

"What makes this guy so special, or is that a secret?"

"No secret. Not for you. He's supposed to be a computer whiz, according to Nicole. I want to see if he is as good as she says."

Schumann threw him a long and thoughtful look. Hummer knew he couldn't hide anything from him. There was a reason why Schumann was the lead detective in his precinct. "Snooping in the wrong places can be viewed as a criminal offence and catch the attention of the FBI, possibly even Homeland Security. For your sake, I hope this guy is as good as your receptionist says."

"I never said he'd be snooping around." Hummer grinned and picked up the bill. "Lunch is on me. Maybe next time I'll let you pay."

"What was the woman's name again?" Schumann asked.

"Rose Miller. I'd appreciate it if you could locate her for me."

Hummer didn't see Tony when he walked into the office. Nicole looked up from her computer. "He's with Mr. Marconi," she said before he could ask.

"Good. I hope he's as eager today as he was yesterday." He opened the door into Marconi's office and walked in.

Tony stood in front of Marconi's desk, holding a notebook. He turned when he heard Hummer coming in. "Oh, hi, Mr. Hummer. I'm just trying to get as much information from Mr. Marconi as I can. He's given me a bunch of names. Who of these people is the most important one? I mean, whom do you want me to check out first?"

"Rose Miller. I want to know everything there is about her. After that, check out Harry Middler. That'll keep you busy for awhile."

"No problem. Which computer can I use?"

"Use the one in Mr. Silvo's office. He's in Miami, on business. He won't be back for a few days." Hummer didn't tell him that Silvo's computer was password protected. It would be Tony's first test. "Ask Nicole to let you into the office."

After Tony was gone, Hummer sank into the leather chair. "I played golf with Schumann today. I asked him to locate Rose Miller. Of course I meant Helen Middler." He rubbed his chin. "I didn't tell him anything. I want to check out Happy Acres Sanatorium first and see if they took Harry Middler there. If he isn't there, then we may have a kidnapping on our hands. It'll complicate things, because the kidnappers have no way to contact Helen Middler."

"You told me you witnessed Harry Middler's abduction. What makes you think that is his real name? And what makes you so sure the woman you met is Helen Middler, his wife? According to all the evidence she is Rose Miller and he's an escaped mental patient," Marconi pointed out.

"Somehow the woman I met does not fit the type of person who would live in that shabby apartment. I haven't shown you the pictures I snapped." He took his cell phone out of his pocket and handed it to

Marconi. "Download the images onto your computer. They may give you a different perspective."

Marconi pulled his lips into the shadow of a smile as he hooked up Hummer's cell phone to his computer to download the pictures. Stroking his goatee with long fingers, he said, "I've studied the pictures in the album. They look genuine to me. If the album belonged to Rose Miller, it is her in those pictures."

"The similarity to the woman I know as Helen Middler is uncanny. They could be twins."

"Perhaps they are."

"You mean a case of separation at birth?"

"It is possible."

Hummer thought about that suggestion. "I guess we'll have to do some deep digging. I hope Tony can deliver what he promised." He rose. "I'm going to take a drive to the Happy Acres Sanatorium and see what I can find out. Have you been in touch with Silvo? How is his investigation going?"

"I talked to him this morning. He didn't say much. Apparently, he's making some progress."

"Good. I hope he's careful." Hummer took back his cell phone and shoved it into his pocket. Then he left Marconi's office and stopped to talk to Nicole. "How's Tony doing in there? Any trouble with Mr. Silvo's computer?"

She gave him a questioning look. "No. Should he have?"

"I didn't expect any if Tony is as good as you said."

Her smile was condescending. "I'm surprised you question my credibility, Mr. Hummer. You should know me better than that."

"One of the reasons I hired Tony was your credibility, Nicole. I didn't think you'd be foolish enough to recommend somebody who is no good. Tony's job wouldn't be the only one on the line."

Her bright-blue eyes showed surprise. "Are you saying you'll fire me if Tony doesn't work out?"

"You got it, Sweetheart."

"I'm disappointed, Mr. Hummer. After working for you for three years I would have thought you value me more than that."

"It's not a question of how much I value you. After working for me for three years you should know that I don't have any desire to waste valuable time dealing with incompetent employees. I want only the best people working for me. If you can't measure up there are plenty of others who fit the bill."

"You are a hard man, Mr. Hummer."

"I didn't get to where I am by being soft." When he saw her eyes misting over, he felt sorry for sounding so harsh and he tried to smooth things over. "You wouldn't have lasted this long had I not thought highly of you, Nicole. You have nothing to worry about and I have a feeling your boyfriend will be all right. Have some faith, girl."

"I have faith in Tony," she said with a low, almost teary voice. "It is you who doubts him."

"I'm looking forward to his report on Monday morning," he said. "I'll be at the Happy Acres Sanatorium, just so you know. Don't look so glum, I haven't fired you, and I gave your boyfriend a job. That should be cause for celebration."

"I'm elated," she said but not sounding happy at all.

He left the office and walked into the parking lot to get his car.

Women! I'm glad I never married. I don't think I could take it. Why do they always have to start crying when you want to discuss serious business with them?

The Happy Acres Sanatorium was about half-an-hour away during light traffic, but since it was Saturday, many drivers were on the road and it took him fifty minutes to get there.

A guard at the entrance asked him what his business was for visiting.

"I want to check on someone who was brought here yesterday," he told him. "Who can I speak to about that?"

"Go to admittance. They'll help you." The guard pointed. "Through that door. You'll have to ring the bell."

Another burly guard opened the door for him and accompanied him to the counter. Then he stood nearby, pretending not to watch, but Hummer knew he was being scrutinized.

The woman behind the counter reluctantly tore her attention away from the book she was reading. "Can I help you?"

"I understand you had a patient admitted yesterday. His name is

Harry Middler."

"Are you a relative?" Her voice was brisk, not exactly friendly.

"No, I'm not. My name is Frank Hummer. I'm a private investigator. Mrs. Middler hired me to find out about her husband."

"Find out what?" She gave him a suspicious look.

Hummer smiled. "She wants to make certain her husband gets the best care."

"He'll be treated like any other patient. We don't make any exception. Everyone admitted to our facility is important to us."

"I wouldn't assume otherwise." His smile could have melted the ice cubes in a glass of Scotch, and he felt like having one right now. It didn't seem to have an effect on her, because she went back to reading her book.

"Can you, please, check your records to make sure he arrived yesterday?" He coughed into his hand. "You know patients sometimes get lost on the way to the hospital. It happened to a good friend of mine, Mayor Gonzales. You may have read about it in the papers. Fortunately, it was only a big misunderstanding. Mayor Gonzales was ready to fire the hospital administration, including the staff at the admittance counter."

She looked up from her book and stared at him. "Are you a friend of Mayor Gonzales?"

He laughed. "We are practically brothers. I was best man at his wedding."

"Oh, I see." She closed her book and walked over to her computer. After a few minutes of searching, she said, "Nobody by the name Harry Middler was admitted. The only patient brought to us was a Henry Miller. In fact, I remember him clearly. He was heavily sedated." She dropped her voice. "I'm telling you this in confidence. From the records we have this Henry Miller is a violent man. He came to us from the *Silver Maple Mental Hospital*."

Hummer slapped his hand against his forehead. "I feel like an idiot." He gave a little chuckle and threw a glance at the guard. "It's only a temporary condition, not to worry. Otherwise I'm fine. Henry Miller is the man I'm looking for."

"But you said Harry Middler."

"A slip of the tongue. Harry Middler is the name of another client of mine. I must have been thinking of him. You can see that, can't you? Middler...Miller. It is easy to make that mistake." He looked at the woman with a dog-eyed expression. "Is it possible to visit with Mr. Miller?"

"I'm afraid not. He is still in Section D where we keep our most violent patients. He'll be there until he calms down." She shook her head. "There is a note attached to his records, from his doctor at Silver Maple Mental Hospital, which strictly advises against anyone communicating with him until his condition improves."

"What's the name of his doctor? At least tell me that."

"Doctor McDermott."

"Thank you so much. I will tell Mrs. Miller he's here. It will take a load off her mind. She's been so worried."

"I'm glad I could help. We are always there for our patients and their families."

"That is good to know. In fact, I'll mention your kindness to Mayor Gonzales next time I have lunch with him. Of course without betraying your confidential information."

"I'd appreciate that. Will you be back for a visit, Mr. Hummer? Perhaps you and I could go out for a drink next time?" Her smile was actually friendly, almost seductive.

"Sounds good to me, Miss...uh...I don't know your name."

"Victoria. I'm usually here."

"Victoria. That's a nice name. My grandmother's name was Victoria. You remind me a little of her." He took out one of his cards. "My number is on it. In case there is a change in Mr. Miller's situation, you can call me."

"I sure will." She took the card from his hand and read it. Then she looked at him with her brown eyes; her earlier hostility seemed to have vanished. "A man with a grandmother named Victoria is almost like an old friend." Her cheeks took on a slightly rosy tint when she said it. "I'm sorry about brushing you off before, but sometimes we get reporters coming here under false pretenses. We do value the privacy of our patients."

"You can't be too careful these days. Anyway, I'd better get going.

33

See you, Victoria." He doubted it would happen, but anything was possible.

Before he turned the key in the ignition of his car, he pulled down the visor and looked at himself in the mirror and smirked at his image. "You're quite some storyteller, my friend, but you'll never get any women that way."

He shrugged and started the car, thinking about Victoria.

That woman isn't bad looking and she's got fire. Any other time I wouldn't mind taking her out for a drink or even for dinner, and maybe some romance later, but I'm afraid you can't build a relationship on a mountain of lies. Sorry Grandma Hummer for calling you Victoria; I prefer Amanda any day, even though I wouldn't have loved you any less had your name been Victoria. Of course, that would have eased my conscience a little today.

When his phone rang, he answered it with, "Yes, what's so important?"

"It's Tony, Mr. Hummer. You might want to come back to the office. I discovered something you may find interesting and a little disturbing."

Chapter Four

Tony handed him a stack of printed pages. "I wrote down and printed everything, in case you want to double-check my findings." He seemed quite proud of his achievement.

Hummer scanned the pages. "You did an excellent job and I'll read it at a later date. There is a lot of information here. For now, give me a short version."

"Well, I have to admit, I had to do some digging, but in a way I'm a bit surprised at how much I found and how easy it actually was. It is not difficult to get basic information on anyone if you know where to look. It is amazing how much information is out there about most people. And most people don't even know this."

"Enough lecturing, Tony," Hummer said impatiently. "You're not telling me anything new. What did you find?"

"Well, first of all I found over eighty-seven million sites with the name Rose Miller. I began narrowing it down and finally ended up with twenty-eight who could have been the one we are looking for. Some were older, some were younger than the suggested age of the Rose Miller in the pictures, and three of the twenty-eight were of the approximate same age. Of course, according to the inscription on one of the pictures, Rose Miller had a brother named Henry, which helped. Anyway, the Rose Miller we want was born June seventeen, nineteen-eighty, in Philadelphia. Her parents, Joseph and Erica Miller, owned a corner grocery store. Worked there much of their time, and, apparently, had no time left for their four children, Henry, Henrietta, John, and Rose.

She was the youngest. Got herself pregnant when she was seventeen and left town. Moved to Denver where she had the child, a little girl, which she gave up for adoption. Got into drugs and made her living as a prostitute. Moved here in two-thousand-seven. Has been living at four-sixty-four Cumberland Street since then. She spent four months in jail in two-thousand-ten for robbing a client. She has auburn hair and green eyes."

Tony gave Hummer a questioning look. "That's pretty well everything in a nutshell. I can go into more detail if you want." When Hummer shook his head, he continued, "You will find all the details in my report, like the name of her girl, what hospital she was born in, what month and day. Even the people who adopted her." He smiled smugly. "I had some trouble finding that out, but with a little bit of patience I managed it."

"What about her brother Henry? Did you find out anything about him?"

"Only the basics. It didn't take long once I discovered all the stuff about Rose. I can start searching on Monday to find out more."

"No, leave that for the time being. I want you to start looking into Helen Middler's background. What basic stuff did you find out so far about Henry Miller?"

"Henry Miller was born August seven, nineteen-sixty-seven, in Philadelphia. He joined the army after getting a degree in literature. He only made it to the rank of Sergeant. Spent time in the Gulf war. Came back and drifted around, became a drug addict and alcoholic, got involved in crime. Did jail time for armed robbery in two-thousand-one, and finally ended up in a mental hospital, where he has been for the last five years."

"Do you know which one?"

"Yes. The Silver Maple Mental Hospital."

Hummer nodded in appreciation. "I have to admit, Tony, I didn't expect you'd find out this much in such a short time."

Tony chuckled, almost in contempt. "Mr. Hummer, there is one thing you need to know about me. I don't brag about things I can't do. I may not be the handsomest man around, not the slimmest, either, but I know computers. They are my life. I play games, I design games, websites, programs, you name it. It's child's play."

"I believe you. I'll let you play on my computer, but don't get too cocky, okay, not when you're on my watch. Don't get caught snooping around on sites that are off-limits to civilians, computer files that have restricted access, like those in government computers, for instance, the Military, the FBI, Homeland Security, or the CIA. You understand?" Hummer gave him a stern look.

"Are you telling me to stay away from those sites and computers, Mr. Hummer?"

"I didn't say that. I said *don't get caught*. By the way, this conversation never took place. Is that clear?"

Tony lifted his hand to salute, but then he let it fall again. "Loud and clear, sir." He lowered his voice to nearly a whisper. "I am so excited, Mr. Hummer. I almost feel like a spy or a secret agent on a covert mission."

"You should feel that way, because what you are doing is illegal, things only spies do. So in a sense you are on a covert mission."

"Oh, wow, this is exhilarating. Almost like playing a computer game. You wouldn't believe how complicated and close to reality some of these games are. I'll just pretend I'm playing a game."

"This isn't a game, Tony. This is real life with real dangers," Hummer warned. "I can't stress it enough. Cover your tail. Be a ghost when you surf the Internet. Make certain nobody knows you are there. Remember, you are not the only computer genius. There are plenty like you out there and some of them are on the other side, protecting the information you are trying to steal."

Tony only smiled smugly. "There is only one like me, Mr. Hummer. I'm the best."

"I hope so. By the way, what was the disturbing stuff you discovered?"

"Nothing I can put my finger on, but it seemed it was almost too easy to get the information I was searching for, as if someone actually wanted me to find it."

"Maybe it's because you are the best, Tony." Hummer grinned. "Things may just come a little too easy for you. That's what happens when you're good at your job." He lifted the stack of papers. "I'm taking this home with me and study everything there. Call it a day and take Nicole to a nice restaurant tonight. Save the bill and give it to me on Monday. I will reimburse you. You don't have to tell Nicole about it. It's our secret, all right?"

"Gee, thanks, Mr. Hummer. I like working for you already."

"Don't thank me too soon, Tony. I'm a difficult boss to work for. Just ask Nicole." Hummer left Tony standing in the office and walked out. Nicole looked up from behind her desk, questions in her eyes. "Time to go home, Nicole," he told her. "Make sure you treat Tony nice tonight."

"I always do," she assured him with a happy little chuckle.

* * * *

He didn't get a chance to look over the printouts Tony gave him. When he came home there was a message on his answering machine.

"Hello, Frank. This is Cheryl. What have you been up to lately? I feel lonely. How about meeting me for dinner tonight? You pick the place. Call me."

Cheryl was the woman he dated off and on. Neither of them had made a commitment, and their relationship was strictly casual. He didn't know if she dated anyone else, and he didn't really care. Her full name was Cheryl Gibson. She was the daughter of Congressman Charles Gibson. Perhaps that was the reason he kept his distance. Charles Gibson was known for his controversial views, and Hummer didn't agree with most of them. If it were up to Gibson, he'd send all the black people *back to Africa* and every illegal immigrant to jail.

Cheryl was a fashion designer and owned a model agency. She and her father didn't see eye to eye because of his radical views.

Hummer hadn't seen Cheryl for nearly two months and when he heard her voice, he suddenly felt like talking to her. She always made him feel good and he certainly needed someone right now to cheer him up.

She answered her phone after the second ring.

"Hi, Cheryl. It's Frank."

He could tell by her voice she was pleased to hear him. "Hi, Frank. You want to come and pick me up at my place?"

"Sure. No problem. I just got home and I'm in need of a shower. See you in a couple of hours?"

"Make it sooner if you can. I'll be waiting."

"I'll try."

She lived in a swanky condominium which her father had bought for her. Even though she didn't agree with his opinions she didn't have any scruples about taking his money.

Hummer parked the car in the underground parking lot and took the elevator up to the fifteenth floor. She answered the door and let him in.

He lifted an eyebrow when he scrutinized her. She was dressed in a clingy, red dress that showed off her slim figure and highlighted her blonde hair. "You look ravishing."

She smiled, put her arms around his neck and purred with a silky, seductive voice, "I'm glad you came."

He kissed her and was surprised at the passion she displayed kissing him back. When they broke apart, he said, "Wow, what was that all about?"

"I've missed you, Frank. It's been much too long since we've been together."

"It'll be two months next Saturday." He held her close. "I've missed you, too. Time seems to get away from us sometimes."

"I know. We should make it a point to go out more often." She moved out of his embrace. Taking his hand and pulling him to the couch, she said, "But tonight I don't really feel like going out. I've ordered pizza. I hope you don't mind."

"You said you wanted me to take you out for dinner. If you didn't want to go out why are you dressed this way?"

"I dressed like this for you. I know you like seeing me in a dress." Laughing, she pushed him onto the couch.

"I do. There is nothing more beautiful than a gorgeous woman in a dress, especially one as clingy as the one you're wearing. And you, my love, are gorgeous, but I've told you so before." He grabbed her hand and pulled her down. Still laughing, she sat on his lap. Her buttocks felt soft on his thighs. "Are you trying to seduce me or am I misreading the signals?" he asked.

"Isn't it obvious?"

He looked into her eyes. They were blue and shiny. Her red lips smiled wickedly, but there was more in her expression than just an invitation to have sex with her. "My birthday is coming up. I'll be thirty-six in two weeks. I've been thinking a lot lately…about getting older, about having someone to love, and to have someone lying next to me every night. I've been thinking about you, Frank—even fantasizing a bit."

He chuckled, tensing inside, almost afraid where this would lead. "I'm flattered. What role did I play in your fantasies?"

Her lips touched his. Opening her mouth, she let her tongue caress his lips. "It wasn't the first time I had those fantasies, you know." Her fingers gently stroked his neck. "I love you, Frank."

"Wow! Where did that so suddenly come from?" This was not something he expected.

"It's not so sudden. I've had these feelings for quite some time. Do you love me?"

"I've never thought about us that way. I'm fond of you, but you know that." He was beginning to feel a bit uncomfortable with the subject.

"There is no love for me in your feelings?" Her eyes searched his face.

He hesitated before answering, not sure how to phrase it. "I suppose I love you, too," he finally said.

"You are saying the words, but do you really mean what they imply? Am I the only woman you are telling so or do you speak those words to other women when you hold them in your arms?" Her blue eyes studied his face.

"Ever since I met you, I haven't been with another woman."

"Is this true? Even though we have never discussed our relationship?"

"I swear." He smiled. "You never told me what you fantasized about me."

"You being my husband. Is that so hard to guess?"

He didn't say anything, trying to digest what she'd said. She also stayed silent. Sitting in his lap, she toyed with his hair, her lips forming a smile. He became aware of her beating heart.

When he didn't comment, she asked, "Surprised? Stunned?"

"I have to admit, I am surprised. You were always the one who kept telling me marriage was not on your list. You wanted to keep our relationship casual. No commitments, remember? Yes, I am surprised."

"I'm actually a bit surprised myself, but would it be such a bad thing being married to me? Have you never thought about getting married?"

"Perhaps I have, but I've never played out any fantasies in my mind."

"When you thought about it, was I in your picture?" She seemed eager to hear the answer but also almost afraid. He could tell by her rigid body.

He stroked her hair. "You are always in my picture, honey."

She leaned into him, her arms tight around his body. "I'm happy to hear that. I was afraid..." The doorbell interrupted her. "That must be our pizza." She jumped from his lap and rushed to the door to open it. It was indeed the pizza delivery man.

"Hang on a second. I'll have to get my purse."

Hummer registered with amusement how the young man's eyes seemed to be mesmerized by Cheryl's buttocks as she walked away from him. He noticed Hummer watching him and grinned with obvious embarrassment, changing the gaze of his eyes toward the ceiling until Cheryl came back with the money.

"Enjoy the pizza, ma'am, and make sure you call us back," he said before she closed the door.

She laughed as she carried the box with the pizza to the counter. "I thought his eyes would pop out of his head the way he stared at my breasts," she said.

Hummer watched her walking toward him, her hips swaying slightly. "I can't say I blame him," he said with a smile. "You are displaying enough of them to give a guy crazy ideas. You should have seen his eyes when he checked out your ass."

Standing in front of him, her hands on her hips, she gave him a mock-angry stare. "Is that all you men look at? A woman's breasts and butt?"

He nodded with a solemn expression. "Yep, you've got it. That's all we look at."

"How about my face? Doesn't it deserve a good look? I spent enough time on it. I don't know why I bother."

Getting up, he put his arms around her and pulled her close. "Everything about you deserves a good look. In fact, I can never get enough of you, and that's the truth. I can't think of another woman I would rather be married to than you."

"But?"

"You are springing this at me out of the blue without a warning, so, please, don't ask me to give you an answer right now or even comment on it." Holding her face between his hands, he kissed her. She responded by pressing her body against his, kissing him hungrily.

Her hands were busy with his belt. "My appetite for pizza is not as great as the appetite I have for you," she whispered. "Let's skip the main course and enjoy the dessert."

* * * *

The tantalizing odor of frying eggs and bacon woke him up. He opened his eyes and found Cheryl gone. Climbing out of bed, he walked naked out of the bedroom.

Cheryl was busy at the stove. She didn't hear him coming up behind her and let out a little yelp when he put his arms around her waist.

"You scared me," she sputtered. "Don't you know it's dangerous to approach a woman holding a spatula?"

He kissed her exposed shoulder. "I had no idea. I've never done it before," he said, his voice muffled by her thick hair.

She turned in his embrace. "It's even more dangerous to approach her naked. Anything can happen."

He chuckled cheerfully. "Nothing will happen. I'm still exhausted from last night. A man my age needs a good night's rest to fully function the next day. You should be aware of that before you become Mrs. Hummer."

"Is this a marriage proposal?" she asked, smiling expectantly.

"No, but it is part of the information package that comes with the product you're showing an interest in…me."

"I have enough information on the…uh…product to know it performs well." She laughed and put her hands on his chest. "Now, let me finish breakfast. You go and take your shower and get dressed. I can't guarantee anything if you stand here much longer looking handsome and naked."

Humming a little tune, he walked into the bathroom. He had to admit, it was nice to wake up in the morning and not feeling alone. He couldn't think of a single good reason why being married to Cheryl wasn't a good idea.

There was only one problem. Charles Gibson would be his father-in-law.

Cheryl was in high spirits and laughing a lot while they ate breakfast, reaching across the table once in awhile to touch his hand. Hummer liked seeing her this way and he had to admit, a man couldn't ask for a better companion to spend the rest of his life with. He didn't remember ever seeing her in a bad mood, except the time he accompanied her to visit her parents. Her mother was a delightful person, busy with doing charity work in her community, but her father was not a pleasant man. Full of hate for people of color or anyone who didn't have a decent job, blaming them for the state of the economy in the US.

There is no reason for a man to be unemployed. There are plenty of decent jobs out there, but all these niggers, chinks, and other riffraff want to do is push drugs or collect welfare checks. It's so much easier than doing an honest job. We should send them all back where they came from! And the Middle East? Nuke the whole damn place and be done with it.

Yes, Congressman Charles Gibson had the answer to everything. If people would only see things his way, the world would be a better place to live in.

Hummer had no love for the man. He could not understand how he ever got as far as he did in politics. Of course, he had one thing going for him. He was rich, one of the richest men in the USA. He was an oilman; his father had been an oilman, and his grandfather before him. On top of that, he was the owner of one of the largest banks. He had influential friends and could afford to shoot off his mouth without worrying about repercussions.

It still didn't mean Hummer had to be his best friend or even like him.

Looking at Cheryl and listening to her talking, he had a sudden unpleasant thought.

Do I have to get down on my knees and ask him for the hand of his daughter? He strikes me as the kind of man who expects it. I'd rather get married in Vegas by an Elvis look-alike.

"So what do you think about that?"

Her question brought his attention back to her and he realized he hadn't heard a word she'd said. "I'm sorry, I haven't really thought about it at all," he said, hoping it was the right answer.

"Well, maybe then you should give it some thought. It is important to me." She finished her orange juice and dabbed her mouth with a napkin. "I'll go change into something more appropriate and then we'll take a little drive into the country. It's a nice sunny day. We don't want to waste it procrastinating in the city."

"Good idea. As long as we're back tonight. I need to go to the office tomorrow. I have a new case and I'm anxious to solve it. A woman's life may be at stake."

"Ooh, sounds mysterious." She got up and walked away. "Don't worry, I'll never pry into your cases, I promise, unless you want my input," she said over her shoulder. Before she disappeared into the bedroom, she stopped. "I want your assurance that you won't take your work with you today. Your mind needs a day of rest. Leave all your anxieties and excitements your cases throw at you behind. Today I should be the object of your attention. I want to make you forget about all your troubles and your problems."

"You are already on my mind," he assured her. "Spending the day with you will be enough excitement."

Her laugh mocked him a little. "I'm not sure if that is a compliment."

It is easy to make a promise to someone, however, keeping it is a different story. When his cell phone rang he was tempted to let his answering service take the call, but his conscience didn't allow that. There was no point in having a cell phone and not answer it when it rang. His reason for having one in the first place was to make himself available to his staff and clients.

Reluctantly, he flipped it open. "Hello?"

"Frank, this is Martin. I went back to the precinct yesterday afternoon and tried to find out where they were holding Rose Miller. There is no record of her being taken into custody by any parole officer. What did you say that officer's name was?"

"Sarah Dalton."

"That's what I thought. I couldn't find a parole officer going under the name Sarah Dalton. Sorry, that's all I can do for you now."

"Thanks, Martin. I appreciate it."

Chapter Five

All good things come to an end. After spending another night with Cheryl, he said goodbye to her in the morning. "Think about what we talked about," she said, clinging to him for a moment and kissing him gently. "Thank you for spending the weekend with me. You've made me very happy. Don't push yourself too hard, Frank. If you need me, I'll be here."

"I know," he said. "And I am glad for it."

He drove away, heading for his office. He recalled Schumann's phone call Sunday morning.

There is no Sarah Dalton.

Then who was that woman who took Helen Middler away from Rose Miller's apartment pretending to be her parole officer? Those two policemen with her? Had they been authentic officers of the law? He blamed himself for not insisting they show their badges. He didn't slip up often, but this one was a major blunder. He had no way of tracing Helen Middler's movements.

He smashed his hand against his steering wheel and cursed loudly, "Damn it!"

Tony was already sitting behind the computer in Silvo's office when he arrived. "I want you to find a Sarah Dalton. She's supposed to be a parole officer," he told Tony.

"How about Helen Middler?"

"I need information on her also. By the way, did Nicole treat you right this weekend?"

Tony grinned from ear to ear. "A gentleman enjoys and keeps his mouth shut, Mr. Hummer."

"Well, I'm glad it worked out for you, Tony."

Tony fished around in his pocket. "Here is the bill you told me to give you. Are you still going to honor it?"

"Of course. I don't make a promise I'm not willing to keep." He took the bill and looked at it. Smiling, he said, "The Steak-and-Lobster Grill. Good choice."

"You said to go to a nice place." Tony defended the bill.

"I said that, didn't I?" Hummer took out his wallet and counted out the money. "Consider it a bonus for a job well-done. As I've said, you don't need to tell Nicole."

"Thanks, Mr. Hummer, but I don't want any secrets between me and her."

"That's up to you, Tony, and quite admirable. Don't let me influence you. Every man deals differently with the woman in his life. Sometimes it's best not to tell her everything; at other times it is a good idea to share things with her. Just make sure you don't give her anything she can use as a bargaining chip should the opportunity arise." He chuckled. "Of course I'm not an expert on women. Perhaps I would be if I were married."

"You are not married, Mr. Hummer?"

"No. Never had the urge to get married."

"Never? Gee, I guess I'm lucky. I'm planning to marry Nicole. If she wants me." Tony grinned. "With the kind of money you're paying me, I can afford it now. I would have thought you'd have women chasing you, Mr. Hummer. I mean...you are good-looking, a successful business man, rich..."

"I don't think I'd want to marry a woman who wants me only for my money." Hummer thought of Cheryl. She had plenty of money of her own, in addition to being the daughter of a billionaire. He didn't have to worry she might be after his money.

"Well, thank you again, Mr. Hummer," Tony was saying. "I'd better get back to earning my keep."

"Okay. If you want to ask me any questions, I'll be in Mr. Marconi's office."

Marconi sat behind his desk, reading the paper. He looked up when Hummer walked in. "Have you seen the morning papers?" Marconi asked.

Hummer shook his head. "No, I haven't had the chance yet."

"There is something in here that might peak your interest. It's on the front page." He flicked through the pages. "Here it is: Two men die in fire at Globe Labs Institute. Names are withheld until notification of next of kin." Marconi looked at Hummer. "What a strange coincidence. Isn't that the company where Professor Harry Middler was employed?"

"Yes, it is." Hummer sank into one of the chairs. "What are the chances of such a thing happening? I'm familiar with the company. Does the article list what Globe Labs produce?"

"It says here they were experimenting with alternative fuels."

"Can you find out more about the company?"

"I'll try. You think there is a connection between Harry Middler's kidnapping and the fire?"

"At this moment I don't know what to think. The questions seem to be piling up and nothing makes sense so far. I have only bits of information, but nothing fits." Hummer leaned forward. "Perhaps you can see things from a different angle. Let's see what we have: I am witnessing the kidnapping of a man by three employees of Happy Acres Sanatorium. According to his wife Helen Middler, his name is Harry Middler. Professor Harry Middler. But I find no record of a Harry Middler being taken to Happy Acres Sanatorium, only a man by the name of Henry Miller, who is a mental patient transferred from another hospital. The woman who says she is Helen Middler cannot prove she is the woman she says. The only things she carries with her identify her as Rose Miller, who incidentally is Henry Miller's sister. Are you with me so far?"

Marconi stroked his goatee and pulled his thick brows into a frown. "I am, but this is already confusing."

"It gets more confusing. Rose Miller, who insists her name is Helen Middler, gets taken into custody by her probation officer, Sarah Dalton. When I tried to find out where they took Helen Middler under the name of Rose Miller I was told there is no record of her. I also have it from a reliable source that probation officer Sarah Dalton doesn't exist. Another woman who apparently does not exist is the pink-haired hooker Raquel who claimed to be Rose Miller's neighbor. Who are those two women and who are they working for? Oh, I forgot, Harry and Helen Middler do exist and they live at thirty-seven Pineridge Cove. I checked that out myself." He had a sudden thought. "I wonder if one of the men who died in the fire will be identified as Professor Harry Middler. It's just a hunch I have."

"Since you've met and checked out the apparently real Middler-couple, it brings up one question: who is the woman who claims to be Helen Middler? By all outward appearances she is actually Rose Miller," Marconi mused.

"It seems that way, but it doesn't explain the whole incident in the mall. I wasn't dreaming it. Rose Miller was a drug addict and a criminal with a low self-esteem. The woman I met as Helen Middler did not fit that picture." He rose. "I want to pursue another lead I have. Helen told me she was a student at the Henry Hopkins University. I'm going to check it out."

Henry Hopkins University was nearly a two-hour drive away. Fortunately, it was a nice, sunny day and an enjoyable ride. The trip also gave him time to think about Cheryl. The idea of marrying her didn't seem so absurd. He knew he was fond of her, possibly even loved her, but she had always insisted marriage was not in the cards for her. Perhaps that was the reason he never thought about it.

She was right when she said the clock was ticking for both of them. She was going to be thirty-six and he was already thirty-eight. People used to get married in their twenties; he knew his parents did. Couples getting married that young were almost guaranteed to become grandparents. Of course, his parents may not live long enough to see any grandchildren. His father was sixty-eight and his mother sixty-five. Derek, his younger brother, was married but so far childless. And may stay that way. He once confided in him that Peggy, Derek's wife, did not want children. She did not want to ruin her hourglass-figure.

Hummer didn't know how Cheryl thought about the future. Did she want children? Since they never talked about marriage, the question of children never came up. Cheryl was a career woman and also quite obsessed with her figure. Her thoughts may mirror Peggy's.

Did he want children? He wasn't sure about that, either. Did he want to get married? Somehow he couldn't picture himself as a married man.

Glancing at the clock on the dashboard, he realized it was close to noon. Deciding to stop for lunch, he drove into a small diner. The place was not yet packed with customers and he found a table in the corner where he could see the TV above the counter.

After giving the waitress his order, he leaned back and watched the screen. They were showing firefighters trying to douse a fire and he realized he was watching the fire at Globe Labs. The sound was turned down, but it was loud enough for him to catch most of what the reporter said. As he suspected, one of the men who died in the fire had been identified as Professor Harry Middler and the other man was the CEO of Globe Labs, Saul Finkbein. According to the reporter, a spokesman for the firefighters said it was fortunate the fire occurred on a Sunday when the plant was closed and nobody was working; otherwise there may have been more casualties.

Watching and listening to the reporter, a gnawing feeling churned Hummer's stomach; the way it always did when something was wrong. Why were Professor Middler and the CEO in the Lab on a Sunday? How did the fire get started?

According to the report, the police suspected foul play. Of course, they did so most of the time.

The announcer didn't say how the two men died. Were they killed in an explosion? An accident? If there was foul play, did that mean they were murdered? Not much information was available.

When the waitress brought his food, he concentrated on eating, paying only little attention to the news. More people had entered the diner and the noise level was high enough to make it nearly impossible to hear the TV. There was a report about Benjamin Simmerman, the man who was running for President, and he would have liked to hear what it was all about. The man had a good chance of winning the coming election. He knew that Cheryl's father, Charles Gibson, did not like Simmerman, because he was not fond of the oil industry. Simmerman was a great supporter of alternative fuels. His goal was to get rid of cars using gasoline within twenty years. He wanted to see only electric cars on the road or cars running on fuels manufactured from renewable resources. The fact, that his son, Fred Simmerman, was the owner and CEO of Green Fuels Development Inc., a company involved in developing alternative fuels from renewable resources, probably played a role in his platform.

Senator Simmerman's policy did not go over well with the oil companies. No surprise there. Neither did the car manufacturers support him, but he had a large following of people who agreed with him, which meant potential votes.

He finished his lunch, paid the waitress and left the diner. He was not into politics and not a supporter of any party. What mattered to him was the man who sat at the helm, the man who would be the President of the United States. Hummer and the Senator were old friends, and he knew Simmerman was a good man. He was tough but honest and sincere; then again, every politician promised the world before the election. Once they were elected they somehow found one excuse after the other to renege on their promises.

Hummer, along with many others, suspected that the President didn't have the power to make decisions, even though it seemed that way. He was just a figurehead, a puppet. His strings were pulled by more powerful people. The ones who financed his campaign, the ones who decided he'd be the next President long before the voters even knew he'd be running for the position of the most powerful man in the world.

Benjamin Simmerman would not be one of those people. He had enough money to finance his campaign and didn't need any backers who would have him in his pocket after he was elected.

Hummer arrived at Henry Hopkins University an hour later. It was a huge place and it took him some time to find Administration. The woman behind the front desk looked up and smiled at him, so he decided to talk to her. "Hi, my name is Frank Hummer. I'm a private investigator and I was wondering if I could ask you some questions."

"A private investigator?" Her smile widened. "I've never met a real Private Eye. I only see them on Television. Is your job really as glamorous as it is portrayed in those shows?"

He laughed. "Don't believe everything you see on TV. My job can be boring and tedious."

"Is it tedious right now?" Her smile mocked him.

"Right now is one of those pleasant moments," he said, giving her a little wink. "Talking to a beautiful woman always is."

"Oh, my, you're a charmer. I guess it comes with the territory?" She chuckled. "Too bad I'm a married woman; otherwise I might ask you to take me out for coffee."

He made a face. "That really sucks. Why are the beautiful women always taken?"

"Oh well, I'm sure there are plenty still out there. Now, what can I do for you, Mr. Hummer?"

"I have a client who said she was taking a course here at the University. I would like to talk to her teacher."

"Is this client young or old?"

"She's thirty-five. She was working on her masters in biology. Her name is Helen Middler."

"You say she's thirty-five? That means she is probably in our adult education program. Let me check it out." She began searching her computer. After awhile she shook her head. "I don't have a file on a Helen Middler."

"Maybe I could speak to the teacher who teaches biology to adult students?"

After more time the woman shook her head again. "That would have been Miss Hartwick. It seems you're out of luck. According to her file, she quit last Friday. There is no other information."

"That is unfortunate," Hummer said. "And quite some coincidence." He hesitated. Taking out one of his cards, he handed it to the woman. "If anything comes up, I'd appreciate a call. Thank you for the trouble you went through."

She gave him a little smile. "Sorry I couldn't be of more help."

"You may have given me more information than seems at first glance," he told her.

"Well, then I'm happy. Perhaps you'll drop in again someday."

"Perhaps. Have an enjoyable evening." He walked away, his head full of speculations. It certainly was some cruel twist of fate that Helen Middler's teacher would quit on the same day her husband gets abducted. He realized he might have all his facts wrong about the woman who claimed to be Helen Middler, but somehow he could not think of her as Rose Miller.

His thoughts went back to the incident in the mall. The man he saw accompanying Helen, who she said was her husband, had not given him the impression of being violent or mentally unstable. He had seen him only for a relatively short time, a few minutes really, but first impressions usually take only moments. Those are the moments when people subconsciously make up their minds, when they decide if they like someone or not.

Then again, most people had many faces. The one the public saw, the one family members knew, and the real one, the face a person wore when alone and unobserved.

He looked at his image reflected in the sun-visor-mirror.

How many faces do I have? Is this the face the people I talk to see or does it change the moment someone looks at me? Do people perceive me as cool and collected, competent in my job, friendly and willing to go out of my way to help, or do they see a man who is not really interested in their problems, a rich man who cares about others only as long as he can make money off their misery and problems.

I like to think of myself as a man who cares, but am I that man? Would I be different if I didn't have any money and would have to work for a living? Do I actually care? Is my past responsible for the man I am today?

Checking the clock, he saw it was still early enough for everyone to be in the office. He decided to talk to Tony.

When Nicole answered the phone, he said, "Nicole, connect me with Tony."

"Sure, Mr. Hummer."

Mister Hummer. She always calls me Mister Hummer, even though she's been my employee for three years. I never asked her to call me 'Frank'. Am I so standoffish? Which of my faces does Nicole see?

"Tony here. If you're calling for information I did find some more stuff, Mr. Hummer."

"What did you find?"

"About eight million sites under the name Sarah Dalton. It takes time to sift through them, but I didn't come up with a Sarah Dalton who is a parole officer in Kansas City or anywhere nearby." He paused. "I checked files in local police computers, jails, and other government offices, no luck. I didn't search any Federal Government files yet. You want me to do that?"

"No, forget about her for now. How about Helen Middler? What can you tell me about her?"

"There are plenty of Helen Middlers out there. Thousands. Obviously, I checked out the people living at thirty-seven Pineridge Cove. According to tax records the house belongs to Harry Middler. Strangely enough, his wife Helen does not seem to be a co-owner, so that was a dead end. Then I looked into the marriage license records at City Hall and found records of a Harry Middler and a Helen Molokov getting married April fifteen, two-thousand-six."

"That sounds about right. She told me she and Harry have been married for five years. Did you manage to find any pictures?"

"No, I'm sorry. I didn't have enough time for that."

"That's okay. You did all right so far. Tomorrow is another day. See you then."

When he arrived home, he had the urge to phone Cheryl but decided against it. He didn't know what to tell her about his feelings on the subject of marriage. He needed time to let it sink in that their relationship had suddenly changed from casual to something more intimate, something more serious.

* * * *

He didn't get a good night's rest. His sleep was disturbed by dreams about Helen Middler. Every dream was the same. She was running after the van that took away her husband but didn't catch it. Coming back, she rushed into his arms and kissed him. Then she changed into Cheryl, but Cheryl was a hooker who wanted to marry him for his money. When he woke up the image of Helen walking between the two officers who arrested her wouldn't leave him. What was going on? Who was Sarah Dalton?

The ringing of the phone ripped him out of sleep that had finally come in the early morning hours. When he answered the phone, it was Martin Schumann. "Frank, I think we found your Rose Miller."

"That's great. Where is she?"

"In the morgue."

Instantly awake, he almost shouted, "Did you say *morgue*?"

"Yes, morgue. I don't think that's what you wanted to hear."

"No, I didn't. Are you certain it's her?"

"I just got the report. According to the I.D. they found on the body it is Rose Miller."

"How did she die?"

"Hit and run. Happened last night."

Hummer rubbed his eyes. "Man, that sucks. How the hell could that happen? Where did she come from? Why didn't she phone me if she was in trouble? She could at least have told me she had been released from custody. She knew I promised to help her. Something doesn't add up here."

"If you want to have a look at her body, I can probably arrange it, Frank."

"Thanks, Martin. I'd appreciate that. I guess you know one of the men who died in the fire at Globe Labs was, apparently, a Professor Harry Middler?"

"Yes, I do. He and Saul Finkbein, the CEO were the only casualties. What's your interest in this case?"

"Remember when I told you I was involved in a bizarre case? Well, Professor Middler is part of it. I really can't tell you much more because it gets more and more confusing. Do you have any idea who identified the bodies?"

"They haven't been officially identified, but according to the guard at the gate, Finkbein and the Professor were the only ones in the plant."

"I see."

"You're making me curious, Frank. If there is anything you want to share with me, I'd be most interested. You wouldn't want to get drawn into an investigation and charged with withholding evidence." Schumann's chuckle sounded almost menacing over the phone. "You know, you and I are good friends, but there is only so much I can do to protect you."

"If I had anything useful to share, believe me, you'd be the first to hear about it, but whatever information and facts I seem to have don't make much sense. If I were to talk with you about it, I'd sound like some kind of lunatic. Believe me when I say I have nothing concrete."

"And Rose Miller is also involved in this...this bizarre case?"

"She is, but I don't know how yet."

"Well, I hope you can unravel your mystery. How is your new computer-spy working out?"

"Tony? He's doing okay. He's helping me in this case. So far, we've run only into dead ends."

"Right. I'd better go. Take care, Frank, and stay out of trouble." Schumann broke the connection on the other end.

I need to talk to Mrs. Middler. The one I met at thirty-seven Pineridge. It seems she's the real one after all. She'll be able to tell me if the man who died in the fire is her husband Harry Middler.

After a hurried breakfast he took his car and headed for Pineridge Cove. Arriving at the house, he was a bit surprised when he didn't see any cars parked in the driveway. One would think there'd be friends visiting to console Mrs. Middler after losing her husband so tragically. He got out of the car and walked up the stairs to the front door. Nobody answered after he rang the doorbell.

He tried to look through the window in the door, but he couldn't see anything in the darkened front hall.

As he headed back to his car, he happened to look toward the neighbor's house and saw a middle-aged woman coming out of the backyard. She carried a small watering can and began watering her flowers. He watched her for a moment, wondering if she might be able to help him. She looked up and saw him watching her. He smiled and lifted his hand in greeting.

"I'm looking for Mrs. Middler," he called.

She stopped watering her flowers and came closer. "Are you a friend of the family?" she asked, her gray eyes studying him with curiosity.

"No, not really. I've only met the Middlers for the first time last Friday. Professionally. It's a damn shame about Professor Middler, isn't it?"

"It sure is. Poor Helen. She may not even know her husband has been killed. It is a great tragedy, but it always is when someone dies so suddenly and unexpected." The woman seemed genuinely concerned.

"Helen left Sunday morning to visit her parents."

"I was wondering why nobody answered the door. That explains it. Do you know where her parents live?"

She shook her head. "Somewhere out of State."

"Have you known the Middlers long?"

"No. We only moved here a few days ago. In fact, I've never spoken to Helen before Saturday." She lifted her shoulders as if to apologize. "You know, we had problems with one of our neighbors where we lived before we moved here and we're not exactly eager to get too chummy with new neighbors."

"Where did you move from?"

"Long Island. We lived there many years, but things changed. We didn't like it anymore. One good thing, we got paid some nice money for our house. The new people who bought up the houses in the area were different from the ones who called Long Island home thirty years ago."

Hummer gave her a little smile. "I know what you mean. Things and people have changed everywhere. We are living in different times now. It seems everything was less complicated thirty years ago."

The woman laughed. "You don't look old enough to remember things from thirty years ago."

"I beg to differ, ma'am. I was eight years old," he said with a mock expression of feeling insulted. "I remember things."

"Eight years old. Why, you were almost a man." Her eyes twinkled with amusement. "By the way, my name is Kim Sikomas. And who are you, if I may ask?"

"Frank Hummer, but you may call me Frank. It makes me feel old when people call me *Mister*." He wasn't sure if he should tell her he was a private detective. People always seemed to clam up when they found out about his profession, as if they had something to hide and they didn't want anyone snooping around in their past.

"What exactly was your business with the Middlers, Frank?"

There it was. Somehow conversations always ended with people asking him what he did for a living. "Ah, nothing serious," he said, evasively. "I work for an insurance company."

"Oh, you're a life-insurance salesman. One of those." Her demeanor seemed suddenly a bit frosty. The truth might be the best way after all to gain her confidence.

"No, I'm not a salesman. Actually, I am an investigator." He chuckled. "Selling life-insurance is not my cup of tea. I assume it isn't yours either."

"Not really. I think life-insurance is a bit of a scam. I'd rather not get into a discussion about that."

"Some people are lucky to have it, though," Hummer said. "I'll bet Mrs. Middler will have a fair chunk of money coming her way."

"Probably," Kim agreed. "But it won't bring back her husband. My father always used to say *if you have life-insurance you're inviting disaster*. He was a great believer in providing for his family by putting money away for a rainy day and not relying on insurance or the government."

"It looks like your father was a wise man, a man of the old school. I remember my father saying stuff like that. Anyway, thanks for chatting with me, Kim, but I must run. Do you by any chance know anything about the neighbors next to the Middler house?"

"Nothing, really. Apparently, they moved in a week or so before us. Like I said, we don't know anyone yet in the neighborhood and we might just keep it that way." Her smile left him with the impression he had been dismissed, the way his teacher in grade four used to dismiss him. "Good bye, Frank Hummer." She turned away and went back to her flowers.

Hummer decided to pay the neighbors on the other side a visit. Walking across the lawn in front of the Middlers' house, he wondered about coincidences. When he rang the doorbell at number thirty-nine Pineridge Cove, he heard the shuffling of footsteps coming from inside the house.

Well, at least someone is home in this place.

The man who opened the door gave him an inquiring look. He appeared tense and apprehensive. "If you're collecting for some cause, we've already donated plenty to various charities."

Hummer put on his most disengaging smile. "Sorry to bother you, sir, but I'm not collecting for any charity. My name is Frank Hummer. I'm a private investigator and I was wondering if I could ask you a few questions about your neighbors, the Middlers. I assume you heard about

Professor Middler's death in a fire Sunday night, or haven't you?"

"Yes, I have. It is a great shame." The man seemed to relax a little. "You said you're an investigator. Is it about the fire? Are you working for the police?"

"No. My inquiries are of a private nature. I understand you've moved here only a couple of weeks ago. Is that correct?"

"Yes." The man seemed to go rigid again. His eyes narrowed when he looked at Hummer. "What of it?"

"I'll perfectly understand if you don't know anything about the Middlers, but you've been here a bit longer than Mrs. Sikomas, who lives in number thirty-five, and you may have talked to Helen Middler or her husband at least on one occasion."

"I may have. What do you want to know?"

"Do you by any chance have an idea how long the Middlers lived next door?"

"I believe about three years. In fact, yes, now I remember. Helen mentioned it to my wife. We just talked about it, wondering if we would last that long in one place." His chuckle seemed strained. "We've moved around a lot since we got married."

"Three years you say. That seems about right. It coincides with the information I have on file. Say," Hummer said in a conversational tone, "Kim, Mrs. Sikomas, and her husband resided on Long Island before they moved here. Where did you live before?"

"Minneapolis. Why do you want to know?" He seemed suspicious again, like a man guilty of something, a man afraid of getting caught. Hummer was good at reading people, a trait he needed to be successful in his chosen profession.

"I'm just curious." Hummer's smile was innocent enough to cover his real interest. "I wondered how long it took you to find a beautiful house like this one in this quiet and nice neighborhood."

"Not long at all. In fact, we were told this house stood empty for nearly a month, but it was put on the market the same day we looked at it, and bought it." The man actually smiled. "We did get a good bargain. Everyone gets lucky sometimes."

"That's true. One more thing, would you know Helen Middler's occupation?"

"I believe she is a student. She wants to become a biologist."

"A biologist. Hmm. Interesting. One would think with her red hair and lovely, slim figure she'd want to be a model." Hummer grinned. "One wonders what a beautiful woman like that found in an older man like Professor Middler."

"Who can figure out a woman," the man agreed. His smile looked almost natural. He turned his head to look behind him. "Don't tell my wife I said this. She gets jealous quite easily," he said in a near whisper. "I have to agree, Helen is a beautiful woman with her red hair and gorgeous figure. She won't have any problems finding another husband."

"I have no doubts. When did you say you saw Helen Middler last?"

"I talked to Harry and Helen just on Saturday. Helen was talking about visiting her parents. She left Sunday morning."

"You spoke to them Saturday. Fascinating. You wouldn't by any chance know where her parents live?"

"No. I don't like to pry into other people's private lives."

"I don't either, but it is my job." Hummer held out his hand. "Well, it was nice talking to you. Thanks for the information, Mr...?"

The man shook Hummer's hand and said, "Larry Krupp. By the way, do you have a business card?"

"Sure." Hummer took one out of his pocket and handed it to Krupp. "Perhaps someday you'll need my services, Mr. Krupp. You never know."

He walked away, aware that Krupp was watching him.

Another mystery. He'd talked to the Middlers on Saturday. He took the bait I put out and confirmed that Helen Miller has red hair, even though the one who lives now in the Middler-house has blonde hair. I guess he doesn't know that I met both women who claim to be Helen Middler, the real one and the imposter. Now I'm totally confused. Which one is the real one? Does he know or did he lie to me about something?

Chapter Six

It might be a good idea to talk to Martin Schumann. Hummer made the decision and drove to the precinct.

He was lucky; Schumann was in and at his desk. The detective looked up when Hummer approached. "Hey, Frank. What brings you here? How's your mystery case coming?"

Hummer plunked himself into the chair in front of Schumann's desk. "Getting more mysterious by the minute. I promised I would fill you in once I had more details and facts. Well, it seems the facts are still eluding me."

"Then how about telling me what you know?" Schumann leaned back in his chair. "Perhaps I can help sort things out. I have more information at my disposal than you."

Hummer couldn't hide his smile.

I have Tony Silvari, my friend. He can probably get information from places you don't even know exist.

He thought it, but didn't say it. Schumann was right, though. He had information readily available, while Tony had to sift through all kinds of files to find what he was looking for. It took time to do that.

Schumann's eyes challenged him to reveal at least something.

"Normally I would be bound by confidentiality between my client and me, but it seems my client is no longer among the living," he started.

"What happened to your client?"

"I was hoping you could tell me that. My client's name is Helen Middler, but that may not be her real name. She might actually be Rose

Miller."

Schumann raised an eyebrow. "Are you talking about the Rose Miller they found yesterday?"

"I'm afraid that's the one. I wouldn't mind viewing the body. You said you could arrange it."

"Let me make a call." Schumann picked up his phone and dialed a number he got from the phonebook he kept in a drawer. "Doctor Norford, this is Detective Schumann. I'd like to come by this afternoon to have a look at the body of Rose Miller." There was a pause as Schumann listened to the person on the other end. Then he said, "I understand. Sure. Thanks."

He put the receiver down and looked at Hummer. "The news is not good. Apparently, the body was so severely damaged from the impact it is nearly impossible to recognize her. She was identified from the driver's license she had with her. The coroner wants to check up on dental records to make a positive identification, but that may take some time. Doctor Norford informed me his office is backlogged quite a bit."

"I'm not really surprised by this news, because everything has gone wrong so far." Hummer stared at Schumann, wondering how much he should tell him. "Remember you told me this morning that the guard at GLI more or less identified Professor Middler and Saul Finkbein as the victims who died in the fire. Any new developments in the case?"

Schumann seemed to hesitate at first, but then he said, "Finkbein died from a gunshot wound in the head. Right behind the ear. Execution style. He was dead before the fire started. It looks as if Professor Middler shot him."

"I wonder why a man would shoot his employer. Has the gun been located?"

"Yes. Middler held the gun in his hand. Apparently, he shot himself after shooting Finkbein." Schumann ran his hand across his bald head. "You're talking about a bizarre case? Well, this one seems to have developed into one. The investigators more or less established the source of the fire. Apparently, it was caused by the explosion of a propane gas tank. Middler was found near the exploded tank. Close enough to have been killed by the explosion. If he is responsible for the explosion and died from it, he couldn't have shot himself, but the wound in his head suggests he died from the gunshot wound, immediately. Also, the angle of the shot is awkward for a self-inflicted wound. Many questions. How did he manage to explode the tank if he was dead from a bullet in his brain?"

"It does sound strange. It seems there was another person on the premises, someone who might have shot both men and then started the fire to cover up the murders," Hummer pondered.

"You might just be right, but the guard at the gate didn't see anyone else entering or leaving the premises. He's the one who sounded the alarm and called the fire department. He says he was there the whole time."

Hummer stroked his chin. "Have both men been positively identified?"

Schumann shook his head. "Finkbein has. His body was not burned as badly as Middler's and the exit wound of the bullet didn't destroy his features. Not so with Middler. His face is unrecognizable. His identity will have to be established through dental records, unless his wife identifies him. We haven't been able to contact her yet."

"I find everything quite coincidental."

"Why?" Schumann queried.

"Because there are just too many flukes in this case. We have only the guard's word that it was Professor Middler in the lab. Helen Middler, his wife, can't be located. Rose Miller's body can't be identified without her dental records." Hummer gave Schumann a thoughtful look. "I have a suspicion the body of Rose Miller is actually Mrs. Middler, the real Helen Middler."

"The real Helen Middler? What the hell are you talking about, Frank?"

Hummer took a deep breath. "I guess I owe you some explanation, since it seems all my clients are dead. Give me another day. I'll meet with you tomorrow and I will fill you in, but there are some things I still need to check out before then." He rose. "I hope by tomorrow I can make some sense out of all this."

"How about giving me just a little?" Schumann didn't look happy. He was a police detective and he hated mysteries. "If you are withholding information associated with this case..." He didn't finish but Hummer understood the hidden warning.

"What I have won't help you with your case. At least you have some dead bodies while I have nothing but missing people. Actually, non-existing missing people. I promise, by tomorrow I'll give you what I have. Who knows, you may even be able to help me." He lifted a hand in a farewell gesture. "See you tomorrow."

* * * *

When he woke up in the morning and looked out of the window, he had a feeling it might not be a pleasant day ahead. Rain never did much to lift his spirits. Getting into his car, he headed for Pineridge Cove. He wasn't quite sure why, but sometimes a man had to follow **his gut** feelings. As the heavy drops hit his windshield, he listened to the soft whooshing sounds of the wipers instead of turning on his radio. It soothed him. Calmed him. He let the events of the last few days run through his mind, trying to find something that made sense, but nothing did.

Pulling into the driveway of Mrs. Kelvin's house, he drove as close as possible. After getting out of the comfortable environment of his car, he pulled up his coat collar to keep the raindrops from running down his neck and walked briskly from his car to the front door. He hoped the old lady, who lived there, would open the door and let him in.

Ringing the doorbell, he waited impatiently, grateful for the canopy over the steps to keep out the rain. He was as elated as a lottery winner when he heard someone coming to answer the bell. The door opened slightly and the lined face of an old woman peered at him out of rheumatic eyes.

"I'm sorry for the intrusion, ma'am. Are you Mrs. Kelvin?"

"Who wants to know?" Even though her face suggested a frail woman, her voice sounded feisty and belligerent.

"My name is Frank Hummer. I am a private investigator representing Mrs. Helen Middler, your neighbor across the street. I wonder if you wouldn't mind answering some questions."

"What kind of questions?"

He was afraid she may close the door in his face by the way she said it, but she kept it open, if only just a tiny sliver. He knew he had only a few short minutes left to convince her he meant no harm. "Professor Middler died in a fire Sunday night. Now Mrs. Middler has gone to visit her parents and can't be reached. I really need someone who has lived on this street for a few years to give me some answers to important questions. You are the only one who probably can. Mrs. Middler told me you can be trusted."

"She did? Well, I'm surprised because I haven't spoken to her for over a year. I don't pry into other people's affairs and I like to keep to myself. I don't trust people. Most people are trying to get something from you." Her eyes narrowed. "What do you want from me? I have no money to give you."

"I don't want your money, Mrs. Kelvin; only information." He hoped his smile was reassuring. He took out his wallet and removed a twenty-dollar-bill. "In fact, I'll give you twenty bucks for talking to me."

"Why would you give me twenty bucks? Is this some kind of a scam? I'm not some poor bag-lady, you know." The door began to close and he realized his approach had been the wrong one. "Please, don't close the door," he pleaded. "I didn't mean to insult you, Mrs. Kelvin. I'm just so used to paying for information." He chuckled. "Even the government doesn't give out anything for free."

"Well, neither do I." A skinny arm darted out, like a snake from its den, and with one quick movement she snatched the money out of his hand, surprising him by her change of attitude. "For another twenty bucks I'll keep an eye on the place across the street for you."

"That would be nice." He reached into his pocket. "Here is my card. If you see anything strange I'd be happy to hear from you. I'll make you a deal, if you have important information, I might be inclined to spring for a C-note."

"A hundred dollars? Either you're crazy or rich...or a liar." She scrutinized him again, suspicion clearly in her expression. "Are you sure you're not trying to scam me?"

He laughed. "You're the one getting the money, not me. Who is scamming whom?"

"You said you wanted information. What do you want to know?"

"Do you know how long the Middlers have lived here?"

"They moved in about three years ago, I think. Yes, it will be three

65

years next month. I remember, because it rained that day, just like today, and I was feeling sorry for them. Especially for their furniture."

"You said you haven't spoken to Mrs. Middler for a year. Do you remember what she looked like?"

"She looked nice. I remember mostly her red hair."

"You're sure about her red hair?"

"Definitely. Red hair and freckles. She used to wear her hair tied into a ponytail. Made her look younger, I guess." She cackled. "She reminded me of myself when I was her age. I used to be quite a knockout, you know. Men whistled when I walked by."

"I'm sure you turned heads," Hummer said. "Nobody whistles after a woman these days. Women get offended. I guess people were not as sensitive about issues as they are now. How about Mr. Middler?"

"He was a little older. Also a nice-looking man. I never talked to him, though."

"Anything else you remember?"

"No. Like I said, I keep to myself."

"I guess that's it then." He tipped his baseball cap. "It was a pleasure talking to you, ma'am, and I'm hoping to hear from you. Perhaps next time you'll invite me in for a cup of tea." Pulling up his collar again, he hurried back to his car. The rain was still coming down and a cool wind blowing from the north made him shiver. He was happy to get back into the warm dry interior.

This confirms it. The people I met at thirty-seven Pineridge were most likely imposters. The blonde woman who claimed to be Helen Middler could have had her hair colored. But if they were pretenders, who was the man who died in the fire?

And why would they play this charade? I guess I'll drive down to the precinct and talk to Schumann.

"I was just about to leave," Schumann said when Hummer walked in. "I have something you may find interesting."

"Anything to do with my case?"

"I'm quite positive it does. Remember the woman who was identified as Rose Miller? Well, here is something weird. She carried an old car registration hidden in one of the pockets of her purse. It was made out to a Helen Middler."

"What?" Hummer sat down in the chair. "This confirms my suspicion. The dead woman is not Rose Miller. She is Helen Middler, my client. Damn!" He punched his fist into his palm. "She was such a nice person. She didn't deserve to die like that." Staring at Schumann, he said, "That was not a hit-and-run accident, Martin. I'll bet you any money, she was killed deliberately. In other words, she was murdered."

"Why would anyone murder her, and why did she come to you in the first place? You'd better level with me, Frank. It seems we have more than one murder case on our hands. Hers, her husband's, and Paul Finkbein's. What is the connection here?"

Hummer shrugged. "That's what we'll have to find out. I met Helen Middler last Friday morning, when her husband Harry Middler was abducted. In fact, I was there when it happened."

"You were witness to a kidnapping?" Schumann sat down in his own seat. "I think it's time you come clean, Frank, and you'd better leave nothing out. I should have pressed you for more information when you asked me to find that Rose Miller." He wiped his forehead. "I've always trusted you, Frank. Don't drag me into a situation as an accessory. I'm a cop and I don't want to jeopardize my position."

"You have nothing to worry about. Like I told you before, this whole case is so twisted and I have so little information, I still can't tell you much. It seems this is not a simple kidnapping—there is much more to it. It may involve identity theft and who knows what else. Whatever happened was out of my control. I wanted to protect the woman who came to me for help, but I failed her. Now she appears to be dead, as is her husband."

"Perhaps you should start at the beginning. I need to know everything you found out so far. Maybe between the two of us we can find something."

"All right," Hummer leaned back in his chair as he explained what he knew. As I said, Helen Miller asked me to help her...and so it seems the people who claimed to be the Middlers were imposters. One question pops up. Who is behind all of this and why? There are a number of people involved, which means it took money and planning for all of this to happen. And what happened to the real Rose Miller?" Even after telling Schumann the whole story, he still didn't know much. In fact, more questions popped into his mind.

Schumann reached for his phone. "Let me find out if there are any more details about the fire and this Professor Middler." He dialed and after waiting for a moment, he said, "Listen, Graham, any new developments in the Globe Lab fire? Really? Well, that's interesting. Okay, thanks." He put down the phone and wiped his bald head with one large hand. "They've identified the corpse by his fingerprints, which surprisingly were nearly intact." His fingers drummed the desktop in a pattern that almost sounded like Morse code. "This gets more bizarre by the minute. You won't believe who the dead man may be?"

"Well?" Hummer waited for Schumann to tell him. "Don't keep me in suspense."

"He is not Professor Middler. It seems his name is Henry Miller, a man with a lengthy criminal record. Apparently, he spent the last five years in a mental hospital." Schumann's expression was one of disbelief when he looked at Hummer. "I have a strange suspicion this Henry Miller is a relative of the Rose Miller you were trying to locate. What a peculiar coincidence."

Hummer nodded. "Rose Miller had a brother by that name. So now we found him, but that still leaves me wondering about Rose Miller's whereabouts."

"I doubt she's still alive. I took the liberty to run her name through the system. She was a drug addict and made her living as a prostitute. She probably ended up in a morgue somewhere from a drug overdose or even murdered by one of her Johns. We've got plenty of Jane Doe's ending up that way." Schumann tried to sound sympathetic, but Hummer knew that a man's emotions hardened after awhile. There is only so much sympathy a police officer can bring to his cases. Hummer couldn't blame him. Dealing with criminals, murder-victims, prostitutes, and drug addicts day after day changes a man and leaves him with little empathy for them.

"She was a human being," Hummer said softly. "Every human being deserves to die with dignity."

"You are right. Everybody does, in an ideal world," Schumann agreed, but his eyes didn't show any pity. He rose from his chair and grabbed his coat. "Let's you and me take a drive to Pineridge Cove. I want to have a look at the Middler house and maybe talk to the neighbors. If we have a couple of impostors living there they'll need to be brought to justice."

Hummer left his car in the precinct's parking lot. They took Schumann's patrol car, which suited him just fine. Schumann's partner, Jerry Martinez, drove the car, with Schumann sitting in the passenger's seat. Hummer sat in the back, feeling like a prisoner.

When they arrived in front of number thirty-seven Pineridge Cove, he got out of the car and threw a look at the house across the street, wondering if Mrs. Kelvin was at her post. He thought he saw the curtains behind her window move slightly, but that could have been his imagination. *She's probably wondering why I'm back again.*

When Martinez rang the doorbell nobody came to the door. Hummer would have been surprised had someone actually answered the ringing of the doorbell.

"I guess nobody's home," Martinez said. He looked at Schumann. "What do you want to do?"

"I want to have a look inside the house," Schumann said. "Open the door!"

"We don't have a warrant," Martinez objected.

"I'm not telling anyone if *you* won't." Schumann glanced at Hummer. "How about you, Frank?"

Hummer shrugged and grimaced. "I know nothing about police procedures. I'm a private eye."

"You hear that, Martinez? Mr. Hummer here is a private citizen. He knows nothing about how the police operate in certain situations. Open the fucking door! I'm getting cold and wet out here."

"No problem. I just wanted to make sure I heard right." Martinez took a few tools from his pocket and started working on the lock. It didn't take long before the door swung open.

Schumann was the first to enter. "Police. This is Detective Schumann. Anyone in the house?" he called. When nobody answered, all three men proceeded to walk into the living room. "Check upstairs," Schumann told Martinez. "Be alert."

Hummer stayed with Schumann. He didn't touch anything, careful not to get his fingerprints onto any furniture, in case they found something that would be cause for the CSI team to check out the house.

Schumann wore gloves, obviously thinking along the same lines as Hummer. The place looked the way Hummer remembered; nothing seemed out of place, but he had only seen the front vestibule and the living room. He thought it strange not to find any pictures, not even in the drawers upstairs, after he followed Schumann into the bedrooms.

There was a computer in one of the rooms, which was obviously used as an office. Martinez turned on the computer but couldn't get into any files, since they were password protected. "We'll have to take it in and have our computer experts look at it. I doubt we'll find anything useful," Schumann said.

"We can't just take it," Martinez said.

"Not us, we'll get the CSI boys to search the place. After we get a warrant," Schumann assured him. "Strange," he said, looking around. "Somebody stripped this place clean of anything personal that would give us some clues about who lived here." He opened one of the closets. "I see only men's clothing in here."

"Maybe they had separate bedrooms," Hummer suggested.

When they checked out the closet in the other bedroom, it was nearly empty, except for a few old dresses, a couple of blouses, a woman's coat years out of date, and one pair of high-heeled shoes. No handbags or small purses.

"It appears there was no woman living in this place. Nobody has slept in that bed for a long time." Martinez used his flashlight to look under the bed. "Dust bunnies," he commented when he was done. "No efficient woman would leave those under the bed."

"I wouldn't know," Hummer said, grinning.

"You're not married?" Martinez asked.

"Nope."

"I am, and believe me when I say my wife drives me crazy with her cleaning. That vacuum never gets a rest. Of course, I can't blame her. The kids try their best to keep her busy. I swear, they're carrying little shovels and pails when they go outside to bring as much dirt into the house as they possibly can."

"How many kids you got?"

"Four and one on the way."

Schumann laughed. "I told him already to put a fucking knot into his pecker or at least put on a rubber."

"Do you wear socks when you take a bath?" Martinez asked.

"No, why would I?"

"Then why would I put a rubber sock over my prick? It ain't natural," Martinez defended himself. "Aside from the fact my wife and I love children."

"So do I but come on, five?"

"We may go for a few more."

"Well, as long as you can feed them and give them the opportunity to get a good education it's none of my business, but the moment they become a burden to society, in other words to me, it becomes my business."

Martinez looked at Hummer who had not commented on the exchange between the two men. It seemed friendly enough, but he detected an underlying tension. "Schumann thinks couples shouldn't have more than two children max. I'm just making up for the ones who have none. Of course, he's already filled his own quota. What are your thoughts on the subject?"

"I never gave it much thought. People do what they think is right, but I'm of the same opinion as Schumann to a degree; if you can't afford to give your children a good home you shouldn't have any."

"I can't argue with you there," Martinez said. "But children don't have to have everything they want. The most important thing is love, and mine have that."

"Well, I'm glad to hear that, Martinez," Schumann said. "Now, let's come back to our situation at hand. I believe we've seen enough here. I don't know what to make out of what we found, or maybe I should say what we didn't find." He gave Hummer a quick look. "What do you think, Frank?"

Hummer lifted his shoulders. "I'm as baffled as you are. From the looks of it this house was occupied by only a man. No woman has lived here for some time. It proves to me the people I met were not the true occupants, but imposters. They disappeared soon after the fire at Globe Labs, maybe even before, which means they are involved deeply. I am left with the question who was the woman I met? Was she the real Mrs.

Middler or was she Rose Miller. Why did Rose Miller have a registration in Helen Middler's name in her purse? How are those two women connected? Is it possible they are one and the same person?"

"I can't answer any of those questions." Schumann rubbed his head. "Let's go. I'd like to speak to the neighbors."

Nobody answered the door at the Krupp residence next door. When Schumann tried the doorknob, the door opened. "I guess we'll just walk in."

The house was as empty as the one they just left; with one difference. It was really empty. No clothing in the closets, no furniture, not even any dishes in the cupboards. It seemed as if nobody had lived in the house for quite awhile.

"Didn't you tell me you talked to a guy here?" Schumann asked Hummer.

"Yes, I did. A Larry Krupp. He told me they moved in a couple of weeks ago." Hummer chuckled. "He was wondering how long they'd be staying in this house, since they apparently moved around a lot."

"Well, it seems they didn't last very long in this one," Schumann said, sarcasm clearly in his voice. "I wonder what made him move out in such a hurry. Was there a Mrs. Krupp?"

"He told me there was. I never saw her."

They left the house and locked it behind them. "I don't want any vandals trashing the place until we've dusted it for prints," Schumann commented. "Let's talk to the neighbors on the other side. I hope they are home."

Mrs. Sikomas was in. Her face lit up when she saw Hummer. "Frank, nice to see you again, and so soon." She looked at Schumann and Martinez. "I see you've brought friends. They look like real cops, even though they are trying hard to hide it."

"Hi, Kim. This is Police Detective Martin Schumann and Detective Jerry Martinez. I believe Detective Schumann wants to ask you a few questions."

"Sure." Her gray eyes were steady when she looked at Schumann. It was clear to Hummer here was a woman with nothing to hide, except possibly her age.

"We were wondering if you saw anything suspicious since

yesterday," Schumann asked.

"Suspicious? How?"

"The people living in number thirty-nine seem to have moved out."

"Yes, they have. Late last night."

"Did you know them?"

Kim shook her head. "No, we just moved in last week. We haven't had time to get friendly with any of the neighbors. I wouldn't know why they moved out, especially since they apparently only moved here a little over two weeks ago." Her eyes twinkled when she smiled. "Perhaps they didn't like the neighborhood."

"Perhaps not." Schumann didn't smile. He was all business, like an undertaker discussing funeral arrangements with the family of a deceased. "Do you have any plans of moving out in the near future, ma'am?"

She laughed at his remark. "I'm happy to have found this place and not at all eager to move any day soon. I hope to stay in this house until I'm too old to take care of it, or maybe I should say until my husband is too old. He's the one doing all the hard physical work."

"Where does your husband work?"

"He's an accountant. He works for Fuller and Sons, a landscape contractor. You find them in the phonebook." Her eyes met Hummer's. "You should tell your friend the Detective here to lighten up a little. Life's too short to be so glum all the time." She looked again at Schumann. "Anything else you want to drill me about, Sergeant?"

"Detective, ma'am," Schumann said. "Thank you for your time, ma'am. We'll be in touch."

"Oh, that sounds so official. Have yourself a pleasant afternoon, Detective." She smiled at Hummer. "Next time I hope to see you alone, Frank. I'll invite you in for a cup of coffee."

"That sounds great," Hummer said. "Perhaps I can meet your husband next time."

Her laughter teased him. "When I said alone I meant alone, just you and I."

"Won't your husband mind?" Hummer asked, wondering if she really meant what she said.

"Why should he mind? He won't know about it. It'll be our little secret."

Schumann coughed into his hand and turned to walk away. Kim laughed softly. "I have a feeling Detective Schumann doesn't approve. He will tell on us. We mustn't let him find out."

"I'll make sure he won't," Hummer joked. "I'd better go with him. I have no other transportation to get home." He could hear her soft laughter as he followed Schumann and Martinez, wondering if she had been teasing him about visiting her when she was alone.

When he sank into the backseat, Schumann turned to look at him. "What the hell was that about, Frank? Are you screwing that woman?"

Hummer grinned, amused by his friend's accusation. "Yesterday was the first time I talked to her. Hardly enough time to get to know her intimately."

"It was quite obvious she invited you for a little nooky," Martinez said, chuckling. Then he added, "You lucky dog."

"Come on, Martinez. She wasn't serious. Wasn't it clear she was trying to get a rise out of Schumann?"

Martinez laughed, backing the car into the street. "What was clear to me was that she wants you to come and visit her, *alone*. You're not married, man. You should take advantage of that invitation. I would."

"I have no problem believing that," Schumann growled.

"I meant I would have before I was married. Anyway, it seems to me we have some missing persons."

"We have a bunch of criminals on the loose, that's what we have. Who the hell are these people? Damn it all!" Schumann cursed, angry about something. "You should have come to me sooner, Frank."

"Maybe I should have, but like I said I didn't have much to go on, only what appeared to be a kidnapping and possibly a case of identity theft. Except I didn't know who did what to whom," Hummer said in his defense, annoyed about Schumann's accusation.

"If those people weren't the real Middlers and the guy who died in the fire wasn't Professor Middler, where is the Professor? Where did they take him after his abduction?" Schumann spoke more to himself than to Hummer and Martinez.

"He's obviously another missing person," Martinez said.

"It's possible he is in the Happy Acres Sanatorium," Hummer

suggested, wondering if his assumption was correct. "Even though I was told the patient they have is Henry Miller. Since Miller is dead, the man could be Harry Middler."

"There is that possibility," Schumann agreed. "It needs to be checked out, but we can't do anything without a warrant, and we may have a problem finding a judge who will sign a warrant, not without probable cause."

"What more cause do you want, Martin? You said yourself the dead man is Henry Miller."

"That's what the coroner tells us. Maybe we'll find out he is also an imposter." Schumann sounded pessimistic. His expression was that of a man who just discovered he lost something important, like his wallet.

"I could go back to the Sanatorium. I think I made a bit of a connection with the woman in admittance," Hummer suggested.

Schumann's laugh sounded like the growling of an old grizzly. "Did she also invite you for a little nooky, as Martinez so aptly put it?"

Hummer smiled good-humoredly. "She suggested we might go for a drink the next time I visit. I could probably persuade her to let me have a look at the man. I only saw Professor Middler briefly before he was led away, but I have a good memory for faces. I'll recognize him."

"I'm afraid I can't let you do that, Frank," Schumann said. "This has now become official police business. I suggest you close the file. By the way, who's going to pay your fees on this one?"

"I didn't take this case for the money."

"Why did you take it?"

"To help out a woman in distress," Hummer explained. "I know you have a difficult time believing it, but once in awhile I do charity work. This is one of them." He knew with Schumann everything was always about money, but he wasn't in Hummer's position. Police detectives never get rich, not with the wages they are paid. He let out a slow sigh. "Unfortunately, I let down my client. I promised to help her but failed."

"Things don't always turn out the way we hope," Martinez said, trying to console Hummer. "Don't beat yourself up over it. It won't solve anything."

"Martinez is right. Take some time off, Frank. Go get drunk or fuck that woman, that blonde model I've seen you hanging out with,"

75

Schumann suggested in his rough way. "Are you two getting serious or are you still at the handholding stage?"

Hummer wasn't offended by Schumann's crude talk. That's just the way he was. They'd been friends since high school, going on double dates, to bars, parties, and they spent a lot of time together on hunting and fishing trips. They still met regularly to play golf and every once in a while they took an afternoon to go fishing.

"I think she wants to get married," Hummer revealed.

Schumann let out a rumbling laugh. "Don't tell me I might see you get hitched? I never thought that would happen. You're much too involved with your job and investments."

"I said *she* wants to, not me."

"You'd be a fool to let her slip away, Frank, a good-looking woman like that. She'll be good for you. I wasn't going to say anything, but you've been getting kinda ornery these last few months. You need some TLC, perhaps even a couple of kids before you get too old to enjoy them." Schumann shifted in his seat and grinned. "Remember when we were teenagers? Remember how we used to say *she needs to get laid* when we bumped into a bitchy woman? Well, my friend, lately you've been acting like those bitchy women. You need to get laid."

"I wasn't aware I was being bitchy," Hummer argued.

"You should listen to yourself sometimes. What do you think, Martinez?"

Martinez concentrated on driving but allowed himself the luxury of throwing a glance at Hummer in the rearview mirror. His grin was friendly and without malice. "I've got to agree with Schumann. You were a little off today. Maybe a night of passion will put you at ease."

"A night of passion!" Hummer chuckled. "You're a romantic, Martinez. Why don't you say what you really want to say?"

After getting dropped off at the precinct, he got into his car and headed straight for his office.

Chapter Seven

Marconi agreed with Schumann about closing the file.

"There are still too many loose ends," Hummer reasoned. "I hate to walk away from a case before it is completely solved."

"We're not walking away. We're only closing the file. What else do we need to find out? It seems our client, Mrs. Middler, is dead. Her husband is still missing, but he wasn't our client. Let the police handle it from now on. We don't know what happened to Rose Miller, but it doesn't matter. She wasn't our client either. She's also police business. Her brother, Henry, has been murdered. That is a murder case for the police to solve." Marconi pulled his black, thick eyebrows into a frown, lending his narrow face the appearance of a satyr, one of the deities out of Greek legends, except Marconi didn't frolic in the woods, chasing nymphs. He hated the outdoors. "We have other cases demanding our attention, Mr. Hummer."

"I just don't feel right knowing the man kept in an insane asylum is probably a sane man. I'm certain he is the real Harry Middler. Who put him there and why? Was the murder of Henry Miller a case of mistaken identity? Was he murdered instead of Professor Middler? If so, who wants Professor Middler dead?" Hummer stared at Marconi. "Isn't it my moral obligation to investigate that?"

"Perhaps it is, but I would suggest we let the police look into that. They have the manpower and the law to back them up. They don't need to sneak around and break into government computers to gather information," Marconi said.

"Why do you say that? Has Tony been misbehaving?"

"Well, he's pretty good at covering his tracks, but he did attract somebody's attention. There are other computer geniuses out there. Some of them work for law enforcement."

"Which one?"

"The FBI is one of them. I got a call this afternoon."

"The FBI, hmm," Hummer mused, wondering why they would call instead of breaking down the door to his company's office, guns drawn, but he had a pretty good idea about the identity of the caller. "Did Agent Mason call?"

"The same one. He wondered why you didn't come to his office instead of snooping around in the FBI's database, and therefore inviting an investigation that might result in you losing your license and possibly be charged with a federal crime."

Hummer chuckled. "That sounds like Mason."

Marconi didn't share his amusement. He hardly did. "Agent Mason is right, Mr. Hummer. This is a serious offense. You're lucky to have a friend in the Bureau."

"I'll have a talk with Tony," Hummer promised.

"And tell him what?"

"Tell him he's been made and to be more careful next time. I can't tolerate sloppy work."

Marconi didn't comment, but it was obvious he was not happy about his employer's assessment of the situation.

Hummer left Marconi's office and went into Silvo's to find Tony sitting behind the computer. He looked up when Hummer walked in. "Hi, Mr. Hummer. I guess Mr. Marconi told you about the call from the FBI?"

"Yes, he did. What happened?"

"I was careless," Tony admitted. "I promise it won't happen again. I'll be a ghost next time." He smiled. "I have to admit that guy at the FBI is good."

"What were you looking for?"

"I tried to get more info on Professor Harry Middler."

"Did you find out anything? I mean more than we already know?"

"He was born September twenty-three, nineteen-sixty-five, in

Liverpool, England. Immigrated to the USA in July eighty-five, became a US citizen in ninety. He married a Liz Sears in eighty-eight. The couple had two children. One boy and one girl. Liz divorced him in ninety-four, when she discovered he had an affair with a woman he worked with. We already know he married Helen, his present wife, in two-thousand-six. He is a chemistry professor and a genius. He developed a revolutionary battery that runs on salt water. He also discovered an alternative jet fuel while working for Globe Labs Institute."

"And you found that out where?"

Tony grinned. "Where else but in the FBI files."

"The FBI has a file on Professor Middler? Interesting. What about his wife Helen? Anything you found on her?"

"That's the strange part. Even though she is mentioned briefly in Harry Middler's file, I can't find any details about her. There is no file on her. Her name doesn't come up. When I tried to dig a little, I hit a protected area." He made a face. "I guess that's when I was flagged."

"Are you trying to tell me that Helen Middler's name may be in a secret file somewhere?"

Tony nodded. "It seems that way. I didn't get a chance to find out anything because I had to close down my snooping program. Unfortunately, I didn't get away fast enough."

In one way, Hummer was not really surprised to find Professor Harry Middler in the FBI files, because the company he worked for was engaged in important research that might be a concern to national security. Why his wife Helen should be in a secret file did not make any sense. Why was there no evidence of her having lived at Pineridge Cove? But he realized none of this really mattered. The case was closed for him. As much as all this new information intrigued him, it served no purpose to pursue his investigation. The woman he met as Helen Middler was dead and her husband missing. Maybe Schumann would carry on with the investigation, or maybe not. It wasn't Hummer's problem anymore.

"You did a good job, Tony, but I'm afraid we've gone as far as we can with this case. It is closed."

"Too bad. Just as I was getting into it." Tony looked disappointed.

"May I ask why you are closing the case?"

"The police are involved now. Besides, my client is dead."

"Oh, I'm sorry to hear that. What happened?"

"Hit-and-run."

"Don't you find that peculiar?"

Hummer smiled grimly. "More than peculiar, but that's how things go sometimes."

Tony seemed suddenly depressed. "I just realized something, Mr. Hummer. I know you hired me especially for this case, but since we don't have a case anymore, do I still have a job?"

"You have nothing to worry about, Tony," Hummer assured him. "We have other cases. Talk to Mr. Marconi. He'll find something for you to do. As soon as Mr. Silvo comes back from Miami, you can be his assistant."

"His assistant? I don't want to sound ungrateful, but I was secretly hoping to work directly with you."

"I'm flattered, Tony, but I don't really need a personal aide. Actually, that is not quite accurate. Every employee of mine works directly with me, so in a sense you are my assistant. In a sort of round-about way. When I need you for a special assignment, I'll let you know."

A big grin spread across Tony's face. "Special assignment. I like that. Sounds so...so secret-agent-like."

"Don't let it go to your head. Speaking of secret agents, I hope you keep everything that goes on in this office to yourself. Any information you gain while investigating places and people or anything you hear while we are discussing a case cannot be divulged to anyone outside this office, you understand."

Tony got up from his chair. His face carried a somber expression when he said, "I swear on my father's grave that I will never reveal any secrets from this office as long as I live. If you want me to I will swear on the bible, Mr. Hummer, or the American Flag."

Hummer had to suppress a smile when he saw the seriousness in Tony's face. "That's not necessary. We are not a government agency nor are we a secret society. Your word will be good enough. Just for your information, if you should discuss what goes on in my company with anyone not in my employ and I find out you will be fired without any explanation."

"I understand completely and I wouldn't even blame you for it."

"Good. Now, gather all of the information you have and keep it in one file. Strange things happen. We may have to look at the file at some later date."

"Shall do, Mr. Hummer. You can count on me. And, thank you again."

"Don't keep thanking me. Do your job well and you'll have a job as long as I own this company."

As he walked across the parking lot to his car, his cell phone rang. It was Cheryl. "Hi, Frank. How would you like to come to a barbeque at my father's place tomorrow? I hope you are free?"

"As it happens, I am. What time do you want me to be at your place?"

She laughed into the phone. "How about coming over right now? I'll make it worth your while."

When she answered the door, she came into his arms, smiling happily. "I've missed you." Then she kissed him with an urgency that startled him.

"It's only been three days since I saw you," he said after they broke the kiss.

"Three lonely days and two cold nights," she whispered, looking into his eyes. "I need to feel your warm body lying next to me. I want to snuggle in your arms when I wake up in the morning." Her smile was almost shy. "Am I scaring you with my crazy talk? Do I sound like some lovesick teenager?"

He stroked her hair. "It's not crazy talk, but to be honest? You do sound a little like a teenager who has just had her first sexual experience with the boy of her dreams." His smile teased her. "Am I the boy, or perhaps I should say man of your dreams?"

"You know you are. You will always be."

"Are we skipping dinner again tonight?" he asked, wondering if he'd be eating pizza once more.

She lifted up and planted a kiss on his nose. "Not tonight. I've made reservations for us at the Lazy Donkey Saloon. We'd better hurry."

"Sure, why not? I hear they make a great steak."

She slapped his arm. "When you go to a Mexican restaurant you eat Mexican Food, you big lug. You can have your steak tomorrow at my father's ranch."

"Well, that'll give me an incentive to visit your father. He may be a Redneck but he serves good food, I'll give him that."

* * * *

Congressman Charles Gibson was a rich man. One of the richest men in the country, probably in the world. Even though Hummer was a multi-millionaire, he was a pauper in comparison to Gibson. The gate to the estate was guarded by an armed security man to keep out uninvited guests. Cheryl pulled up to the gate,

"Good Day, Miss Gibson." He smiled at her but when he turned to Hummer he was all business. "Sir, what is your name?"

"I'm Frank Hummer."

"Are you carrying a gun?"

Hummer nodded.

"No weapons of any kind allowed on the estate, except for the ones Congressman Gibson owns or the guns his guards carry."

Hummer shrugged and gave the security man his gun. He felt naked without it, but he had no doubt there was enough firepower around Charles Gibson to defend him against an army of invaders. Hummer had no intentions of shooting the man. After all, there was a faint possibility Congressman Charles Gibson might be his father-in-law some day.

The security man looked at his log and nodded. "You're on the list. Go ahead."

Cheryl seemed a bit annoyed at the guard's behavior. "Of course he is on the list. Mr. Hummer is my guest."

I may be invited, but am I a welcome guest? After my last visit with the Congressman I'm not sure he'll welcome me with open arms.

As they drove down the long driveway to the mansion, Hummer recalled his argument with Charles Gibson. After Hummer pointed out that many Americans believed the US was in the Middle East only because of the oil, Gibson gave him a lecture about patriotism and the supremacy of the Western World, especially the United States of America. And about his vision of the future.

Bullet of Revenge

We cannot let those camel drivers control the flow of oil, Hummer. It is our duty to keep them from selling it to the Chinese or the Russians. We'll pump and use their oil until all the wells in the region run dry. After that we'll let them get back to riding their camels across the desert, because they won't be able to afford buying our oil.

His words still rang in Hummer's ears. Charles Gibson didn't care if in the meantime the atmosphere of the planet became so polluted by the exhaust fumes spewing from millions of cars people in the future may be forced to wear oxygen masks when going outside. As long as he made money in the process.

Cheryl parked her car in one of the many garages on the property. She still had her personal parking spot.

"It looks like my dear brother Eric and his lovely wife Marilyn are already here," she commented, pointing out the car in a stall two cars down. "I hope Marilyn isn't her bitchy old self this time."

Hummer had never met Eric and Marilyn, because they lived in another state, but from the few times Cheryl mentioned them in conversation, he got the distinct impression she wasn't exactly fond of her sister-in-law.

He knew Eric Gibson was the owner of a large sugar plantation with a great number of employees, the majority of them Mexicans. Some of them most likely illegals, the very same ones his father wanted to deport. Yet, apparently it was okay for his son to hire them. Talk about prejudice being alive and well in the Gibson family.

Cheryl's mother met them by the front door. Dressed in an elegant business suit, she was still an attractive woman with classical features, an older version of Cheryl. Hummer found it comforting to know some day Cheryl would look like that.

She hugged her daughter and gave Hummer a friendly nod and smile. "Nice to see you again, Frank."

"Always a pleasure to come visit you and the Congressman, ma'am," he responded.

Her laughter sounded pleasant and almost a little taunting. "I'm not sure if you enjoy your visits with my husband so much."

"If you're referring to my discussion with your husband last time I was here, you may be correct. Congressman Gibson does have radical views I can't agree with."

"That he does. If it is of any consolation, I don't agree with everything he says, either." She gave Cheryl an inquiring look. "You look nice. I'd almost say there is this certain glow about you. Are you pregnant?"

Cheryl chuckled. "No, I'm not pregnant, just happy."

Her mother's gaze traveled to Hummer. "Happy? That's good to hear. Has anything changed in your relationship with each other since your last visit?" she asked with a mother's perception.

"Like what, Mother?"

"Well, you may think of getting married. The clock is ticking, for both of you. Frank is a handsome man, charming, with good manners, independently wealthy. Everything a smart woman is looking for. I know you two are sleeping together. What healthy couple wouldn't? So what is the problem?" She looked first at Hummer and then at Cheryl.

"There is no problem," Cheryl said, her eyes on Hummer. "Right, Frank?"

Hummer felt suddenly pressured, like a man who couldn't swim being told to jump into the deep end of a pool. He tried to cover up his uneasiness with a polite laugh. "I'm not aware of any problems, either, but marriage plans need to be discussed in private between the two parties involved."

As if sensing Hummer's reluctance to talk about the subject, Mrs. Gibson put her hand on his arm in a friendly gesture. "I didn't mean to pry into your affairs. I hope you two can work it out."

"Don't worry, Mother, we will work it out." Cheryl acted as if she hadn't noticed Hummer's discomfort, but he knew she hadn't missed it. He silently cursed her mother for bringing up the subject. It was something he still had to come to grips with. He was fond of Cheryl, in fact deep down he had to admit he may even love her. He may never find another woman like her, but he needed more time to make up his mind. He also knew he couldn't wait too long. She wouldn't wait forever.

"Everyone is on the patio. Why don't you go and join the crowd?" Mrs. Gibson suggested.

There was quite a large crowd. Some stood around, holding glasses in their hands, while others sat on wicker chairs at tables. From the nearby pool came loud voices and laughter, most likely children of the guests.

One of the women saw Hummer and Cheryl stepping onto the patio. She waved and started walking toward them. It was Suzan, Cheryl's younger sister. Her long, blonde hair bounced around her exposed shoulders as she walked. Hummer always figured her a bubblehead and a bit of a flirt. She hugged Cheryl enthusiastically. "I've got some news, Cher," she blurted out.

Cheryl laughed. "I hope good news."

"The best. I'm expecting a baby. Can you imagine? After trying for five years it happened at last."

"That is good news," Cheryl said, hugging her sister back. "I'm happy for you. How is Larry taking it?"

"Oh, he's ecstatic." She giggled. Then she whispered, "He was beginning to doubt his ability to father a child. I told him if it didn't happen soon I may have to look for a man who could deliver." Her left eye closed in a conspiratorial wink. "But this gave him back his confidence. He's so much more energetic. If you know what I mean. Our sex-life is better than ever." She giggled again, like a little school girl who said something naughty.

"And Father? What does he think about it? He never cared much for Larry."

Suzan waved it off. "You know Father. He doesn't care much for anybody." Her eyes fell on Hummer as if noticing him for the first time. "I see you brought your hunk. Hi, Frank. Nice to see you again." She looked at her sister. "Are you two finally involved? I mean really involved?" She sniggered. "Sexually, that is."

"You're much too nosy," Cheryl said, but she smiled.

Suzan gave Hummer a smoldering look from under hooded lids. "If I weren't married and pregnant I think I would give my sister a run for her money. She'd better hang before some other woman tries to get her hooks into you. I'm surprised you are still single, as handsome as you are."

Hummer laughed good-humoredly. "Well, thank you for the compliment. I may be single, but I'm not looking. Cheryl is enough for me."

"Oh, wow! That sounds almost serious." Suzan threw a questioning look at her sister. "Is it?"

Cheryl looked at Hummer and smiled. "Perhaps."

"I'm happy to hear that. You're not getting any younger, you know."

"Why is everyone mentioning my age?" Cheryl asked. "Even Mother told me my clock is ticking. Thirty-six isn't so old."

"Old enough, Cher." Suzan's lips were smiling but her eyes were solemn when they studied Hummer's face. "I've heard that you and my father have locked horns on occasion, but so have many people. Don't let that scare you away. I love my sister and I don't want to see her hurt. She is a good person and deserves the best. If she thinks you are what she wants, then that is good enough for me." She rushed up to him and planted a quick kiss on his cheek.

Then she broke into cheery, giggly laughter, slipping back into the role she usually portrayed. "Well, have fun, kids, get yourself a drink, and join the merriment of the Gibson family get-together and barbeque."

"Either your sister has matured since I last saw her, or she has been putting on an act all this time," Hummer commented.

"She likes to pretend she is a dumb blonde," Cheryl said. "She figures people underestimate her, which will give her an advantage. In reality she is quite brilliant. She has as degree in psychology, did you know?"

"I didn't, and frankly I'm somewhat amazed. She certainly fooled me," Hummer admitted.

"I thought you were a detective," Cheryl joked. "Shouldn't you spot something like that?"

"I'm a detective not a psychologist," Hummer growled.

"Let's get a drink. I'm thirsty." She pulled him with her to the bar.

The bartender behind the counter looked up when they approached. He was an old guy with a dour face. Hummer had the impression the man wanted to be somewhere else. "What'll it be?"

"I'll have a gin and tonic," Cheryl said. "And don't forget the lime."

"I always put ice and lime into my gin and tonic," the man said, his pride obviously injured. He gave Hummer a sour look. "And you, sir?"

"I'll just have a beer," Hummer said.

"Any preference, sir?"

"Surprise me." Even though Hummer preferred certain brands, he wasn't overly fussy about what brand he drank.

"We have draft, sir."

"Draft is fine." He wanted to add *as long as it is cold* but refrained from doing so, not wanting to arouse the man's indignation any further.

Cheryl hooked her arm into Hummer's and sipped from her drink. She seemed happy and bubbly. "We should go and say hi to my father."

Congressman Gibson sat at one of the tables, his back to the patio door. Obviously, he had not seen them coming out of the house. He was busy talking to a number of men sitting with him. Hummer spotted at least three security men near him. It was not hard to miss them with their dark suits and sunglasses. Cheryl and Hummer walked around the table so Gibson could see them.

He stopped talking when Cheryl said, "Hello, Father."

Gibson took a long drag from his cigar and exhaled slowly, a cloud of smoke obscuring his face for a moment, before he answered. "Well, if it isn't my rebellious daughter, Cheryl, and her detective friend, Hummer. I'm glad you can spare the time to come to our barbeque."

"I wouldn't miss it, Father," Cheryl said cheerily. "I see you're still smoking your smelly cigars."

"They're Cubans, dear daughter. I smoke only the best." He let out a rumbling laugh. With a look at Hummer, he said, "How's the detective business going, Hummer? Any new cases?"

"There's never a shortage of new cases," Hummer said. "There are plenty of people out there who will take advantage of the innocent and vulnerable."

"Nobody is ever really innocent, Hummer. And the vulnerable ones invite trouble as light attracts moths." He put the cigar back between his lips. The tip glowed softly as he sucked on it. "I hear you're taking on a fair amount of cases that don't pay. Why?"

"Because I like to help people in distress."

Gibson smiled humorlessly. "I know about your soft heart. Is that black woman still working for you?"

"If you are talking about my housekeeper Sarah the answer is yes. Why do you ask?"

"I'm just curious. She is young and without a husband. What does she do for you?"

"She cooks and takes care of the house."

"Just like a wife, eh?" Gibson stared at the cigar in his hand. "Not so long ago we used to keep blacks as slaves. We could do anything we wanted with them and nobody cared. We could fuck a black woman and get her pregnant without worrying about the consequences, but now they demand the same rights as white people. Who would have ever imagined that?"

"Who indeed. It's a good thing we've finally come out of the Dark Ages, but some people seem to have a problem with that." Hummer didn't bother hiding his sarcasm. "For your information, Sarah is not my slave nor is she my lover or anything else. She is my housekeeper. The fact that she is young is not important." Hummer was annoyed at what Gibson implied, but he kept his temper under control. There was a time when he would not have been so patient with someone like Gibson, but that was a long time ago. He didn't want to think about those days anymore. Sometimes it is good to let the past lie.

"Why did you hire her?"

"She was in trouble and needed a job, and I needed a housekeeper."

"Like I said a soft heart. It doesn't make you any money."

"Not everything is about money, Congressman. Besides, I have enough money."

Gibson chuckled. "There is no such thing as enough money. I have billions and I am always looking for ways to make more money. If you want power and prestige you need money. Lots of it. People respect you when you have money. People fear you if you have enough money and power. Men with money shape and manipulate the world; they make things happen. They control their own destiny and the destiny of others."

"With all due respect, Congressman, I've heard all that before. Not everyone has the ambition to manipulate the world. Some of us are just happy to be alive." He smiled. "Mind you, I'm not saying money doesn't help."

"Well, there are leaders and there are followers. I call them sheep. Most people in this world are sheep. Which are you, Hummer?"

"I don't think of myself as a sheep. I'm an entrepreneur, a man who makes decisions, a man who takes chances. I fancy myself a leader."

Gibson puffed out a thick cloud of smoke. "Perhaps you are, Hummer. You may think you are a rich man, but your idea of a fortune is nothing but pocket change for some men."

Hummer smiled. "I don't consider thirty million dollars pocket change, sir."

"I know what you're worth, Hummer. Nearly half of your so-called fortune is tied up in a company that may not have much of a future."

"If you're talking about Green Fuels Development, sir, you are wrong. Alternative fuels are the future."

"Maybe in the far future. For now, the real money is still in oil. It will stay that way until we find more lucrative ways to make money."

"Or until the air is so polluted we won't be able to live in the world the men with money are trying to control. If we're lucky the oil will be gone before that happens."

Gibson looked at Hummer with contempt in his eyes. "Why do you care? You and I won't be alive."

"We may not be, but our children and their children will be."

"What concern is that to you? You don't have any children; maybe never will have."

"That is not the point, Congressman. I have a good friend with children. You have grandchildren. Do you want them to inherit a world that isn't fit to live in?"

"I wouldn't worry about that. We'll be developing more efficient cars. Besides, this whole pollution thing is nothing but propaganda by the scaremongers and doomsday-preachers. There was more pollution in the air a hundred years ago when people used horses and buggies to get around. Can you imagine cities like New York and Chicago on a hot July day? Do you know what horseshit turns into on hot, dry days? Dust. Fine yellow dust. The streets were full of it and the wind blew it into every open window, every open door. It covered furniture, floors, walls. The air was alive with horseshit. Try to live with that, Hummer. Now that is pollution."

"I can't agree more," a man with a neatly trimmed white beard sitting at the table said. He exhaled a small cloud of smoke and put down his cigar. "How about all the factories that used coal to drive their machines? Or the locomotives in the nineteenth and twentieth century? They left stink and soot behind. I'm glad I wasn't alive then."

"Maybe you were, Julian," another man said, laughing. "You look old enough. You just can't remember."

"Very funny," the old man said. "That is very funny. Another remark like that, Tessler, and you can kiss your contract for next year goodbye."

"You do that and we'll cut you out as the middleman in our deal with Yemen," Tessler threatened.

"Gentlemen, no business talk today," Gibson said sharply. "I'm having a discussion with the man my daughter is dating." He crushed half of his cigar into an ashtray. "Let me give you some friendly advice, Hummer. Sell your Green Fuels Development shares and invest your money in oil. If I were in your position, I would also sell my shares in Tanner Golds. The price of gold has been artificially inflated. There is no shortage of gold and the price will come crashing down as soon as the governments who hoard it begin selling it off to pay off their national debts. Don't listen to the so-called experts who predict gold will reach five thousand dollars an ounce. Remember what I told you about certain people manipulating events?"

"Thanks for the advice but no, thank you. I'll keep my money invested in GFDI. Once Senator Simmerman becomes President, there will be many changes. The drilling and pumping of oil will stop and the development and use of fuels from renewable resources will be promoted. We've had too many disasters involving oil in the last few decades. Remember the damage the last one in the Gulf of Mexico caused?"

"Disasters will always happen. Some are natural and some are manmade." Gibson reached for the glass in front of him and emptied it. Setting the glass down with a forceful thud, he said, "There is no guarantee Simmerman will be the next President of the United States. I wouldn't count on it."

"He has plenty of supporters and the polls favor him."

"It looks that way but a lot can happen before the election." Gibson gave Hummer a thoughtful stare. "You are running with the wrong crowd, Hummer. I hear you are quite chummy with Simmerman's son."

"I wouldn't exactly say that. We meet for lunch or a game of golf sometimes. After all, he is the CEO of GFDI and I own a large chunk of shares in the company. That's all we have in common." Hummer returned Gibson's stare. "By the way, where did you get your information about my investments? Are you spying on me, Congressman?"

Gibson's eyes were cold. "I keep tabs on people, Hummer, including you. I want to know everything about the man who fucks my daughter."

Hummer heard a sharp intake of breath beside him. "How dare you embarrass me in front of strangers, Father!" Cheryl hissed. "I don't appreciate that. This is one of the reasons I don't come around so often." She pulled on Hummer's arm. "Come, we'll look for friendlier company."

"In just one moment, honey." Hummer glared at Gibson. "You may be rich and powerful, Congressman, but you are a man with no compassion for others, not even your own family. My relationship with your daughter is a private affair. Mine and Cheryl's. What we do is nobody's business."

"It is my business, Hummer," Gibson rumbled. "She is my daughter."

"Sometimes I wish I weren't," Cheryl said, her voice choked with anger.

Cheryl's mother rushed up to her and pulled her away. "Come along, Cheryl. I want to discuss something with you."

Hummer stood suddenly alone. Everyone seemed to ignore him, except for Cheryl's father. Gibson's eyes studied him with the curiosity of a predator watching a potential prey or a possible intruder. "What game are you playing, Hummer?"

"Game?"

"Yes, game. Do you really believe you can get to me through my daughter? If so you are walking into an inferno without a protective suit. You will never be one of the big fish in the pond, because you, like the rest of the sheep, have no idea what is really going on. By the way, watch out for the next market crash. It is coming. Sooner than most people think." His words sounded ominous, but Hummer had the chilling sensation Congressman Gibson was showing his teeth for some unexplained reason.

"Even big fish get caught sometimes," he said. "Especially if they get overconfident. I'd rather stay in the background." He pointed at the cigar Gibson took out of a box on the table. "I'd be careful with those. Tobacco causes cancer. Nobody is immune to that. Now, if you'll excuse me, I'll get myself another beer."

His cell phone rang as he walked to the bar. When he answered it, he heard Schumann's voice on the other end, "Hey, Frank, I know I told you to close the Middler file, but you might be interested in this. We just picked up the guy who apparently started the fire at Globe Labs. He's being interrogated right now."

"What's his name?"

"Felix Erskine."

"How did you find out about him?"

"An anonymous tip."

"Why are you telling me this, Martin?"

"I'm calling you as a friend. Come in to see me tomorrow, Frank. You may be involved in this, by involved I mean *implicated*. I can't tell you more. Not over the phone."

Chapter Eight

"It doesn't look good, Frank." Schumann ran his hand across his bald head. "Erskine confessed to setting the fire. Apparently, he was hired by someone from Green Fuels Development. He got paid a couple thousand for doing the job. He didn't know the man's name, but his description of the man who paid him the money in a brown paper bag fits Fred Simmerman, the CEO of Green Fuels. We're preparing a warrant for Simmerman's arrest." He leaned forward. "I remember you told me you had a fortune invested in that company."

Hummer nodded. "Yes, I do. Why would that be significant?"

"You and Simmerman have lunch once in awhile? Even play golf together?"

"Why do you ask? You yourself played with us a few times. What's this all about, Martin?"

"You may be called in for questioning, Frank. This has nothing to do with me. I don't handle the investigation. I shouldn't even be talking to you, since you and I are friends."

"Then give me a good reason why my name even comes up?"

"You have more than a passing interest in the company and you are chummy with the CEO."

"Okay, but let me ask you another question: Why would Fred Simmerman hire someone to set fire to Globe Labs? What possible reason could he have?"

"A very good reason. To get rid of the competition. Globe Labs was working on the same projects as Green Fuels Development, right?"

"Yes. I wasn't aware of that until recently, but I'm sure what Globe Labs did is no secret."

"No, it isn't, but here is something which is not public knowledge: Professor Middler developed a new type of battery that uses salt water as a medium to create electricity. He also designed an electric car. That puts Globe Labs ahead of Green Fuels. Apparently, Saul Finkbein has been talking to a Chinese conglomerate about a deal involving billions. Whoever builds this battery and the car will corner the market. That is plenty of reason to get rid of the competition."

"Fred Simmerman would never stoop as low as committing murder. I know him better than that. He may be a ruthless businessman, but murder? Never!" Hummer was convinced what he said was the truth. Simmerman was not one of his dear friends, but after associating with the man for years, even on a casual basis, gave him a good idea about the man's character. But then again, he admitted to himself, he could also be wrong. Some people have the ability to fool even their closest friends. "Where does the tip about this Erskine fellow come from?"

"That is confidential, Frank. Sorry. You know better than asking a question like that."

Hummer cracked a tiny smile. "I figured as a friend you would throw me a bone."

"I threw you more than a bone because of our friendship. You know that." Schumann looked at his watch. "I have an appointment in about an hour; otherwise I'd suggest we go for lunch. Sorry."

Rising from his chair, Hummer said, "I appreciate the information, Martin. Just so you know this opens up the file again for me since I'm involved now. I want to be prepared if someone should be coming for me. I've suspected from the moment I took this case there was something not quite right about it, and it seems my instincts were correct, again. Of course, I didn't have a clue I might be drawn into it."

"Let the law handle it, Frank."

Hummer chuckled. "The law is only interested in finding someone to lock up, no matter who gets hurt in the process. Sometimes the evidence lies, the facts are murky, even if they appear clear. Once a case is in the hands of a prosecutor there lies the danger things may get swept under the table just to make a case stick. Cops have to follow rules.

Evidence has to be gained through proper channels; otherwise it is not permissible in court. I don't follow those rules. I don't give a crap how I get my information. Besides, this is personal and I'll be damned if I let anyone accuse me of something just because it seems I am involved or have more than a passing interest."

"Don't let your personal feelings lead you into doing something that involves breaking the law. Just some friendly advice, Frank. Don't forget, I know how you think. You do have the tendency to bend the law and the rules." Schumann hesitated. "I don't want to know what you're up to. Don't even hint at it in friendly conversation. Always remember I'm a cop. I am the law. You understand?"

"Don't worry, Martin, I won't jeopardize your career." He grinned. "You're out of the loop, my friend."

So am I. As he left the precinct, he realized from now on Schumann would not share any more information about the case with him, and he couldn't blame him. There was still the question as to how Henry Miller and Saul Finkbein died. He didn't believe Miller did the shooting. The explanation looked too pat. What reason did he have to kill Finkbein? What was his connection with Finkbein? Did Erskine do the shooting or was there another person with him? The guard at the gate said he only saw Professor Middler and Finkbein. It seems he lied about seeing the Professor, who turned out to be Henry Miller. Was he covering up something? Hummer made a mental note to have a heart-to-heart talk with the guard at Globe Labs.

He stopped at a hamburger joint to pick up something to stop his stomach from growling, not wanting to waste time sitting in a restaurant and waiting for his order to arrive. While eating, his thoughts drifted to Cheryl and the barbeque at her parents' estate. *Damn you, Congressman Gibson! Why couldn't someone else be Cheryl's father? Should I somehow decide to marry her, you'd be my father-in-law. Reason enough not to marry her.*

After finishing his lunch, he drove to his office. Tony sat in the front office, chatting with Nicole. He jumped up when Hummer walked in, looking guilty.

"Tony, I've decided to reopen the Middler case. I want you to find out everything you can about a Felix Erskine. He's the man who apparently started the fire at Globe Labs, the one that covered up the murder of Harry Middler a.k.a. Henry Miller, and Saul Finkbein. I want to know everything about him, like who his friends are, his contacts, the bank he deals with, even his bank account. And this time try to be discreet. Can you do that?"

A hurt expression spread across Tony's round face. "I make a mistake only once, Mr. Hummer. It won't happen again. They won't even have an inkling I was there."

"Good. Now go and start digging." He walked into Marconi's office. "Marconi, I want you to come with me. I'm driving to Globe Labs Institute to talk to the guard at the gate. I need you as a witness in case I have to get persuasive."

"I understand." Marconi opened one of the drawers on his desk and pulled out a couple of glass cases. He handed one to Hummer, opened the other one and took out a pair of sunglasses. Then he reached for his hat and put it on.

Hummer took the offered case and slipped it into his pocket. "Good thinking, Marconi."

When they sat in the car, Marconi asked, "What's going on?"

"I talked to Schumann this morning. They've arrested a guy who claims he was hired to burn down Globe Labs. Apparently, the man who hired him was Fred Simmerman."

"The CEO of Green Fuels Development?" Even though Marconi wasn't a man who signaled his emotions with every gesture or every word he spoke, Hummer could tell he was taken by surprise. "Simmerman is a friend of yours, isn't he?"

"We golf together and have lunches. I'm a major stockholder in his company," Hummer explained.

Marconi coughed into his hand. "I see where this is going. Green Fuels and Globe Labs are competitors. If something were to happen to Globe Labs, Green Fuels would be in a leading position in their research and the development of alternative energy. Since you own a large number of stocks, it stands to reason that you may be a suspect, right?"

"That's about sums it up. There are a lot of open holes in this case, Marconi. I need to find out who murdered Saul Finkbein and Henry Miller. I suspect Miller may have been mistaken for Professor Harry

Middler. Who wanted the Professor dead and why? I am positive Fred Simmerman has nothing to do with these murders and the fire. Why was Henry Miller there in the first place?"

"What is the reason you want to talk to this guard?"

"He's the one who told police he saw Professor Middler going into the building. Now we find out it wasn't the Professor but a man by the name of Miller. Either the guard lied or someone else told him what to say."

"You believe he is involved?"

"I rule nothing out."

"And the cops? What do they think?"

"They want to arrest Simmerman. He's a suspect on the word of a man who claims to have set the fire at Globe Labs and that is good enough for them. They have a lead and they will follow it. Can't blame them for that. There is something else. Someone tipped the cops off about Erskine. Schumann didn't tell me where the information came from. I want to find that source."

Hummer parked his car a block away from the Globe Labs buildings. Before they left the car, Hummer said, "Give me a moment. I want to call Simmerman."

His call was answered after the first ring. It didn't surprise Hummer. Simmerman always answered his phone immediately. It seemed his cell phone was part of his body. "Fred Simmerman here."

"Fred, this is Frank Hummer. I'll make it short. You must be aware of the fire at Globe Labs? Well, arm yourself with an attorney, a good one."

"Why, are they blaming me for that one, Frank?" Simmerman chuckled into the phone.

"As a matter of fact, they are. But that's not all. You are a suspect in the murder of Saul Finkbein. I can't go into details. I shouldn't even be calling you, because I got the tip from a friend."

"Is Schumann behind this?"

"He's involved in the investigation, but the charge is not his doing. They've arrested some guy who fingered you. You'd better not waste any time. This is serious, Fred."

"Damn right, this is serious! Why the hell would I want to murder

Finkbein? Did they say I lit the match that started the fire that killed him?"

"He didn't die in the fire. He was shot before the fire started."

"Shot? And I'm supposed to have shot him? This is preposterous. I don't own a gun or rifle. I'm not a hunter. I hate guns and violence. Never even fired a gun in my life. This must be some kind of joke."

"I'm afraid not, Fred. Take my advice and get a defense attorney, and make if fast. They'll be coming for you as soon as they can get a warrant for your arrest. Do me a favor and don't mention I called you, okay?"

"Sure. No problem. Thanks, Frank. I owe you one. This is fucking crazy. You know me, Frank. I wouldn't hurt a fly, never mind killing someone."

"I know that, you don't have to convince me. Don't waste any time now trying to rationalize this. Get that lawyer and be ready. Good luck."

He didn't tell him about his own involvement or the fact he was going to find out who was behind it all. He didn't want Simmerman to get his hopes up.

"Let's go, Marconi." After he finished talking to Simmerman Hummer put on the pair of sunglasses Marconi gave him in the office. They got out of the car and walked the short distance to Globe Labs. Except for broken windows and a few black streaks on the brick wall on one of the buildings, there wasn't much evidence of a fire. The guard at the entrance to the property gave them an inquiring look when they walked up to the guard house.

"Hi," Hummer said. "Hard to believe there was a fire here a few days ago."

"Yes, sure is. Are you guys cops?"

"No, I'm a private investigator. I have a client who is…uh…involved with Globe Labs. You may be able to help me."

"Is one of the workers suing Globe Labs?"

Hummer smiled at the guard's eagerness to divulge information. Maybe things would go smoothly if he played it right. "You're a member of the union, aren't you?"

The guard nodded. "Sure am."

"Well, then you know there are certain rules to follow. I can't discuss my client with you." He lowered his voice. "I'll tell you this in confidence. You are on the right track."

"Well, I'm not surprised. There are rumors some of the researchers who worked in the lab are angry because Mr. White, who is the temporary CEO of the company, told them there is no work for them at the moment. Not until the lab has been rebuilt."

"That is a shame. Listen, were you here when the place burnt? Must have been something."

"I wasn't working that day. It would have been my weekend to work, but I got a call in the morning not to come in. Some new guy would be taking over my shift. I didn't complain. I get a lot of nagging from the wife because of my working the weekends and I can't even blame her. This way I got to spend a Sunday with my family and I'll even get paid. I'm on a fixed salary, you know."

Hummer was disappointed to hear the guard wasn't there that day, but something about that raised his suspicion. "Do you know who called you and told you not to come in?" he asked.

The guard pursed his lips. "It was one of the girls from the front office. She didn't identify herself, but I'm pretty sure it was Estella. She has this exceptionally high voice, even for a girl."

"Does she have a last name?" Marconi asked.

"I don't know." The guard made an apologetic gesture with his hands. "I spent most of my time in this guardhouse. Don't give me much of a chance to socialize with the rest of the workers. Sorry."

"That's okay," Hummer said. "You were helpful. What was your name again?"

"Victor Laquette. People call me Vic."

"Thanks, Vic. Do you think anyone is working in the front office today?"

"Oh, sure. Everybody is working, except for the lab people."

"Can we just walk in or do we have to register with you, Vic?"

"Normally I would have to take down your name and your purpose for entering the premises, but you just go on ahead." He grinned. "I have certain powers as a guard. I can let people in or turn them away. It's up to me. By the way, the front office is in the first building to the left, the one with *Administration* on top of the door."

"Great. We'll find our way." Hummer and Marconi walked across the parking lot and headed for the indicated building.

"Well, that went quite smoothly," Marconi remarked. "Unfortunately, we still know nothing."

"We have a name. Let's hope this Estella is working today. Somebody put her up to making the call." Hummer opened the door and entered the building, followed by Marconi.

The front office was not hard to find. Large double glass-doors let them see a number of desks, occupied by mostly young women. "This must be it," Hummer said. When they walked into the large office, the woman behind the first desk looked up. "Do you have an appointment with someone?" she asked.

"I'm afraid we have no appointment. We are looking for Estella." Hummer looked around the office, located a door in the back, a potential escape route for someone who didn't want to be found. "Is she in?"

"We have two Estella's. Which one do you want?" the woman asked.

"We have no last name. Just Estella."

"She has a high voice," Marconi said.

"Oh." The woman showed a little smile. "That must be Estella Wilson." She pointed at one of the desks. "She's over there."

Estella was a chubby girl with short hair, dark lips, and heavy makeup around her eyes. She wore at least six rings in her left ear and a couple in her right ear. Another ring pierced her left eyebrow and one her lower lip. The thought why so many overweight men and women assumed if they stuck rings through their ears, lips, and other body parts it would make them more attractive popped fleetingly into Hummer's mind.

Do they ever look in the mirror?

She watched them approaching her desk with visible apprehension. Hummer wondered what she was afraid of. Just by her expression and rigid posture he was certain she felt guilty about something.

"Estella Wilson?" Hummer asked.

She nodded. "Yes."

"We'd like to ask you a few questions. Is there a place here where we can talk in private?" He didn't identify himself on purpose.

Nodding again, she said, "We could go into the lunchroom. There is nobody there right now."

"That'll be fine." He made a gesture. "Go ahead and lead the way."

She got up from her chair and stepped around her desk. Hummer was surprised how short she was. This girl surely didn't have much going for herself. No amount of makeup or jewelry would enhance her looks. She even waddled when she walked.

The lunchroom was just around the corner. As soon as they entered it, Estella said, "I've done everything you people asked me to do. I want no more part of this."

"We're not going to ask you to do anything," Hummer said, picking up on some clue her remark meant. "We only want to make sure you get what's coming to you. What were you promised?"

"A thousand dollars." She squinted at Hummer. "Did you bring the money?"

"Are you telling me you didn't get your money yet?" Hummer asked, acting shocked. He looked at Marconi. "Did you hear that? She never got her money. I'm not surprised. Are you?"

Marconi shook his head. "Hell, no. It's so typical." His dark eyes fixed on Estella. "Nobody told us about the money. Who was supposed to bring it to you?"

"I don't know."

"Well, who did you talk to? What's his name?"

"He never told me his name. Actually, there were two guys."

"Can you describe them?" Hummer pulled out a notebook and a pen. "We may be able to locate those guys for you. We are very concerned when protocol isn't followed."

Looking at the ceiling, she screwed up her face. "One was tall, the other one a little shorter. Both wore sunglasses and hats. Dark suits and dark ties. The shorter one had a deep voice, but he didn't do much talking. The other guy told me what to do and say. Does that help?"

"Your description fits half the guys in the company. Do you remember any details? Like scars, a mustache, a beard, the color of hair, any jewelry. Skin color. Were they of average weight? Old or young? Heavy? Skinny? Stuff like that." Hummer gave her a look of encouragement. "Anything?"

"They were average in weight. Clean shaven. Oh, the short one had a flat nose, you know like a boxer. His skin color was darker, but not black. There is something else I remember. The pinky on his left hand was kind of crippled, like bent funny." She held up her hand and tried to show them. "Something like this."

"That's quite helpful. I'm positive we will be able to recognize who you're talking about," Marconi said.

"It does help," Hummer agreed. "Any other oddities you can recall?"

"Nothing much, except his earlobe was gone. I thought his ear looked, you know, gross. That's about all."

"You have a good memory, Estella. We'll find the man, don't worry," Hummer assured her. He made some notes in his book. "By the way, have you talked to any cops?"

"Oh, no. They told me to talk to nobody, especially the cops. I could get into deep trouble."

"Good girl. Remember that. Don't tell anyone about our conversation, either, okay?"

"Sure. I'm not stupid."

"Nobody said. Did anyone tell you the reason for the call you made?"

Her dark-rimmed eyes suddenly filled with tears. "Yes, they said there would be an important secret meeting taking place between Mr. Finkbein and some government man, but now I feel so bad about Mr. Finkbein and Professor Middler. If Vic would have been at his post, he may have stopped the guy who set the fire in the lab when he snuck past the gate."

"How do you know about the guy who set the fire?" Marconi asked.

"I saw it on the news when I had lunch." She pointed at the TV in one corner. "We always watch the news in here."

"Did they announce any details about the suspect?"

"The police didn't release much. They only said they have someone in custody."

"Okay." Hummer put away his notebook and glanced at Marconi. "I guess we got as much as we can."

"It seems that way." Marconi nodded solemnly.

Before they turned to walk away, Hummer reminded the girl, "Don't forget now, keep this to yourself."

"I will, I promise."

Once they were outside, Marconi said, "Not one of the brightest people I've ever met and quite naïve. Didn't she question why anyone would offer her a grand to make a phone call? She must have realized something wasn't kosher."

"Like you said, not the brightest girl, but I don't believe she's involved other than having made the call to Laquette," Hummer pondered. "She's just some poor bitch who got pulled into something ugly."

When they came to the guard house, Hummer stopped to talk to Laquette for a moment.

"Did you find Estella?" the guard asked.

"Yes, we did. Thanks, Vic. She's been quite helpful." He was about to walk away when Marconi said, "Listen, Vic, that camera up there, is it always connected?"

"It is. Why do you ask?"

"Would it have been recording last Sunday when you weren't working?"

"Of course."

"Where are the recordings stored?"

"In Security. As far as I know they keep everything for a year. After that they delete it."

"Would it be possible to have a look at Sunday's recordings?"

"Not unless you have a warrant."

"That may be difficult to achieve," Hummer said. He had a sudden idea. "I have a friend in the police department. We can give him a call. He can tell you that I'm not just some nosy guy, you know. Sometimes we do work for the police department. He can vouch for me. Do you think that might work?"

"I guess it would."

"Good." He pulled out his cell phone and dialed Schumann's private number. When the phone rang, he handed it to the guard. "Just ask him if he knows a PI Frank Hummer."

Laquette listened to the phone for a moment then he said, "Hi, this is

Victor Laquette. I'm a guard with Globe Labs. I wonder if you can tell me anything about a PI by the name of Frank Hummer...I see...He says you know him. Really? Just a moment..." He held the phone toward Hummer, "He wants to talk to you."

Hummer grabbed the phone. "Hi, Martin."

"What the hell is this all about, Frank?" Schumann didn't sound happy.

"I just wanted you to confirm that you know me. It's not that important."

"The hell it is. Don't give me that crap, Frank. Everything you do is important. Don't drag me into something."

"Give me more credit than that, Martin. I'll tell you everything about it next time we play a round of golf. Got to go. See you." He shoved the phone into his pocket and grinned at Laquette. "He's a good guy but doesn't like to be called on his private line. So can you get us into the security department?"

"Let me see what I can do." He used the phone in the guardhouse. "Hey, Artie. It's Vic by the gate. Listen, I'll be sending you a couple of my friends. They want to look at the recordings the camera outside the gate made on Sunday. Will it be okay if they come now? Perhaps you can have the stuff ready for them...sure...yeah... They just want to look...okay, they'll be there in five. Take care."

He put the receiver down. "Artie says it's okay by him. As long as you can do it quick."

"We won't take up much of his valuable time. Now you'll just have to explain to us how we find this Artie."

The guy they found sat in a chair watching a number of monitors with little or no interest. He didn't even get up when Hummer and Marconi walked in.

"You must be Artie," Hummer said.

Artie nodded with little enthusiasm. "I guess I am since there is nobody else in this room. Vic says you want to check out the tapes from Sunday. Any particular timeframe?"

"Sunday afternoon. Since this place is closed on Sundays it shouldn't take too long," Hummer told him.

"Watch monitor number four. Just give me a second to set it up."

The screen went blank for a few moments, and then it showed the gate and part of the parking lot. "There you go," Artie said. "Let me know if you see something of interest. It bores me sitting here watching nothing all day long."

Hummer had to admit it was boring to stare at a screen showing nothing but asphalt. "Can you fast-forward this?"

"Sure." Artie did something but the scene didn't change much, then suddenly a car stopped by the gate, it opened and the car drove through.

"Can you bring that back, please, and this time in slow motion?" Hummer asked.

The car on the screen rolled backward.

"Okay. Now...stop it right there."

The driver was clearly visible through the front windshield. "That's Mr. Finkbein," Artie said.

"Your CEO," Hummer commented. "At least we know he came alone. Fast-forward it until the next car."

When another car appeared by the gate, Hummer said, "There. Slow it down...now freeze it...zoom in on the driver." He turned to Marconi. "Record these images."

Marconi pulled out a small video camera and began recording.

"There are two people in that car," Artie observed.

"You are right. Do you know them?"

"Never saw either of them before."

"Isn't one of them Professor Middler?" Hummer asked.

Artie shook his head. "Nope. They're both strangers."

"Can you increase the image a little? The face of the driver looks familiar." When the picture became larger, Hummer cursed. "What the hell! That is the guy I saw at Pineridge Cove who claimed to be Professor Middler."

"He isn't Professor Middler," Artie said. He unfroze the image. "Let's see if they drive into the parking lot."

Before the gate opened, another man walked into the picture. The driver of the car rolled down the window and talked to him. When the man turned, his face was briefly visible. Artie froze the picture again. "That's not Vic," he said.

"Vic wasn't working that day," Hummer explained. "Who is this

105

guy?"

"I don't know. Usually Trevor Kelsey takes the other shift, but this guy is also a stranger."

On the screen, the gate opened and the car drove into the lot.

"Keep it going," Hummer ordered. "I want to see when they leave again."

There was no action for awhile, and then the second car drove out again. "Rewind and freeze the frame when you see the license plate," Hummer said. "Okay, zoom in on it."

As the back of the car increased in size on the picture, Hummer noticed something else. "The driver is the only one in the car. Too bad we can't see his face."

The gate opened and the car drove through.

There wasn't any action on the screen until a fire truck raced through the open gate, and then another one.

A few moments later a car pulled up and stopped. The driver opened the window and seemed to talk to someone. Another man came into the picture. It was the guard. He spoke with the driver of the car. The driver got back in and drove through the open gate. As it drove by Hummer saw it was the Fire Commissioner's car.

As soon as the Commissioner's car was through, a man walked briskly away from the guardhouse. "There goes the guard," Marconi said. "Now we know for sure he was in on it."

Hummer addressed Artie. "Are there any cameras in the lab? You know the one with the fire?"

"No. They didn't want any cameras in there to keep sensitive material from being recorded. They had their own local cameras but they were destroyed in the fire." Artie gave Hummer a speculative look. "Who are you guys really? I know Vic said you're friends but I think you are no friends of his. Vic's a nice guy but a bit gullible. By that I mean goodhearted. You talk nice to him and he buys you a drink. If you know what I mean."

Hummer didn't see any reason to lie to Artie. "You are right. We are not Vic's friends. We are private investigators. What we are going to tell you now must be kept in this room, you understand?"

Artie nodded. "No problem."

"Your boss Mr. Finkbein was murdered and so was Professor Middler. That fire was no accident. We figure the guy who drove that car was the one who started the fire and who murdered Mr. Finkbein and the Professor." Hummer's expression was somber when he spoke.

"We never saw Professor Middler coming in," Artie said.

"That's because the man who died in the fire was not Professor Middler." Hummer didn't see any harm in telling Artie.

"Who was he?"

"That's what we are going to find out. We also want to find out who is behind it all and the reason for the murders and the fire."

"I thought the cops are investigating this?"

"The cops are moving in the wrong direction. That's why we are looking into the case," Hummer said, grimly. He didn't tell him about Simmerman and his own assumed involvement in this affair.

"Well, I hope you find the bastards who murdered Mr. Finkbein. He was a good man to work for. It won't be the same without him," Artie said vehemently.

"We'll try our best," Hummer assured him. He was quite happy with their discoveries. At least now they had names and faces. Of course, the task of finding out who exactly these people were and who they worked for would not be easy, but he was confident about being successful.

"Why haven't the cops checked out these recordings?" Artie asked.

"Because, as I said, they are on the wrong track. They have someone in custody and that is good enough for them. I compare the people who are in law enforcement to horses wearing blinds. They see only what's in front of them," Hummer explained.

"That's why sometimes innocent people get convicted of crimes they did not commit," Artie mused. "I understand what you're saying."

"That's right. We want to prevent that in this case." Hummer held out his hand. "Thanks for allowing us to look at the recordings. You did the right thing, Artie. By the way, there is no reason to broadcast it, right?"

"Right. Good luck with your investigation." Artie shook Hummer's hand. "Let me know how it turns out, okay?"

They stopped to talk to Laquette at the gate and then they walked back to their car.

"Let's go back to the office and find out who these men are," Hummer said.

Chapter Nine

Tony was ecstatic to hear more important work was waiting for him. "I've got the information you were looking for on Felix Erskine," he told Hummer.

"Okay. Shoot."

"He was born June third, nineteen-seventy-four, which makes him thirty-seven years old. His father, Dan Erskine, was a truck driver; not much info on his mother. A native of New York, Felix grew up in a poor neighborhood, got into trouble for the first time when he was twelve. Stole some other poor kid's bike. At fourteen, he and a couple of his friends robbed a grocery store. He got caught and spent a year in juvi. That was just the beginning of his criminal career."

Tony looked up from his printed report. "The list is long. I don't believe you want me to bore you with details. To sum it up, Felix Erskine is a drunk, drug addict, thief, and armed robber but no murderer. He spent much of his adult life going in and out of jail. He doesn't have a fixed address. Usually lives in run-down hotels. A couple of weeks ago he was released from jail, apparently through a clerical error."

"Do you by any chance have a picture of him?" Hummer asked.

Tony nodded proudly. "Yes-sir. Here it is." He held up a sheet of paper. It displayed a skinny, unshaven man with unkempt, dark-blond hair.

"Let me look at the face," Marconi said. He peered at the picture. "This is the guy who walked away after the Fire Commissioner's car arrived. The guard at the gate to Globe Labs on Sunday was Felix

Erskine, shaved, with combed hair, but I recognize him."

"I agree with you," Hummer said. "This means Erskine was never inside the building. He lied to the cops because he wasn't the one who set the fire. That other guy did, the one who also murdered Finkbein and Henry Miller."

"Which means the police may have arrested the right guy but for the wrong reason," Tony commented.

"He's involved, that's for sure," Marconi said. "He may know the identity of the other man. I wonder why they didn't kill him. Obviously, he is only a small fish in this operation."

"He is the fall guy," Hummer mused. "I'll bet you anything, once Fred Simmerman has been convicted, Erskine will suffer an unfortunate accident in jail. He is a liability."

"I wouldn't take the bet," Marconi said. "I'm certain I would lose it. He definitely is a liability to the people who are behind the fire and the murders." His dark eyes rested on Hummer. "We know Fred Simmerman had nothing to do with the murders. He is being framed, but why?"

"I think I have a good idea why," Tony piped up.

"Let's have it." Hummer and Marconi looked at him with expectation.

"I read the news on one of the websites," Tony began, giving them an almost apologetic smile. "I'm interested in certain things. Anyway, there was an article about Senator Simmerman in there. He stands a good chance of becoming our next President, but there are those who oppose him. They don't like his policies of going green. The oil companies hate him, the car manufactures are not anxious to see him as President, and neither are the big banks. The Federal Reserve Board members are totally against him, because he wants to change legislation when it comes to the powers of the Federal Reserve. He wants to transfer the power for the ultimate approval of decisions the Board makes to the office of the President. Other Presidents have tried and paid dearly for their attempt."

"You're a smart guy, Tony. You may be detective material after all, because I have a feeling I know where you're going with that," Hummer interrupted.

Tony smiled smugly. "Just let me know if I'm on the right track with this, Mr. Hummer. Senator Simmerman is the father of Fred Simmerman, right? So any scandal involving his son will ultimately have some kind of backlash against Senator Simmerman. Am I correct?"

"Unfortunately, you may just be," Hummer growled. "I have this suspicion we are dealing with a group of powerful people, possibly high up in the government or men who are secretly behind the scenes, pulling strings and controlling certain events."

Men with money shape and manipulate the world; they make things happen. They control their own destiny and the destiny of others.

Congressman Gibson's words echoed inside his head.

"You are talking about a secret government that in reality runs our country, and possibly the whole world," Tony said. "I've heard about such conspiracy theories."

"They are not just theories, Toni. I'm afraid those people exist," Hummer said grimly, his mind going back to a time he wanted to forget. "You know, I fought in Operation Desert Storm. I was young then, eager to defeat the evil in Iraq. Both of my brothers were in Iraq when the US went in to capture Saddam Hussein. I have since come to the conclusion the war in Iraq had nothing to do with getting rid of an evil dictator, or of liberating the people of Iraq. That was just a smokescreen. I'm not saying Hussein was not an evil man; he was, but he was only an excuse, a convenient fall guy. The only reason we were there was the oil. The only reason we are in the Middle East right now is oil. Everything else you hear is propaganda."

The real money is in oil. It will stay that way until we find more lucrative ways to make money.

"I have a friend who is in Afghanistan right now," Tony said. "Are you telling me he is putting his life on the line for a bunch of money-hungry bastards?"

"It is a bit more complicated than that but, yeah, that about sums it up." Hummer felt cynical and bitter about any of the wars. His brother Robert died in Iraq. For what? So the oil would keep on flowing? Most people didn't see it his way, especially the parents who lost sons or daughters in that war. To admit their deaths wouldn't make any difference in the scheme of things would be cruel. To admit the ultimate sacrifice of their children only made certain individuals richer and more powerful would almost be sacrilege. They deserved better than that.

"That is not right," Tony broke into Hummer's contemplation.

"No, it isn't, but these people don't care about right or wrong," Hummer said.

"If this is true, what's the point of finding the people who orchestrated everything that has happened here?" Tony queried. "They will never be punished. If they are so powerful they will get rid of all of us and we will have no means of defending ourselves."

Hummer smiled. "They won't know we are going after them. I'm counting on you to be a ghost when you break through their defenses. Talking about wars, we're on the verge of starting one. We'll be taking on a powerful enemy but I am intending to emerge the victor. And you, Tony, will have a large part in this war. Are you up to it?"

"Now more than ever, sir," Tony said with conviction. "What do you want me to find out next?"

"Mr. Marconi recorded something I want you to download onto your computer. I'm talking about faces. Find out who these faces belong to. There also is a license plate you may want to trace. It probably is bogus, but check it out anyway. Before you do, though..." He tore out a page from his notebook and handed it to Tony. "This is a description of two men; one is more detailed than the other one. Maybe you can put names to these two. These guys sound like their working for one of the government agencies. Possibly FBI, but I doubt that. I suggest starting with files in the CIA."

Hummer put a finger on his pursed lips, following a thread of thoughts. "According to the police reports, Henry Miller was the other dead man in the fire. Which means one of the two men in the car is Henry Miller. See if you can confirm that. You shouldn't have any problems getting a picture of Henry Miller."

Tony looked at his watch. "It is nearly quitting time, Mr. Hummer. Do you want me to stay late or come in tomorrow?"

"I'll leave that up to you since I made you work last Saturday."

"If it's okay with you I'll come in tomorrow." He grinned as his stomach growled. "Nicole promised me one of her fabulous meals."

"I won't be here," Marconi said. "I promised my father I'll take him to a soccer game. He will be terribly disappointed if I don't."

"That's okay. Don't worry about it. Tony can handle it all by himself."

* * * *

When Hummer watched the evening news, he was not surprised to hear about Erskine's arrest, but no mention was made about his accusation.

I guess they haven't got the warrant for Fred's arrest yet. I hope he takes my advice and gets himself the best attorney he can find. He'll need it. If what I fear is true, the net will be tight. He'll have a hard time wiggling out of it.

He thought about what Tony said and what he suspected all along. Somebody tried to get to Senator Benjamin Simmerman through his son. Senator Simmerman was to all outward appearances an upstanding citizen with no scandals or any skeletons in his past. He was a true American who believed in his country. He would make a good President. Unfortunately, he was for the common people and didn't care about big business interests. He promised to pull the troops out of the Middle East and other countries. The money wasted on military operations would be put to better use like getting a good healthcare system for all Americans. He'd make sure senior citizens didn't lose their homes and possessions when they fell ill, because they couldn't afford expensive operations or hospital stay.

Even though he had the popular vote, there was plenty opposition. Oil companies, weapon manufacturers, drug companies, insurance companies, even doctors, the list was long. All were afraid they may become victims of Senator Simmerman's reform. And some would. The oil companies would be the biggest losers.

To have a son accused of murder would certainly create a huge black mark against the Senator. It may mean the difference between winning and losing.

But why would I be affected by it? Who is after me?

He suddenly remembered the black car he saw following him from his office parking lot on the Friday when this whole thing started. Perhaps he had not imagined it.

He looked up when he heard someone coming into his living room.

113

It was Sarah, his housekeeper. "Will you be staying home for supper tonight, Mr. Hummer?" she asked.

"Yes."

"Good. I am making a pork roast. I will serve it in about half an hour in the dining room. Will you be ready?"

He smiled. Good sweet Sarah. She never complained much, even when he didn't come home for supper without letting her know or wasn't home for breakfast. She was used to his erratic lifestyle. The food never went to waste because she was allowed to use it for herself. In addition to free food he paid her well and let her live in the guesthouse with her two children, a boy and a girl. Her husband died in a car accident when the children were still young and left her without any means of support. At first, Hummer had been reluctant to hire her because of her youth, but for some reason he had felt pity and never regretted his decision.

"Will you join me for dinner?" he asked. "I feel lonely tonight."

"If you wish, Mr. Hummer. Roy and Denise went to camp with our church over the weekend. I'm kind of lonely too."

"Good. That is settled. See you in half an hour."

He went into the dining room thirty minutes later. The tantalizing aroma of roasted meat made his mouth water. Sarah had set the table nicely. Even two bottles of his favorite beer were already standing beside a glass.

He remembered Charles Gibson's words at the barbeque.

Just like a wife.

Would Cheryl cook for him? Would she even know his preferred brand of beer? Probably not. But then again, she wouldn't have to, since Sarah would still be around. There was no reason to let her go just because he may get married.

He looked at Sarah as she sat across from him at the table. She was in his employ now nearly six years. When he hired her she was twenty-four years old with two young children, a scared black young woman with no place to go. Had he not hired her, she probably would have ended up somewhere in the ghetto, perhaps spent the rest of her life as a prostitute. Her lack of education left no other avenue open for her to make a living.

He liked to think he made a difference in her life and the life of her children.

She noticed his scrutiny of her. "Why are you looking at me like that, Mr. Hummer? Is something wrong?"

"No, nothing is wrong." He smiled. "I just realized how long you have been part of my life. I don't know what I would do without you."

Her face showed concern when she looked at him. "Are you thinking of replacing me? I work very hard to keep your house nice and clean."

"I know you do and I'm not complaining."

"I planted some flowers in the garden today."

"That sounds great. I will make it a point to look at them tomorrow. By the way, the roast is very good, and so are the mashed potatoes and the peas. You are not only a good housekeeper; you are also a wonderful cook. Maybe someday you will get married again and you will be a good wife to your new husband. I'll miss your cooking."

She chuckled softly. "I am not looking for a husband. Nobody will ever take the place of my Jake."

"He's been dead for over seven years now, Sarah. Isn't it time you moved on with your life? You can't mourn forever for someone you loved."

"I can." She sipped from her soft drink and looked at him across the rim of the glass. "How come you're not married, Mr. Hummer? You have lots of money, are good looking, not too old, not yet. Maybe you don't like women? You like men?"

He laughed. "I like women a lot. I'm always busy with my job. No time to socialize, although I do have a lady friend I spend some time with."

"How come I've never seen her?"

"Because the only time I brought her over to the house you weren't here. It was your day off."

"You like this lady?"

"Yes, I do."

"You love her?"

"Maybe."

"She loves you?"

He chuckled. "She wants to get married."

"Oh." Her face fell a little. "When?"

He shrugged. "Probably not for awhile. I'm not even sure if I want to get married."

"Will she move in with you here in this house should you marry her?"

"I hope so. She lives in a condominium in the center of the city. I don't think I'd like to live there."

Her dark eyes studied him intently. "Maybe I won't have a job here anymore after you get married, Mr. Hummer."

"You will. Somebody still has to clean the house and cook for us. You'll just have to get used to cooking for one more person."

"I don't think that will be a problem." Sarah looked happy. "Perhaps when you're married you will stay home more often and I won't waste my time cooking a nice meal for somebody who is gone most of the time."

"I hope so also. It will certainly change my habits. A married man has to lead an orderly life." Deep down, he wondered if that would ever happen. Cheryl's job as the owner of a model agency forced her to an irregular lifestyle, and his clients wanted to meet him sometimes at the oddest hours. "Well, we won't worry about those things, yet, Sarah."

"Okay, I won't." Her eyes were still on his face, but she seemed a bit more relaxed. "Would you like dessert?" she asked.

"What do you offer?"

"I made rice pudding for Roy and Denise, but now they are not here." She giggled cheerfully. "You and I could eat the whole thing until we're sick from overeating."

He smiled at her silliness. "Sure, why not. I don't remember the last time I ate rice pudding."

"I made it last year for Christmas," she said with a little smile. "For a detective you sure don't remember stuff like that. You are lucky I am not your wife, otherwise I might just be a little upset." She got up from her chair. "It's in the fridge. Maybe I'll also bring a little whipping cream."

He leaned back in his chair and finished the rest of his beer, watching her as she rushed away to get the pudding. She moved her slim body with grace and lightness of feet.

She's a delight to have around, and she has a childish sense of humor. She also wiggles her ass in the most tantalizing way. If I weren't going around with Cheryl, I might even make a pass at her right now. That's how I feel at the moment. Strange, I never really noticed her. She was just Sarah, my housekeeper. Maybe I'm not such a good detective after all.

Congressman Gibson's insinuation popped into his head. His veiled suggestion Sarah may be doing more for Hummer than just cook and clean the house had roused his anger. Could it be deep down he did have some secret feelings for her? If so, Gibson would have nothing but contempt for him. In that man's eyes black people were not the equal to white people.

We could fuck their women and get them pregnant without worrying about the consequences.

That attitude was one of the reasons Hummer did not care for him. Gibson had no compassion for anyone who was different, be it the color of skin, the spiritual belief, or the state of a person's wealth. He condemned them all.

Sarah came back, carrying a tray with two dessert dishes, a large container filled with pudding, and a small bowl with whipping cream. She put everything on the table and filled one of the dishes to the rim with pudding. Then she topped it with a generous amount of whipped cream. "If you don't eat everything you'll have to go to bed early," she said sternly, her eyes twinkling with mischief.

"I'll try my best," Hummer said, grinning. "But I'll blame you if I get fat."

"It'll take a little more than just my pudding to make you fat, Mr. Hummer. Maybe once you are married and you will eat more of my cooking you might develop a big belly." She laughed, obviously picturing him with a large belly.

He joined her laughter. It felt good to have someone to joke around with. Perhaps he should get married. Maybe it was time for him to put down roots. He might even feel happy like this all the time. Unfortunately, other thoughts, more somber thoughts, spoiled his feeling of temporary joy. Somebody was trying to involve him in something ugly and he had to find the individuals responsible before they managed to tighten the snare they set out for him.

Ghosts from the past reached out toward him and a dark mood of dismay settled over his thoughts. He knew now the abduction of Harry Middler had been the beginning of something much more sinister than a simple kidnapping. Even the murder of Middler's wife Helen and that of Saul Finkbein and Henry Miller was only part of a much larger conspiracy. They were only expendable pawns in a game played by ruthless people who didn't care about how many lives they destroyed in their search for power and wealth. They needed to be stopped and brought to justice!

Who would stop them? Was it time to turn back the clock and awaken again the man he buried a long time ago? The man he thought would stay dead forever?

"I think you should go to bed and get some rest, Mr. Hummer."

He opened his eyes to look into Sarah's smiling face. "Did I fall asleep?" he asked.

She nodded. "I guess I'm not very interesting company."

Rubbing his neck to get out the kinks, he mumbled, "It is not you, Sarah. You are great company and I thank you for spending a little time with me. I've been pushing myself lately and I guess it is finally catching up with me. I will take your advice and go to bed."

"So will I. Good night, Mr. Hummer."

* * * *

He got up early in the morning. The sun was shining and it promised to be a warm, dry day. Another beautiful summer day waiting to be enjoyed. If only he could shake this feeling of dread. Sarah had breakfast ready by the time he took his shower. "Join me for breakfast," he said, but she shook her head. "I already ate."

"Did I say something last night at dinner to upset you?" he asked.

"No. Everything was fine and I enjoyed having dinner with you, but you are my employer, my boss, and I think we should not forget that." Her eyes were large when she looked at him. "I will make it no secret, Mr. Hummer, I have…uh…feelings for you and last night I saw something in your eyes that should not be there. You told me you may be getting married. For me it means you love somebody who loves you. I don't want to jeopardize that for you and I don't want to jeopardize my job. I like it here. We mustn't do anything we both would regret, and that could easily have happened last night."

"You are a very perceptive young lady," he said, smiling sadly. He knew she was right with every word she said. "You are also quite levelheaded and honest. An admirable quality. Other women may have taken advantage of an opportunity and tried to further themselves financially. You are truly a great treasure, Sarah, and I am glad to have you."

"And I am lucky to have you as my boss, Mr. Hummer. Not many men are like you." She poured his coffee. "And now you must eat before your eggs get cold. I will go into the garden and water the flowers."

He picked up the paper, which Sarah had laid on the table, and looked at the headline. *Police have new lead in fire that killed Globe Lab's CEO Saul Finkbein and Professor Harry Middler.*

He skimmed through it but no names were mentioned. It meant Fred Simmerman probably hadn't been arrested yet. It would have been all over the news. Monday's news may be different from this one.

When his phone rang, it was Tony. "Mr. Hummer. I have found something that will be of great interest to you. Something about Mrs. Helen Middler. I don't want to talk about it over the phone."

"Okay, Tony. I'll be there in an hour. I'm surprised you already found something interesting. When did you get to the office?"

"I got here at six. This case doesn't let me sleep very much."

"Well, join the club, but I have reasons to be nervous, because my future is at stake here."

Tony made a little sound that could have been a chuckle. "If your future is at stake it will also make mine precarious. My employment depends on you being around to pay my salary. I have a lot invested in making sure you stay in business."

"Okay, you make a good point. I'll see you then."

Hummer wondered what Tony could have discovered. Helen's file had been in a protected area of the FBI files. It could only mean one thing. She was in a witness protection program. At least that was the logical explanation. But why?

When he arrived, Tony seemed excited and eager to share his

discovery. "As I already told you," he began, "Helen Middler's name was the one that got me into trouble the last time. Anyway, I found her buried in the witness protection files of the FBI. When she married Professor Middler, her maiden name was Molokov, but…" Tony made a dramatic pause. "That is not her real name. She was born with a different name, and you will have a problem accepting this." He paused again, chucking like an evil sorcerer getting ready to put a spell on an unsuspecting victim.

"Don't make me beat it out of you," Hummer threatened.

"She changed her name in nineteen-ninety-four, as soon as she turned eighteen, because she was a witness in a murder case involving a prominent mobster. Her real name, get this, her real name was Henrietta Helen Miller."

"Are you certain about that?" Hummer did have a problem believing it. The coincidence was too much.

"Quite certain. She is Rose Miller's older sister."

"No wonder she looked so much like Rose. Unbelievable."

Tony's chuckle made him narrow his eyes. "What?"

Tony rubbed his hands gleefully. "There is more. Professor Middler and Helen separated a year ago. She hasn't lived at Pineridge Cove for a year. I also found her current address. She now lives in the suburbs of Dallas, Texas."

"You mean she did live in Dallas, right? She died in a hit-and-run accident a few days ago."

"I don't believe she did. I called her number this morning, pretending to be a telemarketer, and she answered the phone. She's alive and well in Dallas, Texas."

Somehow Hummer felt a great relieve hearing it, but at the same time the news about her being alive opened up a whole new line of questions. The fact that Helen was alive somehow explained in a roundabout way the link between Professor Middler, Rose, and Henry Miller. But why did she go along with the charade? Why did she pretend to have lived with her ex-husband still? Had that whole thing with her stolen purse and the exchange of her ids been an act? Why? What had been real and what faked that day when Professor Middler was abducted? Had she been there or was the woman he knew as Helen

Middler a double?

Many questions screaming for answers.

If Helen was still alive, it left him with only one conclusion. The woman who died in the hit-and-run was Rose Miller. What a mess! Nothing made sense. It was obvious, somebody was trying to tie the murder of Saul Finkbein and Henry Miller into a web of knots and illogical acts that were nearly impossible to untangle.

This proved it beyond the shadow of a doubt Fred Simmerman had nothing to do with the murders and the fire at Globe Labs, and it was clear to Hummer everything that happened was engineered to implicate Senator Benjamin Simmerman.

He made a quick decision. "I need to talk to Helen Middler. I'm going to fly to Dallas." His gaze rested on Tony for a moment. "I want you to come with me."

"Me?" Tony pointed a fat finger at his chest.

"Yes, you, my young genius. I may need you to find out more stuff in a hurry after we've interviewed Mrs. Middler. Also, somebody has to record everything that is being said. You wanted to get some field experience. Here is your chance."

"When are we flying?"

"Today. We'll be back tomorrow."

"Today? Actually Nicole and I…" He stopped in mid-sentence and shrugged his beefy shoulders. "We just have to change our plans. Nicole will understand. She wants me to succeed."

"Good. I'll tell Nicole to book us two tickets with the next available flight."

Tony hesitated. "Mr. Hummer, I don't have an overnight bag. You know, a change of underwear, a shirt, pants, pajamas…"

"We'll take Nicole along. That's one way of keeping her happy because she'll still be with you. She can go shopping for us while we visit Mrs. Middler."

Tony's round face lit up like a full moon on a clear night. "I think I like this in-the-field stuff already."

Hummer had to laugh. "It doesn't always work out this way. Now, what else did you find out?"

"The passenger in the car driving into the parking lot at Globe Labs was Henry Miller. It was easy to find that out since I already had Miller's name. I just searched for a picture of him. I haven't identified the driver of the car yet. That may take a bit more digging, but I'll find him eventually." Hummer was pleased to hear the confidence in Tony's statement. He thanked his lucky stars for hiring Tony that day instead of brushing him off.

An hour later the three of them were on their way to the airport.

Chapter Ten

The plane landed in Dallas shortly after twelve noon. They took a taxi to a swanky downtown hotel. Hummer booked two rooms on the sixth floor. Then he took Tony and Nicole to lunch.

"Wow," Tony exclaimed when they sat in the dining room. "I've never been in a place like this. I'm almost afraid to touch the glasses. They look so fragile."

Hummer chuckled amused. "They are fragile. Even water in this hotel is expensive; that's why they have to serve it in proper glasses."

"It doesn't taste any different," Tony commented after taking a sip.

"It probably comes from the same source as our bottled water," Nicole said.

"Before I forget," Hummer pulled out his wallet and removed a few bills. He handed them to Nicole. "Here is five hundred dollars. Go shopping. Buy Tony some underwear and a nice shirt for tonight's supper."

"How about you, Mr. Hummer?" she asked. "What should I buy for you?"

"I put on new underwear this morning." He grinned. "We'll be flying home tomorrow. I'll be okay. Buy yourself something nice. I don't want you to be bored or unhappy."

"That's a lot of money you're spending," Tony observed.

Hummer waved it off. "It's deductible. This is a business trip, remember?"

It was Tony's turn to grin. "It's a holiday for me."

"It may appear that way, but we are working. As soon as we're finished with our meal we'll be leaving to visit Helen Middler."

Their server was quick with their lunch, and soon Hummer and Tony sat in a taxi heading for the address Hummer gave the driver. When they arrived in front of Helen's house, Hummer paid the driver and told him to wait for them. "It may take a couple of hours, but don't worry about that. Listen to music or whatever to amuse yourself. I'll pay you double for the time you spend waiting, okay?"

The taxi driver shrugged. "As long as you don't try to stiff me, and you don't commit some horrible crime in there, I have no problem with that."

"You'll get your money, and if it'll make you happy no crime will be committed anywhere," Hummer assured him. "Just wait for us. I don't feel like getting stuck in this neighborhood trying to find a cab. Here, take a look at my business card."

The driver took it and read the front, "Hummer Investigations. Hmm…a couple of private dicks. You guys are on a case?" He gave Hummer a shrewd look. "A divorce case? Maybe fraud or something?"

"Read the back of the card," Hummer suggested.

The driver turned the card around in his hands. "Discretion guaranteed," he read.

"There is your answer, so please don't pry." They climbed out of the taxi and walked toward the house.

The place was nothing fancy; just a small bungalow with a neat front yard and flowers along the front of the house. The houses in this part of the city were old, but most of them looked well-kept. An older man was busy raking the grass a few houses down. He looked up for a moment and watched Hummer and Tony walking on the narrow sidewalk that led to the front door.

After ringing the doorbell Hummer turned to Tony. "You are here only to observe and to record everything the woman says, understand?"

Tony nodded. "There is a lock on my lips, Mr. Hummer. I won't say a word."

Hummer smiled. "You can talk if you feel it is necessary."

The door opened and a woman stuck out her head. Her eyes widened when she saw Hummer.

"How did you find me?" she stammered.

"I'm a detective, Helen, remember? You may also remember when I told you I don't give up until a case is solved." At first he thought she may not be the same woman who came to him asking for help. She wore jeans and a checkered shirt, open at the collar to reveal the crease between her breasts. Her auburn hair was tied back with a yellow band, and the makeup she wore was not overpowering. But her reaction and words proved it was definitely her.

"Why did you come? What do you want from me?"

"The truth, Helen. I want the truth," he said softly. "May we come in?"

She opened the door and stepped back. Hummer and Tony entered the house and waited for her to close the door.

"Please, go into the living room and take a seat," she said, her voice trembling.

Hummer walked to the indicated couch and sat down, while Tony planted his bulk into the leather chair. "Nice place you have here, Helen," Hummer commented to break the ice.

She sat on the edge of the loveseat and looked at him, her green eyes studying his face. "You didn't come here to give me compliments." She had her hands folded in her lap, appearing calm and collected, but he observed the slight twitching of her right eyelid.

"No, I didn't." He smiled grimly. "First let me say I am happy to see you alive. I assumed you were dead. A woman who looked like you was killed in a hit-and-run accident and it seemed somebody wanted the police to think her name was Rose Miller, but she had an old registration in your name. Can you explain that to me?"

Helen put her face between her hands as a sob escaped her lips. She sat like that for a long moment then she looked up. Her face was tearstained. "I didn't know about Rose's death. They told me Rose was in a safe place. She was my sister."

"I'm sorry about your sister. I don't believe her death was an accident."

"Why would they kill her? She had nothing to do with any of this." She pulled a tissue out of a jean pocket and dabbed her eyes. Her face showed sudden panic. "They also told me Harry would be safe. He'd be given a new name and a new place to live. Now I'm not so sure if that was also a lie. I don't know where Harry is."

"I think I do," Hummer said. "You don't make much sense. Who are *they*? Why don't you start at the beginning and fill me in what exactly happened and why?"

She sat up straight and took a deep breath. "It seems you already knew Rose was my sister. What else do you know about me?"

"Well, in a nutshell, we know that you were born in Philadelphia and baptized Henrietta Helen Miller. You had to change your last name to Molokov and dropped *Henrietta* when you witnessed a murder and were placed into a witness protection program. You married Professor Harry Middler in two-thousand-six but separated last year."

"You know more about me than you should. I was told nobody would ever find me and I would be safe, but now…" She didn't finish the sentence.

"Normally when the Feds put somebody into a program they are quite safe, but we knew your present name and only had to do a little digging." Hummer glanced at Tony who sat quietly in his chair. "I can assure you getting information like this is not as easy as it sounds. You should still be safe." He didn't tell her that the very people who promised her protection may be the ones who would want to eliminate her if she became a liability. "Give me the reason why you and your husband separated."

"My husband was going to be a public figure after the announcement of his inventions. I was scared the people who I testified against would find me through pictures in the papers or on TV. We had discussed it at length. Our plan was for him to disappear after his company sold his inventions and he was no longer needed. He'd be getting a large payout which would allow us to live in peace and away from public eyes."

"Sounds logical. Who were the people who were going to help you achieve this?"

"The same people who put me into the witness protection."

"Did you contact them?"

"No, of course not."

"You said the same people helped you. Are we talking about the exact same people here?"

"No, these were different people. What I meant they were people involved in the witness protection program. They told me so."

"I see. Why did you take part in your husband's abduction-charade?"

"I was promised after this was all over my husband and I would be reunited."

Hummer nodded, mulling over what she'd said. So far everything made sense but it didn't explain anything. "What was the reason for that whole abduction scene? Surely not just to make your husband disappear from the public eye?"

She shrugged. "I'm not really sure and I didn't care. As long as I could go back to my life of seclusion."

"Something must have gone wrong," Hummer said. "I mean, here you are, still alone. You don't even know where your husband is right now."

"They told me to be patient a little longer. There were...complications."

There was little humor in Hummer's chuckle. "I'd say so. Did you know that Mr. Finkbein, your husband's boss, was murdered and fire set to the lab your husband worked in?"

Her face fell and her eyes were large. "Mr. Finkbein is dead? Murdered?" Her voice was nearly hysterical. "What about my husband?"

"There was another man who died in the fire, but it wasn't your husband." He hesitated, reluctant to tell her, but there would never be a good time to give her the bad news. "The other man who died with Mr. Finkbein was Henry Miller, your brother."

"No." Her wail was heartbreaking. "Not Henry!" She pressed her hands against her temples and closed her eyes. "Rose and Henry, both dead!" she cried. "This can't be real. I'll wake up any moment and realize this is nothing but a bad lucid dream."

Hummer got up and sat beside her on the loveseat. Putting an arm around her shoulder, he said soothingly, "If it's any consolation neither of them suffered. Their deaths were instant and painless."

She leaned against him. "It is my fault. I should never have testified against those murderers and none of this would have happened. My life would have been completely different, more relaxed and peaceful. I lived these last seventeen years in constant fear, always looking over my shoulder."

He rubbed her back, not knowing what to say. He had never been good with words of comfort. "You can't blame yourself, Helen. Sometimes things are beyond our control. They just happen."

"But why did they murder my brother and sister? What reason could they possibly have?" She sobbed uncontrollably, but finally calmed down. "I'm sorry about my inability to control my emotions."

He dropped his arm and moved back to his place on the couch. "No reason to apologize. You've lost two people you loved, your husband is missing. Nobody can blame you for being a little overwhelmed by it all."

She tried to smile, but it came out like a grimace. "You probably know everything about Rose and Henry. They were not exactly model citizens, but they were my sister and my brother. Actually, I haven't been in touch with them for years; that's why this is so much harder." She wiped her nose with her tissue. "I'm usually better in controlling my feelings. I have had lots of practice this last year. I joined a local theatre group and did some acting."

"No wonder you fooled me completely," Hummer commented. "You were quite convincing as the hysterical wife whose husband has been abducted and whose identity stolen."

She smiled through her tears. "I was as shocked as you when I saw my sister's apartment. That wasn't an act."

"How about your husband? Is he also an actor?"

"No. He'd never make a good actor. He's too much of a scientist with both feet on the ground." She pulled out another tissue and blew her nose.

"I'd say he played his role quite well in that abduction scene."

"That's because that man was not my husband. He was an actor, just like the people in our house. They were all actors."

Hummer pursed his lips. "You know, we've been dancing around the real question I've wanted to ask. Who are the people who set this whole thing in motion?"

"They are government people. Who else would they be?"

"Did they ever tell you what branch of government?"

"No, and I didn't ask. I assumed they worked for the FBI, you know, the way they dressed and talked, wearing sunglasses and hats, just like you see them on TV."

Hummer looked around the living room. "May I ask you who set you up in this house?"

"They did. The government people. They moved me in here. The house was furnished with everything I needed. They even supplied me with clothes and food." She sighed. "They've been good to me. That's why I don't understand any of this." Tears burst from her again. "But why all these killings? What is the purpose? Do you think my husband is also...?"

"Dead?" Hummer didn't want to give her false hopes, but he had his suspicion about the whereabouts of Professor Middler. "No, I don't think so. I may know where they are holding your husband, but I can't be sure. I would suggest you fly back with us and get him before something happens to him."

"It would be nice to have Harry back. This last year has been a strain."

"Good. We're flying back home in a few days. We'd like to do some shopping first. Can you be ready with such short notice?" He looked at Tony, telling him silently not to question the change in plans.

She laughed, suddenly appearing happy and hopeful. "I'm ready now."

Hummer got up and stretched. "I wouldn't mind walking around a little in your backyard and getting some fresh air. I can see the flowers through the window, they look nice." He chuckled. "We've been sitting in the airplane, after that we had lunch, sitting again. My legs are becoming restless. Do you mind?"

"Of course not. I could use a bit of fresh air also." She rose and led the way to the patio door. Hummer and Tony followed.

The backyard was small with flowerbeds and a couple of old trees by the back fence, their branches hanging low and thick with leaves. There was a bench under one of the trees and Hummer headed for it, seeking protecting from the hot sun.

Tony sat down on the bench, but Hummer preferred to stand in the shadow of the tree branches. Helen leaned against the thick tree trunk and looked expectantly at him. "You must have a different reason than just restless legs for coming out here."

"You are quite perceptive. Yes, I had a different reason," Hummer said with a low voice. "I don't want to sound like an alarmist or a man obsessed by paranoia, but I have a strong suspicion your home may be bugged."

"Bugged?" Helen gave him a perplexed look. "Why would anyone bug my house?"

Hummer's laugh was sarcastic. "Why do government people do the things they do? It is in their nature, that's why. Law enforcement agencies want to keep tabs on the people they are interested in."

"And they are interested in me?"

"Definitely."

"I'm just an average woman with nothing interesting in her life. I have little they could want."

"You have a genius-husband who invented something that could change the world," Hummer told her.

"You are right, my husband is a genius, but my knowledge about his inventions is limited. He didn't talk about it at home. He told me it would be better if I didn't get involved in his work, and that suited me just well. I'm not at all interested in mechanical stuff. I know how to pump gasoline into a car but I don't have a clue what the gasoline does inside the motor. Even if he would have told me about the things he worked on I wouldn't have understood it anyway." She looked toward the house. "Are you serious about them having microphones and cameras inside my house?"

"I am. Your phone is in all likelihood also bugged."

"What makes you so sure that I'm under surveillance?"

"I suspected it, but I was sure the moment you told me the FBI moved you into this furnished house. I know how they work."

"Then what are we going to do?"

"We will act as if we don't suspect anything. You will pack your bags right away and you will come with us to our hotel. We're leaving for Kansas City tomorrow."

"What about your shopping plans?"

Hummer smiled grimly. "We don't have any. I only said that for the benefit of anyone listening. I want to make sure they don't spoil our plans. Now, let's go inside and maybe you can make us a cup of coffee or tea. While Tony and I drink the tea you can pack a few little things into your purse, like makeup and stuff, but don't be too obvious about it. Take nothing else with you, okay? No clothing, no dresses or blouses. You can buy everything you'll need. Don't forget your wallet with your I.D."

"You're scaring me. Do you really think they've been watching me all this time? I mean, even in my bedroom?" Her face looked flushed when she asked it.

"I'm afraid so." He had no reason to lie to make her feel better. She deserved to know the truth about the people she dealt with. They didn't shy away from murder and would have no scruples about prying into her deepest secrets. He wanted her to be afraid of them.

Tony, who had been silent till now, coughed delicately into his hand. Hummer threw him an inquiring look. "Is there something you wanted to say, Tony?"

"Yes, if I may. I'm quite familiar with electronic spying devices. I could very discreetly walk through the rooms to see if I can spot some of them." His eyes were barely visible behind their folds of fat as he peered against the sun.

I should have given him a pair of sunglasses. He doesn't look like a cool detective with his round face and squinting eyes.

"It would be a good idea to know where they are, but don't try to touch any of them," Hummer said.

"I can do that."

"Okay, let's go back into the house."

"Won't they get suspicious if I leave with you?" Helen asked.

"I'll invite you for dinner tonight. It won't look suspicious."

They strolled back to the house, just in case there was a camera surveying the backyard. Hummer reclaimed his seat on the couch, but Tony said, "Where is your bathroom, Mrs. Middler?"

"Just down the hall," Helen told him. "I'll make some tea, is that okay?"

"Sure. I'll drink a cup." Tony headed for the bathroom. Hummer watched him open one of the doors and step through it. He came out shortly after and opened the second door.

Hummer suppressed a grin, admitting Tony may make a good detective some day. The first door had obviously led into Helen's bedroom. If Tony was as good as he said, he was it would take him only a moment to spot a camera. Microphones were a bit more difficult to detect.

He surveyed the living room with a practiced eye while Helen was busy in the kitchen, and it took him less than a minute to discover the location of one of the cameras. It was almost too obvious, hidden inside the head of a tall statue, standing in the corner, facing the living room and dining area. One of the eyes was just a bit too shiny.

When Helen came back into the living room, he said, "Your place is nicely decorated. I like the pictures. They all carry a theme, even those two statues fit into the décor."

"Yes, the pictures depict scenes from Greek mythology. The statues are supposed to be Zeus and Aphrodite." She laughed. "Even if I didn't like them; they are too big and heavy to move."

"You have good taste," he complimented her.

"I'm afraid I can't take credit for choosing the décor. Everything was already here when I moved in. The praise goes to the former owners of this house. It is lucky I actually like everything."

"So you do have good taste after all," he said.

Tony came out of the bathroom and claimed his seat again in the big leather chair. "The bathroom is nice and clean," he said, glancing at Hummer, who knew Tony meant he couldn't find any surveillance devices in the bathroom. Tony gave Helen an apologetic look. "I accidentally walked into your bedroom. That's quite some chandelier you've got hanging there right above the bed. It is beautiful but heavy-looking. Aren't you afraid it might fall down and injure you?"

She dismissed his fear with a wave of her hand. "It hasn't fallen on me yet. I was told it's an antique and apparently worth a few dollars."

"Maybe you should sell it," Hummer joked.

Helen shook her head. "It's not mine to sell. I'm only renting this place." She heaved a small sigh. "I'm actually growing quite fond of this little house. It has character and the neighborhood is quiet and peaceful. It's an old area of this city and doesn't attract too much crime. When

Harry and I get together again I wouldn't mind moving here for good."
The whistling of the water kettle made her turn her head. "I'd better pour
the water onto the teabags." With that she hurried back into the kitchen.

Hummer looked at Tony. "I didn't know you were interested in old
chandeliers."

"I'm interested in anything that glitters," Tony said. "That
chandelier caught my eye the moment I opened the door. Nicole would
love it. She loves anything old and huge." He chuckled. "That's why she
loves me. I may not be old but I'm huge."

"You should go on a diet, Tony. I don't want you dropping of a
heart attack some day," Hummer suggested. Even though they were
making light conversation in which Tony told him the camera was
hidden in the chandelier, Hummer meant his advice about the diet. He
kept his body in shape by eating sensibly and exercising regularly and he
had a difficult time understanding why so many people didn't seem to
care about the health and condition of their body. He pointed at the statue
of Zeus. "Take a lesson from the old Greeks. They were believers in a
healthy, trim body."

"I know what you mean," Tony said, obviously getting the hint
about the hidden camera. "Perhaps when we get back home I'll start an
exercise program."

Helen came back, carrying a tray with three cups and a teapot. She
placed the tray on the table and sat on the loveseat. Pouring tea into the
cups, she said, "I hope you like it. I only have fruit tea."

"It'll be fine. I won't know the difference. I'm not much of a tea
drinker," Hummer said. "I usually drink coffee."

"I'm sorry, I could have made coffee. I thought it would take too
long to make it." She apologized with a little lift of her shoulders.
Picking up her cup, she daintily sipped from it.

"You must live a lonely life without your husband," Hummer said,
picking up his own cup.

She nodded. "It does get lonely living here all by myself. I don't
really have many friends except for the people in my theatre group, but I
don't associate much with any of them."

"How about joining us for dinner tonight? In fact, you could stay
overnight in the hotel. You can keep my secretary Nicole company for

the day, take her shopping maybe, while Tony and I do some man-stuff. It'll do you good. What do you say?"

Helen hesitated. "I don't know. I wouldn't want to impose on you."

"You won't be imposing. It'll be nice to have dinner with two women instead of just my secretary and my assistant Tony." Hummer sounded enthusiastic.

She looked down at herself. "I want to change though. I couldn't go in jeans."

Hummer laughed. "We'll give you fifteen minutes to change. I know it isn't much time for a woman, but it is getting late. I'd like to get back to the hotel before dark. Besides, we have a taxi waiting and I promised our driver double pay for the time he's waiting for us. I don't want to blow my budget on him."

Helen rose. "I'll make it quick. I can be ready in ten."

She actually made it in eleven minutes. When she came out of the bedroom, she wore a pair of black slacks, high heels, and a light-green blouse. Her hair curled past her shoulders, its auburn color complimenting the green of her blouse. She looked as beautiful and confident as the day Hummer saw her for the first time in the shopping mall.

Tony apparently couldn't suppress a low whistle when she stepped into the living room. "I'm sorry," he mumbled. "I know it's not polite to whistle, but you look so…stunning."

Her eyes lit up and a smile brightened her face. "Thank you for the compliment. I've never had a problem with having a man whistle when I walk by." She looked at Hummer. "I'm ready to go."

He was satisfied to see she only carried a small handbag slung across her shoulder. Finishing his second cup of tea, he put down the empty cup. As if reading his mind, she said, "Don't worry about cleaning up. I'll put everything away when I come back tomorrow. It'll give me something to do to take my mind off things."

Hummer rose and nodded to Tony. "Well, let's go then, partner."

Tony got his bulk out of the leather chair, groaning a little. "I was just getting comfortable."

As they walked to the waiting taxi, Hummer said, "I have to compliment you, Helen. You are a damn fine actress and that was a convincing show you put up in there."

"I am playing the most important role of my life, Mr. Hummer," she said. "I'll do anything to go back to my quiet life."

"Anything?"

She threw him a sidelong glance. "Anything."

Chapter Eleven

"I never did ask you this. What happened after the probation officer Sarah Dalton took you away?"

Helen sipped from her wine. She looked at Hummer with a little smile. "Sarah Dalton doesn't exist. She was part of the act. They all were." Her face was suddenly sad. "The only thing real was Rose's apartment. I still can't get over it how my sister could have sunk so low to have lived in a place like that. I wish I would have searched for her, but I was afraid for my life, afraid to call attention to myself. Now she is dead." She wiped a finger across one cheek. "And I am asking myself if her death was caused through my actions."

"You were only a pawn in a much larger game," Hummer assured her. He studied her with curiosity. "I worried about you. Of course, now I see I had no cause to worry."

Her hand touched his with a casual gesture. "Thank you for worrying, Frank. I'm sorry I caused you all this trouble. How can I make it up to you?"

Suddenly uneasy about her calling him Frank and not Mr. Hummer, he downed his beer. When he put down the empty glass, he looked into her green eyes. "You don't owe me anything, Helen," he said. "You were a woman in distress, at least I thought you were, and I wanted to help you. I still want to help you."

She pulled away her hand. "You are a descent man and I'm sorry for pulling you into this mess."

"I just happened to be there. You have nothing to be sorry for."

Lowering her lids, she stared at her wineglass. "You don't know everything, Frank. It wasn't by chance it happened when you were present. They knew you'd be there. Apparently, you have coffee in the mall every Friday morning. You were part of the plan. We put on the show for your benefit. You were supposed to be the one taking my case."

He sat up straight and stared at her. "Why?"

She shrugged. "I was never told. I only played my part. I wasn't concerned about the reason. My concern was my own safety and my husband's return to me."

"That hasn't happened and may not happen without my help." Hummer leaned back in his chair, disturbed by her revelation. It was becoming clear to him that Helen and Harry Middler were only part of a conspiracy involving the murder of Saul Finkbein, of which Fred Simmerman was to be tried for, and ultimately Senator Benjamin Simmerman's falling out of grace with the American public. His own role in the whole scheme was still a mystery.

"How do I fit into the picture, Helen?" he asked.

"I told you I don't know. And that is the truth."

"I want to believe you, Helen. I'd be disappointed to discover you held something back from me."

The flickering flame of the candle on the table reflected in her green eyes and he had the sudden desire to bend over the table and kiss her.

What the hell am I thinking? She's a married woman in distress and I am dating a woman whom I may even marry. I'm not a cheater.

Her hand was warm on his when she reached out toward him. "I would never do anything deliberately to hurt you, Frank. You are my protector. My friend in need."

God, she is beautiful. I'd better get a grip on my emotions. What is the matter with me? Last night I almost took Sarah to bed and today I'm having the hots for Helen. Where the hell are Tony and Nicole? How long does it take to have a drink at the bar?

He turned his head and looked up when somebody coughed. It was Tony. He pulled away one of the chairs to let Nicole sit down. "Are we interrupting anything?" he asked.

"Like what?" Hummer countered, his voice coming out almost too sharp.

Tony lifted an eyebrow. "Never mind. It was only a routine question."

Hummer forced a laugh. "A detective never asks routine questions. Every question has to produce information, even if it seems insignificant."

Tony's face was without expression when he said, "I'm watching everything you say and do to become a good detective." His lips formed a little smile. "And believe me, Mr. Hummer, when I say I gained plenty of information with my routine question."

"Well, I'm happy to hear that." Hummer had regained his cool composure, glad for Tony's little bit of bantering. Not for the first time he was pleased to have hired the young man. Tony brought a bit of fresh air into his company, not to mention the fact he was bright and showed great insight. He was also a good observer. Maybe a little too much of an observer.

I think I'll keep him around as a chaperone and watchdog to keep me on the straight path. My big guardian angel.

"Have you ordered already?" Nicole asked, studying the menu.

"No, not yet. I told the waiter to wait until you joined us."

As if on cue the waiter, dressed in a tuxedo, came over and asked, "Are you ready to order?"

"Almost," Hummer told him. "Can you bring us another bottle of wine and a bottle of beer for me? We'll be ready to order then."

"As you wish, sir." The waiter bowed and walked away.

"You certainly know how to live, Frank," Helen said. "The detective business must be profitable."

He chuckled. "If I had to rely on the money my agency brings in I'd starve. I have other means of making money."

"Like what?" She seemed genuinely interested.

"I buy shares in businesses, play the stock market. I'm always on the lookout for new investments. Boring stuff like that."

"Oh, I'm sure it is exciting if you know what you're doing, especially when your stocks go up." She laughed. "I don't know much about stocks and bonds."

"I have a good stockbroker and lawyer." Hummer closed his menu. "Everybody ready to order? Here comes out waiter."

* * * *

Helen hung onto Hummer's arm as they waited for the elevator to take them up to the sixth floor.

"I think I drank too much wine," she said, giggling like a teenage girl coming home from a party.

Hummer glanced at Tony, who gave him a knowing look. "I think Nicole also had more wine than she can handle. That last bottle did them in," Tony said.

Nicole joined Helen's giggling. She planted a kiss on Tony's cheek. "I get real naughty when I had too much to drink. I hope you are up to it, lover."

Tony looked uncomfortable under her open display of affection. "We're not alone," he whispered fiercely.

"I don't care," Nicole said. "Mr. Hummer knows I love you, don't you, Mr. Hummer?"

Hummer chuckled. "Everybody loves Tony. He's a lovable hunk."

The elevator doors opened and they piled into the elevator. "Take us up to the sixth floor," Nicole told the elevator after the doors closed but nothing happened.

"I think you have to push the button," Helen giggled. She stabbed at one of the buttons but hit the fifth floor. "Oh, oh. Wrong floor."

"I believe this is a man's job," Tony said, pushing the correct button.

Helen looked at Hummer and smiled wickedly. "Which button does a woman have to push with you to get the right one, Frank?"

"Nobody pushes Mr. Hummer's buttons," Nicole said, waggling a finger at Helen. "I've tried." She looked at Tony and smiled. "That was before I met you."

The elevator stopped and Nicole tried to rush out, but Tony pulled her back. "One more floor," he told her.

Everyone got off on the sixth floor. Tony and Nicole headed for their suit which was across from Hummer's. He opened the door to his own suit and waited for Helen to enter first. She staggered over to the couch and sank into it. Looking at him with a silly smile, she said, "I think I'm drunk, Frank. Maybe a cold shower will help."

"Go ahead," he told her.

While she was in the shower, Hummer turned on the TV, wondering if there would be news about Saul Finkbein, but nobody mentioned anything about him or Globe Labs. They showed the flood situation in North Dakota and across the border in Canada and talked about the fires in the southern states and the widespread flooding of the Mississippi.

The weather sure is crazy these days.

When he heard the door to the bathroom opening, he turned his head. Helen stood naked in the open door. She looked beautiful and seductive with her green eyes large and her mouth slightly open. He couldn't help but notice her heart-shaped pubic hair. It was the same color as her hair, a gorgeous auburn, and still glistening from the shower. "I didn't bring a nightgown," she said, not sounding drunk at all. "I guess I'll have to sleep in the nude." She took a few steps toward him. "You never told me where I would sleep."

"You can sleep in my bed," he said.

"Okay." She turned and walked toward the bedroom and he realized she wore her high-heeled shoes. A woman always looked good in high heels. He watched the way her round buttocks moved and remembered admiring them that first day when they were looking for her car. Only this time he didn't have to imagine what they looked like.

Before she entered the bedroom, she stopped and turned around. "Are you coming?" she asked with a throaty voice. "I don't know how long I can stay awake."

He pulled his gaze away from her lovely shaped breasts and concentrated on her face.

Damn! This is going to be hard.

"Don't worry about not being able to stay awake. Get some rest. We'll get up early tomorrow. Our plane leaves at eleven."

She pulled her mouth into a pout. "Are you saying you won't be sleeping with me?"

"That's what I'm saying."

"I thought, I mean since I'm sharing your room. Why didn't you get me my own room?"

"Because the hotel is filled up."

"I guess I misunderstood, but that doesn't change anything. I am offering myself, Frank. Freely and without any conditions. My way of thanking you. Don't embarrass me." Her eyes almost pleaded with him.

"You are a married woman, Helen," he said.

"I'm married only on paper, Frank. My husband and I haven't been together as man and woman for years."

"Why not? I thought you loved him."

She gave a strangled laugh. "I don't, but let's not go into that now. I need someone to comfort me and make me happy. I want you, Frank. I can see you want me also. What is the problem?"

Why do I have to be such an upstanding guy with high morals? She can't make it any more obvious or easier. She is right. She wants me and I want her. Damn it.

"Yes, I want you," he admitted, reluctantly. "At this moment I'm probably the horniest guy walking this planet, but I can't. I have a girlfriend who wants to marry me. I'm not going to cheat on the woman I may possibly marry. Besides, you're my client, and I don't get involved with my clients."

Her laughter teased him. She put her hands under her breasts and lifted them. "I've always been proud of my breasts. Somebody told me they are nearly perfectly shaped. Most men would give a lot to suck them, but I haven't had a man touch them for a year. Don't you want to be the first one to do so?"

He smiled sadly. "Believe me, I want nothing more, but it would be wrong. You had a little bit too much wine tonight and this is the alcohol talking. If I accept your offer you'll be sorry in the morning, and so will I. Now, go to sleep."

"Okay. Your loss. The offer is good all night if you should change your mind. But after tomorrow morning it won't be repeated." She turned and opened the bedroom door.

He watched the door closing behind her, the image of her white, full buttocks etched into his mind. *Some men might call me a fool, but I'd be an even greater fool to accept her invitation.*

He finished watching the news but couldn't get the vision of her out his thoughts. When he went into the bathroom he saw her slacks and blouse hanging on a hook but her panties and bra lay on the floor, and he wondered if she had done so on purpose.

The pull-out couch was comfortable enough, but he spent a restless night, tossing and turning. At one time he was almost ready to join Helen in the bedroom but suppressed the terrible urge. Falling into an uneasy slumber toward morning, he woke up with a dull head and blamed it on the four bottles of beer he consumed but knew there was more behind it than just the beer.

He got up and went to brush his teeth. Helen wasn't up yet when he was finished and he knocked on her door. "Time to get up," he called. She came out of the bedroom a few minutes later and headed for the bathroom. When she saw him sitting on the couch, she crossed her arms over her bare breasts and said, somewhat sheepishly, "Good morning. Are you up already or are you still sitting there from last night?"

"I'm up," he said, his eyes studying her black, lacy panties.

She noticed his look. "I did manage to pack an extra pair of panties into my handbag," she said. "I think I made a fool of myself last night." A hint of rosy color crept into her cheeks. She made a move with her head toward the bathroom. "I'll get dressed and make myself presentable. I promise I won't be long."

"It's still early," he said, smiling. "We have enough time."

* * * *

Sarah's face displayed surprise when he brought Helen home with him. She looked at Hummer. "Aren't you going to introduce me to your girlfriend, Mr. Hummer?"

"This is Helen. She is not my girlfriend, Sarah. She's a client."

"Oh, a client." Sarah lifted her eyebrows a little. "Since when are you bringing your work home with you?"

Hummer was amused by Sarah's misunderstanding of the situation. "Don't read anything into this, Sarah. This lady is from out-of-town and she has no place to stay. One more thing, I don't want it broadcast about her staying here, you understand? This may be a matter of life and death. Make up the bed in the guestroom for her, please. By the way, are your kids back from camp?"

She shook her head. "No, they won't be coming home for another couple of days."

"Then you should join us for supper tonight. I don't want you to feel lonely." He smiled. "After all, I consider you part of my family." He paused. "There may be another guest, so prepare for four people. We'll have supper on the patio. It is a warm evening."

"Is there anywhere I can freshen up?" Helen asked.

"Sure. Sarah will show you your room. It has its own bathroom. There is also a small library and a TV in the room. You'll find privacy there. Nobody will disturb you. Now, if you'll excuse me, I'm going into my office to make a couple of calls." He walked away without waiting for an answer. Being near Helen all day had been somewhat disturbing and he needed to be alone to collect his thoughts. Her exceptional beauty bewitched him, and having seen her flawless nude body and her offer to have sex with him kept stewing in his mind.

In all his years of being a detective he had never gotten involved with a female client. Many of the women had been in distress and vulnerable and easy to take advantage of. That was not the kind of man he was. He took pride in being honorable and decent. In his younger years he had been different, but that was a long time ago. That man did no longer exist, but it seemed he still lurked in the dark recesses of his mind, waiting to be awakened and freed from his restraints, ready to unleash violence and create mayhem.

The first call he made was to Martin Schumann.

It seemed Schumann was not happy to receive Hummer's call. "What the hell, Frank, this is the second time in two days you're calling me on my private cell. Do I have to change my number?"

"My apologies, Martin, but this is important."

"It is Sunday, dammit, Frank. I'm having a family barbeque. Can't a man have at least one day off?"

"I'll make it up to you, Martin. I promise. Did you get that warrant for Simmerman?"

"No but I'll get it tomorrow."

"Do me a favor. Hold on with the arrest. Simmerman is innocent. I have proof. If you arrest him, you'll be destroying a good man's reputation and future. Not only will he suffer from it but America will be the big loser."

"What the hell are you talking about, Frank?"

"I'm talking about Senator Benjamin Simmerman, Fred Simmerman's father. You must be aware he is running for President."

"Of course I am. Who isn't? His picture is on every TV screen."

"If you arrest his son you'll ruin his chances of ever becoming President of the United States."

There was a pause on the other end. Then, "What kind of proof do you have about Fred Simmerman's innocence?"

"Not only do I have proof of Simmerman's innocence, I also know Felix Erskine did not set the fire at Globe Labs, he also didn't kill anyone. He was there but not inside the building. He was the guard at the gate. The Fire Commissioner will confirm it if you show him Erskine's picture."

"How do you know all this?" Schumann showed sudden interest.

"I suggest you drive to Globe Labs tomorrow and talk to Artie. He is the guy who watches all the security screens. Ask him to show you the recordings taken by the camera at the gate, the ones from Sunday, the day of the fire. Ask him to zoom in on the guy by the gate and the guys in the car."

"Where did you get your information from?" He paused again. "Fuck it, Frank," he cursed. "Now I get it. That call last week. You used me for something. I warned you, Frank."

"Don't get hot under the collar, Martin. I only used your name. You have nothing to worry about. Go and check out what I told you and you'll see what I mean. Maybe by tomorrow I can give you a couple of names."

"I want more than names, Frank. I want you to do some explaining. I want to know what the hell is going on."

"And you will, as soon as I know. I told you this was a bizarre case; well, it still is."

He clicked off, hoping Schumann would trust him and do the right thing. If he ignored his request and suggestion and followed through with the arrest of Fred Simmerman it would set in motion a series of events carrying worldwide critical, possibly dire consequences.

Walking over to his liquor cabinet, he took out a bottle of cognac and a glass. Luckily, alcohol didn't go bad; otherwise he would have had to discard most of the bottles in the cabinet. He didn't usually drink hard liquor, but today he had a sudden craving for a stronger drink than beer. Pouring some of the cognac into the glass, he put back the stopper and stored the bottle away again, making sure it didn't click against the others, like a collector worried about damaging his beloved, valuable treasures.

Sniffing the glass, he closed his eyes, recalling the first time he tasted cognac. Paris, March seventeen, nineteen-ninety-one, a month after his eighteenth birthday and a couple of months before he joined the army. He had accompanied his father on a business trip to France. While his father was busy promoting one of his companies, he was busy enjoying the local entertainment.

She had been some hot and wild little French girl, the spoiled daughter of rich parents. He met her at a bar in a night club where she and her girlfriends celebrated her eighteenth birthday. Actually, she had been the one to speak to him first. He didn't speak French and she only spoke a little English, but who needs to talk at all when all you want is to get into a girl's pants?

She carried a bottle with her when she approached him and offered him a drink, straight out of the bottle. He didn't know it was cognac and he didn't particularly like it, but the horny fool that he was, he drank more than he should have, totally spellbound by this beautiful girl who chose him from all the other single guys in the nightclub. After spending the whole night with her doing things he'd never done before with any girl, he found himself the next morning with a huge hangover and totally exhausted in a strange hotel room.

The girl was gone and she left him with the bill for the room. His father had been furious with him, not because he had to pay for the room but for his stupidity to get involved with a complete stranger, no matter how beautiful or hot.

His father's words stayed with him all his life.

The world is full of predators preying on unsuspecting victims. You could have been one of those victims. You could be dead now, son. Never trust a beautiful woman who comes on to you for no reason at all. No reason you can see. She may have a hidden agenda that usually doesn't end in your favor. Never forget that.

And he never did. He also never forgot that beautiful French girl.

Sighing, he emptied the glass, letting the strong liquid trickle down his throat, washing away old memories, some pleasant and some best forgotten. His thoughts came back to the present. Did Helen have a hidden agenda?

Always think with the head on your shoulders, son. Never with the one in your pants.

Picking up his phone again, he dialed Cheryl's number.

She seemed surprised to hear his voice. "I tried to call you a couple of times but all I got was your automated message. Did anything happen?"

"I'm sorry; I should've let you know. I was in Dallas on business. I didn't answer my calls because I didn't want to be bothered. Are you busy tonight?"

"I don't have any big plans. What do you have in mind?"

"I'd like you to come over to my place for supper."

"Why not come to my place?"

He would have liked that but knew it would not be polite or fair to leave his guest alone. That was not the only reason. He preferred if Cheryl came and met Helen at his place instead of hearing about the female houseguest sleeping in his guestroom. He realized he needed to have Cheryl staying with him the night to take his mind off territory it should not be dwelling in.

"I can't, honey. One of my clients is staying with me for a few days and I promised her protection."

"Her?" Cheryl asked.

"Yes, a woman. It's complicated and I can't talk about it on the phone. That's why I want you to come here." He made a pause. "Besides, I've missed you and I need to see you."

"Just see me?" she teased.

"Naked, if possible," he said, laughing.

She returned his laughter. "In that case I can't justify refusing your request. Besides, I want to meet that woman who is staying with you. I'll be there around seven, is that okay?"

"Sure. See you then. The door will be open; just walk in. We'll eat on the patio in the back."

"Looking forward to it. I love you," she said before she broke the connection.

She was there shortly before seven. When she walked through the patio door, he asked himself why he would even be tempted to cheat on her. She looked absolutely stunning in her tight black pants and red sleeveless sweater. She didn't wear a bra and she had no need for it. Her breasts, while not large, were no less perfect than Helen's. She had her blonde hair pulled back and tied into a ponytail, leaving her ears exposed to show off her gold teardrop earrings. He knew the sparkle in them was caused by diamonds most people couldn't afford.

He got up and took her into his arms. "What are you trying to do?" he whispered into her ear.

"What do you mean?" she asked impishly, sounding innocent.

"You know what I mean, looking like a love-goddess."

She laughed and kissed him on the cheek. "You always know the right things to say to a woman." Her gaze fell on Helen, who was sitting in one of the lounges. "Is that your houseguest?"

Hummer made a gesture, indicating Helen. "This is Helen Middler, my client. She is my latest case. Her husband has been kidnapped in my presence and I'm trying to help her find him."

Cheryl took a few steps toward Helen. She looked genuinely concerned. "I'm sorry to hear about your husband. I hope you find him soon."

Helen smiled. "I have no doubt we will. Frank has been really helpful so far."

"Frank?" Cheryl threw a quick look at Hummer. "Yes, Frank is a good detective. By the way, I am Cheryl Gibson. I'm sure Frank has talked about me."

"He's mentioned you briefly. You are a lucky woman."

Oh, oh! The claws are already coming out. I'd better step in.

He walked up to Cheryl and put his arm around her shoulder. "This is the woman I told you about, Helen. She has captured my heart and soul."

Helen picked up the glass standing on the patio tiles beside her lounge and held it against her lips but didn't drink from it. "Sounds serious. You make a good couple. Any plans to get married?"

"We haven't made plans yet," Cheryl said, throwing a quick glance at Hummer. "But I'm working on it."

They were interrupted by Sarah who came out of the house, carrying a large tray. "Supper will be served in ten minutes," she announced. Then she walked over to the large table which was already set with plates and cutlery. She took two covered bowls from the tray and put them onto the middle of the table. Taking the empty tray, she started walking back to the house.

"Sarah, wait a minute so I can introduce you to Cheryl." Hummer said.

Sarah gave Cheryl a friendly smile. "I am pleased to meet you, Miss Cheryl. Mr. Hummer told me all about you and I'm looking forward to someday taking care of you the way I take care of Mr. Hummer."

"What do you do for Mr. Hummer?"

"I clean his house, I make the beds, I do the laundry, I cook for him, I shop for groceries and other things Mr. Hummer may need." She smiled sweetly. "I do everything a wife usually does for her husband."

"Everything?" Cheryl asked, a little taken aback. "Do you sleep with him?"

"No, Miss Cheryl. I don't sleep with him. He is my boss, not my husband. I work for Mr. Hummer and he lets me and my two children live in the guesthouse."

"How long have you worked for Mr. Hummer?"

"Six years, ma'am."

"And you've lived in the guesthouse since then?"

"Yes, ma'am. And I hope to live there still after Mr. Hummer marries you."

Cheryl looked thoughtful when her eyes met Hummer's. "I thought I knew everything about you, Frank. How come you never told me anything about Sarah? I knew you had a housekeeper but I didn't know she lived with you. And I didn't know she was so young and pretty."

"It never came up," he said with an apologizing lift of his shoulders. "Why, is that a problem?"

"No, it's no problem. I'm surprised to discover you actually have a soft spot in your heart. I only know you as this tough detective who does nothing but solve cases."

"I take on a lot of cases that don't pay any money," he said. "Does that not count as proof I have a soft heart?"

"It is still considered business and doesn't really count. It's like advertising and brings new clients. This is different. This is part of your personal life I don't really know much about." Her face showed sympathy when she gazed at Sarah. "I would never make you move out of the guesthouse and I'm looking forward to have you look after me the way you do with Mr. Hummer."

Sarah laughed happily. "Maybe you'll change your mind after you've tasted my cooking. But now I'd better get the rest of the food before everything gets cold." She whirled around and hurried back into the house.

"She's a delight," Cheryl said, sweetly. "I like her. We'll have to discuss her future at another time. You and I."

Chapter Twelve

He woke up to find Cheryl standing naked in front of the large mirror in his bedroom. She turned her body slowly and looked at herself with a critical eye.

"You have a perfect body," he said, still a little sleepy. "Come back to bed and make love to me before we get up."

She laughed and struck a pose. "This is all you'll get, lover. Didn't I give you enough last night?"

"You did, but this is morning."

She padded closer and bent to plant a quick kiss on his lips. Her breasts swung freely in front of his eyes and he reached for them. She evaded him by stepping backward. "I have a show coming up next weekend and have a lot to do to get ready. I'd better get going," she said.

"Will I see you during the week?"

She shook her head as she slipped into her panties. "I'm afraid not. Don't even bother to call. I won't have any time. I'll be working day and night." She laughed when he made a face. "Don't pout. I promise I'll take some time off the week after. Maybe we can go away for a couple of days."

Propping himself up on his elbows he watched her getting dressed. "You are so beautiful," he said.

"Thank you for the compliment, but it won't get me back into your bed. Now let me put on some makeup. I don't have much time."

"I'll call Sarah to have breakfast ready for you," Hummer said.

"Don't bother. I won't stay for breakfast. No time." She disappeared into the bathroom.

He stretched and lay back to stare at the ceiling.

I hope we'll have more time together should we ever get married.

Turning his head to look at the alarm clock he noticed it showed six-thirty-two. He usually got up at seven. Since he was already awake he decided he might as well get up. He did a few stretching exercises while waiting for Cheryl to come out of the bathroom.

She walked out looking fresh and lovely, her hair hanging loosely around her shoulders instead of having it pinned back. She looked older that way, more mature but still beautiful and desirable.

"You're up," she said, giving him a bright smile. "Do you always exercise in the nude?"

He grinned. "It's the only way, but I would have preferred a different exercise this morning. One that involves you."

She came close to him and stroked his chest with a soft hand. "I'm happy you want me this badly. I want you too, but I really can't this morning. I promise I'll make it up to you. Hopefully, next week. I love you." Then she kissed him and turned to walk away. Before she closed the door to the bedroom, she blew him a kiss.

He sighed and walked into the bathroom. It smelled of her perfume. Closing his eyes, he took a few deep breaths, trying to bring back the memory of the night. He could almost feel her warm body touching his, and her hot breath on his face as she gasped above him.

Memories are like wisps of smoke in the darkness of the night, insubstantial and elusive like a dream, like ghosts that never existed in reality. Are they memories of things that transpired or are they just wishful dreams of things that may or may not come to pass?

He read that somewhere, but he didn't remember where. Opening his eyes, he looked into the mirror and saw his unshaven face.

What does a woman think of a man when she wakes up in the morning and sees this? Does she think he's a handsome hunk or does she think he looks like a bum?

He grinned at his image. "You look like a bum," he said. *An unshaved man always looks grubby no matter what the ads on TV tell you.* Then he shaved and brushed his teeth. He didn't have to fuss much with his hair because he always wore it short. As he studied himself, he wondered if Cheryl would try to change the way he looked once they were married. Women did do that sort of thing to a man. Was Cheryl already thinking about the things she would change in him? He liked himself the way he was.

Am I already getting cold feet? I haven't even proposed to her yet. I'm an independent man, not used to having someone plan my day for me. Will she tell me to stop wearing my suit and tie every day? Tell me to wear a hat instead of a baseball cap? Or dress more casual? Damn it! Perhaps married life may not be for me after all!

He climbed down the stairs, wondering what the hell he should do.

"Good morning," a woman's voice called when he was halfway down the stairs. He looked to see Helen standing in the middle of the living room, gazing out of the window. Dressed in her black slacks and light-green blouse, her long, red hair highlighted by the morning sun falling through the tall window, she looked attractive and more desirable than ever.

That instant attraction for her came over him again and he realized having made love to Cheryl had done nothing to keep him from wanting Helen. He wondered how he would feel toward Helen had he accepted her offer to have sex with her. Would he still have this desire inside him? Forbidden fruit were the sweetest and most desirable but once tasted they seem to lose their appeal.

Maybe I should have fucked her and gotten it out of my system!

"It promises to be a nice day," she said. The color of her blouse and the sunlight magnified the green of her eyes, making them appear large and shiny.

"It appears that way," he agreed, climbing down the rest of the way. "Did you have a good night's rest?" *God, I love her beautiful eyes. Especially when she looks at me like this.*

"I had a good rest. Did you?" Her smile seemed to mock him. "I saw your girlfriend leaving already. Everything still okay between you two?"

"Why shouldn't it be?"

She shrugged her slim shoulders. "I don't think she likes me. Don't think she likes your housekeeper either."

"She'll get used to Sarah."

"And me?"

"She doesn't have to get used to you. Once we have you reunited with your husband and safe you'll be out of the picture. We will probably never see each other again."

"Perhaps we will. Life is funny that way. It seems once you meet someone there is a certain bond connecting you with that person. You will never be completely free of each other." She turned away from the window and came walking toward him, a cryptic smile on her lips. "Ever. It has something to do with karma."

He was not a believer in karma and cosmic intervention. As far as he was concerned, people made their own decisions, created their own destiny. Actions spawned consequences. It was as simple as that. To blame something on fate or a higher power was to refuse responsibility. Of course, he could not deny that sometimes things happened that defied logical explanation, but he was certain everything could somehow be explained in scientific terms.

Helen stood in front of him and looked into his eyes. "Yesterday, when I asked your girlfriend about any plans to get married, she said she is working on them. You didn't comment. She is a beautiful, self-assured woman and probably loves you, but are you willing to submit to her ego and forfeit your own? And she will try to influence you. It's in a woman's nature to want to change the man she marries. Are you ready to be changed? Will you wonder someday how your life would have been with another woman? Or perhaps without one?"

Her hand touched his chest and her fingers played with his tie. "Do you always wear a suit and a tie?" she asked.

He felt uncomfortable having her so near. Her feminine scent made his head spin. She wore perfume, but it was hardly noticeable. "I feel most comfortable in a suit," he said, his voice gravelly.

"Most men are quite comfortable dressing more casually. A suit may mean you are rigid in your thoughts and actions. Wearing a tie at all times only confirms it." She spoke softly. Her tongue played across her lips and her eyes were half-veiled by her lowered lids. With a sudden quick move, she put a hand behind his neck and pulled him close.

Her lips were soft and warm on his and she opened her mouth to push her tongue against his teeth. With a loud groan, he kissed her back.

When they broke apart, she smiled up at him. "We're both adults, Frank. Yes, I'm a married woman but in name only. My husband and I are practically strangers. And you are not married. From your reaction yesterday, I sensed you're not ready or even willing to make a commitment to Cheryl. It will be all right to make love to me. You won't be taking advantage of me, because right now I'm sober and not influenced by alcohol."

He knew she was right in everything she said. He wasn't married and he had made no commitments to Cheryl. Looking into Helen's green eyes he saw promise and suppressed passion. He was not immune to a woman's charms, especially when she was as beautiful and willing as Helen.

With a silent curse, he scooped her up in his arms and carried her upstairs.

* * * *

Sarah was ominously silent when she served them breakfast. When he asked her if she wanted to join them, she declined with a shake of her head. "I already ate breakfast earlier this morning."

"You didn't sit with us last night either," he said, "Even though I invited you."

"I didn't think it would be proper. I'm the hired help. I work for you, sir."

"We'll discuss that another time," he said. He didn't think she knew what had transpired between him and Helen, but she probably sensed something had changed. Helen sat across from him at the table, a satisfied, almost triumphant smile playing across her full lips, while he felt guilty as hell.

He didn't really know why he should feel so guilty. Perhaps it was the fact the bed had still been warm from Cheryl's body when he had taken another woman into the same bed he shared with her. He told himself he hadn't really cheated. How can you cheat on someone when you've made no promises? But his reasoning didn't help much. Helen had portrayed him quite accurately when she said he was rigid in his thoughts and actions.

Looking at his watch, he realized it was after ten. "We have to hurry," he said.

Her expression was amused when she looked at him. "Why the sudden rush?" she asked.

"We need to drive to my office first to make plans. After lunch we'll drive to the Happy Acres Sanatorium to get your husband," he told her.

"Is that where Harry is?" she asked.

"I'm not quite sure, but I'm confident we'll find him there, because the man who is supposed to be there is dead."

"Who was that other man?"

"Your brother Henry."

"Oh." Her face fell when he mentioned her brother. It brought her back down from her amused state. Her demeanor suddenly changed. "You are right. We should hurry." Her eyes seemed to have lost their sparkle when she stared at him. "For a short time I forgot the ugly world I live in and it felt good; now I must face reality again."

He saw the moisture in her eyes and his heart went out to her. Forgotten was his guilt. "We'll get your husband back," he said softly. "Your life will be better soon, I promise."

Using her napkin to dab her eyes, she said, "It would be nice, but you can't promise me that. Having my husband back won't change much in my personal life, but there is much more at stake here than you can possibly know. My life will never be the same again." Her eyes looked into his as she added, "And neither will yours be."

He didn't know what exactly she meant, but she was right. Having succumbed to her charms was definitely going to have an influence on his future. "What happened this morning was not right," he said. "You know that. Neither of us will ever mention it to anyone, okay?"

She gave him a sad smile. "Women don't usually brag about their conquests the way men do. You have nothing to fear about me broadcasting I spent a couple of joyful hours in your bed. We both needed this. You can't deny that. I have no feelings of guilt. What we did felt good and right. I didn't force you, only nudged what you wanted all along, and I don't remember hearing you complain when you lay in my arms."

He finished his coffee and wiped his mouth. "Well, it happened. I can't change that. Are you ready to go?"

"I am, just give me a moment to brush my hair and apply a little makeup."

"As long as it doesn't take too long." He was getting impatient. Time seemed suddenly of the essence.

"Ten minutes is all I need," she promised. Then she hurried down the hallway toward the guestroom.

Women! They spend more time powdering their noses than any man ever spends admiring himself in the mirror.

He took the time to call the office. When Nicole answered, he asked, "Is Mr. Silvo back from Miami?"

"Yes, he's in his office right now."

"Ask him not to leave. I'll need him this afternoon. Also tell Mr. Marconi to stay. Tell them we'll be paying the Happy Acres Sanatorium a visit."

"Okay, Mr. Hummer. I will let them know."

"Is Tony there?"

"Yes."

"Put him on?"

It took a few moments until Tony answered. "Yes, Mr. Hummer?"

"Did you get a chance to do some more digging?"

"I'm sorry, Mr. Hummer. I've been kicked out of the office I was using. I'm a man with no office right now. A man without a home, so to speak."

"That's okay. I'll be coming in and we'll sort things out. You'll be accompanying us this afternoon on another mission. Be ready."

"Will do, Mr. Hummer." Tony sounded happy and excited.

Helen came back into the dining room, her hair pinned back and her lips showing a hint of red. "Ready to go," she said brightly. "How do I look?"

"You look great. Your husband will be pleased to see you."

Her face didn't show much enthusiasm when she said, "I hope so."

They drove to Hummer's agency office in relative silence. When they walked into the office, Tony was sitting with Nicole. He jumped out of the leather chair when he saw Hummer, looking guilty and apologetic. "I didn't put my feet on the table, Mr. Hummer."

Hummer couldn't help but chuckle. "I never said you did, Tony. Are you ready for this next assignment?"

"Sure am. Do I get to carry a gun?"

"I'm afraid not. First of all, you don't have a license and second I don't want you to shoot anyone accidentally. If you want to carry a gun you'll have to learn how to handle one first." Hummer told him. He turned to Helen. "Please, take a seat. I'll have to talk to my associates first." With that he walked into Silvo's office.

Dennis Silvo looked up from his computer screen. "Mr. Hummer," he said. "Good to see you. Nicole told me we'll be visiting someone in the Happy Acres Sanatorium."

Hummer smiled grimly. "Not visiting. We'll be rescuing an innocent man. By the way, how are things in Miami? Any progress in the case?"

Silvo moved his thick shoulders inside his jacket. "I found the man who swindled Mrs. Sardovsky out of her money, but I couldn't get anything from him. He's a slick son-of-a-bitch and not easily intimidated. We'll have a hard time building a case against him."

"As soon as we're done with this business I'll take a look at the case myself. My new assistant Tony is good at finding out things. Maybe we can dig up some dirt on your man. Come with me into Marconi's office, I want to talk to you and him about what's going to happen."

"Sure." Silvo got up from behind his desk and followed Hummer into Marconi's office. Marconi was busy reading the newspaper. When Hummer and Silvo walked in, he put down the paper. "The price of gas is going down again, but for how long? This is just another teaser. The oil companies are playing with us. It's time we get more electric cars on the road to stop their monopoly. In other news: A bunch of Taliban radicals blew themselves up again in Afghanistan. Nothing but good news these days."

He folded the paper and shoved it into a drawer. "So, what's the plan?"

"I want to get Professor Middler out of the Sanatorium," Hummer said. "Problem is we can't just waltz in there and tell them to hand him over. In addition, we have another dilemma: He is listed under Henry Miller, the man who died in the fire at Globe Labs."

"If we had a court order it would be relatively easy," Silvo suggested.

"Say, wasn't Henry Miller transferred from another hospital?" Marconi asked.

"From the Silver Maple Mental Hospital."

"He must have been transferred there under a doctor's orders."

"You are correct." Hummer pulled out his small notebook and rifled through it. "Let's see, I was at the Happy Acres Sanatorium Saturday, June eighteen and talked to a Victoria Sommers. According to her the doctor who signed Henry Miller's transfer papers was a Dr. McDermott."

"Why not give him a call?" Marconi suggested.

"And ask him what?"

"Ask him to send us a copy of the transfer orders."

"Hmm, I guess it wouldn't hurt." Hummer looked thoughtful. "We could copy their form and print a note which allows Mrs. Miller to take out her husband for a day, under our supervision. It might just work."

"I think it's a good idea," Silvo said.

"Okay, let me make the call." He went to the door and called out, "Nicole, get me the Silver Maple Mental Hospital. Ask to talk to a Dr. McDermott."

"Sure thing, Mr. Hummer."

While they waited for the call to go through, Hummer asked Silvo to give him more details about how things went in Miami. It took only a few minutes of waiting though until Nicole came into the room.

"Well?" Hummer asked before she could say anything.

"There is no Dr. McDermott working at the Silver Maple Mental Hospital."

"I'll be damned," Marconi said.

"Actually, I am not surprised." Hummer gave Marconi a scrutinizing look. "You'd make an impressive doctor," he mused.

"I'm afraid to ask what you have in mind." Marconi pulled his thick eyebrows together into a frown.

"I'll get Tony to make up a file for Henry Miller and print out some scientific sounding document which you will present to Victoria Sommers. You'll tell her you want to take Mr. Miller back to the Silver Maple Mental Hospital for a few days of observation."

"And who exactly will I be?"

"You will be Dr. McDermott. Since he doesn't exist, nobody will know what he looks like, right? Tony can print a couple of business cards to make it look official. You can give one of the cards to Miss Sommers at the admission's counter." Hummer grinned. "Tell her she's a good-looking woman. She'll like that."

Marconi gave him one of his sardonic smiles. "I'm not a ladies' man like you, Mr. Hummer. Lies don't come easily past my lips."

"It won't be a lie. She is quite pleasant to look at. It's not like you'll be taking her to bed."

"I don't think I'd go that far, Mr. Hummer. I never mix pleasure with business and I never get involved with my clients."

Ouch, that hits close to home. I did just that this morning.

"A good policy," Hummer said, feeling guilt rising up inside him again.

Nicole was still standing in the doorway. "What do you want me to do, Mr. Hummer?"

"You heard what I said?"

"Of course I did."

"Then you know what I want Tony to do," Hummer told her.

The team left shortly after lunch. Hummer, Marconi, Silvo, Tony, and Helen. When they arrived at the Happy Acres Sanatorium, Marconi told the guard at the gate he was there to check up on a patient. The guard didn't give them any trouble getting into the compound.

Victoria recognized Hummer immediately. Her face lit up with a bright smile. "Hi there, Mr. Hummer. Is this by any chance a social visit?"

Hummer returned her smile. "Hi, Victoria. I'm pleased you remember me, but I'm afraid I didn't come here for personal reasons; maybe next time. This is Dr. McDermott, but I'll let him speak for himself."

Marconi handed her his card. "I'm here for one of my former patients. Mr. Henry Miller. He was admitted to your facility June seventeenth of this year." He waved his hand in a dismissive gesture. "I'm sure you have all the details in your records." Then he turned to Helen who stood beside him, "Nurse Sandler, show her the document."

Helen leafed through the file folder she carried and pulled out a

159

sheet of paper. She handed it to Marconi. "Here it is, Dr. McDermott."

"Thank you, Nurse."

He waved it in front of Victoria's eyes. "I don't think it is necessary for you to read all the small print. This says the Silver Maple Mental Hospital has arranged a separate room for Mr. Miller where I can keep him under observation around the clock. I need to do some more tests on him."

Victoria tried to get a better look at the document, but Marconi handed it back to Helen before she could read anything. "Make sure you don't lose any of these documents, Nurse Sandler. I'll hold you personally responsible for them." He turned back to Victoria. "Mr. Miller is a special case, you know. I've actually grown a little fond of him." He pulled his goatee and chuckled. "I know it's probably hard for a pretty young lady like you to understand that I may feel sympathy for such a violent man as Mr. Miller."

Hummer had to cough to keep his lips from grinning. Marconi might give the impression of being a dull, serious and boring man, the perfect rep for a funeral parlor, but that was far from the truth. In reality he had quite a dry sense of humor and a sharp wit.

Victoria looked at the card Marconi had given her. "We all have our little weaknesses, Dr. McDermott. Anyone who calls me a pretty young lady cannot be all bad, right?" She smiled up at him.

"My lips only speak the truth," Marconi said, "Now. I hope you've been taking good care of my patient?"

"Our patients are treated like family," Victoria assured him.

"I have no doubt." Marconi drummed his fingers on the desktop, indicating his impatience. "Can you arrange for us to see Mr. Miller?"

Victoria looked at the burly guard standing not far from them. "Karl, accompany Dr. McDermott and his staff into Section D."

"Sure. No problem," Karl grunted.

"Perhaps you can get the release papers ready for me to sign, Miss Victoria," Marconi said.

"Don't worry, I'll have them ready."

"Nurse Sandler, there is no need for you and Jerry to come with us. Please, go outside and wait for us there," Marconi told Helen.

They had discussed everything beforehand and decided it would be best if Professor Middler didn't see his wife until they were outside to prevent him from bringing down their charade. Helen nodded. She and Tony left the front lobby while Hummer, Marconi, and Silvo accompanied the guard.

An elevator took them to Section D, which was below ground. Hummer was reminded of an ancient prison as they walked down a dimly lit corridor, past iron doors with small windows in them. It was eerily silent in this wing of the Sanatorium. Silent and gloomy. They stopped in front of one of the doors. The guard produced a key and unlocked the metal door. It swung into the room with a creaking of rusty hinges.

"This is not a friendly place," Marconi remarked before he entered the room behind the metal door.

"It's all part of the therapy," the guard assured them.

"Therapy?" Marconi said sharply. "Are you a doctor?"

"No, I'm not, but that's what I've been told."

The man sitting on a wooden bench against the wall didn't even look up when they entered the room. He stared at his hands with a blank look on his face, like a man lost in a world of his own, or a man heavily drugged. Hummer knew the latter was the case with Professor Middler.

Marconi walked over to the Professor and touched him on the shoulder. Middler responded by lifting his head and giving Marconi an uninterested look. "We'll take you out of here for a little while. Can you walk?"

Middler nodded slowly. Marconi turned to Hummer and Silvo and said, "Perhaps you and Dr. Marsh should help the patient, Mr. Hummer."

"Certainly, Dr. McDermott." He put one hand on Middler's arm and pulled him gently to his feet. "Come," he said softly. "How would you like to look at the sun?"

Middler's face lit up a little; a sign he wasn't quite out of it and understood them. "Yes, I would like that," he said, his words coming slowly, like someone who has to make an effort to speak. He walked between Hummer and Silvo without creating any fuss.

They led the Professor past the admittance desk, while Marconi stopped to pick up the release papers. He joined them just before the guard opened the door to let them out.

When Middler stepped into the fresh air he let out a soft groan and squeezed his eyes into tiny slits. It was obvious the bright light of the burning sun caused him discomfort. Tony and Helen stood not far from the entrance. Helen came rushing up to them, but didn't touch the Professor.

"Is this your husband?" Hummer asked with a low voice.

She nodded, but her face didn't show much emotion.

They began walking toward their cars. A crashing sound and the squealing of tires made Hummer look toward the entrance to the Sanatorium's parking lot. Two cars had broken though the gate and sped toward them. The cars stopped and four men in suits and wearing sunglasses jumped out. When he saw the machine guns in their hands, he warned Marconi and Silvo. "Do nothing!"

One of the four men pulled out a flat wallet and flipped it open. "Federal Agent Keller. We'll take the Professor off your hands." He was the only one not carrying a machine gun, but he held a 9mm pistol in his hand. He waved it threateningly. "Don't try to be heroes and interfere with FBI business. We have orders to shoot if necessary."

"Who gave the orders?" Hummer asked.

"None of your business. Just hand over the Professor!" Keller spoke sharply. Hummer detected a slight accent but couldn't place it. This didn't look and feel right, but he had no intentions making any threatening moves. Those machine guns would cut them down before he or his companions could even draw their guns, and he did not believe the four men were bluffing. They looked grim and determined.

"Can I get a closer look at your badge?" he said.

"You've seen it," Keller said. "Now, I'm getting impatient." He lifted his gun and fired a shot into the air. "The next bullet might hit one of you clowns."

"Let him go," Hummer said to Silvo, who was holding onto Middler's left arm.

"Go with those men," Hummer told Middler. Like an automaton, the Professor walked toward the agent holding the gun. Keller grabbed Middler the moment he was close enough and led him toward one of the cars. Hummer looked at the license plate, trying to memorize the number.

Keller shoved Middler into the backseat. Before he joined the Professor, he looked at Helen and said something in a foreign language. Helen shook her head vehemently. The man shrugged and said something else in the same language. Then he climbed into the backseat of the car. The other three men walked backward toward the second car, keeping their weapons trained at Hummer and his companions. Once they were in the car, both cars sped away with screeching tires.

Hummer looked at Helen. "What was that all about?"

"He asked me if I wanted to join my husband."

"He didn't speak English. What language was that?"

"Russian."

He gave her a curious look. "You speak Russian?"

"Only a little, but I understand most of it."

"Why would he speak to you in Russian?"

"Because he knew I would understand him. He's one of the men who helped me get established in Dallas. He told me at that time about his Russian ancestry. My parents came from Russia. They changed their name from Molokov to Miller after they came to the US. Why are you surprised to hear I understand Russian?"

"Perhaps I shouldn't be surprised. It seems I'm learning new things about you every day." He scrutinized her, speculating why the agent would ask her to join them. He also wondered about something else. "How did they know we would be here?"

"Didn't you tell me my place was bugged?" Helen asked. "They probably heard us discussing our plans."

"We didn't discuss any details inside your home."

"But you asked me to come with you to get back my husband," she said.

"They probably guessed our intentions," Tony suggested. "Maybe I shouldn't have mentioned the chandelier in the bedroom. It may have tipped them off. They are federal agents after all and not stupid."

Hummer chuckled. "I was an FBI agent for eight years and I can say with confidence not all federal agents are smart. I've met a lot of stupid ones, believe me." Pulling out his notebook, he jotted down the license plate number before he forgot it. Then he patted his pocket. "Oh damn, I must have forgotten my cell phone in the office. I need to call Detective

Schumann and report this incident. I don't like to be threatened with a machine gun by anyone, not even the FBI." He looked at Helen. "Do you have your cell phone handy?"

She nodded and took her phone out of her purse. "Here."

He took it and flipped it open. Pressing redial, he listened to the dial tone. Somebody picked up after the second ring and answered it.

He didn't speak English. Hummer recognized the voice of the man who had introduced himself as *Agent Keller*.

Chapter Thirteen

After using Helen's phone to call Detective Schumann it took less than fifteen minutes before two police cars came racing through the gate with blaring sirens. Hummer could never understand why the cops always had to use their sirens. There certainly was no reason for it now.

"What the hell happened here?" Schumann shouted with a blistering voice. "We get a call from the guard about two cars busting down the gate and shots being fired and then you call me with this ridiculous story. What are you doing here in the first place, Hummer?"

Schumann called him by his last name only when he was extremely upset.

I guess he's upset now!

"Calm down, Martin. I can explain everything."

"I'm listening." Schumann stood wide-legged before him, his eyes cold with suppressed anger.

"Did you check out the recordings at Globe Labs?" Hummer asked.

"I did. We confronted Erskine and he admitted not being inside the building. The records confirm it." He lifted one hand to rub his bald head the way he always did when troubled but changed his mind. Instead he stabbed a finger at Hummer. "You are making my life complicated, Frank. I thought we had the case sown up."

"And you would have convicted an innocent man of murder."

"Erskine is not innocent. He is involved as the recording showed. Now he's talking about making a deal."

"Did he identify the man who is probably the one who set the fire and murdered Finkbein and Miller?"

Schumann dashed Hummer's hopes with the shake of his head. "He has little to give us."

"What about his claim Fred Simmerman paid him to set the fire, which he incidentally didn't start?" Hummer asked.

"He still sticks to the story about Simmerman paying him money."

"He lied about his role in the whole affair. Doesn't it stand to reason he would also lie about Simmerman?"

"I can't work on assumptions. My hands are tied. I can't hold off much longer with arresting Fred Simmerman." Schumann's face looked pained. "Unless you can give me more, Frank."

"If we can establish the identity of the man who drove the car into the parking lot at Globe Labs we may know who he worked for," Hummer suggested. "I'll bet you any money he doesn't work for Green Fuels Development."

"Maybe. Coming back to my first question, what are you doing here, Frank?"

Hummer pointed at Helen. "Meet Mrs. Helen Middler. We came here to get her husband, who was held in this facility against his will. Perhaps you want to bring charges against Happy Acres Sanatorium?"

"I can't press any charges unless I talk to the man who was held here against his will." Schumann studied Helen for a moment. He had a way of looking at people that made them uncomfortable, but Helen didn't seem to be intimidated. She gave him a smile and held out a hand. "I'm pleased to meet you. What is your name again?"

"Detective Schumann." His eyes were still scrutinizing her. "We assumed you were dead, but here you are alive and well."

She gave a small laugh. "Alive yes, well..." she shrugged. "I'm not so sure about that. After all, my husband was just abducted, again."

"I thought the FBI took him." He looked at Hummer.

"They claimed to be federal agents," Hummer said.

"Didn't you check their I. Ds?"

Hummer's grin was less than pleasant. "They did not cooperate well and it is difficult to argue with four men pointing automatic weapons at you."

Schumann scratched his head, his eyes taking in Silvo, Marconi, and

Tony. "I see you brought your whole company just to get one man out of a hospital. What were you prepared to do?"

"Whatever it would have taken to get an innocent man out of there."

"It seems you weren't too successful," Schumann stated with an ironic twist of his lips. "All this manpower and you let them take your man."

"We didn't expect anything like this. Besides, we have only three guns while they had four and possibly a couple more inside the cars. Half of our group was unarmed and not trained to deal with a hostile situation. We did the only thing we could do," Hummer defended what happened.

"I'm not criticizing and I'm glad this didn't turn into a bloodbath." Schumann smiled grimly. "I would have hated to go to a good friend's funeral. It would totally spoil my weekend not being able to golf with someone who is only half as good as I."

Hummer laughed. "Don't let the fact you beat me last time go to your head." He became serious. "Fred Simmerman is not guilty of any crime, Martin. This whole thing stinks to high heaven. Give me twenty-four hours to put a name to the face of the man in the car. After that..." he shrugged. "You do what you must do."

"Okay. How about giving me a few details about what just happened so I can write up a report?"

"There is little to tell. We were heading for our vehicles when these two cars came screeching into the parking lot, four men with automatic weapons jumped out, one identified himself as Federal Agent Keller and demanded we hand over Professor Middler. We did and they left, with Professor Middler. Then I called you." Hummer spread his hands. "That's about it."

"That's not much, is it?" Schumann looked disappointed and suspicious. "Any details anybody remembers?" He looked to the others.

"That's pretty much the way things went down," Marconi said.

"Everything happened so fast," Silvo added.

Schumann nodded, gazing at Hummer. "You have a good team here, Frank. I wish my men would stick with me the way yours do. If you remember anything worthwhile you know where to find me."

Hummer reached into his pocket and took out his notebook and a pen. Copying the license plate number he wrote down, he tore out the page and handed it to Schumann. "Maybe you want to check out this plate."

Schumann took the note and stuffed it into his breast pocket. "Better than nothing." He waved to the other cops who stood around fingering their holsters as if expecting some kind of showdown. "Let's get back to the precinct. There is nothing we can do here."

"Aren't you going to look for my husband?" Helen asked.

"It appears the FBI has him. I have no case here."

Hummer watched the police cars drive off. Turning to Tony, he said, "We'll have to work overtime, young man. You heard what I told the detective. We have twenty-four hours to find our man. Are you up to it?"

"Sure, boss," Tony said with conviction. "I'll find him for you."

"Good. You and Mrs. Middler go with Mr. Marconi. I want to check out something with Mr. Silvo. When you get to the office, tell Nicole to let you into my private office. Use my computer for your search, but don't start snooping around, okay? I'm trusting you, Tony."

"You can trust me, Mr. Hummer. Scout's honor."

The three left in Marconi's car. Silvo joined Hummer. Once they were seated, Silvo said, "How did you know I had something to discuss with you?"

Hummer's chuckle sounded anything but pleased. "Your grandmother was Russian, right?"

"Yes she was. If you're asking do I speak Russian the answer is *yes.*"

"Then you know what that agent said to Helen Middler?"

Silvo nodded slowly. "That woman lied to you, Mr. Hummer. She is deeply involved in this whole scheme."

"What did he say?"

"His first sentence was *are you coming?* When she declined his invitation he said *you did your job well.*"

Hummer had suspected something like that and wasn't greatly surprised. "She's the one who called them," he told Silvo. "It was the last call she made on her cell phone. The man who answered was the same guy who said he was Agent Keller."

Silvo smiled knowingly. "I wondered why you borrowed her phone, but I had a hunch you might already be suspicious of her."

"She was the only one who could have told them." He stared grimly out of the window. "The bitch fooled me," he said angrily. "Those guys weren't FBI. I know you have a talent for drawing faces and a near photographic memory. Do you think you could make sketches from all four of them?"

"Give me a couple of hours and you'll swear you are looking at photos from them."

Hummer started his car. "Then let's get to work. A man's reputation and the future of a whole country are at stake here."

* * * *

Helen sat in the front office reading a magazine. She looked up when Hummer and Silvo walked in. "Any news?" she asked.

"It's been barely an hour," he said curtly. "But we have our suspicions."

"Oh, good. Anything I can do?"

"I'm afraid it's going to be a long night. There is no need for you to hang around. I'll have Nicole drive you to my place. She can stay with you over night. If something develops I'll let you know."

Helen gave him a strange look. "I don't need a babysitter."

"Not a babysitter, a guard. Nicole is not a full-fledged detective but she's pretty good with a gun. I taught her myself. Your life may be in danger. We can't be too careful." He didn't tell her the real reason Nicole would be there, not to protect her from harm but to keep her from disappearing. He gave Nicole a barely noticeable sign with his eyes. Then he went into his own office in the back where he found Tony busy at work.

Nicole joined him a few minutes later. "Yes, Mr. Hummer?"

"We have a bit of a situation here, Nicole. Mrs. Helen Middler is not the woman she appears to be. She is hiding something. She may even be dangerous. I want you to drive her to my place and stay with her until tomorrow. Keep an eye on her and make sure she doesn't try to escape."

"How can I do that? I'm only your secretary not a trained detective. And what about that remark about me being good with a gun? You know I hate guns. I won't be taking a gun with me." She looked distressed.

"Don't worry. I'll give you a holster with a fake gun inside. She won't know the difference. Just pretend you're a tough female but don't overdo it." He went to his gun cabinet and took out a holster and a belt. Handing it to Nicole, he said, "It should fit you."

"I'd rather carry a gun in my purse, even if it's a fake one."

"This will make you look more dangerous, believe me."

She took the belt with reluctance and put it around her waist.

Hummer stepped back and grinned. "You're a natural, Sweetheart. You look absolutely smashing. If you and Tony weren't an item, I might even make a pass at you."

"Don't get carried away, Mr. Hummer. I'll do this for you but it'll cost you." Nicole advanced toward Tony, who was concentrating on his computer, and stood wide-legged in front of him. One hand on the holster of her fake gun, she said with a hard voice, "Hey, Mister, I want you to get up slowly and face the wall."

Tony lifted his head and stared at her. "What?"

"You heard me, Mister. And don't make any sudden moves or I'll have to draw my gun."

Hummer grimaced, amused by Nicole's playacting. "I'd advice you not to give in to your impulse to draw that gun. It's only a toy, Nicole."

She stared at him with a hurt look, shoulders slumped. "Did you have to spoil it, Mr. Hummer. Tony didn't know that."

"Didn't know what?" Tony asked.

"Never mind, Tony," Hummer said. "I'm sending Nicole on an assignment. She needs a gun to protect herself."

"How come she gets to carry a gun and I don't?"

"It's only a fake gun." Hummer became impatient. Turning to Nicole, he said, "Go on, Nicole. I'm counting on you. Your performance was cute but don't take your task too lightly. This is deadly serious. We are not playing a game here. The people we are dealing with are ruthless and have no problem killing anyone who gets in their way. Please, be careful."

Nicole's expression was suddenly sober. Gone was the playful child. "I was only kidding around. Probably just to cover my unease, but I'm all right now. Don't worry about me. I can handle it."

"I know you can. Now, go on. Get Mrs. Middler out of the office. We have a lot to do."

After Nicole left, Hummer turned his attention toward Tony. "Any luck with your search?"

Tony leaned back in the chair he sat in, making Hummer cringe. The chair was not designed to have a heavy man like Tony lounge around in it. "Take it easy with my chair, Tony," he said, trying not to sound upset.

"Oh, sorry, Mr. Hummer. Sometimes I need to stretch my legs. Anyway, I managed to get into the CIA database. I'm in it right now. I'm in the process of downloading my face-recognition program into your computer. It is quite sophisticated I might add. With any luck we'll find your man."

"You're not sure?"

"I've never tried this program. I developed it only a short time ago but I'm confident it will work." He bent forward. "There we go. Okay, I've already downloaded the images from Mr. Marconi's recorder. Let's see, I'll have to make a copy of the frozen image. Here we go. There, the program is searching."

The chair creaked when he leaned back and stretched, but Hummer didn't comment. He was ready to forgive Tony anything if he came up with positive results. The chair could be replaced. Tony moved suddenly forward and gave the computer screen a wet kiss with his thick lips. "Gotcha!"

Hummer stepped around the desk and looked at the two faces displayed on the screen. There was no doubt it was the same face displayed twice.

"That's him," he said, trying to keep his voice calm. "That's the guy who pretended to be Professor Middler and the same one who drove the car. What's his name?"

"Evan Pacholuk. Let me do a search in the CIA files using his name and face," Tony said, sounding as excited and eager as a young man on his second date.

"Wow," Tony exclaimed. "There is a special file on Agent Pacholuk. He goes under many names. Perhaps you want to have a look at this yourself, Mr. Hummer?" Tony heaved his bulk out of the chair, vacating it for Hummer.

After sitting down, Hummer stared at the displayed information. Moving his finger slowly across the screen, he scrolled down the pages.

"It seems Evan Pacholuk is not just your average CIA agent," he murmured more to himself than to Tony. "I believe he is a skilled assassin. Just look at his list of accomplishments. There is enough material here to send him to jail for many lifetimes, possibly even to the electric chair. Unfortunately, we can't use any of it without exposing how we came by the information." He looked at Tony with respect in his eyes. "You are a friggin' genius, Tony. Now I hope your infiltration into the CIA database went undetected. Otherwise we may have Homeland Security knocking on our doors. This information was meant only for people with top level clearance. I won't even ask how you managed to break into these files."

Tony grinned with satisfaction. "It's easy when you understand computers and how to program them."

"Can you find an address where Agent Pacholuk resides when he is not on assignment?"

Tony took the chair again and let his fingers move across the keyboard. "I'm going to save this file first if it's okay."

"Sure. Go ahead." Hummer watched as Tony saved the file into his computer. Then Tony began to search for an address.

"He doesn't seem to have a permanent address. Oh, wait a minute. Here is something. By the way, Evan Pacholuk is not his real name. He was born Wilfried Meyers. He has one sister, Edith Meyers. Not married. She lives with her mother, Wilma Meyers. What do you know. Wilfried Meyers alias Evan Pacholuk receives his correspondence at his mother's address. His mother and sister live in Lincoln, Nebraska."

"I'm blown away. If the wrong people find out about this gift of yours, your life may not be worth much." Hummer was impressed and he didn't mind telling Tony. "How do you do it?"

"Unless you are knowledgeable about computer programming you wouldn't understand the technical jargon, Mr. Hummer. I mean no respect by telling you so. To put it in laymen's terms, my program automatically erases every step it takes. It leaves no trace. You told me to be a ghost." He chuckled gleefully. "I've downloaded everything into your computer, Mr. Hummer. The information will be at your fingertips whenever you want it."

Hummer looked at his watch. "There is still time to get this information to Detective Schumann. Put the various names of Evan Pacholuk and the address of his mother into a file, add a picture, and e-mail everything to Detective Schumann at his precinct. His e-mail address is in my address book."

"You want me to do that now?"

"Right now. The sooner he gets it the better I will sleep tonight. Let me know when it's done so I can call him and explain a few things to him. After you've done all that do a search for Helen Middler in the CIA files. Remember, her maiden name was Molokov, before that she was Miller."

"My files are in Mr. Silvo's computer."

Hummer smiled. "Surely if you can break into the CIA database it should be child's play for you to get into Mr. Silvo's computer and retrieve your files or am I wrong?"

"No, you're not wrong. I just wanted to get your permission." Tony grinned. "Mr. Silvo will never know his computer has been invaded."

"As long as you only take what's yours and don't snoop around in his files. Now, go and send that e-mail to Detective Schumann."

Hummer dialed Schumann's number fifteen minutes later. "Have you checked your e-mail?" he asked without introducing himself.

"Frank, what the hell? I'm busy with another case. I have no time to constantly check my e-mail."

"Well, take the time and check it now. I sent you some stuff you may be interested in."

"Okay. Just hang on." A few moments later, Schumann said, "Where did you get this from?"

"You know better than to ask, Martin. I can't tell you without implicating myself."

"I can only guess how you obtained this information. You know I can't use any of this."

"Evan Pacholuk is an assassin, a cold-blooded killer. He needs to be stopped."

"He is CIA, for heaven's sake, Frank. He's a man with a dozen aliases. We don't even know his real name."

"Sure we do. His real name is Wilfried Meyers. On his off-days he lives in Lincoln, Nebraska with his mother. He probably banks in

Lincoln. Have Lincoln police put a tail on his mother and sister. Who knows, they may have him in their files already for some minor incident. When he shows up they can nab him."

"Even if all this is true I still have no legitimate reason to go after the man."

"At least this confirms Fred Simmerman did not kill Saul Finkbein and Henry Miller. You can act upon that information." Hummer was getting irritated with Schumann's attitude, but he knew Schumann was right, which made it even more frustrating.

"It still doesn't mean Simmerman didn't hire this Pacholuk or whatever his name is," Schumann said doggedly.

"Come on, Martin. Surely you don't believe that. You said it yourself. Pacholuk is a CIA agent. He was hired by somebody all right, but not by Simmerman." Hummer didn't hide his annoyance.

"Okay, you win," Schumann said. "I guess I can keep the warrant for Simmerman's arrest in my drawer indefinitely if need be. I don't know what you fell into, Frank, but it doesn't smell good. Take my advice and tread easily. Don't mess with government agencies. You can only lose."

"Thanks for the advice, but I'm already deep in this shit, and my instincts tell me things are only going to get rougher. I need to find out who is behind it before I drown in this."

Schumann's sigh was clearly audible over the phone. "You can be so pigheaded sometimes, but I guess that's what makes you a good investigator. You should have stayed with the FBI. Maybe you wouldn't be in this mess right now."

Hummer echoed his sigh. "You may be right, but eight years of doing what I did was enough. I didn't like the man I had become and I liked the man I was going to be even less. I know I made the right choice."

"Perhaps you did. For one thing, you probably wouldn't be the rich man you are today. Sometimes I wonder why you still associate with me, an underpaid, overworked public servant." Schumann chuckled into the phone.

"You are my friend, Martin. A cherished friend. Money doesn't buy real friends," Hummer said. "Don't disappoint me again by questioning my motives for associating with you. I'll let you know when I have more information to give to you. Maybe next time it will be something useful."

He hung up with a feeling of relief. Schumann would not arrest Simmerman, at least not for now. However, things were far from being back to normal. Professor Middler was still missing, seemingly in the hands of a Russian group pretending to be federal agents. He wished they would have had the chance to get Middler into hiding, but it hadn't gone as planned. Helen had betrayed them and given away the plan to rescue her husband. Why?

He felt suddenly quite tired. Spending the night with Cheryl and his episode with Helen in the early morning had sapped his strength.

I must have been running on adrenalin all day.

Checking his watch again, he realized it was getting late. Simmerman was safe for the moment and everything else could wait. He turned to Tony, "Take a break, Tony. Go home and relax. You can continue with your search tomorrow."

It seemed Tony was reluctant to stop. "I'm on a roll here, Mr. Hummer. I don't mind working a little longer."

Amused by Tony's eagerness, Hummer said, "I appreciate that but there really is no need. Tomorrow will be soon enough."

"Okay, but let me shut down everything first."

"You do that. I'll see you tomorrow." Hummer left his office. Before he walked out, he stuck his head into Silvo's office. "How are the drawings coming?"

"Quite well. I've done two so far. Just working on the third one. Want to have a look?" Silvo held up what he created. "What do you think?"

Hummer recognized them immediately. One of the drawings was of the man who had introduced himself as Agent Keller. "Very good. You are in the wrong profession, Silvo. You should have become an artist."

Silvo laughed. "And starve to death?"

"You could work for the police department or the FBI."

"No, thank you. I'll keep this job." He tilted his head. "Or are you giving me some kind of hint here?"

"No hint. I wouldn't want to lose you. Capable and dedicated professionals are hard to find these days. Can you scan those two pictures and print them out for me?"

"Sure, just give me a moment."

Hummer waited while Silvo put the drawings into his scanner and then print them. He took the prints from Silvo and put them into his briefcase. "I'm going home. I already told Tony to quit for the day. Why don't you do the same? Schumann is going to hold off with the arrest of Fred Simmerman. Tony found the identity of the man who murdered Saul Finkbein. He is a CIA assassin by the name of Evan Pacholuk."

"Wow. How did he manage to get the information so fast?"

Hummer grinned with satisfaction. "He's a genius. I'll fill you in tomorrow with the details."

He popped his head into Marconi's office. "I'm leaving. I suggest you call it a day, Marconi."

"I don't understand. You seemed so worried?"

"I was, but Tony saved the day. I'm too tired to explain, just take my word for it. I have a feeling by tomorrow night we may have unraveled this mystery."

"I'm curious how this will end. What a lot of twist of turns from the simple kidnapping of a man."

"Not so simple it seems," Hummer said. "Well, anyway, I'll talk to you in the morning."

When he drove home, his mind was trying to sort out the events of the day. It had started with an unexpected passionate encounter that should never have happened. Thinking about it made him feel guilty, especially since it seemed Helen Middler deceived him from the beginning. What was her motive for seducing him? Or did it just happen by accident? It had never been in his plans, even though he felt an attraction toward her ever since Dallas.

Who is Federal Agent Keller really? I don't believe he even works for the FBI, but then I might just be wrong. Did Helen lie to me how she and Keller met? It probably isn't his real name anyway. He spoke Russian. Keller is not a Russian name. But neither is Miller. Helen's parents changed it from Molokov.

He gripped his steering wheel with both hands and said under his breath, "What a fucking mess! What kind of a deep hole did I fall in?"

When he drove down his graveled driveway and into his garage, he wondered why he didn't see Nicole's car in the small parking lot in front of the house. The door into his house was not locked. He walked in and called, "Hello, I'm home," but nobody answered.

"What the hell!" He rushed into the living room. Then he bounded up the stairs taking two steps at a time and shouted, "Nicole? Sarah? Helen?"

A faint thumping that seemed to originate in his bedroom caught his attention. The door was closed. He ripped it open and stared at the two bodies on the floor. One of them was Nicole, the other one Sarah. Their legs were wrapped tightly together with ropes and their arms were bound behind their backs. A rope tied each one to the bedposts. He reached them with two steps that seemed to take forever. A quick examination revealed they were alive. Bending over Nicole, he saw the tape over her mouth, but her eyes were open. She blinked when she saw him and made a snorting sound through her nose.

As gently as possible he removed the tape from her mouth and asked, "What happened?"

The fury in her eyes spoke louder than words. "That bitch used some kind of fancy moves on me, and before I knew it I was hogtied on the floor. Why do you keep rope in your bedroom closet, Mr. Hummer?" The anger in her voice didn't quite hide the fear she felt and her relief at seeing him.

"What were you doing in my bedroom in the first place?"

"She said she needed to go into your bathroom to retrieve something." Nicole didn't have to elaborate what she was thinking, but she did so anyway. "What did she leave in your bathroom?"

"I wouldn't know." He tried to untie the rope but gave up. "I'll have to get a knife. These knots are impossible to open." Moving over to Sarah, he pulled the tape from her mouth. "Are you okay?" he asked.

Sarah let out a deep breath. "I'm fine, now. I knew that woman would be trouble from the first moment I saw her," she complained. "That's what happens when you bring your work home with you, Mr. Hummer."

Her outburst made him smile in spite of the grave situation. "I promise from now on I'll leave my work at the office." Rising to his feet, he said, "Let me get that knife."

He went downstairs to get a knife from the kitchen. After that it didn't take long to free the women. They stomped their feet and rubbed their wrists to restore circulation. "If I see that woman again I'll wring her neck," Nicole promised. "I suppose she took my car?"

Hummer nodded. "She did."

"Damn that bitch!" Nicole cursed. "I hope she doesn't wreck it. I just had my brakes fixed."

"Maybe it wouldn't be so bad if she did wreck it. Then you would finally buy a new car," Hummer commented.

"How will I get around now?"

"You can borrow my Porsche until things settle."

"Your Porsche? Are you kidding, Mr. Hummer? That is your baby. You hardly drive it." She stared at him, obviously not believing she heard right.

"Like you said I hardly drive it. It's only a car."

"Only a car?" Her laugh bordered on hysteria. Looking at Sarah, she said, "Did you hear that? It's only a car. The Porsche is only a car!"

"I guess to Mr. Hummer it is. Me? I'll never drive one." She smiled. "You must mean a lot to him if he lets you have his Porsche."

Hummer lifted each of their hands. "Ladies, let's not make a big deal about the car. Right now we'd better report Nicole's car as stolen, but we won't go into any details when the cops ask. We'll say it was stolen from my driveway. No other explanation necessary, okay?"

"Okay by me. It will spare me the humiliation of revealing I was tied like a steer in a rodeo," Nicole said. She snickered. "Perhaps I wouldn't complain so much if a handsome cowboy had done the deed."

"Don't let Tony hear that," Hummer joked. He was glad to see Nicole and Sarah weren't too traumatized by the whole incident, unpleasant as it was. "Did Mrs. Middler give an explanation for her actions?" he asked.

"No explanation, but in her defense I have to admit she did apologize for tying us up," Nicole said somewhat reluctantly. "But that doesn't mean I have to forgive that crazy bitch! Her luck the gun you gave me was a fake gun."

"It probably was a good thing the gun was a fake. Somebody might have gotten hurt," Hummer said. "Guns are dangerous in the hands of inexperienced people." He put his hand into his pocket to take out his cell phone. When he looked at it he realized it wasn't his, it was Helen's. He forgot to give it to her. She must have discovered it and known he would check out her contacts. That's what triggered her desperate action. He didn't think she'd be going back to her house in Dallas. In any event, she would ditch Nicole's car at the earliest opportunity and either rent a car or take a plane somewhere. In all likelihood she wouldn't use her real name.

"We won't report the theft today; we'll do it tomorrow. I think you should stay here overnight, Nicole, and leave in the morning. You can drive home first and get whatever you need or drive straight to the office from here. It's up to you." His gaze took in Sarah. "I assume the guestroom has been cleaned and is ready for Nicole?"

"It is. You never told me if that woman would be coming back to stay another night, so I cleaned the room," Sarah told him.

"Then it's settled. How about getting us something to eat?"

"I made some stew. All I have to do is warm it up. I hope that's all right?"

"Stew is fine. Go and set the table for three. You'll eat with us, Sarah, and I don't want to hear any arguments. I'm going to call Detective Schumann and tell him about my client's escape. Maybe he can still catch her before she boards a plane."

Putting Helen's phone back into his pocket, he went into his office to call Schumann.

He won't be overwhelmed with happiness by getting a call at home from me, again, but what are friends for?

Chapter Fourteen

After Nicole left the next morning, Hummer decided not to go the office. It was time he talked to an old colleague. Taking his briefcase, he left his home and headed for the offices of the FBI.

He knew Rick Mason would be in his office. After getting shot in the back during a gun battle with a gang of would-be-bank robbers, he was left paralyzed from the waist down. Even though they offered him early retirement, he chose to stay and work behind a desk.

"I was shot in the back not my head," was his argument.

Hummer and Mason had been members of *The Third Unit*, an elite team of federal agents. They had never been close friends, but there was a bond between them only shared hardship and danger can form, a bond nothing could break.

Before he left his car, he called the front desk of the FBI and told the officer on duty to let Agent Mason know about his visit. "Please, tell him it is of utmost importance I see him. I'll be there in five minutes."

Eight years of being a federal agent gave him enough time to learn protocol, but his knowledge was nine years out of date. Time changes behavior and procedures. He walked up to the front desk and gave the woman behind the desk a friendly smile. "My name is Frank Hummer. I called a few minutes ago to make an appointment with Special Agent Mason."

The woman gave him a scrutinizing look. "May I ask what it is all about?"

Hummer's smile deepened. "You may, but I'm afraid it is for his ears only."

"Special Agent Mason is quite busy at the moment." Her blue eyes were two pools of arctic ice and her voice matched their frostiness. "Why don't you have a seat? It may take some time."

Hummer leaned across the desk, looked into her eyes and said softly, "If the life of the President of the United States were in danger and seconds would make the difference in a life and death situation, would you tell the man who could save him to wait?"

She stared. "Of course not."

"Then why are you telling me to wait?"

"Are you saying the President's life is in danger?"

"Not the President's. I only used him as an example, but somebody's life is in danger. I'm talking about yours. Maybe not your life but your job may be on the line if Agent Mason finds out you told me to wait." Hummer gave her a friendly chuckle. "I guess you don't know who I am."

"You are Mr. Frank Hummer. You told me so yourself."

"That's right. I suggest you call Special Agent Mason right now and tell him I'm here to see him. Do yourself a favor, will you?"

She did so reluctantly; obviously not wanting to take a chance she might offend someone important.

"Sir, there is somebody here who wants to talk to you. I told him you were busy. His name is Mr. Frank Hummer." She paused and stared at Hummer. "He wants to know if you are *the* Frank Hummer?"

"Tell him that's me." Hummer grinned, amused by the way she looked at him.

"He says that's him," she told Mason. "Okay, sir. Sure, sir." She disconnected her link with Mason. "I apologize for giving you a hard time, but we get too many kooks coming in here wasting our agents' time. He says to come up right away." A certain respect seemed to have replaced the coldness in her eyes. "Who exactly are you, sir?"

He could only imagine what Mason told her on the phone. Mason had always been a bit of a jester and made it a habit of messing with other people's minds. Hummer didn't believe that his unfortunate accident and the past years had changed him much. "I am *the* Frank Hummer," he said. "Who else would I be?"

She seemed reluctant to give him more trouble. "May I see what's in your briefcase, sir?"

He handed it to her. After opening and checking its contents, she nodded, closed it again and gave it back to him. "Do you carry a weapon?" she asked.

He flipped open his jacket and showed her the empty holster. "I left my gun in the car." He smiled. "I know the drill."

She nodded again and told him it was okay to go ahead. "Use the elevator, Mr. Hummer," she called after he stepped through the body scanners. "Special Agent Mason is on the third floor, room thirty-four."

Mason was genuinely happy to see Hummer. He rolled his wheelchair around his desk and met Hummer halfway across the room. "Great to see you, Frank. I notice, you're still wearing a gray suit, maroon striped tie, and a baseball cap," he said, laughing, and pumping Hummer's hand with great enthusiasm. "Don't you ever get bored with it?"

Hummer shrugged and grinned. "I also have a brown suit with a brown striped tie."

"Even more boring. If you were married, your wife wouldn't let you walk around like that," Mason joked. "She'd tell you to lighten up, to take off that awful tie and put on something more comfortable. Something to go with that baseball cap glued onto your head."

"Maybe that's why I'm not married. I don't like any woman telling me what I should do," Hummer countered, his mind automatically thinking of Cheryl. Would she demand he changed his manner of dressing?

"It's a small price to pay for all the benefits being married to a woman brings. I don't know what I would do without Miriam." Mason let go of Hummer's hand. "Did Annette at the front desk give you the third degree?"

"She tried to keep me away from you, but when I told her I was *the* Frank Hummer she gave in. I don't know what you told her about me, but her attitude toward me changed."

Mason's grin was as mischievous as Hummer remembered. "I told her to make sure you were *the* Frank Hummer and to handle you with kid gloves and not to mess with you."

"I'm glad you didn't tell her I was some kind of dangerous terrorist," Hummer said dryly. "I see you've moved up in the ranks."

Mason grimaced. "And you've become this rich big shot who has no more time for his old buddies. How long has it been?"

"Three years." Hummer walked over to one of the chairs and sank into it. "Time has a way of getting away from us."

Mason rolled his wheelchair back behind his desk. "You are right. Time has this peculiar ability." His face became serious. "I'm not going to assume this is a social visit, Frank. What's in your briefcase?"

"Some pictures I want you to look at." He opened his briefcase and took out the two drawings Silvo made. Shoving them across the desk at Mason, he said, "These men pretended to be federal agents. This guy said his name was Keller, but I don't believe it is his name. Neither do I believe he works for the Bureau."

"Who made these drawings?"

"My associate Dennis Silvo. He drew them from memory. There are a couple more he is working on."

"He's got talent. He should be working for us."

Hummer laughed. "That's what I told him, but he likes working for me better."

"Better working conditions, I guess." Mason put down the pictures. "Obviously, there is a story attached to these pictures. How about filling me in?"

Hummer told him a condensed version of his case, not wanting to bore Mason with unimportant details; unfortunately, sometimes these small details told the story more accurately than what seemed most obvious.

Mason listened intently without interrupting Hummer. When Hummer was finished, he said perceptively, "That's why you had one of your people snoop around in our files. He was looking for information. Tell him to cover his tracks better the next time."

Hummer gave a little chuckle. "He assured me it won't happen again."

"He won't snoop around in the FBI files?"

"He didn't say that. He meant he won't be caught again."

Mason looked impressed. "He's that good?"

183

"Better."

Mason's expression became somber. "Whoever your man is, tell him not to get cocky. We have sophisticated security programs in place, so has Homeland Security, the CIA, the military, and the rest of the government institutions. If he gets caught breaking into any protected files he'll be up for charges, and so will you. When I called I did that as a friend, remember that. Anyone else would have visited you at your office, with a warrant for your arrest."

"I appreciate that, Rick." He didn't tell Mason about Evan Pacholuk and the CIA's involvement in the case. It would have meant telling him about Tony's sophisticated face-recognition program. He decided it would be best nobody knew about it. He pointed at the drawings on Mason's desk. "Can you run those through? I'm anxious to find out who I'm dealing with."

Mason pushed a button on his intercom. "Schroeder, come into my office, please. I have a task for you."

The young man who walked through the door a few moments later was tall and lanky. He reminded Hummer of Tony, even though he was skinny instead of fat. He gave Hummer a curt nod. Then his pale eyes fixed on Mason. "What's up?"

Mason gave him the drawings. "Run these through the system and see what you come up with. Apparently, they are FBI agents."

Schroeder grabbed the two sheets of paper and disappeared without another word.

"He's one of our researchers," Mason said after Schroeder was gone. "A strange young man but a genius. He's the one who discovered your man's break-in into our system." He formed a steeple with his fingers. "You know, Frank, I miss the old days. You and I, we made a good team. Hopkins and Lee are in Washington now, protecting the President. I don't know if you've heard, Timmins was killed a couple of months ago in a car crash. He always liked his fast cars. He left the Bureau last year to work for a Private Security Company. Too bad about him. He was a good man."

"I didn't know about his accident." Hummer took a moment to absorb the news. "You're right, Timmins was a good man. I lost track of everyone after I left. Simmerman warned us not to stay in touch. It was for our protection. After all, the Third Unit wasn't exactly on the up and up, but you know that."

"No, it wasn't." Mason nodded grimly. "But I don't regret anything we did. It was for the good of the country." He gave Hummer a thoughtful look. "I've often wondered why you left, Frank, but I can guess the reason. You didn't always agree with the things we needed to do."

"It was time for me to leave," Hummer confirmed Mason's assessment. "After our last assignment I realized how my job was changing me. I didn't want to be judge and executioner anymore. I'm happy with what I do now."

"Who wouldn't be? A millionaire living in a huge mansion, driving expensive cars, a playboy..." Mason grinned. "You are a lucky man."

"It's not as glamorous as it sounds, my friend. I'm talking about my investigating business. My money allows me to help people in trouble who cannot afford to hire a good investigator. That gives me the most satisfaction. My way of redeeming myself."

"I assume the case you're on right now is one of those charity cases?"

"It started out that way, but then it turned personal. Somehow I am involved in this and I need to find out how and why."

Both men looked toward the door when it opened. Schroeder walked in, holding a couple of printed sheets in one hand. He put them on Mason's desk. "I printed out some of the stuff I discovered. You want me to go through it quickly?"

"If you don't mind."

"Neither of these two men works for the Bureau. This one here," he pointed at the one who said his name was *Keller*. "His real name is Viktor Lebedev. He is a Russian national and an employee of the Russian Embassy. The other one is Anton Putin. He came to the United States two years ago on a visitor's visa and never left. Immigration has been looking for him ever since. Lebedev has a long list of offences from rape and suspected murder to driving while under the influence of alcohol. You name it, he's done it, but we have not been able to touch him because he has diplomatic immunity. We suspect he is in reality a member of the Russian Secret Service."

"Where can we find these men?" Hummer asked.

"Lebedev probably resides on the Embassy grounds in Washington. Putin?" Schroeder shrugged his bony shoulders. "He can be anywhere. If we knew where, he would have been caught a long time ago. Apparently, he has a sister who married an American, a Collin Jackson. He brought her to the States in two-thousand-three. They met on the internet."

"Do you have her address?"

"Sure." Lifting his pointy chin, he indicated the two sheets on Mason's desk. "It's on page two."

"Good work, Schroeder. I'll call you when your services are needed again."

Schroeder left. Mason picked up one of the sheets and scanned it with a practiced eye. "Amazing," he commented. "How you can get information on practically anyone these days. Privacy is a thing of the past. Of course, not everything is available to the general public, which is a good thing." He gazed at Hummer. "This Professor Middler. Any theories why the Russians kidnapped him?"

"He is a genius who developed a battery that runs on salt water, a formula for a new kind of jet fuel, and he designed an electric car. There may be other inventions. I can see why the Russians would want him."

"And why did the CIA stage his death in such a bizarre way? Obviously, they stashed him away in that Sanatorium for some reason or other. And why do you believe you are involved in this…this conspiracy? Whatever it is."

"Helen Middler, Professor Middler's estranged wife, told me the whole kidnapping scene was staged for my benefit. She didn't know why. Saul Finkbein, the CEO of Globe Labs, and Helen's brother Henry were murdered. Senator Simmerman's son, Fred, was implicated in the murders. I have a large chunk of shares in Fred's company, GFDI, which, apparently, makes me also a suspect."

"You probably mentioned this when you told me your story, but refresh my memory. What would be Fred Simmerman's reason to murder Saul Finkbein?" Mason scowled, obviously trying to connect things.

"Globe Labs and Green Fuels are both working on finding alternative energy sources. With Professor Middler and Finkbein dead,

Globe Labs has lost its competitive edge over Green Fuels." Hummer shrugged. "That's the theory anyway."

"But the Professor isn't dead," Mason injected.

"Officially he is dead."

Mason shook his head, not quite understanding. "If the CIA staged the kidnapping of Professor Middler, the murder of Finkbein and Mrs. Middler's brother, and then hid the Professor in the Sanatorium under a false name, what would be their reason?"

"I'm trying to find that out. There is one scenario I came up with. Fred Simmerman was falsely accused of the murders and the fire that destroyed the lab of GLI. If he is arrested, there will be a backlash. His father is running for President. A scandal like that will destroy his father's chances of becoming President. It might even cost him his seat in the Senate."

Mason thought about that for a moment. "The reasoning is logical, but what is your place in this theory? And it still doesn't explain why they kept Professor Middler alive instead of having him murdered as well."

Hummer made the decision to tell Mason about Evan Pacholuk. "There is still one tiny bit of information I held back," he said. "Remember I told you about the man who drove the car into the parking lot of Globe Labs? The one who probably committed the murders? Well, his name is Evan Pacholuk. That is one of his names. His real name is Wilfried Meyers. He is an assassin for the CIA."

Mason stared at Hummer, a look of incredulity on his face. "And you remembered that only now? Come on, Frank, consider who you are talking to." He lifted both hands as if to ward off an attack. "Perhaps you should not explain why it only came to you now. I may not want to know." He rolled his wheelchair around the desk. "Let's pay Schroeder a visit. He'll find this assassin."

Schroeder seemed to be busy at his computer. He looked up when Mason and Hummer came through the door into his office. "Must be important if you come into my dungeon," he said.

Hummer looked around and he had to agree with Schroeder. His office did look like a dungeon, but only because of all the stuff cluttering the shelves on the walls and the printers and scanners standing all over the room, leaving little space for maneuvering. One wall was covered with computer screens.

"I want you to find a CIA agent by the name of Evan Pacholuk, also known as Wilfried Meyers. He may have other names, but try these two," Mason told him.

"Are you going to wait for the results?"

"Yes, we are. Is that a problem?"

"Well, I was just busy with something else." He shrugged and sighed. "I guess it will just have to wait." He looked at Hummer, his strange pale eyes large in his narrow face. "If Special Agent Mason wants something we have to drop everything we are doing. That's how it works around here."

Mason chuckled in good humor. "Don't forget to mention that Special Agent Mason is also the one who protects your ass when you screw up."

"And it is Special Agent Mason who has these unusual requests that usually get me into trouble in the first place. Now, before I start, I want to have this made clear. You want me to break into the CIA files?"

"That's what I'm asking you to do," Mason said.

Schroeder began his search without making another comment. It took only a few minutes before he said, "Wilfried Meyers has been with the CIA since nineteen-ninety-five. According to this file, he is a low-level agent who handles unimportant tasks. There is a link to another file here which refers to one of his tasks, but the link leads nowhere, or so it appears. I'm being shunted to another file asking me to enter my clearance number. Well, let's see, oh wow! You were right, Wilfried Meyers has many names. Evan Pacholuk is only one of them. He uses that name for certain assignments, and there are many. It seems Mr. Meyers is not such a low level agent after all."

His pale eyes searched out Hummer. "I assume you are the man who is interested in this Wilfried Meyers or whatever name he goes under?"

"You assume correctly."

"You weren't actually introduced to me, which means I don't know who you are, but since Special Agent Mason brought you into my office, I assume you must be someone authorized to see all of this. Am I correct?"

"This is Frank Hummer, an old friend," Mason answered Schroeder's question. "What I am telling you now, Schroeder, is meant only for agents with top level clearance, and it stays in this room. You understand? Mr. Hummer was a federal agent for eight years. He was a member of the Third Unit. He has permission to hear anything you find."

"The Third Unit," Schroeder repeated. "There are no files about the Third Unit in the system. I know because I've checked."

"What reason did you have to check?" Mason asked softly.

"I was curious, because I've heard rumors about a special team operating outside the regular teams, a team that didn't exactly follow protocol and procedures." His smile made him look like a schoolboy trying to hide something. "I seek information the way a missile seeks its target."

"And you know what happens to the missile when it finds its target," Mason said. "Sometimes it's best not to be too curious."

"To be curious is my second nature. Were it not for that I wouldn't be here gathering information for you, Special Agent Mason," Schroeder countered.

"Okay, Mister *Curious* who has an answer for everything, you must have a reason for trying to establish Mr. Hummer's right to be here. Spit it out."

"I discovered a link to a hidden file in Evan Pacholuk's assignments. The file doesn't have a name, only a number, and it is locked."

"Can you open it?"

"It will take some time. I have to penetrate several layers, but I can do it. There is an alarm attached to it. Anyone not authorized will set off the alarm. Here goes. Uh, not so difficult after all. Here we are...a list of names with addresses and links to a file behind every name. I'll read you some of the names without the addresses. Harry Middler, Helen Middler, Henry Miller, Rose Miller, Saul Finkbein, Felix Erskine." He paused and threw a look at Hummer. "You will find this interesting, Mr. Hummer. Your name is also on the list."

"That *is* interesting," Hummer said, somewhat disturbed by the news but also not overly surprised. It was obvious the file represented the Middler case. It also proved he was part of whatever plan the CIA had cooked up. Hidden somewhere had to be the reason for the plot to kidnap

Professor Middler and his part in it. "Is there a link to a file behind my name?" he asked.

"Yes, there is."

"Check it out."

"No problem. Frank Hummer. Born February sixteen, nineteen-seventy-three. Founder and owner of Hummer Investigations. Founded on April twelve, two-thousand-two. Served in the military from nineteen-ninety-one to nineteen-ninety-four. Took part in Operation Desert Storm in Iraq. Federal agent from nineteen-ninety-four until two-thousand-two. Member of the Third Unit. Was Commander of Operation Emerald." Schroeder paused. "There is a link here to Operation Emerald. I can link to it now or later." He waited for Mason to make a decision.

"Skip it," Mason said.

"All right. Let's move on. Hummer is six feet tall, weighs two-hundred-twenty pounds. Black hair touched with gray on the temples. Military style haircut. Gray eyes. Usually dresses in a gray business suit with a maroon, striped tie. Wears baseball cap. No sunglasses. He has one brother, Derek Hummer, born June nineteen, nineteen-seventy-five, who is the CEO and owner of Hummer Enterprises, a construction company. Another brother, Robert Hummer, born June fifteen, nineteen-seventy-eight, died in Iraq. Frank Hummer is single but dates Congressman Charles Gibson's daughter Cheryl."

Schroeder paused. "The file is long and there are links behind every name mentioned. Shall I go on?"

"I believe we've heard enough," Mason said. "What do you think, Frank?"

Hummer nodded, disturbed by what Schroeder found. Why would the CIA keep such a detailed file about him in Pacholuk's file? Why even mention Cheryl? How would they know about the Third Unit and Operation Emerald? Somebody leaked information.

"Enough about Mr. Hummer," Mason said. "What else is in the locked file?"

"The list of names goes on. A couple of names sound familiar. Fred Simmerman. CEO of GFDI. Benjamin Simmerman, Senator. I think it would be best if I save everything and print it out later."

"Go ahead and do that. Can you locate any other links to hidden files in this one?"

"More than one, but some of them are protected better than Fort Knox. I will need more time to break through the layers of each one. The information stored in them must be of great importance. There is one not protected. It is a list of names. Evan Pacholuk's is at the top. Apparently, it is a list of people belonging to a unit called White Ops. Probably all of them CIA agents. Oh, oh, it seems I was wrong. Here are two I recognize. They work for us. Not in this office but out of Washington. I'll save the file for you to look at, Agent Mason. Done. I'm partially in another file now. It seems to refer to an organization called the Order of Capricorn. That's all I can get for now. It'll take hours to sift through all this information. I think I need a break. My mind is spinning."

"You've found more than I hoped for," Mason said. His eyes searched out Hummer. "Right, Frank?"

"Much more," Hummer said solemnly, agreeing with Mason.

The Order of Capricorn!

Oh, yes, he was quite familiar with that organization.

"What is the Order of Capricorn?" Schroeder asked. Hummer had expected him to ask.

"A secret society of powerful business men," Mason told him.

"Are you talking about a secret world government? I'm quite familiar with those conspiracy-theories. How much truth is to them?"

"Good question, Schroeder. There are plenty of conspiracy-theories abound about a secret world government. People are talking about a new World Order. Well, those conspiracy enthusiasts are not far from the truth. The members of the Order of Capricorn are oil men, bankers, lawyers, white supremacists, weapon manufacturers, and high-ranking members in the military, even officials in the government. They are seeking world domination, the control of oil and other commodities, manipulation of world money markets, control of the space program, and eventual control of the Moon and Mars. These people are thinking and planning decades ahead."

"That sounds like something out of a Science Fiction novel," Schroeder said.

"It does, but it is real. It would be a breakthrough to get their names, but unfortunately, it wouldn't do much good. None of them will ever be accused of anything. They are either too rich or too high up in government. Anyone brave enough to go after them will find out quickly how ruthless and merciless these people are. There have been occasions when a team of dedicated men and women have tried to interfere with the group's plans. This is usually done in secret. The public never hears of it."

"Like the Third Unit?" Schroeder asked, his sharp mind drawing the obvious conclusion from the information he gained.

Mason nodded slowly, his eyes on Hummer as if asking for his permission to go on. Hummer didn't see the need for Mason to explain certain things to Schroeder, but the young man would eventually dig up the information anyway. His curious mind and thirst for knowledge would not permit him to forget about what he had seen in the files. "Like the Third Unit," Mason said. "Men who are not afraid to take on even powerful organizations like the Order of Capricorn, men who believe in a just law for every man, woman, and child on this planet, no matter their color or faith, no matter how rich or poor."

Schroeder focused his attention on Hummer. He couldn't hide the excitement and a certain respect in his pale eyes. "In your file it said you were commander of Operation Emerald. Any connection to the Order of Capricorn?"

Considering all the information Schroeder had already gained there was no reason not to talk about Operation Emerald. Schroeder was sworn to secrecy. His position in the FBI gave him access to information not many in the Bureau would ever know about. "Everything we did had something to do with the Order of Capricorn. We foiled a plot to shoot down the Mir Space Station, which would have sparked a conflict with Russia. Certain men always make money in a war after the motto *when the blood runs in the streets fortunes are made.* No matter how many lives are lost in the process and how much damage a conflict with another nation causes."

"Wow!" Schroeder exclaimed. "The Mir Space Station. That would have been monumental."

"Yes, it would have been. The last thing we needed was a war with Russia to end the twentieth century. Those people who believe in Armageddon may have gotten their wish."

"Since the International Space Station is still circling the Earth it is safe to assume you were successful. Did you get the people involved?"

"We did." He didn't tell him about the execution of the assault-team's operatives. Yes, they got them, but the people who organized and planned the destruction of the space station were never caught.

"I'm just thinking about something. What about 9/11? There are conspiracy buffs who say the CIA was behind it. What are your thoughts on that?"

Mason chuckled. "I won't even comment on that."

"The result of those attacks was the war in Iraq. There are plenty of people who got rich on that. In fact, the war still goes on in that part of the world and many companies and individuals are getting fat on it. Do you think the Order of Capricorn orchestrated that attack?"

"We have to be careful with our accusations," Mason warned. "There are other forces out there who are trying to create chaos. We have religious extremists who have their own agenda about who should dominate the inhabitants of this planet. They would prefer to see a world inhabited only by peoples of their faith, living in fear and suppression. The terrorists are a real threat to world peace. We finally managed to kill Osama Bin Laden, who was the brain behind all those terrorist attacks on our country, but that doesn't mean the threat has been eliminated. He had many followers."

"Some people say Osama Bin Laden worked for the CIA," Schroeder insisted.

"He was trained by the CIA when the Russians tried to invade Afghanistan. That doesn't mean he was still working for the CIA. Of course, nothing is impossible, but there are some things nobody will ever be able to prove. And sometimes it is best people don't know the real truth." Mason shrugged off Schroeder's suggestion, seemingly reluctant to follow the young man's threat of thoughts. He turned to Hummer. "Did you find out what you wanted?"

"I wouldn't mind knowing why my name is in that file," Hummer said.

"I'll have Schroeder dig around. If the information is there he will find it."

"Good. One more thing. Do you have a file on Helen Middler?"

"I can find out." Schroeder did something to his computer. It took only a few seconds before he said, "Yes, we do. I'm going to skim over her file. Helen Middler, born May seven, nineteen-seventy-six, in Philadelphia to Ivan and Alexandria Miller. Her maiden name was Helen Henrietta Miller. In nineteen-ninety-three, at age seventeen, she witnessed a murder and was put into a witness protection program shortly after she turned eighteen. She changed her name to Molokov and moved to Chicago. In nineteen-ninety-five, she went to Russia as an exchange student. She came back to the States nineteen-ninety-nine. That's about it in a nutshell. According to a note here, we didn't have any reason to keep tabs on her after she got married."

"Hmm, I didn't know about her having been in Russia. Interesting. Did you say her file is inactive?"

"Yes. It was locked away. Like I said, we had no reason to keep her under surveillance."

"I find that also interesting." Hummer checked his watch. "It is almost lunch time. You want to join me, Rick?"

Mason shook his head. "We have a lunchroom. Maybe one day you come and visit me at my place. Miriam will cook up a nice meal for us. She's a real good cook. I don't like to go out to eat. You never know what they put into food these days. Never trusted restaurants."

Hummer laughed softly. "I still remember. When this is blown over I'll make it a point to visit you." He shook Mason's hand. "Let me know what you find out. Perhaps you can go after this Pacholuk. He's a psychopath and needs to be stopped." He waved to Schroeder. "Nice meeting you, Schroeder, and thanks for your time."

When he walked past the front desk, he gave Annette a big smile. "Enjoy your day," he said.

"Thank you, Mr. Hummer."

Walking across the parking lot, he heard what sounded like a song coming from his pocket. Reaching in, he looked at the cell phone in his hand, realizing it was Helen's.

It rang again and he flipped it open. "Hello."

"Frank, it's me. I need your help." Helen's voice sounded urgent and scared.

Chapter Fifteen

It took him a moment to get over the shock of hearing her voice. "Frank?" she asked when he didn't answer right away. "Are you there?"

"I'm here all right," he growled into the phone. "Where the hell are you?"

"I'm at home. In Dallas. It seems you have my phone."

"It seems so. Are you calling me because you want your phone back?" he asked, putting dripping sarcasm into his voice.

She didn't laugh or even chuckle. "You must be pretty angry with me."

"Angry?" His laugh was cruel. "Angry is not the word. You stole Nicole's car after tying her and Sarah against my bedpost. You sold out your husband to some Russian terrorists and you think I'm angry? I'm pissed off at you, Helen, for what you've done. I thought you were a decent person and I tried to help you. You've been using me all along."

"I'm not the bad person you think I am. I'm sorry about Nicole and about what I did to her. Her car is not damaged. I left it near the airport, locked. I put the key and instruction where the car can be found into an envelope and mailed it to your office."

"I guess that makes it all right," he said mockingly. "What do you want from me?"

"I want your help. My life is in danger and I have no one to turn to."

"What about your Russian buddies? I'm sure they'll help you out. Or how about your CIA friends?"

"The Russians are not my buddies and I have no friends in the CIA.

You must believe me." The fear in her voice was evident and convincing, but then he remembered her telling him she was a member of a theatre group. An actress.

"Why should I believe you, Helen? You've lied to me from the first moment I met you."

"I'm sorry I had to deceive you like that, Frank, but I was also deceived. Nobody told me anything about the involvement of my sister and my brother. Nobody ever hinted that harm might come to them, and now they are dead. I've been lied to and I want the people who did this to pay." Her voice broke as she talked and her loud sob sounded genuine. "Please, Frank, help me. Don't turn away from me."

"After all you've done you ask for my help?" He chuckled, grimly. "What reason would I have to even listen to you, Helen? You can't be trusted. You've made that pretty clear."

"Frank, please. I'm sorry for everything that happened, for everything I've done. If I could I would change things, but nothing went right from the beginning." She sobbed again. "Frank, I'm pleading with you. You are my last hope."

"What can I do to help you out of the mess you've created for yourself, Helen?" he asked, trying to make his voice sound harsh but heard it softening against his will.

"Come to Dallas and I will explain everything."

"I can't just fly to Dallas on a whim. How about explaining it to me right now?"

"Not over the phone. You told me my house is bugged, remember?"

"Are you calling from at home?"

"Of course not. I'm on a payphone. I'm using my credit card. This call cost me a fortune already. Please, come," she begged.

"It will cost me much more to fly to Dallas," he said, already half convinced by the panic in her voice.

"It won't break you, Frank. Please, you're the only one I trust. Don't give up on me."

"All right, I'll come," he said, against his better judgment.

"When?"

"Today."

"Thank you, Frank." He heard the relief in her voice. Perhaps she wasn't acting after all. He hoped he wouldn't be sorry giving in to her plea, hoping she was not trying to play him for a sucker. If nothing else came out of his trip, he could always alert the authorities to her whereabouts.

Before he started his car, he called his office. "Hi, Nicole. Something came up. I'll be flying to Dallas to check up on something."

"When will you be back?"

"Probably not before Thursday. Tell Tony I want him to find out everything he can about a group called White Ops. Evan Pacholuk belongs to White Ops. The group may be CIA, but not necessarily, because apparently a few FBI agents seem to be members."

"Okay, I'll tell him. By the way, your Porsche runs great. Plenty of muscle under that hood. Makes a gal feel reborn and powerful."

"I want to see my car, Tony, and you undamaged when I return, you hear?"

She laughed into the phone. "The car is hot and so am I, Mr. Hummer, but don't worry, I won't overheat the car, Tony, or me. We'll all be fine. Have a good trip."

Putting the phone back into his pocket, he shook his head.

Give a woman a fast car and she thinks she's a dominatrix. I hope Tony is happy with the new woman I created.

He was lucky to catch a plane leaving for Dallas within one hour after his arrival at the airport. This time he didn't have any luggage with him. It didn't matter. Anything he'd need he could buy in Dallas. Before he boarded the plane, he rented a locker and put his gun and house keys into it.

When he finally sat in his seat on the airplane, he relaxed and leaned back, closing his eyes.

I hope I'm not on a wild-goose-chase, Helen. You better make this trip worthwhile by giving me valuable information or I'll haul your sexy ass into the closest FBI office faster than you can blink those pretty green eyes.

* * * *

He told the taxi driver not to wait and walked up to Helen's front door. She must have been watching for him, because he didn't even get a chance to push the doorbell button before she opened the door.

Her bright and happy smile melted away all of his accumulated anger. She looked the way she had the last time he and Tony came to visit her, wearing jeans and a checkered shirt, with her hair tied back into a loose ponytail. Except this time, she had put on some makeup, making her appear younger than her thirty-five years.

She looked absolutely stunning and more attractive than he wanted to admit.

"I'm so glad you came, Frank. I'm sorry I'm putting you through all this and I want to make it up to you. I'm not some evil monster. I'm only trying to stay alive and make the best out of the cards fate has dealt me."

Digging her fingers into his arm, she pulled him into the living room. "Come, sit down. I'll make you a drink. You must be thirsty."

"You're right, I am thirsty. Do you have beer? I'm not much for hard liquor or mixed drinks." He let her push him onto the couch. His resolve to stay angry dissolved when he looked at her standing in front of him, a cheerful smile on her full lips, obviously happy to see him. This was not the evil, scheming witch he thought of while sitting in the plane, the bitch he wanted to bring to justice.

"No problem. I have beer. Bottle or glass?" she asked.

"Bottle is fine. As long as it's not a can. I hate beer out of cans."

She laughed. "Funny, so do I. I never buy cans." She rushed into the kitchen to get the beer.

Stretching his legs, he made himself comfortable. Letting his eyes roam around the room, his gaze fell onto the two tall statues in the corners.

Zeus and Aphrodite, still keeping a watchful eye on the people in the room. Actually, it was only Zeus who had one eye a bit shinier than his other one. The remote camera behind the eye had a good view of the entire living room and part of the dining room. He was tempted to show the statue his middle finger, but that would have betrayed him to the watchers. Even though Helen told him the FBI set her up with this house, he didn't believe it. He had a hunch it was the CIA who received the recorded images.

Helen came back with two bottles of beer. Handing one to Hummer, she chose the easy chair across from him and sat in it, pulling up her legs. "Here's to mutual understanding," she said, lifting her bottle.

He raised his bottle but didn't say anything. Taking a long draught from the bottle, he let the cold liquid slowly run down his throat. Then he put the bottle onto the table and leaned back. Looking at Helen and watching her take a few tiny sips, he realized she was stalling and at the same time trying to cover up her nervousness. The gaze of her green eyes met his and she lowered her lids. He could see the rise and fall of her chest and knew whatever bothered her was real. She was indeed scared about something. He didn't think she was that good of an actress.

"I feel much better now that you are here," she finally said.

"Why did you run away?" he asked softly.

"When I realized you still had my phone, I panicked. I knew you would check it out and discover it was I who called the Russians. The only thought on my mind was to get away from there as quickly as I could. I know what I did was wrong and now I'm sorry I acted so hastily." She spoke with a barely audible voice. He could scarcely hear what she said.

"Yes, what you did was wrong," he said, rising from the couch. Walking slowly toward the statue of Zeus, he took off his baseball cap and put it on the statue's head, covering both eyes. Then he returned to his place on the couch. "I got the feeling that statue was watching me," he said with a little chuckle.

She smiled. "I'm glad you can still make jokes."

"It wasn't really a joke," he picked up his bottle and studied it. "I'm surprised you're not drinking Russian beer."

"Why would I drink Russian beer?"

"Well, your parents were Russians. You changed your name back to your old family name Molokov. You spent four years in Russia doing who knows what. You sold your husband out to some Russian terrorists. I'd say you have pretty strong ties to your fatherland Russia."

"Appearances are not always what they seem. Russia is not my fatherland. That's a cheap shot, Frank. How did you know I was in Russia?"

Hummer gave her an almost friendly chuckle. "Are you forgetting I'm a detective? It's my job to find out things like that."

"Yes, it's true; I was in Russia, as an exchange student." She sighed deeply. "I said I would tell you the truth. There is no reason to keep anything about me from you. I want you to understand why I did what I did. When I was in Russia the Russian Secret Service recruited me and trained me as a spy. Don't forget, I was only nineteen years old, impressionable and easily influenced. Being a spy sounded so romantic and adventurous." She chuckled. "I never did any actual spying. When I came back to the States, I worked in a clothing store. Not very exciting. They told me to wait for an assignment, which I got in two-thousand-five, when I received the order to meet a scientist by the name of Harry Middler. My orders were to marry him."

"Did they tell you why?" Hummer asked.

"They said he was working on something important. My job was to keep an eye on him and report any developments in his research. That's all." She gave Hummer a thoughtful look. "I never loved my husband. He hardly paid me any attention. His love was his job. Even at home he spent most of his time with his journals and his computer. When we had sex it was over before I could even get into the mood."

"Did you ever cheat on him?"

Hesitating with her answer, she finally said, "Not in the beginning, but later on I did. There were a few men, but none of them meant anything to me. I'm not ashamed to admit it was strictly sex. I'm a passionate woman and I need the undivided attention of a man. I need to give myself to him completely." She smiled. "But you found that out already."

He didn't comment but couldn't stop images of her writhing nude body and the memory of the tremendous pleasure he experienced in her arms from rising up unbidden in his mind. "You left your husband a year ago. You told me it was because you didn't want your picture to be seen on TV or in the papers."

"I told you that, didn't I? Well, that's not the complete truth. I needed to get away from him and pursue my own happiness."

"So the FBI helped you get settled here?"

She shook her head. "Not the FBI. The CIA came to me a year after I married Harry. They made me an offer. They said they knew about my connection to the Russian Intelligence Agency. They offered me a deal. If I worked for them they would not charge me with spying against the

United States. I had no choice but to agree to their terms."

"In other words you became a double-agent," Hummer stated.

"In a sense I did. I never gave it much thought."

"What did you have to do for the CIA?"

"Nothing until now."

"You're talking about that little play in the mall?"

She nodded. "The pretend-abduction of my husband."

"Which you put on for my benefit. What is my role in this game?"

"I really don't know. They didn't tell me much."

"Who did you deal with?"

"The agent I dealt with introduced himself as Evan Pacholuk. He said he knew my sister and my brother, but I don't know anything about him."

"Probably a good thing. Why did you betray the CIA to the Russians?"

Her lips tightened and her face became a mask of hatred. "They killed my brother and my sister. I never knew they lived in Kansas City. So close, and yet nobody ever told me. Had I known, perhaps I could have helped them."

"You brother was a drug addict. He did jail time for armed robbery and spent the last five years in a mental hospital. I don't believe you could have done much to help him. And your sister Rose was a prostitute, a petty criminal, and an addict. Maybe it was better you didn't know about her either."

"Are you saying they were bad people and their deaths don't mean anything?" The agony and sudden resentment in her face made him feel sorry for what he'd said.

He bent forward and took her hand into his. "Nobody deserves to be murdered. I'm talking about the way they lived. It was their choice and you shouldn't feel guilty about what happened to them. It's not your fault. I doubt it would have made much difference in their lives had you known about their whereabouts. It only would have meant more agony for you."

Her face softened. Squeezing his hand, she said, "You're probably right, but I'll always keep wondering from now on."

Hummer pulled his hand away. "Tell me about the Russians. Who are they and what is their agenda?"

"I know nothing about them, and that is the truth. The only one I was in contact with was Viktor Lebedev. He is a guard at the Russian Embassy in Washington."

"He's a dangerous man, wanted for rape, murder, and other offences," Hummer said. "Your relationship with him may have ended up badly for you."

She looked hurt. "I didn't have a relationship with him, Frank. I'm not my sister Rose. I don't jump into bed with every man I meet."

He smiled lopsidedly. "You said you had many affairs with different men?"

"That still doesn't make me a prostitute. I didn't charge for it." Her smile matched his. "You never paid for it."

"I didn't ask for it. You seduced me."

"You didn't struggle too much. Admit it; you wanted it as badly as I." Reaching for her bottle of beer, she put it to her lips and drank deeply. He could see her throat working as she swallowed the golden liquid. He noticed his own bottle was empty. When she put hers down, he said, "Do you have another beer for me?"

"Sure." Her lips seemed to mock him a little. "I stocked up for you."

"Wasn't that a bit presumptuous taking for granted I would be coming?"

"Maybe a little, but I knew you'd be furious with me and would not let the opportunity go by to get back at me." Her expression changed from playful to solemn. "I wasn't kidding when I said I'm afraid. I screwed with the CIA and they'll be coming for me. It's only a matter of time."

Hummer's face was grim. He knew Helen spoke the truth. Evan Pacholuk would not let her get away with what she did. He was a psychopath and would find great pleasure in killing her. He'd probably do it legally with orders from his superiors. Nobody screwed with the CIA. The problem was he couldn't do much about protecting her. He saw only one way to keep her alive. She needed to disappear. If he could convince Rick Mason to put her into another witness protection program it might work. It would have to be done without creating a file for her and that would be the tricky part.

"You'll have to come back to Kansas City with me, Helen," he told her. "Only the FBI can help you now."

"I'll be arrested. I stole a car, remember?" She didn't look enthused about his proposal.

"I have friends in the Bureau who will help you. You'll get a new name, a new identity." He studied her beautiful features. "It will mean a new look. Different hairstyle, different hair color, different makeup. Helen Middler will disappear without a trace. Nobody will know where you are."

"Not even you?"

Shaking his head, he said, "Not even me."

"I will miss you, Frank." Her green eyes were moist when she looked at him and he could see genuine sorrow in her expression. "I never had many real friends. All the men I knew only saw me as a good lay and the women looked at me as some kind of troublemaker best avoided. You seem to be the only one who cares about me without asking anything in return. I regret we never met under different circumstances."

"So do I," he said. It wasn't a lie.

Wiping a finger across her cheeks, she gave a little laugh to cover her emotional state and jumped up. "I'll get you that beer," she said. "Wouldn't want you to go thirsty."

"Actually I'm quite hungry. It's been hours since I ate and the food on the plane is not exactly gourmet these days."

She looked at the watch on her wrist. "Oh, my God, I didn't realize it was this late. I'll make us something to eat."

"Isn't there a restaurant nearby where we could go? I don't want to create any work for you."

"Well, there is a little place I go to sometimes. It's only about a fifteen-minute drive." She chuckled. "It's not the fancy place you're used to eating at, and the waitress doesn't pay you much attention, in fact sometime she ignores you totally. The food they serve is pretty basic, but it is good, wholesome fare."

"Just because I have a few dollars in the bank doesn't mean I don't appreciate good, wholesome food," he joked. "In fact, I prefer a quiet dinner without the waiter hovering at my elbow constantly. Let's go there."

"Good. Then I don't have to change. I can go in my jeans."

Even though it was already late in the evening, the heat was still stifling and he was grateful for the air-conditioning in Helen's car. She parked it in the small parking lot of the restaurant. There were only a few cars parked there which meant it wouldn't be busy. Helen hooked her arm into his when she walked beside him and he didn't mind at all.

They chose a table by the window and waited for someone to come and take their orders. The waitress, an older woman, gave them a sour look when she approached their table and said, "Hi, Helen. Haven't seen you around. What'll it be for you and your new boyfriend?"

"Hi, Marge. You look great. By the way, he's not my boyfriend, just a good friend."

"Whatever. You want the *special*?"

"Sure. Bring us your *special*. At least then we won't have to wait too long."

The waitress walked away without saying another word. Helen laughed softly. "Good old Marge. She's like an old dog. Her bark is worse than her bite. I'm going to miss her dearly." Her hand reached across the table to touch his. "You're a good man, Frank. I don't know how I can ever thank you for your kindness. Your girlfriend is a lucky woman. I'd trade places with her in an instance."

"I'm not so sure if she'd feel so lucky if she knew I'm having supper with you and that you and I had sex right after she left my bed yesterday morning. She'd probably shoot both of us." He felt guilty thinking about Cheryl. His feelings toward her had changed; there was no doubt in his mind. How could he look her in the eyes with a clear conscience? Images of him and Helen having sex in the same bed, on the same sheets, she and he had shared only hours before would spoil their intimate moments for a long time, maybe forever.

He remembered telling her she was the only woman in his life right now. It had been the truth then, but not anymore. He had cheated on her. Other men would probably laugh at his reasoning and his uptight morals, but he wasn't *other men*. He was Frank Hummer, who prided himself to be honest and of high standards. A man of honor and integrity.

Obviously not so honorable and with little integrity.

When the food came, he cleared his mind of any unpleasant thoughts. He couldn't change what happened and would have to live with it. He had another beer, while Helen drank three glasses of red wine.

"Maybe I should drive," he offered. "Your alcohol level is probably higher than it should be."

She laughed gaily. "As long as I can walk straight I can drive. Besides, it's only a short hop home. Relax and enjoy the ride."

He shrugged, feeling a bit uneasy about letting her behind the wheel, and breathed a sigh of relief when they arrived safely at her house.

"I'm going to take a shower," she announced, throwing off her shoes. "Maybe you want to get the bed ready for us."

"Us?" he asked.

She threw a look at him from under lowered lashes. "I have only one bedroom and one bed."

"I could sleep on the couch in the living room," he suggested.

"I don't have extra sheets. Don't argue and get the bed ready." She giggled and disappeared in the bathroom.

He opened the door into the bedroom, switched on the light and looked at the bed.

It's wide enough for two. I guess I have no choice. It'll be more comfortable anyway.

He drew back the covers. There was only one pillow. He shrugged and laid it to one side. Then he undressed. Since he didn't have any pajamas, he stripped down to his briefs and climbed into bed. Lying on his back, he stared at the chandelier, trying without success to find the camera hidden in the fixture. Tony said there was one and he believed him. However, there was a slight chance Tony could be wrong.

Helen came into the bedroom naked. She stood in the doorway for a moment, letting him look at her. The bright light from the chandelier made her smooth, white skin glow with golden fire. Smiling, she switched off the light. The image of her slim but voluptuous body glowed in his mind like a bright beacon and when she came into his arms, he groaned and kissed her hungrily.

After breaking the kiss, she whispered huskily, "You're not naked," and pulled down his briefs.

* * * *

They didn't speak much during breakfast. Hummer was racked again by feelings of guilt and remorse, questioning what happened during the night. He had come to Dallas to make Helen explain to him her role in this whole, nasty affair, to bring her to justice if needed, yet he had acted like a lovesick teenager, had fallen for her heads over heels. This was not typical for him. This was not what the hardnosed Frank Hummer was famous for. He did not jump into bed with every woman who rolled her pretty eyes at him, and yet, that's exactly what he had done. Why? Was it possible he had fallen in love with her?

Helen seemed happy and without any worries. "When do we have to leave?" she asked suddenly while spooning out yogurt from a plastic cup.

"We shouldn't wait too long," he said.

"What about all my things?"

"Take only the most personal things but nothing that can identify you. No pictures or letters. Remember, nothing must connect you with Helen Middler or Helen Molokov or Henrietta Helen Miller. They are all dead."

"How about my driver's license and passport?"

"Take them with you. You'll still need those until we have established your new identity." He looked at her with sadness. Sadness for her and for himself. Something had happened between them while they made love during the night. It had not been just the stilling of their animal lust for each other. She had been passionate but with such tenderness he didn't remember ever receiving from Cheryl. He knew his feelings for her were true and genuine and he knew he cared deeply for her. He shouldn't, but fate had a strange way of throwing obstacles into the lives of humans at the most inconvenient time.

"Why are you looking at me like this?" she asked.

"You are so beautiful," he said softly. "I think I love you."

"You think?" She laughed, licking her spoon.

"I know I love you," he said. "You've bewitched me from the first moment I saw you in the mall."

Her face was suddenly miserable and her eyes filled with tears.

"You know you mustn't talk like that. It will make everything much harder. You can't love me. I gave you all I can give you; I can't give you my love, Frank."

"Don't you think I know that? I feel so helpless. I've been trying to come up with a solution but I see no way out."

She got up and came around to sit in his lap. "I feel a deep attraction toward you also, Frank. I've never felt like this with any man; not even my husband. Maybe this is love, I don't know. I feel safe in your arms, and last night I wished the night would never end. You made me happy, not just physically but also emotionally, yet I'm not fooling myself. Our love can't be. They won't let it be." Her tears flowed freely now.

Her arms hugged him tightly and she kissed him tenderly. He held her close and didn't want to let her go. "Let me pack my things." She put her hand on his cheek and stroked it with tender fingers.

"All right." Reluctantly, he let her go. "I'll call us a cab. Can you be ready in an hour?"

"I'll try."

He didn't rush her, even though he felt an urgency to get away. The taxi pulled up in front of the house on the opposite side of the street exactly one hour after he called. Helen came out of the bedroom, carrying a small suitcase. Taking one last look around, she said, "I won't miss the furniture. It wasn't mine to begin with. It is amazing how little I actually own, aside from the clothes I'm wearing." She heaved a loud sigh. "Even when I lived with Harry I didn't accumulate much of my own stuff. He was a dominating man and thought only of himself. I'm longing for a place of my own and a place where I feel free and safe. Is there such a place for me out there, Frank?" She looked back at him. "Tell me, is there?"

He shrugged. "I don't know, but we'll do our best to find you one." He held out a hand. "Come, say goodbye and let's go. The taxi is already waiting outside."

"Don't forget your cap," she said, crossing the living room to get it. Taking it off the statue of Zeus, she gave the statue a little kick with her sandaled foot. "I've never really cared for this statue. I've always had the feeling it was watching me with those lifelike eyes. If I ever get statues again, they'll be of tiny fairies and angels."

Coming back, she gave him his cap, took his hand and leaned against him as they walked out of the door. Locking it carefully, she said, "We don't want anyone breaking in. I wonder how long it will take the neighbors to realize I've moved out." Her laugh was almost pleasant. She sounded as happy as someone going on a pleasure trip. "Of course, I've always kept a low profile. They may not even notice my absence."

She still hung onto him as they crossed the street to get to the taxi.

The cabdriver stepped out of the cab and gave them a friendly smile. "Let me take your suitcase, ma'am." He took the suitcase from her and stowed it away in the trunk. Then he opened the car and said, "Ladies first."

Helen laughed and slid into the backseat. Hummer was about to join her, when he heard the squealing of tires. Looking up, he saw a black sedan coming to a stop behind the cab. With an eerie feeling of déjà-vu he watched as the doors flew open and three men dressed in dark suits, wearing sunglasses, and carrying automatic weapons, jumped out and headed for him.

With an instinctive movement his hand came up to draw his own gun, but he stopped halfway as he remembered his gun was in a locker at the airport back home. Before the men reached him, the taxi took off and drove away, leaving him standing to face the three armed men.

"Hello, Detective Frank Hummer," the first man said, giving him a big smile.

"Hello, Pacholuk," Hummer said, forcing a chuckle. "If you've come looking for Professor Middler, you're too late. The Russians have him."

"Thanks to you, Hummer," The CIA assassin growled. "You had to put your nose into affairs that didn't concern you. Now you'll have to pay for your stupidity."

He shoved his gun into Hummer's belly. "Get into the car and don't try anything heroic!"

"What about Helen?"

Pacholuk grinned. "Don't worry about your hot little girlfriend, Hummer. I'll take care of her in good time."

Chapter Sixteen

They drove to a private airport and put him onto a plane. Before they entered the airport, they took off his baseball cap and pulled a hood over his head.

Once aboard, they removed the hood. Thrust into a seat with the barrel of a gun digging into his ribs, he winced from the pain. Glaring at the big man who shoved him, he snarled, "Next time you try to hurt me I'll ram that gun up your ass, you son-of-a-bitch!"

The man laughed. "Be nice or I'll knock out some of those pearly-white teeth of yours with the butt of my gun. We have orders to bring you in alive. Nobody said anything about the condition you have to be in. By the way, you're free to move around and use the bathroom if you have to. Remember, you're in an airplane. There is no place for you to run. Oh, by the way, give me your cell phone. Can't have you making calls all over the place."

He waited until Hummer gave him his phone. "And the rest of the stuff you've got in your pockets."

Hummer emptied his pockets and handed over everything.

"I'm surprised you don't have a gun or knife hidden somewhere on your body," the big man rumbled. Opening Hummer's wallet, he shook out the change. The coins rolled onto the floor. "That's quite a wad of dough you carry there. Must be nice to be rich." He held out the wallet. "Here, I don't rob people. I do have certain rules."

Hummer put the wallet back into his pocket. "Good to know I'm dealing with honorable people," he said, sarcastically.

The big man grinned, took the seat across and strapped himself in.

Hummer looked around the interior of the cabin. It was luxurious, and it was obvious the plane belonged to someone of wealth. There were three other men in the cabin. All three were armed. They didn't pay much attention to Hummer, but he didn't miss their glances in his direction when they thought he wasn't looking. He didn't see Pacholuk, but that didn't mean he wasn't on board.

The plane began to move and climbed into the air with roaring jets, but the noise was muffled by thick, insulated walls. Hummer relaxed into his seat, cursing himself for not staying vigilant when leaving Helen's house. He had expected a move against her and possibly him, but not so soon. They must have been watching her house to know he was there. Of course, her home was bugged, and his arrival at her place was probably transmitted the moment he showed up in her living room. Covering up the statue of Zeus with his cap had obviously been useless.

Always think with the head on your shoulders, son. Never with the one in your pants.

His father's words of advice came unbidden. It would have been good to heed them. He may have been more alert and clearer of thought had he not given in to his desire for Helen when she offered herself.

Before a warrior goes into battle he conserves his strength. He does not weaken his body by stilling his animal desires.

Wonderful words of advice, but just a little bit too late. There was nothing he could do right now, so he might as well not waste his time thinking about the mistakes he made. He was alive and he would try his best to stay that way.

"What's your name?" he asked the big man sitting across from him.

"Not that it's any business of yours, but what the hell. My name is Maxwell."

"Where are you taking me, Maxwell?"

"You'll find out soon enough. Until then, shut up. I don't feel like having a conversation," Maxwell said gruffly.

"Why?" Hummer sneered. "Too much strain on your tiny brain?"

"Watch your mouth. I don't have to listen to your stupid remarks." Maxwell glowered at him with open hostility.

Hummer chuckled jovially. "I couldn't help but notice for a big man you have small hands. I read somewhere men with small hands have small penises. Is that true? Enlighten me on that one."

"Keep this up and you'll be talking with a lisp," Maxwell warned him.

"I wouldn't take that shit, Max," one of the other three men said, chuckling.

"Nobody asked you, Kramer." Maxwell took off his sunglasses and rubbed his eyes. "I haven't had a descent night's sleep for the last week and I'm not at my best mood. So everybody shut up and leave me alone." His eyes met Hummer's. "I'm trying to be civil here, Hummer. You're not making it easy."

"Sorry," Hummer said, realizing there was no good reason antagonizing the man. "I've had some shitty days lately and I'm not at my best, either. You know my name, which means you're not just a lackey who came along to party when you got me."

Maxwell laughed with a rumble. "Oh, you're correct when you say I know your name. I guess you don't remember me?"

Hummer shook his head. "No. Should I?"

"You had a reputation then, Hummer. I'm talking thirteen years ago. September twelve, nineteen-ninety-eight, to be exact. Does Operation Emerald ring a bell?"

"What do you know about that?"

"Enough. I was part of the assault team that was supposed to destroy the Mir Space Station. Your team ambushed us and prevented us from completing our mission. You executed all the men in my team." His face turned ugly when he said that. "I lost some good friends that day."

"If you were part of the team, why are you still alive?" Hummer asked.

"If you and your men hadn't left in such a hurry after shooting everyone, I probably would be dead." He pulled his shirt out of his pants and exposed his chest. An unsightly scar ran along his ribs just under his left armpit. "I was lucky I moved when I got shot. The bullet meant for my heart grazed my side, shattered a couple of ribs but didn't do any major damage. I played dead."

Pushing his shirt back into his pants, he gave Hummer a speculative look. "You were a cold bastard, Hummer. I saw and heard you give the order to kill everyone."

"I was a different man then," Hummer said, trying not to recall that day; in fact, trying not to recall any of those years in the Third Unit. He and his team members had done things that would have been considered criminal offenses had they been committed by regular lawmen, but they had operated outside the law, given a blank check by the President himself to do anything necessary to protect the citizens of the United States of America.

Somebody has to do it. Why not me? I'm a patriot and I have sworn to keep law and order in this great country of ours. The price of freedom can never be too high.

He had told himself that to ease his conscience, until the day came when he couldn't justify it any longer, the day he quit the FBI. "How did you know I was the one who gave the order and how did you find out my name?"

"In the fall of two-thousand-two, I saw an article in the papers about a former FBI agent who founded a new detective agency. I recognized you then. I did some research to find out more about you. I stumbled across a reference to a secret file with the heading Operation Emerald. Couldn't find out much, but I found out the name of the agent who led the assault. He was referred to as The Hammer. His ruthlessness and lack of mercy was whispered about among certain agents of the CIA and FBI. Nobody knew his identity. Since I saw you that day when you smashed our mission I knew you were him." Maxwell gave him a calculating look. "Are you really a changed man or is this just one of your hidden identities?"

"Whatever you may have heard about The Hammer was blown out of proportion, but he was not a pleasant man, regardless. However, that man is gone," Hummer said.

"Is he? Sometimes we try to run from our past, but eventually it catches up with us and demands redemption. Eventually we all have to pay for the things we've done, the crimes we've committed. I have a feeling this is the day you have to do penance for your sins, Frank Hummer."

Hummer looked into Maxwell's eyes. "Are you the man who will demand payment? You must be quite exhilarated for finally having caught me."

"I feel nothing, Hummer," Maxwell said, his voice as emotionless as his words. "This is just another job for me. We are both professionals and we do what we must do. I hold no grudge against you, but there are others who hate your guts. Those are the ones you have to fear. Now, if you don't mind, I want to relax. No more questions."

The rest of the flight went by in silence. Hummer spent it relaxing as much as was possible. There was nothing he could do while the plane was in the air. As Maxwell had pointed out, there was no place to run. It would be different once they arrived at their destination.

After the plane landed, one of the other three men covered his head again with a hood and cuffed his hands behind his back.

"Just a precaution," Maxwell said beside him. "I don't trust you, Hummer."

A blast of hot, humid air enveloped him as he was led down a staircase and then pushed into a car. Before the car door closed, he heard the sound of a foghorn. He also caught a whiff of air laced with salt and the odor of fish, and realized they were near a harbor. It might be worthwhile filing away that information. Hopefully, he would have the opportunity to use it.

He could smell the perspiration of the two men who sat on either side of him.

It's probably the heat making them sweat. I don't think it's because they're scared of me. It would have been different in the old days. They would have had a reason to be afraid. "Hot day, isn't it?" he said, but neither of the men reacted to his remark.

Settling in as comfortably as he could between the two men, he acted relaxed but his brain was working overtime trying to find a way out of this situation. He had to admit it didn't look promising. Trying to escape from a moving car was just as impossible as escaping from a plane. He knew there were four men with him in the car. He had no doubt all four were armed, but he didn't know if any guns were aimed at him. He didn't think so, but had no desire to find out. There was no other way but to wait and see where they were taking him.

None of the men talked. They drove in silence.

"You guys are certainly a quiet lot," he said, trying to get them to talk, but he didn't receive an answer. Either they were afraid he might recognize their voices or they had nothing to talk about.

When they finally stopped and the driver shut off the car engine, he estimated about thirty minutes had gone by. He filed it away, but since he didn't know which direction they'd been driving, he had no idea if they were still near the water or far away from it.

"Out!" one of the men ordered him. He recognized the voice as that of the man who Maxwell had identified as Kramer. He climbed out of the car, keeping his head low to avoid hitting it against the doorframe. Stretching his legs, he wriggled his shoulders to get out the kinks.

"How about taking off the cuffs," he said. "There are four of you with guns and only one of me, and I'm without a gun. Besides being blindfolded."

"Shut up and walk," Kramer said, punching him between the shoulder blades with his fist.

Hummer stumbled forward. Clamping his jaws together to suppress the sudden pain, he growled, "I'll remember this, Kramer. Maybe I'll get a chance to pay you back."

Kramer laughed. "I don't think that is going to happen. I listened to your friendly conversation with Maxwell. It seems you two know each other from years back and apparently you had some sort of reputation? Well, I don't know you and I don't give a shit what kind of tough guy you were back then. You don't look so tough now, so forget about getting your revenge." He shoved Hummer again.

Hummer growled deep in his throat, but refrained from reacting violently. Blindfolded and with his hands in cuffs behind his back, his chances of doing much damage to any of them were slim.

The way Kramer talked about Maxwell, Hummer didn't think the big man was with them. He didn't know if that was a good sign or not. Somehow he had made some kind of connection with Maxwell, who, according to his own words, didn't feel any animosity toward Hummer.

Faint echoes of their footsteps suggested they were in an indoor parking lot. They hadn't removed the hood, but he was quite sure there were no other people around. The stink of humid dust, rancid oil and mould-covered cement hung unpleasant in the air.

Probably an old, deserted warehouse or factory.

One of the men sneezed and cursed, "What a fucking place! You'd think they find a better location to meet!"

"Someday we'll move into a plush palace," Kramer sneered and laughed.

They halted and waited for something. Hummer heard the groaning and squealing of old machinery and knew they'd be boarding an elevator. When the noise stopped, he was pushed forward, and he took a few steps. The elevator began to descend, taking them below ground. It stopped almost immediately, indicating they had gone down only one level.

Hummer was led down an empty corridor, judging by the loud echo their shoes created on the hard floor. The air smelled dank and felt cold. It was almost a relief from the heat outside.

"Well, here we are," Kramer said.

The whooshing sound of an opening door told Hummer he was about to enter a room. Kramer gave him another shove, but Hummer was already moving forward and Kramer's flat hand ended up as a gentle slap.

Someone pulled the hood from his head. Hummer blinked a few times to get used to the sudden light, dim as it was. He stood in a room devoid of any furniture except for an old wooden table and a chair on either side. A single bulb hanging from the ceiling on an extension cord was the only source of light. He didn't see a window, which probably meant they were below ground level, as he already suspected.

"Take a seat," Kramer said, extending his right arm with a flare. "Your company will arrive soon."

Hummer studied the other man for a moment. Kramer was of average built, maybe five-ten, slim. He wore a black suit and black tie, sunglasses, and a black hat. *The embodiment of a typical CIA agent.* He watched Hummer with a cynical smile on his thin lips.

"How about taking off the cuffs now?" Hummer asked.

"The cuffs stay on. It's for the best." Kramer grinned broadly. "Our benefactor wouldn't appreciate it should you decide to attack him."

"Aren't you going to stay as a chaperone?" Hummer put a sarcastic tone into his question.

"We'll be right outside the door. If for some miraculous reason you

should manage to get free, you won't get far. You can't outrun a bullet."
Kramer moved his hand toward his chest and inside his jacket, indicating
he had a gun. "Unless you're Superman." He tipped the rim of his hat
and walked out the door.

Hummer took another look around, registered the cold, bare walls.
They had once been covered with paint, but now the paint was peeling
and the cement showed through holes in the plaster. The ceiling didn't
look much better.

Might as well make myself comfortable.

Squatting, he lowered his cuffed hands down behind his back. Even
though he was a big man, he was agile enough to push his feet backward
across the short chain, first one and then the other, to bring his hands to
the front. Then he moved behind the table and sat down on the hard
metal chair. Resting his hands in his lap, he waited.

The wait was not long. He heard voices outside and then the door
opened.

"Hello, Frank Hummer," said the man who walked in. He carried a
laptop computer in one hand.

At first Hummer was surprised to see him, but only for a moment.
Deep inside, he always suspected that the man was involved in more
than just amassing a fortune.

"Good to see you, Congressman Gibson," he said.

Gibson chuckled evilly, puffing on his cigar. "I'm not here to rescue
you, Hummer."

"I didn't think so," Hummer replied.

Another man came in with Gibson. Agent Pacholuk. He grinned at
Hummer and stationed himself in front of the door.

Gibson took the seat across from Hummer and put the laptop onto
the table. "I hope you had a good flight."

"It was fine. I assume it was one of your planes? It would have been
nice to get something to eat," Hummer said pleasantly.

"I'll put it into the suggestion box." Gibson took another drag from
his cigar. Bending forward, he blew the smoke in Hummer's face.
"You're probably wondering why you and I are here...in this dismal
place."

Hummer tried not to cough as he inhaled the acrid smell of the cigar smoke. "The thought has occurred to me."

"Well, let me enlighten you then. Are you a religious man, Hummer?"

Hummer shook his head. "Not in the traditional sense, but I believe in some kind of super intelligence that runs this universe, though. Don't you?"

Gibson laughed. "Only fools and the weak-minded believe the irrational ideas the church has been feeding the soul-searching public for centuries. I'm a rational man. I don't believe in some benevolent entity who watches over us humans. Look at the world around you. Take for example what's happening in Africa right now. Would a loving god allow millions of people to starve to death? Or would a loving god allow a bunch of zealots strap bombs around their bodies and blow themselves up murdering innocent people in the process, in his name? I could go on. There is no shortage of examples. No, Hummer, I'm afraid there are no benign gods. Gods were created by clever, wise men to scare the shit out of the stupid masses. Scared people are easy to control; they will do anything to appease the gods or the ones who claim to be emissaries of the gods."

"America is a free country. You are allowed to believe what you want. I won't hold it against you, Congressman," Hummer mocked him. "It must be sad not to believe in anything."

"I never said I didn't believe in anything. I believe in power, especially the power intelligent men and women seize for themselves when the opportunity arises. I believe in the power that makes it possible for me to mold and manipulate the forces behind world events." Gibson knocked the ashes off his cigar and stuck it between his lips. Blowing the smoke out of the side of his mouth, he stared at Hummer. "Gods don't make things happen, Hummer, men do. Men like me."

"Are you saying you are responsible for the drought and famine in Somalia?"

"Don't be an idiot, Hummer. We can't control the forces of nature, not yet. We can't do anything about the drought. It is unfortunate about all those people dying, but to some degree they have themselves to blame. Why do they bring so many children into the world if they can't even feed themselves? The country is run by murderers, and ruthless, but stupid people. Most of the countries in Africa are. What they need are people with the skills to manipulate the masses, men who are able to bring order into the chaos existing in Africa today. The opportunity is there, but it takes more than just ruthlessness to create a powerful elite. It takes time and a willingness to wait."

"Why don't you take advantage of this opportunity?" Hummer asked.

"Who says we aren't?" Gibson chuckled good-humoredly. "Certain people will get rich, or perhaps I should say richer, from the suffering of those millions of people."

"Don't you feel guilty doing that?"

"Guilty? Why should I feel guilty? Do the owners of a funeral home feel guilty ripping off people just to bury or cremate their dead family members? Does a surgeon feel guilty making millions from the illness of sick people? That's how the world runs. People make money from other people's misery. People who suffer will give up the power over their own destiny and life to the ones who promise to help. Take the church for example. For centuries it has ruled Europe and beyond. The church is so powerful because people are searching for a better life, if not here than in the so-called hereafter. People can be poor and have nothing to eat but they will still donate what little money they have to the church freely. Now that is power." Gibson leaned forward. "Enough of this chit-chat! It seems we've strayed away from our topic. You want to know what this is all about?"

"It would be nice to know."

"You've caused me and my fraternity brothers a lot of grief by meddling, Hummer. Everything went according to plan until you started digging." Gibson's voice sounded cold and cruel. "You should have left things alone!"

"What was this grand plan I supposedly meddled with?"

"The plan was to make certain Senator Simmerman never gets a chance to become President of the United States," Gibson snarled. He stabbed a finger at Hummer. "You managed to fuck that up, you stupid son-of-a-bitch! This was the second time you achieved that."

Hummer grinned. "Is that any way to talk to the man who might become your future son-in-law?"

"You must be joking. That was the other part of my plan to make sure you'll never marry my daughter." He laughed cruelly. "At least that part of the plan is still intact."

"How so? Cheryl doesn't listen to you. I'm going to propose to her the moment I see her next. She'll marry me in spite."

Gibson flipped open the laptop and turned it on. "Not after I show her this." He waited for the computer to load then he turned the laptop so Hummer could see it.

It took Hummer a moment to realize what he saw. He had known about the camera in the chandelier, even though he never located it, but had not guessed its sophisticated capability. It had been dark in Helen's bedroom; however, the two naked people on the bed were easily recognizable, even from the bird's eye view. Anyone who knew about the tattoo of an eagle on his right shoulder blade would recognize him.

He watched until the moment came when he disengaged himself from Helen and rolled onto his back. His and Helen's face couldn't have been displayed any clearer.

"You're a sick bastard!" he growled between clenched teeth.

"I believe you have that wrong. I'm not the one fucking one woman while stringing along another one." Gibson closed the laptop and shoved it aside. "There is a way we can make this scene disappear if you tell me what I want to know."

"What would that be?"

"Have you ever heard of the Third Unit and Operation Emerald?" Gibson looked at him with a calculating expression. Before Hummer could answer, he waved a hand. "Of course you have. There is no need to play cat and mouse. You were the man who led the assault that wiped out one of my best teams and screwed up a brilliant plan."

"To destroy the Russian Mir Space Station. You call that a brilliant plan?"

"Had it been successful it would have created huge opportunities."

"At the cost of how many lives? Millions possibly?" Hummer could not believe Gibson's casual attitude.

"What are a few million lives? This planet is overpopulated as it is. It would probably be a good thing to make room for the untold millions already growing in the bellies of women in the third world countries. The human race is multiplying like a bunch of rats. Soon people will be eating each other because there is not enough food to feed everyone." Glaring at Hummer, Gibson said, "Every time a building gets destroyed, a new one will have to be built. Destruction is a good thing. Wars are good for the world economy. They create jobs, they create money. Look what happened after the two world wars. Countries moved forward, people prospered. People made money."

Hummer shook his head in disbelief. "Is that all you think about? Money and power? Don't you have any compassion for people?"

"Of course I do. I care for my family. I cared for my brother who took his life after you and your do-gooders exposed his involvement in the plan to shoot down the Mir Space Station," Gibson said with a hoarse voice.

"I know nothing about that." Hummer tried to remember the names of the companies they investigated during Operation Emerald. There had been weapon manufactures, construction companies, banks, even a garment factory.

"You know nothing about it? Aren't you the one who preaches compassion? Did you ever think about the people who owned the companies you put out of business? The families you ruined by taking away the jobs of the people who worked in these businesses?" Gibson slapped the tabletop with his flat hand in anger. "My brother was the owner of Silver Eagle Manufacturing. The company built warplanes for the government. When the stocks in his company took a dive, my brother lost everything he worked for. He lost his friends, his wife and children. He couldn't accept the shame and shot himself on Christmas Eve. You have that on your conscience, Hummer!"

"No, not me. He did it to himself by getting involved in a terrible plot. Don't blame me for that. I took an oath to defend my country, to guard it against all evil. What your brother planned was wrong, an evil act against the citizens of the United States of America and the rest of the world. He needed to be stopped." Hummer spoke calmly, even though he was seething inside.

"Who the hell are you to judge what is right or wrong? You were a federal agent, nothing more, supposed to follow orders not take matters into your own hands. But no, you and that idiot Simmerman decided to open up your own little *judge-and-jury* business. You had to play god and screw things up!" Gibbons bellowed.

"Our missions were sanctioned by the President himself," Hummer said coolly.

"Oh, yes, the President! He lived under the illusion he had the power to do whatever he felt like. We'll deal with him in good time. The only ones who decide what happens in this country and the rest of the world are the members of the Order of Capricorn. Men who are not afraid to seize power and use it to build fortunes. We control the events. We shape the world." Spittle formed in the corners of Gibson's mouth as he shouted at Hummer, pounding his fist against the tabletop.

Hummer was reminded of some crazy dictator who announced he was taking over control of the world. "You are suffering from megalomania," he said. "I suggest you take some lessons in being humble. It might get you what you desire much sooner."

"Don't lecture me, Hummer!" Gibson growled, wiping his mouth with the back of his hand.

"I wouldn't dream of lecturing you, Congressman. You're beyond lecturing. I'm curious. Are there only men in your little country club or do you also have women who are lusting for power?"

"It's not a country club. We are the real world government and we answer to no-one, not the President of the United States, or the members of the United Nations, who are under the illusion they actually have control over world affairs. To answer your question about women-members in the Order of Capricorn, no, there aren't any. Women have their place but they are not ruthless enough to be in such responsible positions."

"You mean they are not smart enough, don't you?" Hummer commented dryly, pretty much knowing Gibson's real thoughts on that subject.

"Women think differently from men. Besides, our women run the Capricorn Society, which keeps them busy and out of trouble. I'm sure you are familiar with that charity. It does a lot of good in the world. It also diverts attention from our Order."

"May I offer a suggestion? Make damn sure your wife and daughter never find out what you think about their intelligence." Hummer's lips formed a cold, stark smile. "Of course, Cheryl probably knows already about your attitude. That's why she shuns you. She's not as dumb as you think."

"Leave my wife and daughter out of this," Gibson snarled. "Now listen. I want you to give me the names of all the members of the Third Unit."

"To what purpose?"

"So we can deal with them."

"You mean have them assassinated?"

"They will have to pay for what they did."

"I'm afraid I'm suffering from memory loss," Hummer said. "It's been nearly thirteen years. I put it all behind me."

"Don't feed me that bullshit, Hummer! You were a tight-knit unit. I'll bet all their names are still in your head. You're probably thinking about some of them right now. So start talking."

Hummer smiled gently. "You must think I'm stupid, Senator. As long as I have those names in my head I'm alive. The moment I spill my guts, I'm dead. I'm sorry, no deal."

Gibson grabbed his laptop and rose. "Then you leave me no choice. You will talk one way or another." He looked at the agent in front of the door. "He's all yours, Pacholuk. I'll be back tomorrow." Without a backward glance he walked outside.

Pacholuk gave Hummer an evil grin. He waved his gun around. "You heard the Congressman. It seems you and I will get to know each other quite intimately. You can make it easy and give me the information now or we can do it the hard way. I really don't care. I'm an expert in giving people pain without killing them, not right away anyway."

"You'll never get close enough to even touch me," Hummer warned. "I'll kick your balls into your belly so deep people will think you have a cunt."

"I'm not worried, tough guy." Pacholuk opened the door. "Kramer and Spence. Come in here. We have a job to do."

The two men came in with their weapons drawn. Pacholuk aimed his gun at Hummer's head. "Get up and stand over there."

Hummer followed his order and walked over to the wall Pacholuk indicated.

"I've noticed you managed to put your hands in front of you. I want you to put them behind your back again," Pacholuk ordered.

Hummer hesitated. He'd be pretty much helpless with his hands behind his back, but he knew they wouldn't hesitate to shoot him if he didn't comply. Reluctantly, he bent down and stepped through the loop his hands formed.

"Turn around!"

He did and stood facing the wall.

A hard fist hitting him between his shoulder blades felt like the blow from a sledgehammer and made him gasp from the sudden pain. Another whack caused him to fall to his knees in a fit of weakness.

"Stand up, you son-of-a-bitch and take it like a man," Pacholuk said harshly. "You want to talk now?"

"Go and fuck yourself," Hummer cursed. Then he cried out involuntarily when a fist hit him hard in the kidney.

Chapter Seventeen

A soft hand stroked his cheek. Turning his head, he saw Helen kneeling beside him. "Where did you come from?" he asked. "I've always been here," she said and bent down to kiss him. Her lips felt warm and pliable. He put his arms around her and pulled her on top of him. He hadn't realized she was nude.

"You feel so good in my arms," he murmured. "I love you."

"I love you too," she said, kissing him again.

A sudden dull pain in his back from a hard object he seemed to be lying on caused him to let out a loud moan. His arms were numb and his face hurt. He opened his eyes and stared at the cracks in the ceiling above him.

"Helen?" he asked. His voice came out as a croak. The effort to speak brought more pain to his split, swollen lips. There was no answer and he realized he had been hallucinating. As he regained consciousness, pain raced through the rest of his body. He lay on his arms, the cuffs around his wrists digging into his back. Sitting up painfully, he wriggled his buttocks backward until his manacled wrists rested in the hollow of his bent knees. Then he pushed his wrists under his feet and forward until his hands were again in front of him. The whole maneuver took all his will to complete because his arms didn't want to obey his commands. He must have been lying on them for a long time, and when the blood rushed back into his hands and fingers, the pain was excruciating.

His shoulder blades and back felt numb, almost beyond pain. When he moved his shoulders, he suppressed the urge to scream. His chest hurt with every breath he took and he wondered if they broke or cracked some of his ribs.

Memory came back with a rush. They had worked him over first with their fists; when he lay on the floor they used their feet to kick him. Kramer and Spence had done the beating, while Pacholuk watched, mocking him. Only once Pacholuk gave him a kick in the solar plexus with the heel of his shoe after Hummer told him to fuck his grandmother.

He hadn't given them anything, he was certain of that. The last thing he remembered was Kramer's foot above his face, but he didn't remember passing out. Bringing up both of his hands, he touched his nose; it hurt but didn't seem to be broken. When he looked down at himself, he noticed crusted blood on his shirt and tie.

"I'll make you pay for this tie, you bloodthirsty bastards. This tie was my favorite." He wanted to chuckle but it came out like the grunt of a pig. Getting to his feet brought nothing but agony to his limbs, but he managed to stand without keeling over, even though his head seemed to be full of construction workers with sledgehammers. He stood listening to sounds from outside but didn't hear anything. Taking shallow breaths, he found the humid air reeked of vomit, human sweat, and stale cigar smoke, each one equally nauseous. When he looked at the floor he didn't have to guess where the vomit came from. The rumbling in his belly reminded him that his last meal had been breakfast with Helen, and he didn't know how many hours had passed since then. Checking his watch, he discovered its crystal shattered. It was still running but the hour hand was missing.

"Somebody will pay for this also," he muttered. "That watch was expensive."

If I could only get out of these cuffs.

The sound of muffled footsteps outside made him move against the wall at the hinged side of the door. When it opened, the door hid him from view.

"What the hell!" somebody cursed and stepped into the room. Hummer came up from behind the man, wrapped the chain around his neck and pulled hard, strangling him. Struggling violently, the man reached up to get a hold of the chain, but it was too tight for him to get his fingers to find a hold. He kicked back against Hummer's shin, but it

225

was a feeble kick. Moments after, the man went limp and hung like a heavy giant bag of beans in Hummer's grip. Hummer let him slide to the ground. Looking into the man's blue face, he recognized Spence.

Hummer knew he was dead, but he checked his pulse anyway. Then he searched for the man's gun and shoved it into his own holster. Rifling through Spence's pockets, he removed a couple of clips for the gun and put them into his pocket. He hoped he didn't have to use the gun. Firing it with manacled hands would not make it easy to hit a target, especially one that shot back.

Poking his head into the corridor, he didn't see anyone else. Spence had been alone. He stepped out of the room and pulled the door closed. Listening, he tried to decide which way would be the safest to go. He couldn't take the elevator. It might trigger an alarm, but there had to be stairs. They should be somewhere near the elevator.

Suppressing the pain each step caused him, he limped as fast as he could manage down the dimly lit corridor. When he came to the end, he saw the elevator on one side. There was a door on the other side of the short corridor to the right. He decided to take a chance and headed for it. Opening it carefully, he was elated to discover the staircase. Looking around again and listening for any noises, he didn't hear anything. In fact, it was almost eerily silent.

The stairs only went up so he climbed them, trying not to moan. His head wanted to explode and his whole body was on fire from the pain lifting his legs caused him. Much of the pain originated from his lower back where they must have kicked him repeatedly.

The stairs ended on the next floor. The upper floors of the building were not accessible from this location. He saw a door and headed for it. Opening the door, he peeked out and saw nothing but what looked like an indoor parking lot. The place was poorly lit but he spotted one lonely car parked against a wall not far from him.

Probably the car that brought me to this place.

Tempted to try breaking into it, he decided against it. Too risky. He had no key to start it and no tools to shortcut the ignition. Somebody may just decide to take a stroll in the parking garage while he was wasting valuable time trying to get the car going. It was probably nighttime outside, since he didn't see any light shining in from any windows or other openings.

Listening for footsteps or any other sounds betraying the presence of people, he heard nothing but faint traffic noises. It was now or never. He left the safety of the staircase and dashed across the empty concrete floor, feeling like a rabbit trying to run from a pack of hunting dogs. His destination was the wall on the other side. Like the rabbit on the run he knew safety was not in the open but in the protection of a wall.

The mad dash across the empty garage seemed to take forever, but he finally reached the other side and leaned against the damp wall, gasping for breath but getting only warm, humid air into his aching lungs.

The run had left him weak. His legs felt wobbly and his whole body throbbed with dull pain, but he knew there was no time to waste, so he pushed on. Running as fast as his aching muscles allowed, he kept close to the wall, his shoulders sometimes scraping the cold, moist concrete.

When he saw an opening in the wall, he rejoiced, hoping it would lead him out of the building. He was not disappointed. The door was not locked and when he opened it, he almost fell outside. Where once used to be a short staircase was now just an empty hole. But the drop was only a couple of feet and he managed not to fall flat on his face, only jarred his ankle and knee. It didn't matter. A bit more pain didn't make much difference anymore.

He knew he was in some back alley. Another building on the other side loomed above him like a black cliff dotted with dark square holes. Craning his neck, he could see a sliver of the night sky above him. It was a clear night and the stars were sparkling dots of light in the black sky.

A sudden clattering noise behind him made him swing around. A dark form ran across the alley and disappeared into the shadows of the other building. *Probably a cat or maybe even a large rat.* He relaxed and began walking. It didn't matter which direction he chose, as long as it got him out of this alley and into a street where he could find people to help him.

When he finally came to the end of the alley, he found the street just as empty but better lit. It seemed he had ended up in a part of the city that was either full of abandoned buildings or factories that only operated during the day. Listening for sounds of traffic, he decided to turn right and hurried on. He needed to get away from this area as quickly as possible before somebody discovered his escape.

The rumbling sound of a car coming out of a side-street made him hug the nearest building. When the car turned into his street and headed for him, the headlights seemed to search him out and he felt like a fly caught in a spider net, waiting for the spider to come and devour him.

The car came to a screeching halt beside him and a couple of men jumped out. One from the passenger's side in the front and one from the back.

"Hey, what's a fancily dressed white guy like you doing out so late in this neighborhood?" one of them asked, coming closer.

Hummer knew by the pitch of his voice that he was young. He couldn't make out his face in the dark but he knew both of them were black. The white of their eyes seemed to be the only clearly visible feature.

"You wouldn't believe it if I told you," Hummer said.

"You saying we are stupid?" the other one said.

"Never, brother. Nobody would believe what happened to me is what I'm saying." Hummer tried to sound pacifying. The last thing he needed was a confrontation with a couple of young punks.

"Why don't you tell us? You'd be surprised what we believe," the first youth said.

"I was kidnapped and held prisoner by some guys," he said. "I escaped."

"Funny story," the first one commented.

"You don't believe me. Didn't I tell you so?"

"You got money?" the other youth asked.

"What if I have?" Hummer watched them warily. None of them seemed to be armed, but they could hide a gun inside their wide pockets. Or a knife. Most of these young men carried guns and knives.

"Maybe you should give us your money," the youth suggested.

"What do I get in return?" Hummer asked.

"What you get?" The youth laughed. "You get to stay in one piece. Maybe." He snapped open a switchblade. "Or maybe I'll cut you a little just for fun."

"I wouldn't try anything stupid," Hummer warned him. "You might get hurt."

"You talk brave for a guy wearing cuffs. Cops after you?"

"No cops after me." Hummer held up his cuffed hands. "You mean because of these? I told you I was held captive. Don't let the cuffs fool you. They don't make me a helpless victim. Listen, nobody needs to get hurt here. You asked if I have money. Sure I've got money. Lots of it. It would be much more profitable if you boys helped me instead of trying to rob me. I could be very generous."

"How generous?"

"I'll give you a couple of grand each."

"That's a lot of money." The young man nodded, apparently thinking. Then he grinned and said, "I don't trust you. I think I'll take your watch and all the money you got on you." He waved the knife in front of him. "Don't make no wrong moves. Take off your fancy jacket."

It was Hummer's turn to grin. "I guess you're not so smart after all. How can I take off my jacket with these cuffs on?"

"You can't take it off," said the first youth, "that's true, but we can pull it down behind your back. You'll be helpless then."

Hummer was getting impatient and angry. His body ached and he wanted nothing but rest. However, first he needed to put some distance between this place and himself. He didn't have time to waste with these idiots.

"Move back against the wall," the second youth ordered him, threatening Hummer with his knife.

Instead of moving back, Hummer took a step forward and kicked the knife out of the youth's hand. Then he whirled and smashed his foot against the side of the young man's head in a roundhouse kick, knocking him out cold. Without pondering his next move, he let his instincts lead him. The first youth seemed to have frozen on his spot. Hummer kicked him in the chest, sending him reeling against the car, where he slid to the ground to lie dazed on the cold stones of the sidewalk.

Intuition and a gut-feeling made Hummer drop and roll away. A shot rang out and, looking at the car, he saw a third man coming around the hood, gun in hand. Hummer rolled again as the man fired a second time, took refuge behind the car. Hindered by the cuffs, he managed to draw his own gun from its holster. Old instincts took over. His mind was suddenly cold and without mercy. He had been attacked and he reacted to the threat. There was no time to think about consequences. Acting automatically and without thought, he aimed the gun at the target looming in front of him and squeezed the trigger.

The enemy fell, clutching at his chest. His weapon cluttered onto the street. Hummer rose from his kneeling position and looked down at the man he had shot. Even in the dim light he could see the dark stain forming on the pavement. Bending over him, he looked into the slack face, regret rising in him for what he had been forced to do.

He's only a kid, no more than fifteen or sixteen. Why the fuck did he have to shoot at me? I'm a trained killer. He had no chance.

The he shrugged. What was done was done. He could feel sorry later. Without another look at the other two youths he jumped into the car, threw the gun onto the passenger's seat and drove away. At least now he had transportation. To question fate served no purpose.

He had no idea where he was or what city he was in. Suddenly there was more traffic and the street was lit up by bright lamps. It was time to ditch the car and the gun. When he came to another side street, he took it, drove a hundred yards or so and parked the car. Then he wiped the gun down with the sleeve of his jacket, did the same with the clips, and threw them under the front seat.

Locking the car door, he briskly walked back to the main street. There he began looking for a cab.

He didn't have to wait long. When the cab stopped, he climbed into the backseat. "Take me to the next precinct," he told the cab driver. If there was a place to get his cuffs off, a police station was the most logical place to go to. He'd have some explaining to do how he'd acquired the cuffs. They'd be doing some checking to make sure he wasn't a convict on the run, but there should be no problem. He still had his I.D. with him. They would only have to verify his identity. He'd call Mason at the FBI and, of course, his office, but those calls would have to wait till morning.

"This may be a stupid question," he said to the driver. "But can you tell me what city I'm in?"

The driver looked into the rearview mirror. "It is a peculiar question. Have you been in some kind of accident? You look like shit."

"Accident? Yes, you might say I've had an accident. It seems I've lost some of my memory."

"Maybe I should take you to a hospital instead to have you checked out, buddy."

"No, I need to go to the police first. It is important I report what happened to me."

"Okay. Whatever you say."

Hummer relaxed into his seat, weary and in pain. That last exertion had taken all of his willpower and last bit of strength. Now his body demanded payment for the punishment it received. He noticed the driver throwing glances at him through his mirror. He kept his hands in his lap, close together, and pulled back into his sleeves. If the driver had seen the cuffs, he didn't let on. It didn't really matter if he had. He was taking Hummer to the police.

"You never told me what city this is," Hummer said.

"New York. You're in the Big Apple, buddy."

"New York. That's good. I remember I have friends here." It was true, he did have a friend in New York. He hadn't seen Mac Snyder since Hummer left the FBI. Snyder left soon after Hummer did, to start his own company. A private protection service. That's all Hummer knew. They hadn't kept in touch. None of the members of the Third Unit communicated with each other. It was best that way.

But things had changed. Snyder needed to be warned about the danger looming over all of them. He needed to know about the White Ops. As did all of the other agents.

"Here we are." The driver's voice woke him. He hadn't realized he had drifted into an uneasy slumber.

He groped for his wallet and asked, "How much do I owe you?"

"Sixty bucks."

Hummer took a hundred-dollar bill from his wallet and handed it to the driver. "Keep the change," he said.

The cabbie looked at the cuffs. "Do you think it's a good idea to go into a cop-shop wearing those?"

"Probably not, but I'll take my chances."

"Well, good luck. I wouldn't go in there, but it seems you've made up your mind. Take my advice. Don't say anything about an accident. Just make up some story. You'll have less trouble that way." He grinned. "Tell them your wife likes to play rough. They'll understand."

"Thanks for the advice." Hummer closed the door and watched the cab drive off. Then he walked up the steps into the police station.

The female cop at the front desk watched him come in. Hummer limped up to the desk, a silly smile on his face. Smiling didn't come too easy with his swollen, cracked lips and cheek.

"Can I help you?" she asked.

"This is somewhat embarrassing," Hummer said. "I've had a bit of a mishap." He chuckled. "I drank more beer than I should have last night and picked up this woman. We went to a hotel room and we…you know…we played some games. I must have passed out, because when I woke up, she was gone, but she left me with these…" He held up his cuffed hands, smiling sheepishly. "No key. So I thought what better place to get a key but in a police station."

The cop didn't smile. "You look like you had a rough night. Did this woman beat you up and rob you by any chance?"

"Oh, no. She wasn't that kind of a woman. She wasn't in it for the money, just kicks, you know."

"No, I don't know. I'm not into weird sex." She kept a straight face as she spoke. "May I see some identification, Mister…?"

"Hummer. Frank Hummer. By the way, I'm a private investigator."

"Evidently not a very good one. You should have investigated that woman a little closer before you got involved with her." Her eyes narrowed slightly as she scrutinized him. "Did you…uh…play with your clothes on?"

"Why?"

"Your handcuffs. You'd have to be a magician to get dressed with those cuffs on your wrists."

He tried a chuckle, feeling like someone caught in a lie, which of course he was, his mind racing to come up with a plausible explanation. "I have to admit this whole thing sounds a bit bizarre. Come to think of it, it is bizarre. She wanted to play cops and robbers. She was the cop, actually she said she was a CIA agent, and I was a spy. To make it more real, I had to be dressed. That's how I ended up wearing my suit."

The woman shook her head. "You know I've heard wacky stories before, but this one beats most of them. Show me some I.D."

Hummer fumbled around in his pocket to get his wallet.

"I notice you're wearing a holster," the cop commented.

"I told you I'm a PI. and I have a permit to carry a gun."

"Where is the gun now?"

"In a locker in Kansas City. I couldn't take it on the plane."

"So you came to New York in a plane?"

"Yes, I did." That was not a lie, except he couldn't prove it if they asked for a plane stub. He managed to retrieve his wallet and pulled out his driver's license and his business card. Handing it to her, he said, "Hummer Investigations. That's me. To nail down the facts you need a Hammer."

Reading the card, she said, "Your motto would make more sense if your name were *Hammer*."

"It did make sense when I started my business, but somehow it doesn't mean anything anymore." People forget over the years, which is a good thing, unfortunately not everyone forgot about *The Hammer.*

"Give me a moment to run your name through the system," the female cop said.

"I wouldn't mind getting these cuffs off and using your bathroom," Hummer said.

"All in good time. This shouldn't take long." She was busy working her computer. When the phone rang, she picked it up and answered it. Hummer didn't really listen to her conversation but couldn't help hearing what she said.

"I understand...Yes...I'm on it now...I'm retrieving the picture...I'll keep watch...Sure, will do." He didn't miss her sudden rigid stance as her eyes flickered from her screen to glance at him.

"Is there a problem?" he asked, suddenly wondering if he'd made the right decision to come to a police station for help. He felt like leaving, but knew it wouldn't look good, besides it was too late for that. When the female cop aimed a gun at him, he knew he should have listened to the cabbie.

"One wrong move and I'll blast your head off your shoulders," she said with a cold voice.

"That's quite a strong reaction to my story," he said. "I admit I made it up. You would never have believed the real one, but I can tell you what exactly happened."

"Spare me your lies, Mr. Hummer." She activated her intercom and spoke into it. "I need some help at the front desk. I've got a live one."

Moments later two burly cops came out of a side door. Guns drawn, they advanced toward Hummer. "Put up your hands," one of them said sharply.

Hummer lifted them. "I'm already cuffed," he said.

The cop looked at the woman behind the desk. "How'd you manage that, Serge?"

She shrugged. "I did nothing. He came in like that."

"Who is this guy?"

"Apparently he escaped the custody of the CIA."

"The CIA?" He stared at Hummer. "Are you some kind of spy?"

"I'm not a spy. I'm a private investigator who stumbled onto something so big and unreal nobody will believe." His eyes searched out the woman cop. "Whatever information you received I can tell you is wrong. If you let me explain my side of what is going on, maybe we can divert a disaster and the murder of an innocent man."

"Whose murder?"

"Mine. And possibly that of a number of federal agents."

"How do federal agents come into the picture?"

"It's a long and complicated story. I used to be a federal agent. My team and I pissed off the wrong people and now they want revenge. Those CIA agents who will certainly come and pick me up are rogue agents working for some powerful people. Everything they will tell you is nothing but lies, but I have no way to prove them wrong." He lifted his hands and pointed at his face. "They did this to me, this and more. But this is nothing compared to what'll they'll do to me once they have me back."

Her eyes seemed thoughtful. "You should have become an actor or writer. You tell a convincing story, Mr. Hummer, but I don't buy it.

Maybe you shouldn't have told me that stupid story about having kinky sex with a mysterious woman."

He gave her a tired smile. "Blame the cabdriver who brought me here. He suggested it."

"The cabdriver. It's always the cabdriver's fault." She shook her head, trying to decide what to do. "Your credentials seem to check out, but that means nothing. I can't ignore my orders from Headquarters. They told me to hold you. Apparently, you're a threat to National Security. That's quite some accusation."

"I'm not a threat. In fact, I'm trying to avert a threat. Do me a favor and call the office of Senator Benjamin Simmerman in Washington. Insist you talk to the Senator himself. Tell him about me and what is happening. Also call Special Agent in charge Rick Mason at the FBI Field Office in Kansas City. He is a good friend of mine and will vouch for me. And as an added favor call my office in Kansas City and let them know I'm alive...still." He was suddenly feeling faint and he remembered he hadn't eaten since breakfast the previous day with little time to rest in-between, except for the time when he lay unconscious.

There was a bench against one wall. "I'm going to sit down if you don't mind. I'm not feeling well. I'm aching and my stomach is convulsing. It would be generous of you if you could bring me a sandwich and a painkiller, and maybe a glass of water." He didn't wait for them to react to his request and headed for the bench.

"Do you believe this guy?" The two cops followed him slowly, their guns still aimed at him.

"The whole thing sounds so crazy I'm almost inclined to believe him," the woman said. "I can't make any calls until morning, and then I'll let the captain decide his fate. He doesn't look too good. I don't want him to collapse and die on us. Go get him some water and an aspirin. Ask Jackson if he still has a sandwich or something."

One of the cops disappeared through the door. The other one kept his eyes focused on Hummer.

Hummer sat on the bench, grateful for the chance to rest. The pain in his back was excruciating and a swarm of bees seemed to have taken up residence inside his head. He took only shallow breaths to keep the stabs of pain at bay whenever his chest expanded past a certain point.

The cop came back, carrying a glass of water and a small wrapped package. Giving it to Hummer, he held out his other hand. "Here, I got you a couple of aspirins. I hope they help."

Hummer took the pills with a shaking hand and put them into his mouth. Then he washed them down with a long gulp from the glass. Unwrapping the sandwich gave him a bit of trouble, and eating it made his jaws ache, but he didn't care. It tasted better than the juiciest steak he ever ate.

The cops watched him while he ate, obviously unsure what to do with him. Swallowing down the last bite, he burped. "Thanks, guys," he said, grinning feebly. He could barely keep his eyes open. "It wasn't the usual fare I'm used to but it tasted great. Whoever sacrificed this sandwich is a lucky guy to have someone who makes a delicious sandwich like that."

"His name's Jackson and he isn't married," one rumbled.

"Tell him he's a creative genius and a king among sandwich makers," Hummer mumbled. The bees inside his head seemed to be settling down. "Have you told anyone about me?" he asked the woman.

"Not yet, but I can't hold out much longer. I'll have to notify HQ about your presence here. They'll let the CIA office know."

"I wish you'd wait until your captain arrives. I'll have a talk with him, man to man."

"That may be a bit difficult," the desk sergeant said. "Captain Mansfield is a woman."

Hummer smiled. "That's probably even better. She may show compassion and let me go before my executioners arrive."

"I doubt that. Captain Mansfield is the toughest captain I ever served under," one of the two male cops said. "One might say she's got big balls."

The second cop laughed. "Don't let her hear that or she'll have yours."

Hummer slouched on the bench, feeling exhausted and sleepy. He closed his eyes and listened to their friendly bantering with tired interest.

When rough hands shook him, he opened his eyes and stared into a familiar face.

"You didn't really think you'd get away, Hummer. There is no place for you to run on this planet. We'd hunt you down and find you wherever you are." Agent Pacholuk turned and looked at the stern-faced woman in uniform behind him. "You did the right thing calling us immediately, Captain Mansfield. This man is a dangerous criminal, a threat to our great country. We'll make sure he never gets away again."

Chapter Eighteen

Hummer lifted his hand to rub the sleep from his eyes and remembered he was still cuffed. He stared up at Pacholuk. "Did you come to finish the job beating me to death? Because that's what you'll have to do. You'll never get anything out of me."

Pacholuk let out a cheerful laugh. "We don't beat people to death, Hummer. We are the CIA, the Law. We protect our country from terrorists and other criminals from people like you. We let the courts handle your punishment."

Hummer sat up straight, moaning as dull pain rushed through his body. "You are the criminal, Pacholuk, or perhaps I should say Wilfried Meyers. That's your real name, isn't it? We know who you are, Meyers. You told me there was no place for me to hide. Funny thing, I was going to tell you the same thing. My people will find and eliminate you. That's a promise."

"Are you threatening me, Hummer?" Pacholuk put his face close to Hummer's.

"Damn right I am." He looked at Captain Mansfield. "Things are not always what they seem. If you let him take me away, you are signing my death warrant and you will suffer the consequences. I have friends in the FBI and connections to Senator Simmerman. They will not let my death go unpunished. You help this man and you will be held accountable. You'll spend the rest of your life in jail, I promise you that."

The woman returned his look with a cold face. "I've checked their credentials and I'm satisfied. They are federal agents while you are a private citizen. And don't you threaten me! I don't take kindly to being threatened."

"It was no threat, just facts. By the way, I never got my call."

"You didn't get arrested by us, which means you get no calls. They cost money and we are on a tight budget." She turned and stalked away. Pulling open the door to the back offices with an angry movement, she disappeared.

Pacholuk and one of the other two agents with him grabbed Hummer by the upper arms and pulled him up. "Let's go, Hummer!"

"I'm in pain," Hummer complained. "I need a painkiller." His gaze searched out the desk sergeant. She had been watching the whole time without saying anything. When she saw him looking at her, she shrugged and lifted her hands in an obvious apology.

"Do you think you can get me another aspirin and a glass of water?" Hummer called to her.

"I believe I can," she said.

Hummer shook off the hands of the two agents who held him. "Give me a moment of dignity before you drag me out of here." He walked toward the desk and leaned upon it. The Sergeant handed him a couple of pills and said, "I'll get you that glass of water."

Before she got up, Hummer whispered, "Please, make those calls. You still have my card. If nothing else, call my office. Make it a collect call. Tell my people what happened, please."

She nodded and then walked away to get his water. It seemed to take a long time before she came back, carrying a glass filled with water. As she handed it to him, she said in a low voice, "I spoke with Special Agent Mason in Kansas City. That's all I can do for you. My hands are tied."

He took the glass and gave her a grateful look. "Thank you. I will remember your kindness."

"What's taking you so long, Hummer?" Pacholuk walked up to the desk and dug his fingers into Hummer's shoulder. "Are you trying to make a date with her?" He threw a look at the female cop. "I'm afraid Mr. Hummer won't be able to make it. Other obligations, you know." He laughed and pulled at Hummer's shoulder. "Let's go. You have a date with Congressman Gibson. He is anxiously waiting for you. He doesn't like to wait."

"He can go fuck himself," Hummer cursed. "And you, too."

"Now, now. Is that any way to talk to an old friend?"

"We aren't friends, Pacholuk."

The agent grinned and pulled Hummer away from the desk. Leaning closer, he said, "We've been watching you for quite some time. It seems I've known you for ages and I feel close to you. We'll even be closer after I fuck your redheaded girlfriend. She's a slut, just like her sister Rose, you know. You may be interested, I used to fuck Rose until she became a liability and I had to get rid of her. I'll bet Helen is as hot as her sister. You should know. I saw the tape."

"You're a filthy bastard," Hummer cursed under his breath. "If I'll get the chance I'll kill you."

"I believe you but forget about that notion. You'll be dead before that could happen."

They pushed him out of the door toward their car. Hummer knew he couldn't let them put him into the car, but there was no way he could prevent it. His hands were still manacled, and he wasn't in any shape to fight three highly trained agents. They'd probably shoot him down like a rabid beast.

"Into the back," Pacholuk ordered and put his hand on Hummer's head. The pill he took seemed to be doing its job, but the hunger pains were beginning to chew on his stomach linings. The sandwich he ate had not been enough to satisfy his appetite.

Hummer slid into the backseat with a feeling of déjà vu, except the last time he had been blindfolded. The fact they didn't do it this time was not a good sign. They didn't worry about him being able to identify them or the place they'd be taking him.

"I hope you had a good rest, because you'll need it. We have a long day and night ahead of us," Pacholuk said from the front seat, speaking in a jovial tone. "You shouldn't have killed Spence. He was a good man."

"He was an asshole just like you," Hummer said. "I have him and Kramer to thank for the condition I'm in. I wish I could have done Kramer also."

"You don't seem to have a problem killing people."

"Not when they deserve to die," Hummer said harshly.

"Maxwell told me about you. He said they called you The Hammer. Why?"

"Just a nickname. It meant nothing."

The hell it didn't.

Bitter and unpleasant memories stirred deep inside him and tried to poke their ugly heads through the barrier it took him years to build, wriggling and hissing angrily like a thousand poisonous vipers disturbed in their pit.

"Maxwell said he knew you from before."

"So he said. I didn't know him. Besides, the man he knew is dead."

"I couldn't help but overhear your friendly conversation with Congressman Gibson. He must really hate you for what you and your unit did so many years ago. Strange, I've never heard of you."

"We didn't advertise our presence. Much like you and the White Ops."

Pacholuk chuckled softly. "Seems to me no secret is safe these days. What do you know about the White Ops?"

"Enough to know you are not working for the good of the country the way my old unit did. We were patriots, you are traitors."

"It's all relative, depending who you work for."

"Who do you work for?"

"I work for the Order of Capricorn, the new world government. I work for men who have a vision, men who want to bring order to the world under one rule. Their ultimate goal is for the common good of the people. If sacrifices have to be made to bring about this new order, we are prepared to make those sacrifices."

Hummer laughed angrily. "In the meantime millions of people will suffer and many will die to achieve the goal of a few power-hungry, ruthless madmen who are under the delusion they are gods. I will do my best to stop this mad scheme."

"Brave words from a man who is in no position to make such promises. If anyone is mad, it is you, Hummer." Pacholuk shook his head and settled back into his seat.

Hummer had been looking out of the window during their conversation. The traffic was heavy, unlike during the night. There had

241

not been many cars around at four o'clock. He didn't know if this was the same route the taxi had been traveling.

"I need to get gas," the driver said suddenly.

"Now?" Pacholuk seemed annoyed.

"Yes, now! Unless you want to walk the rest of the way."

"All right, get gas."

The driver pulled into a gas station and stopped at one of the many pumps. Hummer saw it was a self-serve and it wouldn't take long to fill up and pay. He checked out the gas station and took notice of the large restaurant. A plan began to form in his head. This might be his chance to escape.

"I need to go to the washroom," he announced.

"I don't think so," Pacholuk said.

"You want me to crap all over the backseat?" Hummer threatened.

"Don't you dare!"

"Well, then let me go."

Pacholuk sighed. "This seems to be one of those days again. Swenson, Margolis, you two go with him."

"How about taking off these cuffs?" Hummer held up his hands. "I can't very well wipe my butt this way. And I wouldn't mind washing my face a bit."

"Okay." Pacholuk searched in his pocket and came out with a key. He handed it to Margolis. "Take his cuffs off just before he goes into the shitter and watch him. Shoot him in the foot if he tries to run or acts suspicious."

"Sure. No problem."

Margolis was a big man, even bigger than Hummer. Swenson was of average built but with a neck like a wrestler. Both agents walked behind Hummer into the restaurant.

"You should be able to handle him by yourself," Swenson said to Margolis. "I'll get myself a coffee and a donut."

"Sure, go ahead. Bring me a fritter and a coffee, okay?"

"No problem."

Margolis and Hummer headed for the washroom. As they entered, a couple of teenagers were standing by the urinals. "Beat it!" Margolis told them.

"What?" One of the youths threw him a look of disbelieve.

"I said get out of here."

"I'm not finished. Who the fuck are you anyway?"

Margolis flashed a badge. "Police business. Zip up and get out! Now!"

"I want to wash my hands," the youth protested.

"Out or I'll arrest you for interference."

"Interference of what?" The young man stood with a defiant expression on his face and stance. "I haven't done anything."

"Come, let's go," his friend said, his voice urgent and shaky.

"Fuck him," the young man said. "This is America, a free country. I'll take a piss whenever I want to. No cop tells me otherwise." He showed Margolis his middle finger and said, "I'm going to wash my hands now."

Hummer had to admit the kid had balls defying a big man like Margolis in a washroom. Not a good idea.

Margolis growled and grabbed the youth by the scruff of his neck and hauled him toward the door. Ripping the door open, he practically threw him into the corridor. Glaring at the other kid, Margolis asked, "You need help getting out of here?"

The youth held up both hands. "No, sir. I'm leaving."

When Margolis closed the door, Hummer saw his chance. Slamming into him from behind with all the strength he could muster, he brought up his hands and banged the big man's head against the door. Margolis slumped to the floor, knocked out cold.

Working feverishly, Hummer searched the agent's pockets for the key, found it and unlocked the cuffs. Then he took the big man's gun and shoved it into his empty holster. Finally, he dragged Margolis across the floor into one of the stalls. Wrapping the agent's arms around the back of the toilet, Hummer put the cuffs around his wrists. Then he threw the key into one of the other toilets and flushed it down.

Let them have fun getting this asshole free.

He took the time to relieve himself and wash his hands and face. Looking into the mirror, he wasn't happy with what he saw. "You look like crap," he told his image, grimacing at the way his split lips moved. He ran his hand across his hair, grateful for his crew-haircut but still wishing he had his baseball cap. He felt naked without it. Straightening his tie, he walked to the door.

Time to leave.

Luck was with him. There was nobody outside. Swenson, the other agent, was still standing in line for his coffee and donut. His back was turned toward Hummer, which was another stroke of luck.

On the way in, Hummer had noticed a side door. Keeping his head down, he walked briskly toward it, and moments later he was outside. Joining the group of people who waited for the traffic light to change, he crossed to the other side of the intersecting street and then followed the side street to the next crossing, where he turned right to trace his way back.

When he saw a young woman coming out of a store and heading for her parked car, he stopped and said, "Excuse me for bothering you, ma'am. I wonder if you can give me a ride to the field office of the FBI."

She gave him a startled look. "Can't you take a taxi?"

"I could but I can't wait for one to appear. This is a matter of urgency. One might even say life and death." He took out his wallet and removed a bill. "I'll pay you a hundred bucks if you take me." He held out the money.

She hesitated, looking him up and down. "I'm not sure if I can trust you. You could use a shave and you look kind of...beaten up."

He let out a harsh chuckle. "That's an understatement. I feel the way I look and I need to get away from here as quickly as I can."

"If you were in some kind of accident or fight, there is a police station not far from here."

"No police. I have to talk to an FBI agent. They are the only ones I can trust."

Her eyes widened a little. "I saw your gun when you got your wallet. Are you an agent under cover?"

He smiled and nodded. "Deep under cover. Do you see my problem now?"

"Okay, get in." She grabbed the money and stuffed it into one of her jean pockets. Then she pressed the remote for her car. Hummer heard the click as the lock opened and grabbed for the handle. Opening the door, he slid into the passenger's seat, taking a deep and grateful breath and settling back.

The young woman took her seat behind the steering wheel. Before she started the car, she looked at him. "I have no idea where the FBI office is."

"Do you have a cell phone?"

"Yes."

"Then call information. They'll give you the address. I notice you have a GPS. Just put in the address and it will lead you there." Hummer forced himself to keep his eyes open. The exertion of overcoming Margolis and his fast walk were taking their toll. His headache had come back and his muscles screamed for more painkillers. To make matters even more uncomfortable he felt somewhat lightheaded from the lack of food and the hot interior of the car.

"By the way, my name is Frank Hummer," he said. "Remember that, in case I pass out."

"Please, don't do that, Mr. Hummer. I wouldn't know what to do. How could I explain your presence to the police?" She looked suddenly afraid.

With an assuring smile, he said, "Don't worry. I'll hold on. Call me Frank. What's your name?"

"I'm Crystal."

"Okay, Crystal. Let's call information to get the address. Ask for the field office of the FBI."

She pulled out her cell phone and entered the number for information. "I'm looking for the address of the nearest FBI office," she said after a moment of waiting. "My location? I'm on..."

Hummer closed his eyes, his mind drifting.

Everything will be all right now. I'm safe. All I need is a good night's sleep.

He was startled into wakefulness when someone touched his arm. "Yes...?"

"I'm ready to go. I've got the address," a woman's voice said. His eyes focused on the face looking at him, momentarily confused. When he saw the green eyes he thought it was Helen but then realized where he was. "Crystal," he said. "You look so much like a woman I know, except she has red hair."

"Your wife?"

"No." He shook his head. "Just someone I very much care for. I have to find her and make sure she is safe."

"Then we'd better get going. I already entered the location of the FBI office into my GPS."

"Then go."

"You scared me for a moment. You looked dead." She eased her car into the street. Traffic was light until they came to the next intersection. She followed the prompts of the GPS and turned into another street. Suddenly the traffic was dense and they moved slowly ahead.

The air in the car was cooler now and Hummer didn't feel like he'd lose consciousness at any moment. His headache was only a dull humming, but his belly still complained. He wished for a thick steak and a cold beer.

"I guess you were lucky it was me who parked there," Crystal said. "Not every woman would have given you a ride. People are suspicious and wary of strangers."

"And with good reason," Hummer agreed. "There is no shortage of people out there who want to do harm to others." He thought of the Order of Capricorn, of Charles Gibson and his fraternity brothers, who had no scruples letting millions of people perish to satisfy their hunger for power and money.

He turned his head to look at Crystal. She was quite pretty; blonde, like Cheryl, but her face and green eyes reminded him of Helen. "You are right, it was lucky for me, but consider this your lucky day also."

"Why?" She gave him a questioning look.

"I'd like to repay you for your help."

"You gave me a hundred dollars."

"I know, but consider it only a down payment. Are you married?"

"No."

"A boyfriend?"

"Yes. Actually he's my fiancé."

"So you're planning to get married?"

"Next year, hopefully." She gave a little chuckle. "Weddings are expensive. Neither mine or John's parents are wealthy."

"What would you say if I pay for your wedding?"

246

She almost slammed on the brakes. "Please, don't try to make a fool out of me."

"I'm serious. Consider it my wedding gift. One stipulation though."

"I knew there was a catch."

"No catch, Crystal. I want you to invite me and my...my woman to your wedding." It wasn't Cheryl he was thinking of.

"If this is no joke then today was truly the luckiest day of my life."

"No Joke." Hummer had a smug smile on his face.

"Why would you do that? I mean, I'm only giving you a ride to the FBI office."

"Yes, you are. When I told you I couldn't wait for a taxi it was only part of the truth. Taxis can be traced and intercepted. It was safer to have a private person drive me. You may have saved my life. That makes me your friend forever, and I am generous with my friends."

"Are you so rich you can afford to be this generous?"

"I have been fortunate to accumulate considerable wealth, even though there are richer men out there, much richer men than me, who have told me I am nothing but a pauper." His thoughts drifted to Congressman Gibson, who was probably fuming by now, unless Pacholuk hadn't given him the good news yet. Pacholuk may still have the notion he might be able to recapture him.

"Okay, so you're rich. Most rich people don't throw their money around. They are usually tighter with their money than poor people. I still don't understand why you are so generous."

He thought about his answer for a moment. It was not something easily put into words. Sometimes he himself couldn't understand why exactly he had this urge to help people in distress and to be overly generous with his money.

"I guess it is just something I have to do. It helps me come to grips with my past. I had to do things I'm not proud of. At the time I thought it was my duty. I was doing it for the greater good of my country, and I thought it would make the world a better place to live in. Since then I've come to realize whatever I thought I accomplished really means little in the scheme of things. The so-called do-gooders in this world probably would condemn me, and most of the others don't give a damn." His words came out more harshly than intended.

Crystal threw him a curious glance. "You sound bitter."

He laughed, winced when sudden sharp pain in his chest reminded him of the abuse he had suffered by the hands of a couple of overzealous rogue agents. One of them had paid for it with his life, and Hummer didn't have any feelings of remorse. Maybe he hadn't shed his old skin completely. There was much hatred and anger still left inside him. How easily one could slip back into old habits and feelings!

"Maybe I'm bitter," he said. "But mostly disappointed with my fellow humans, disappointed, and in a way, sad."

"Why sad?"

"Sad because people are so easily influenced by politicians who lie through their teeth to get their vote, therefore gaining power over them. Sad because whatever I do doesn't make a hell of a difference."

She shook her head, obviously trying to make some sense of what he was saying. "You must have led an interesting life," she said. "You sound like an intriguing man. Perhaps we can get to know each other better some day. You may find a fan in my fiancé. He loves mysteries. You know, conspiracy theories, suppressed inventions and information, secret world governments, old religions, aliens from outer space, and stuff like that."

"I'm looking forward to meeting your fiancé." He shifted in his seat to find a more comfortable position, trying to relieve the pain in his buttocks and back. His throat was dry and the effort of talking made his jaws hurt. He wished for a drink. Looking at the GPS, he saw that they were close to their destination.

Crystal noticed his interest. "We'll be there in a few minutes. Too bad it took so long but traffic is extremely heavy today."

"Monday is the Fourth of July. I guess people are preparing for the celebration." He gazed out of the window and realized they had arrived.

Crystal drove into the small parking lot and was lucky to find an empty spot. When she was parked, she turned to Hummer. "I guess this is where we part company."

"I want you to come in with me," he said.

"It may not be such a good idea." She gave a little laugh. "I have nothing to hide but I don't feel like being in a FBI file."

"They probably have one already. There is no more privacy in this world, not in our country anyway. Do you have an e-mail account? A blog? Are you on Facebook, Twitter, or any other social media?"

"Yes to all of them."

"Then you can be sure you're in somebody's files. I want you to give them information how I can contact you. It will be safer than if I have it on me." He reached out and touched her hand. "Thank you again. You are a special person and I won't forget what you did for me. So, come on." He opened the car door and got out, feeling stiff and in pain.

She got out on her side and, seeing him limp toward the entrance of the building, put her arm around his waist and helped him. "You are in bad shape, Frank," she said. "Maybe you should go to a hospital."

"I might do that after I make my report," he said, grateful for her assistance.

The agent at the desk was on the phone when they entered the front office. Hummer made it with Crystal's help to reach the desk, but then he leaned heavily against it; his legs felt rubbery and weak. The agent finally got off the phone and gave Hummer a questioning look.

"My name is Frank Hummer," he said, "I'd like to talk with the Special Agent in charge."

"He's busy at the moment. Perhaps I can help you?" The agent's dark eyes studied Hummer with open interest. "It seems you've had some kind of mishap. If you want to report an accident you're in the wrong place. You should go to the police."

"What I have to report is for the ears of the Special Agent in charge alone. I don't trust anyone else with it." Hummer spoke calmly, even though he felt like grabbing the agent by his neatly pressed collar and shaking him.

The agent's gaze fixed on Crystal. "Are you this man's wife?"

"No. I gave him a ride to your office, that's all. Whatever he's involved in I had no part of it, but..." she paused. "He asked for my help to bring him here, because what he has to report is a matter of life and death. That's what he told me. By the way, you may notice he needs medical treatment. He seems badly injured."

"Then you should have taken him to a hospital."

Crystal gave the agent a sweet smile. "I would have had he asked me. But even though he is in rough shape, he still insisted I drive him to the office of the FBI. That's how important his information is. So why don't you get your superior on the phone and tell him about Mr. Hummer and his wish to speak to him. If you don't I will open the door and scream, making a big scene. Maybe that will bring him out here to see what's going on."

Hummer had to smile despite his discomfort. This was some feisty young woman he managed to find. She'd make a good sergeant in the army. And a pretty one at that.

Even the agent cracked a tight smile. "If you put it like that I guess I'd better call Agent Simcoe. He is the Special Agent in charge. By the way, he is not my superior." He pushed a button. A voice answered with "Yes?"

"A Mr. Hummer insists he see you. Apparently, it is important."

"Frank Hummer?"

"That's what he said his name was."

"Send him in. I've been expecting him."

"Okay." He nodded to Hummer. "You heard. It seems you've been expected. Go through that door. Walk down the corridor. His office is at the end. You can't miss it. He's got his name on the door. Curtis Simcoe."

Hummer turned to Crystal. "Please, give the agent the information I asked you to. I'll get in touch with you as soon as this blows over. I promise. I'll see you at your wedding."

She put her arms around his neck and kissed him on the cheek. "Good luck, Frank Hummer. I hope things work out for you."

"Thank you." He pushed himself away from the desk and walked heavily toward the indicated door, hoping Agent Simcoe would be able to help him.

Chapter Nineteen

Special Agent Curtis Simcoe turned out to be a short, wiry man with a dark, square mustache under a nose that was a touch too big. He came around his desk when Hummer walked in and held out his hand. "I am pleased to meet the famous Frank Hummer. I spoke to Agent Mason less than ten minutes ago. He told me a little bit about you. I'm glad to see you alive and well."

"Alive yes, but well? I'm afraid not so well." Hummer managed a grin. "I've had a meeting with some people who didn't have my best interest at heart."

"So I've heard." The little man stared at Hummer. "You do look a little pale, unless that is your normal skin color. Come, have a seat and take a load off." He chuckled jovially. "You're a big man. And your knees are probably screaming for you to sit down. I hate craning my neck just to look into your eyes."

Hummer followed his invitation and took the offered chair. "You wouldn't by any chance have something to eat and drink, would you? My knees aren't the only parts of my body screaming right now. My stomach is not used to being neglected."

"The only thing I can offer you is a glass of water, but we can go across the street later. There is a nice diner there with decent food. But first, tell me about what happened to you." Simcoe walked back to his seat behind the desk and sat down, looking expectantly at Hummer.

"What exactly did Rick Mason tell you?" Hummer learned a long time ago never to expect people to know what you're talking about and never give more information than necessary, especially when representatives of the government were involved. Hummer was not a federal agent anymore. He was a civilian and therefore more restricted than certain government employees. He didn't know Agent Simcoe. His jovial act could be just that, an act.

"Well, he told me you used to be a federal agent. He and you were members of an elite unit and you were quite a legend in your time. In fact, he said you two are good friends and he'd accompany you into hell, if necessary. He told me to make sure you were safe and lend you any assistance you may require. He also mentioned Senator Simmerman. That info is good enough for me. You should know Rick Mason and I went to the same Academy?"

"You were a cop?"

"That's right. A member of New York's Finest. Walked the beat for five years. Made detective. Then the FBI made me an offer." He motioned with his hand. "And here I am now after all these years."

"Did he tell you anything about the special unit he made reference to?"

Simcoe's jovial expression was suddenly sober. "He told me it was in my best interest not to know too much or ask questions. I've been an agent for a long time and I have learned not to stick my nose too deep into other agents' affairs." He chuckled and touched his nose with one finger. "Even though mine is large enough to attract attention, and sometimes I do stick it into matters that don't concern me, against my better judgment. It comes with the territory."

Hummer smiled politely. "I appreciate your candor, Agent Simcoe. Did Mason tell you that I'm a private investigator now?"

Simcoe nodded.

"Good. Well, I've stumbled upon a case that became more and more bizarre…"

* * * *

Agent Simcoe stared at Hummer for a long time before he said, "It seems to me you are in deep shit, Mr. Hummer."

"That's putting it mildly." Hummer grimaced. "I'm up against powerful people. I have no doubt my name is already on the watch list at the airport. By the time I get there, the CIA probably will have agents waiting for me at every terminal. I'm stuck here in New York. If I get captured again I'm a dead man for sure. Congressman Gibson won't give me any more chances to escape again."

"I know about Congressman Gibson and his hardliner attitude. He is quite popular in certain circles. Some people are even afraid of him."

"And with good reason. When you listen to him talking about certain men shaping the events in this world you'd like to believe they are the ravings of a madman, but unfortunately, he is telling the truth. The Order of Capricorn exists. There are indeed powerful and ruthless men in control of our government. They are manipulating the markets, igniting wars among nations, and creating unrest in the world to satisfy their cravings for wealth and power. When I was a federal agent, I was involved in trying to thwart some of their plans. We managed on occasion but most of the time not. How can you fight men who have the power and the money to buy Politicians, Senators, Congressmen, and even Presidents? They have no respect for the law. In fact, they create laws to suit their purpose. They control the big banks, the credit, the interest rates, in other words the money. They manipulate the flow and price of oil and gasoline. In a sense they own the country and do pretty much what they want. There is nobody who will bring them to justice. If you get in their way, they will ruin you."

Hummer stopped talking and studied Simcoe with a critical eye. "You become paranoid and wonder if you can trust your neighbor who you have known for most of your life, or your superior. You even look at your best friend with suspicion. How do I know you're not on their payroll?"

Simcoe pulled his lips into a grim smile. "You don't know, but be assured I'm not. Until now I've never even heard of the Order of Capricorn. Oh sure, I've read and heard plenty about conspiracy theories, but you have to admit most of them are pure fantasy of very paranoid people or published by speculators and sensationalists."

Hummer sighed. "I wish this one were one of those. Then I could fly home and carry on with my business. As it is, I'm not even sure if I still have a bank account when I get home. Somebody may have frozen all of my assets."

"Are they really that powerful?"

"I rule out nothing. Maybe I'm starting to get fixated with his whole thing. Gibson told me to watch out for the next market crash which is supposed to happen soon. If they can cause the collapse of world markets, what else are they capable of doing?"

"If they indeed create a crash wouldn't they also stand to lose their fortunes?"

Hummer laughed. "Only for a short time. While everyone else panics and sells at a loss, they are buying up stocks, mutual funds, and other investment vehicles at bottom prices. They will be the ones emerging even richer and more powerful than before."

"It doesn't seem fair. What if investors don't panic at the first sign of trouble and just sit tight. Nothing would happen then."

"That would be great, but investors are jittery these days. They lose their nerve easily and will sell at the smallest hint of a rumor. Gibson and his people take advantage of this uneasiness and non-confidence investors have in the market today." Hummer grinned humorlessly. "I call it the monkey-syndrome. You know, monkey see, monkey do. Somebody sounds the alarms, probably orchestrated by the people in power, and announces he is selling his stocks, and everyone follows the leader, therefore creating exactly what investors constantly fear, the down-spiraling of the stock market. Instead of doing their diligence, investors rely on so-called gurus and investment advisors. I have to admit I have an advisor. I don't have the time and interest to sit in front of my computer day and night watching the markets and looking for deals. Most people are like me."

"But you aren't selling off your stocks at the first indication of trouble?"

"No, I won't. As long as I know the company I've invested in is solid there is no reason for me to sell."

"I assume you are invested in such a company?"

"Yes. Much of my fortune is in GFDI. The company is involved in the research and development of alternative fuels. You may recall I already mentioned Senator Simmerman's son Fred is the major stockholder and CEO of Green Fuels Development. Had Charles Gibson been successful with framing Fred for the murder of Saul Finkbein, the stocks of GFDI would have plummeted, along with Senator Simmerman's chance of ever becoming the President of the United States."

"Senator Simmerman is a friend of yours?" Simcoe asked.

"He was my superior officer in Operation Desert Storm. He persuaded me to join the FBI." Hummer's gaze was watchful when he looked at Simcoe. He decided to give him another fragment of information. "Senator Simmerman was the one I answered to when I was a member of the elite unit."

Simcoe's expression was one of surprise. "I didn't know about Senator Simmerman being a former federal agent." His smile was thin and somewhat apologetic. "After getting Mason's call I went into our databank to check you out and I was a bit surprised to find so little information. Not only because I didn't have much time to search, but because there was nothing there. You telling me about Senator Simmerman being a former federal agent somehow clears things for me. You were in a ghost unit, right?"

Hummer nodded but didn't say anything.

"There was a rumor." Simcoe pursed his lips. "There are always rumors. Some are based on facts some are pure fantasy."

"What about this rumor?" Hummer asked.

"About an agent they called The Hammer. He was ruthless and without mercy, an assassin. In fact, there was a whole group of assassins who operated outside the law, but The Hammer was the most feared." Simcoe's eyes hid his thoughts. "One wonders. Hummer...Hammer. Add the suppressed and lack of information about your years with the FBI. I'm trying to make a connection here as you can see. Am I on the right track?"

Hummer didn't smile. The past just wouldn't leave him alone. There was a reason for the lack of files. There never were any. Even the information that survived should never have been out there. The members of the Third Unit had been specially trained agents, but then their names were removed from the roster of federal agents. They were ghosts. They didn't exist. The only man who knew about them was Benjamin Simmerman. The President knew about the Third Unit but he didn't know the names of the men who belonged to it.

"You said it yourself about not sticking your nose into affairs that are not your business," Hummer said mildly. "Let's keep it that way, Agent Simcoe, okay?"

Simcoe lifted both hands in a defensive gesture. "No problem, but I believe you've answered my question." He leaned forward and said in a conspiratorial tone, "Your problem with Congressman Gibson won't go away unless you take steps to protect yourself. You know what you have to do, don't you?"

Hummer knew what Simcoe suggested but asked anyway. "What would you do in my shoes?"

"I'd eliminate him." Simcoe stared at Hummer with a smug expression. "It's the only solution to your problem, and you know it."

"I know what you're saying, but I can't just go and shoot the man. It would be murder."

"It is either you or him. There is no way out, Frank. You don't mind if I call you Frank?"

Hummer smiled tiredly, suddenly feeling every muscle and bone in his body. "Frank is fine, Agent Simcoe."

"Curtis. Call me Curtis."

"Okay." Hummer closed his eyes for a second. "I think I've exhausted my supply of adrenalin. I wouldn't mind a painkiller and something to eat. How about going to that diner across the street?"

Simcoe rose and looked at his watch. "I didn't realize it's already almost one o'clock. No wonder I'm feeling hungry myself. Let's go then. We'll ask Albert at the front desk to give you a painkiller. He carries a whole drugstore in his wallet. Always gets headaches. There's a water cooler in the front office."

* * * *

After consuming a steak and a beer Hummer felt much better. The painkiller had done its job and his body didn't ache as much anymore.

When they were back in Simcoe's office, the agent said, "Like you said before, you'll probably never get on a plane. They'll intercept you for sure, but there is a way out. You'll go in disguise. I can supply you with false papers and a great disguise. Nobody will recognize you, not even your own mother." He chuckled gleefully. Getting up, he walked to a safe in the corner, opened it and pulled out a number of large envelopes. Handing one to Hummer, he said, "Check this out. I think you'll like your new persona. It has never been used yet. Actually most of our supplies here are unused. We've been at this location only for three months now. I used to be at the New York main office at twenty-six Federal Plaza. The office there is on the twenty-third floor. I always hated those elevators."

"Well, I'm glad you were so close. The lady who was kind enough to bring me here may have refused to take me to your other location," Hummer said. He opened the envelope and took out the contents, Social Security card, a driver's license, an automobile insurance card, and a passport. Looking at the picture of a man in the passport, he said, "I don't see much of a resemblance. This man has thick, black hair, a full mustache, and he wears glasses."

"No problem." Simcoe seemed excited. He went over to a tall filing cabinet and took out a plastic bag. Opening it, he shook out something. He unfolded it and held it up. "A latex mask, see. These masks are so life-like, nobody will ever realize you're wearing one. And here are the glasses. They are clear glass. You'll have no trouble seeing." He brought Hummer the mask. "Let's put it on. We'll transform you from Frank Hummer to Mr. John Davenport in a flash. By the way, these papers are real. They will withstand any scrutiny by airport officials and even the police. The address is real. It's a rooming house. Not in the best area of the city, I have to admit, but that's what makes it an ideal address."

After Hummer finished pulling the latex mask over his head, Simcoe held up a mirror so Hummer could look at his image. He had to admit it…suddenly he looked exactly like the man in the picture, especially since the picture was not crystal clear.

"We'll have to do something about your clothes, though," Simcoe said. "Your pants should be all right. The tie and the jacket have to go. They're a dead give-away. You're a big man, but I believe we have a jacket that'll fit you. Give me a moment." He hurried out of the door, humming a little tune. It was obvious he was enjoying himself. It didn't take long until he came back, carrying a blue sport's jacket with a logo on it.

"I want all the stuff back again. We may need it for someone else."

Hummer slipped into the jacket, moved his arms and shoulders. "A little tight," he said, "but it'll do. By the way, what is my occupation?"

"You're a freelance photographer."

"I assume you have a camera for me?"

"You don't need a camera. You're going on vacation to Kansas City, away from your job for a couple of weeks."

"Speaking of my hometown. I wouldn't mind leaving as soon as possible."

"Perhaps you should rest before you leave," Simcoe suggested. "You look tired and not well."

"I'm fine. I can rest much better in my own home."

Simcoe shrugged. "Albert and I will accompany you to the airport and make sure you get safely on your plane."

"I'd appreciate that."

"Let me make a call to see when the next flight leaves for Kansas City."

It took less than five minutes to get the information. Checking his watch, Simcoe said, "The next plane leaves in three hours. We should leave immediately if you want to catch that one."

"I'm ready. The sooner the better." Deep down Hummer knew it would have been smarter to go see a doctor and have himself checked out and then spend a day resting, but he also knew the CIA might have already alerted all the hospitals to watch out for an injured man of his description. Once sitting on the plane, he could relax and rest a bit.

They were sitting in an unmarked car fifteen minutes later on their way to the airport. Even though traffic was heavy, they made good time. Simcoe walked beside Hummer as they headed for the ticket counter, while Albert walked a few steps behind them, alert for any possible danger.

The clerk at the counter barely looked at the false papers Hummer presented. She handed him his ticket with the words, "Have a nice flight, Mr. Davenport. You'd better hurry, they are boarding right now."

Hummer clasped the little agent's hand. "Thanks for everything, Curtis. Maybe someday you'll come to Kansas City and visit me so I can pay you back for your help."

Simcoe dismissed it with a careless wave of his hand. "You'd do the same for me. It was a pleasure. Now you take care of your injuries and think about what I said about that other matter. Sooner or later you will have to deal with it."

Hummer nodded grimly. "One step at a time. I will do what is necessary."

Simcoe smiled. "I know you will. Good luck."

Hummer walked through the scanner and headed for the gate indicated on his ticket. Minutes later he sat in his seat on the plane to Kansas City. Taking a deep breath of relief, he put on his seatbelt and closed his eyes.

Good bye, New York. You were not kind to me.

* * * *

After the plane landed, Hummer went to retrieve his gun and keys from the locker. Then he boarded a taxi and gave the driver a bogus address. Old habits seemed to take over and he wasn't quite sure if he liked it, but he had never gone wrong following his instincts. To be careless was to be a fool, and right now was not the time to be a fool.

The cabbie dropped him off at the given address. Hummer walked a block. When he found a coffee shop he went inside. Nobody saw him go into the bathroom. It was empty which was also lucky. He took off his mask, folded it into a little bundle and put the mask and glasses into his pocket. Simcoe wanted them back; otherwise he would have discarded them. Feeling hungry and thirsty, he sat down at a table and ordered a hamburger and a drink, enjoying both immensely. He knew he wasn't out of the woods yet. Congressman Gibson would not rest until Hummer was dead. He'd send his goons after him to finish the job. Gibson knew where he lived, but it was a two-way street.

Hummer knew where Congressman Gibson lived.

After eating, he went across the street into a gun shop to buy ammunition for his gun. It was always good to be prepared. On impulse, he bought a second gun and stuffed it into his belt.

He flagged down a taxicab and gave the driver his home address, but when they were close to his house, he told the cabbie to let him out. "I'd like to stretch my legs a bit," he said. "A short walk will do me a world of good."

Walking slowly, he was alert to everything around him, feeling like a hunter one minute and like prey the next.

He felt quite drained and couldn't wait to fall into his own bed. Should his enemies decide to strike now he wasn't sure if his reflexes would be fast enough to defend himself. Neither would he have the strength to ward off a physical attack.

He made it to his front door without an incident. The door was locked and he used his key to open it. Glancing at the alarm panel, he noticed that the alarm had not been set. He didn't know if that was a good sign or not. Drawing his gun, he walked slowly into his living room and looked around. Then he walked up the stairs, gun still in hand. The door to his bedroom was closed. He opened it with trepidation, but there was nobody there.

Chiding himself for being so paranoid, he let out a small chuckle.

Damn, my nerves are as taut as a hunter's bow. I need to relax before they snap.

He took off his newly acquired jacket and hung it in the closet. He was just about to take off his pants to take a long overdue shower, when he heard noises from downstairs. Grabbing his gun again, he tiptoed out of his bedroom and down the short hallway toward the stairs.

Somebody was downstairs in the dining room. He could hear the sound of shoes walking on hardwood floor.

Taking the safety off his gun, he eased down the stairs, stopping and listening at every step. When he reached the bottom stair, he walked on soft soles toward the dining room.

Stepping around the corner, he aimed his gun at the intruder.

Chapter Twenty

"Frank!" Helen almost screamed it. Then she was in his arms and covered his face with kisses. "I thought you were dead," she sobbed and held him tight. Then she looked into his face. "You look awful. What did they do to you?"

He laughed and planted a kiss on her lips. "They gave me a bit of a work-over, but I'm fine now. I was worried about you since I didn't have any idea where you might go or what they might do to you."

"I didn't want to go back home and I didn't know where else to go but here." She smiled under tears. "Your housekeeper wanted to call the police, but when I begged her to listen to what I had to tell her, she didn't call them and even let me stay here. She almost forgave me for tying her up. Almost." Her green eyes studied his face. "How did you get away?"

"With luck, but we're not out of danger. They'll be coming for us, of that I'm certain. We should be fine for a day or so."

"Who are these people who want you so badly?"

"Actually it is only one man who is after me. The man who hired Pacholuk. The same man who hired you and who orchestrated the whole thing. His name is Charles Gibson."

Her eyes went round. "Are you talking about Cheryl's father?" she gasped.

"That's right. He made it quite clear he wants me dead."

"Because you are dating his daughter? Isn't that a bit drastic?"

"It seems it plays a small part in his reason for wanting to get rid of me." Hummer smiled. "I guess he wants to eliminate the possibility of me ever becoming his son-in-law. He has other, much larger reasons, but I don't want to discuss them right now. I need a shower badly and then a good night's rest."

"Have you eaten? I was just about to make myself a sandwich."

"I had a burger half an hour ago and a big steak for lunch. You go and make your sandwich while I take a shower." He pulled her close and held her for a moment. "I'm just so relieved to see you here. You did the right thing seeking refuge in my house."

"I wasn't sure if it was the right thing to do, since I caused you so much grief. I feel responsible for what happened to you. I wouldn't even blame you if you didn't trust me. Possibly even believe I may have lured you to my place so you could get captured." Her eyes seemed to plead with him. "I have nothing to do with that. You must believe me."

"You're correct. I shouldn't trust you, but something Pacholuk said convinced me you're in grave danger. I will do my best to protect you."

He climbed back up the stairs, feeling so much better already. Maybe things would turn out okay. Discarding his clothes, he climbed into the shower stall and let the warm water soothe his battered body.

When he was finished, he took a painkiller. Standing in front of the mirror, he studied his reflection and grimaced when he saw the black and blue marks all over his body. Touching his ribs, they felt tender. He didn't think any of them were broken, only extremely bruised.

After he dried his body, he went into his bedroom and found Helen pulling back the bedcovers.

"I thought you were eating a sandwich."

"You need my help more that I need a sandwich," she replied. She fluffed up his pillow and straightened the covers. Then she came close to him and stroked his chest with soft hands. "Those are ugly bruises. Do you have some ointment I could put on them?"

"I'm sure there is something in the medicine cabinet."

She went into the bathroom and came back a couple of minutes later, carrying a tube. "Lie down on the bed."

He stretched out on his belly and closed his eyes. The ointment felt cool when she squeezed it out of the tube, but her hands were warm and soft. She worked his aching muscles with gentle, but still forceful movements, starting with his neck and shoulders and all the way down to his calves.

"It seems your buttocks and lower back have taken the brunt of the beating you received. They look swollen and are turning all kinds of colors."

"They did try their best to ruin my kidneys and my ass," he joked.

"Your ass still looks nice," she said, kneading his buttocks.

"That feels so good," he moaned. "Where did you learn to do that?"

"I worked as a masseuse in my summer holidays at a friend's beauty salon when I was a teenager to make some extra money. When you're good at something, you never forget it."

"You're good at many things it seems," he murmured.

She laughed softly and gave him a gentle slap on one buttock. "Turn around so I can work your front, but don't get any ideas. You are in no shape to do anything but sleep after this. And sleep you will, I promise you that."

He turned around to lie on his back. "I'm sure I will. I took a couple of painkillers before, but I might be able to postpone sleep."

"Never mind. Just lie still and let me do my job. There is plenty of time for what you have in mind tomorrow, or maybe the next day. We'll see how you feel in the morning."

"Hmm, that's nice," he murmured, concentrating on her hands as they traveled across his aching body.

When he opened his eyes, it was dark in the room. He found himself lying on his bed, covered up with a blanket. Turning to find a comfortable position, his hand touched a soft body lying beside him. "Helen?" he asked, but she didn't answer. He could hear her gentle snoring and pulled his hand away.

Smiling, he closed his eyes again, happy and content for the moment.

* * * *

"You're a miracle worker," he told Helen at breakfast. "I feel hundred percent better today."

"Just don't get too confident. The way your back looked last night, you might hurt yourself if you abuse it too soon. Those muscles and tendons have been pounded hard and need to heal, so give them time."

She reached across the table. "I'm just so happy to see you alive, Frank. You said you worried about me? Just think how I worried, because I saw them take you away and I know what they did to my brother and sister. I never expected to see you alive again, but I still had hope. Miracles sometimes happen."

"The danger is not yet over," he cautioned her. "You told me not to get overconfident. Well, let's not forget that. We are not safe until I take care of some unfinished business."

"What unfinished business?"

"It is best you don't know, Helen. There are things about my past, the man I used to be, you must never find out. Unfortunately, my past is catching up with me. Certain people are carrying a grudge and seeking revenge. I will fight back and take measures to eliminate the threat."

Her expression showed sudden fear when she looked at him. "You're scaring me, Frank."

"Don't be scared. I told you last night I will protect you."

"I'm not afraid of the people who will come looking for us. I'm afraid of the man I just saw behind your eyes when you spoke. I saw coldness and cruelty."

He didn't speak for a moment. "Was it that obvious?" he asked after awhile.

"I don't think I ever want to meet that man," Helen said, shivering. "I feel sorry for the men who will."

Before he could reply, the phone rang. He rose and picked it up. "Yes?"

"Frank, what is going on? I've tried your cell a few times, but you never answered. Where were you?"

"Hi Cheryl." He smiled into the phone. "I was kind of tied up. What's happening?"

"What's happening? Are you kidding me? My father called me this morning asking me for your whereabouts. He said to let him know the moment I hear from you. What does he want?" Cheryl sounded upset and annoyed. "I told him I'm not your babysitter."

"I guess your father is concerned about my wellbeing. Call him and tell him I'm home and feeling fine. Also tell him I'm looking forward to his next move."

"What does that mean? I don't understand any of this."

"Just tell him. He'll know what it means."

"I want to come and see you. Something is wrong. I can feel it."

"It is best if we don't see each other for awhile, Cheryl. I need to straighten out a few things and I don't want to endanger you."

"What are you involved in, Frank? Does it have something to do with that redheaded woman? I had a bad feeling about her all along. Don't shut me out, Frank. If we are going to be married, you can't keep secrets from me."

"I'll tell you everything in good time." He hesitated. "If you talk with your father, he may show you something. It will be...uh...self-explanatory. You may want to ask him how he got that information, though."

"What information are you talking about?"

"It has to do with the case I'm involved in. If he doesn't say anything then don't ask him, okay? It is of no relevance at the moment. More important issues need resolving right now. Listen, I have to go. Talk to you soon." He disconnected the phone before she could comment and put it back into its cradle.

Perhaps it would be best if Gibson showed her the recording of him with Helen. It would save him from explaining why he was going to break up with her. He glanced at Helen who had followed his conversation with Cheryl.

"Your girlfriend, huh?"

"Yep."

"Will you still date her after all this?"

He shook his head. "How can I date a woman whose father wants me dead?" he asked grimly. Moving behind her chair, he put his hand on her shoulder and bent down to kiss her neck. "Besides, things have changed. I've fallen in love with you."

Her hand reached up to touch his. "I love you, too, Frank," she whispered. "It's happening so fast, but I know I've never loved anyone like this. That's why I'm so scared things may turn out badly for both of us. My life has always been full of turmoil and unhappiness. I deserve to be happy."

She lifted her face and looked up at him. "Will I ever be, Frank?"

"We both deserve some happiness. I've suppressed my feelings for too long, always trying to be this tough, emotionless guy. The cold, unshakable Frank Hummer. You've changed me, Helen. You brought back my humanity and I want this. Neither one of us is perfect, but we can be happy together. We just have to make it happen." He kissed her open lips. She responded by kissing him fiercely. When they broke apart, he smiled down at her. "How can I not be happy with a passionate woman like you?"

She nodded bravely and smiled back. "I wish you and I could be happy together." She sighed. "We're forgetting one thing—I am a married woman. I've been cheating on my husband."

"You two have been separated for a year. You told me yourself your marriage was practically arranged and you never loved your husband. I don't call that cheating." He tried to justify having sex with a married woman, but he knew, even though she and Harry Middler hadn't been living together, she was still legally married to him, and therefore anything she did with another man would be considered cheating on her husband.

He looked out of the window. The sun was already high and there were no clouds in the sky. It would be another scorcher of a day. He wondered what had happened to Professor Middler. Helen got up from her chair and began putting away the dishes. He watched her putting them into the dishwasher. Even though he truly loved her, his thoughts were still filled with doubts. Did she love him, or was he just a tool she was using? Was the passion she displayed toward him only an act or was it real? After all, she was an actress, and a very good one.

"Do you have any idea where the Russians took your husband?" he asked.

She gave him a surprised look. "Does it matter?"

"It might. Is he still alive?"

"I'm sure he is. They wanted his inventions and his talent. They wouldn't kill him. I'll bet he's probably on his way to Russia by now. If not, he'll be held in the Russian Embassy. Nobody will find him there."

She came to stand beside him. "It's a beautiful day. I don't want to spoil it by talking about a man I never loved. Let's not worry about him." Her fingers dug into his arm. "You are the man I worry about—the man I want to be with from now on. I'll divorce my husband. It can be done without his presence, right?"

"I'm not a lawyer, but I'm sure it's possible. When this is over I'll talk to a lawyer-friend of mine." He put his arm around her shoulder and pulled her to him. "Let's not think about that right now. There will be enough time for it later." He let go of her. "I have to call my office and tell them I'm okay and at home. They need to be warned about a possible threat to their lives. By the way, has Sarah been here since you arrived?"

"No, she hasn't. She told me I'll have to look after myself."

"All right. I guess I'd better let her know I'm back." He picked up his phone again and dialed Sarah's number. She answered on the second ring.

"Hi, Sarah. This is Frank Hummer."

"Mr. Hummer. Oh, I'm so happy to hear your voice. Are you okay?"

"I'm fine and back home. I'd like you to come over. We have something to talk about."

"About the woman in your house?"

Hummer chuckled. Sarah's voice had taken on a defensive tone. "No. It's not about her. I suppose your children are back from camp?"

"Yes, they are in school right now. What about them?"

"We'll discuss everything when you come over. Are you free now?"

"Yes."

"Okay, come then."

While he waited for Sarah, he called his office. When Nicole heard his voice, she let out a little sob. "Is it really you, Mr. Hummer?"

"Yes, in the flesh, so-to-speak."

"I can see from my display you're calling from your house. When did you come home?"

"Last night, but I was in no shape to call anyone."

"Why? Are you injured or anything?" She sounded concerned.

"Nothing serious that won't heal in a few days. Is everyone in the office right now?"

"Yes."

"Call them all to the front office and put me on the speaker, okay? I need to talk with all of you."

"Why don't you come to the office? Are you really okay?" she asked with even more concern.

"Things are moving fast. There is no time to lose. Call them, Nicole!"

"All right."

He could hear the doors opening and voices over the speakerphone.

"Hey, Mr. Hummer. This is Marconi. I hear you're back. Agent Mason called us yesterday and said you were in New York and you were injured. Beaten up or something. He didn't know any details. What the hell did you do in New York?"

"I wasn't there on business that's for sure," Hummer said.

"That woman Helen Middler called us Wednesday. She was hysterical and told us you'd been kidnapped by the CIA. In Dallas. She said she was staying at your house. Why were you in Dallas?" It was Silvo who asked the question.

"I went to visit Mrs. Middler to get some answers. It's a long story and I'll tell you all about it. For now, I want you to be on guard. Don't go anywhere unarmed. I'm going to talk to Detective Schumann and request police protection for Tony and Nicole."

"Give me a gun, Mr. Hummer, and I'll protect myself and Nicole," Tony said fiercely.

"No way," Nicole protested. "You'll kill yourself and me. You don't know how to handle a gun."

Hummer laughed softly. "I'll talk to Schumann."

"Is that Middler woman in your house?" Nicole asked.

"Yes. She is here."

"You tell her she's lucky nothing happened to my car. By the way, I still have your Porsche, Mr. Hummer. I guess you want it back now?"

"I wouldn't mind, but there is no hurry. There are more important things on my mind right now than my Porsche."

"I managed to find some information on White Ops and this Evan Pacholuk, Mr. Hummer," Tony said.

"That's great, but it doesn't make much difference now."

"Are you still coming in today?" Silvo asked.

"I don't think so. I want to pay Detective Schumann a visit. I need to speak with him personally."

Hummer turned around when he heard the door. It was Sarah. Her face showed fear and anticipation.

"I'll have to go now," he told his staff. "You stay vigilant. I don't want anything happening to any of you."

He put the phone down and smiled. "Don't look so worried, Sarah. I'm fine and everything will be all right."

She ran toward him and threw her arms around him. "I was so scared. When Mrs. Middler told me about you being kidnapped I expected the worst." When she looked up at him, tears rolled down her cheeks like tiny diamonds on a dark satin cloth.

He stroked her back. "I'm here now and nothing serious happened to me. Nothing that won't heal in a couple of weeks."

She let go of him and wiped her cheeks with her fingers. "Sorry for my show of misplaced affection, but I just couldn't help myself. I'm so happy to see you alive and well."

"No need to apologize. I'm touched by your concern. I need to tell you this. It is important. There have been some developments that put everyone I know in danger, including you. I want you and your children to go to a friend's place for a few days until it is safe to come back here."

"It sounds serious." Her dark eyes showed her sudden anxiety. "When do you want me to go?"

"Call the school and tell the principal not to send your children home today. Tell him you will pick them up from school, okay?"

She nodded. "Should I pack some stuff to take along?"

"Only what you need for a week or so. This matter should be resolved by that time." Even though he felt anxious on the surface, deep inside him something cold and oddly familiar had taken hold of him. He knew what it meant and he was afraid of the final outcome. Had all these last years been for nothing? Had the man he came to loathe been waiting patiently for this occasion to be brought back to life?

"I'll go and start packing," Sarah said. Then she left.

Before he picked up the phone again, he said to Helen, "Remind me to get another cell phone."

Detective Schumann happened to be in his office. "I don't have much time, Frank. I'm busy with a case."

"I won't keep you long, Martin. Just wanted to let you know I'm back from New York."

"New York? I didn't even know you were gone. What did you do in New York?"

Telling somebody about an unpleasant event never had the same impact when told over the phone, but Hummer didn't want Schumann hearing it from somebody else. "I was taken there by my new friends from the CIA. One of them was Evan Pacholuk. The same man who murdered Henry Miller and Saul Finkbein. I don't think I have to tell you I didn't accompany them without some encouragement from a gun."

"When did this happen?" Schumann sounded professional but Hummer could tell by the tension in his voice he was a bit unnerved by the news.

"It happened Wednesday morning. I was in Dallas at the time"

"You sure do get around these days, Frank. What is in Dallas?"

"Mrs. Helen Middler."

"You're confusing me. I thought she was with you here in Kansas City?"

Hummer had to chuckle. Schumann would be even more confused after hearing what Hummer had to tell him next. "She was but she went back to Dallas after her husband was abducted by the Russians."

There was short pause. Hummer knew Schumann was trying to digest this bit of news. "When did the Russians enter this picture? I thought the FBI took Professor Middler?"

"They were not FBI. The man who identified himself as FBI agent Keller is in reality Viktor Lebedev, a Russian national, and probably a spy. He is with the Russian Embassy and therefore untouchable."

"Son-of-a-bitch! What the hell did you stumble into, Frank?"

"A deep quagmire of shit, Martin. There is much more I have to tell you, but it would take too long and not something I want to discuss on the phone. Are you free tomorrow?"

"Yes."

"Then how about coming with me to play a game of golf at a private golf course?"

"Whose private golf course?"

"Congressman Charles Gibson's."

"Did he invite you?"

"No. I'm inviting myself."

"I'm not sure, Frank. We can't just go and crash somebody's private course."

"Sure we can. Congressman Gibson and I have a special connection. We're practically family. I'll tell you all about it tomorrow. And make sure you bring your gun. I hear it's a dangerous course."

"I always carry my gun, but that doesn't mean I want to use it constantly."

"You won't have to. It's only a precaution, like an insurance policy. You'll understand tomorrow. I'll pick you up at your place around eight-thirty. See you then, Martin."

After he hung up, his gaze met Helen's. She had been listening to his conversation with apparent great interest and, so it seemed, with increasing agitation.

"You are going to meet with Charles Gibson? Have you lost your mind?"

He gave her a grim smile. "Sometimes the safest place is in the lion's den. He won't try anything on his own property, especially not in the presence of a policeman."

"I don't trust him, Frank." She came up to him and put her arms around his neck. "He is a ruthless man. You got away from him once. He won't let it happen again."

Stroking her cheek, he looked into her green eyes. "You're so beautiful and sexy when you worry," he said, smiling. "I love you and it seems the more I look at you the deeper I fall in love with you."

She leaned into him and caressed his back with gentle hands. "I love you, too, Frank. Don't let anything happen to you. Promise me, you'll be careful."

"I will be. I am Frank Hummer, the Invincible, didn't you know?" He pushed out his chest. She let go of him and laughed at his antics.

"Nobody is invincible, Frank," she said with a somber expression. "Not even you."

"I have to make another call, Helen. If you will excuse me." He dialed Fred Simmerman's number, hoping he'd be in his office.

Simmerman was surprised to hear from Hummer. "Frank, what is happening? After you called me last Friday I've been expecting the cops to break down my door and arrest me. Was that some kind of prank you've played on me?"

"I wish it were, Fred. I don't want to sound too optimistic, but I believe this last week's developments have removed the suspicion of murder from you. Are you up to playing a round of golf with me and Schumann tomorrow morning?"

"I could make the time. Haven't seen you for months, and I don't remember when I played with Schumann last. What's the occasion?"

"I want you to meet someone. Somebody special."

"Sounds mysterious. Who is this mystery man?"

"Congressman Charles Gibson."

"Charles Gibson? I've seen him on TV a few times. He's got radical views. Apparently he hates my father with a passion."

"He hates anything not connected with oil and making money."

"Then he'll hate me. I'm not into oil. I develop alternative fuels. Why do you want me to meet him?"

"Actually, I want him to meet you. I want him to see his nemesis."

Simmerman laughed. "That's what I am? His nemesis?"

"You certainly are. You're one of the people who will eventually put him and his oil out of business."

"Okay, I'll buy that."

"Good. We'll take my car. I'll pick you up at around nine o'clock."

His next call was to Agent Rick Mason. "Hi, Rick. I'm coming to your office to talk to you."

Chapter Twenty-One

After looking Hummer over with a critical eye, Agent Mason acted surprised to see him up and about. "You look like someone who took a ride down Niagara Falls in a drum. You should be resting in bed."

Hummer answered him with a grim smile. "I should, but I doubt I'll get much chance to rest for the next few days. Evan Pacholuk won't let me."

"He's the bastard who worked you over?"

"He only kicked me a few times." Hummer pointed at his face. "He did this. His friends did the rest."

"Agent Simcoe from the New York field office called me after you boarded the plane and gave me the rundown. He said you didn't look good but refused to stay to heal up. I guess he told you he and I go way back."

"He said you were in the police academy together."

"Yes, we were. He's a good man, and quite capable, despite his small size. Many have been fooled by his appearance and sometimes jovial manners." Mason let his gaze roam over Hummer's frame. "Take a seat, Frank, and tell me everything that happened to you since you left my office on Tuesday."

And Hummer did.

* * * *

Mason sat in deep thought after Hummer finished talking, like a man who had been told something he could not believe and needed to come to grips with. His fingers formed a steeple on his desktop. "So what is your next move?" he finally asked.

"My next move?" Hummer knew what his next move would be, but he wasn't going to tell anyone. It was clear in his mind what he had to do. Agent Simcoe had known it too. He also knew he couldn't expect any help from the FBI or any other law enforcement agency. He wasn't even thinking about the CIA. The Order of Capricorn had agents everywhere. Who could he trust?

"I know you, Frank. You won't let this rest and you won't wait for them to make a move. Whatever you're planning, remember you're not a lawman anymore, and you don't have your elite team at your disposal. There is nobody who will protect you and back you up."

Hummer grunted loudly and laughed an ugly, hollow sound. "Like old times, isn't it?"

"We were never really alone. We always had Simmerman and even the President who would take full responsibility for what we had to do. You don't have anyone, so don't go out and do something you will regret," Mason warned.

"I will defend myself should I be attacked. I will strike back if anyone who is even only remotely connected to me is hurt. Aren't I allowed to do that?"

"Of course you can, just make sure the law is always on your side."

"How about Congressman Gibson? Is there any way he can be investigated? You must have files on him. I'm sure if your man Schroeder starts digging he'll discover some dirt on Gibson."

Mason laughed, obviously finding what Hummer said amusing. "Congressman Gibson is one of the richest men in the world. You do not investigate a man like him without dire consequences. I know much about him. His wife is the chairwoman of the Capricorn Society. Everyone knows that society. They do a lot of good."

"Sure they do. The Capricorn Society is just a front for The Order of Capricorn. Nobody would even dare question a wonderful society like that," Hummer said. "It's the old deception game. Like a magic trick. While your eyes are watching one hand, the other one steals your wallet."

Mason sighed and rubbed his chin. "You don't have to explain anything to me, Frank. We've heard about the Order of Capricorn, but members are tightlipped, and so are their death squads. They don't advertise their membership in this exclusive club."

"Well, I know at least one name now," Hummer growled.

"How do you prove it? If you'd go with your story to the media, nobody would print it or even mention it on the news. Hell, Gibson owns the media. Who would you rather believe? The word of a PI. or the word of a well-known member of the government, who also happens to be one of the richest men in America?"

"I'm well aware of that. Even though everyone knows his extreme views, he has a large following. He cannot be touched by anything or anyone, but that doesn't make him invincible," Hummer said between clenched teeth.

"You should talk to Senator Simmerman. He's the only one who could launch a secret investigation without raising any alarms," Mason mused. "Now that we have one name, it might lead to others. Some of Gibson's super-wealthy friends are probably members as well."

"It's possible. You know about predators and how they blend into their environment; they will even masquerade as their prey. Nobody suspects them until they strike. By then it is usually too late." Hummer rose from his chair and stretched his arms and legs to get out the cramps. He grimaced. "I think it's time again for another painkiller."

"Have you seen a doctor?" Mason asked, concern on his face.

"No time for that." He reached across the table to shake Mason's hand.

Before he shook the offered hand, Mason gave Hummer a piece of paper. "Here is my private cell number. You can reach me anytime."

Hummer took the note and shoved it into his pocket. "Thanks for listening, Rick. I wanted to thank you also for contacting the field offices in New York and letting them know about me. You may just have saved my life." He grinned. "It's not the first time."

"No, it isn't, old friend, but I can never repay you for what you did for me." Mason rolled his chair around the desk. "Come by the house some day, Frank. Maybe we can talk about the old days."

Hummer nodded and walked out of the door.

The old days!

He was trying to forget about those days, but it seemed the ghosts of the past never rested, never slept, never died. They insisted to be kept alive and make his life miserable. It didn't matter how hard he tried, he would never be able to get rid of the memories that belonged to another man. This man would insist to be a part of him as long as he lived.

He stopped on the way home to buy another cell phone to replace the one they took away from him. He also got a new number and had the old one deactivated. They probably had destroyed his phone, but he wasn't taking any chances.

When he drove up his driveway, he was happy to be home and looked forward to a restful evening with Helen.

He unlocked his door, satisfied Helen had been sensible enough to lock it.

When he saw Sarah sitting on a chair in the living room, he wondered why she hadn't left yet to pick up her children.

Then he saw the tape covering her mouth and the fine wire tying her to the chair. He also saw the two probes connected to either side of her temples.

By instinct his hand went to draw his gun, but he knew rushing in to see if she was injured somehow may turn out to be a fatal mistake.

For her and for him.

He didn't see Helen and a terrible sense of foreboding made him feel almost ill. He took a step forward but stopped when Sarah struggled violently in her bonds, her eyes wild and the fear in her face enough to convince him the danger was imminent and great.

There was something about the probes on her temples. When he looked closer, he saw the box beside the chair. An extension cord connected it to an outlet nearby, and he knew what it was.

A device that would send a strong electric current through Sarah's head should the switch be triggered, and he had a suspicion he knew how. It didn't take him long to spy the two lasers on either side of the front entrance. Had he taken two more steps, he would have broken the circuit and sent ten thousand volts through the probes and fried Sarah's brain inside her skull.

He didn't see anyone else in the room.

"Where is Helen?" he mouthed.

Sarah shook her head. Her eyes moved sideways and looked toward the hallway. The guestroom was in that direction, but he couldn't see the door from his position.

"Anyone else in here?" He wanted to shout it but moved only his lips.

She nodded.

"How many?"

She moved one finger.

"Just one man?"

She nodded again.

All right. He was up against one man and it didn't take a genius to figure out who that man would be. The realization Helen was in the guestroom with Pacholuk made him furious. He remembered Pacholuk's promise.

We'll even be closer after I fuck your redheaded girlfriend.

Sick with frustration and enraged, his mind raced to find a solution to the problem. There wasn't any way to get to the guestroom. The window to that room was barred from the outside to prevent intruders from entering, as were most of the windows on the ground floor.

Before he could make a decision, he heard the sound of an opening door and the sobbing of a woman. Then Pacholuk came into view. He had his arm around Helen's naked waist and a gun to her head. The look of sheer terror in Helen's face made Hummer want to put a bullet between Pacholuk's eyes, but he knew Helen would be dead before he could even bring up his gun.

"Well, looks who's here. My old wayward friend Frank Hummer." Pacholuk grinned hugely. "I just fucked your girlfriend, but she was a bit of a disappointment. She didn't come up to my expectations. Her sister Rose was much hotter and so much more satisfying. Too bad I had to snuff her."

Helen cried out and struggled in his grip, but he pushed the gun harder against her temple and hissed, "Behave you stupid slut or I'll end your life right now!"

She stopped struggling. Her eyes stared at Hummer in despair and horror. He had never before felt so helpless, and at the same time full of hatred for anyone the way he felt toward Pacholuk at the moment.

"I see you discovered my little contraption," Pacholuk said. "I'm quite proud of it. I was hoping you'd stumble into the room, electrocute that black bitch, set off the little bomb I attached to the underside of her chair, perhaps injuring yourself in the process, but even there I was disappointed."

"What do you want, Pacholuk?" Hummer asked between clenched teeth, trying to stay calm.

Pacholuk's laugh was the sick sound of a man who enjoyed seeing people suffer and in pain. "What do I want? Frank, Frank. Do you really need to ask?"

"Tell me anyway." Hummer was stalling, hoping to come up with an idea.

"I came to kill you. My employer cannot afford to have you walking around alive."

"Your employer?"

"You know him well, Frank. Don't play dumb. Congressman Gibson, of course."

"If I give myself up, will you let them live?"

Pacholuk moved his hand up to fondle Helen's breast. "It all depends how these two bitches behave. After I kill you I'll fuck her again and then I'll fuck that black cunt. Maybe she'll be a bit livelier than this redheaded bitch. If I'm satisfied I may just let them live."

Hummer didn't believe him, but he was trying to distract Pacholuk, hoping he may give him an opportunity to kill him before anything happened to Helen or Sarah.

"How about putting down your gun," Pacholuk said. "It makes me nervous seeing it in your hand."

Hummer bent and put the gun carefully on the floor.

"Kick it over here," Pacholuk ordered.

Hummer gave it a kick and sent it gliding across the carpet toward Pacholuk.

"Good boy." Pacholuk grinned. "I didn't think you'd go down this easily. Another disappointment. This is becoming boring. No action at all. I was made to believe you were this hot-shot, cold-blooded killer who didn't really care about anyone. As long as the job got done. Your job was to kill me, but you missed your chance. What's going to prevent me now from shooting these two bitches and then you?"

"I was hoping you were a man of your word," Hummer said, in full knowledge of what he said was a lie. Pacholuk was a psychopath and would kill them all. It was only a matter of when. He played with his victims like a cat plays with a mouse or bird it caught, deriving pleasure, not from the killing but from the suffering of the prey.

"You shouldn't have done that, Frank," Helen said with a weak and trembling voice. "He would have killed me anyway, but you could have saved yourself and Sarah."

"Shut up, bitch!" Pacholuk cursed and pushed the gun into one of her breasts.

Helen cried out sharply from the pain and kicked backward, hitting his knee with her heel.

Pacholuk let out a grunt and let go of her. His free hand touched his knee and rubbed it. "That was a big mistake," he growled. He lifted his gun and aimed it at her belly.

Helen screamed and attacked him, her fingers going for his face. Lashing out with his foot, he kicked her in the stomach. She went flying backward and ended up on her back.

Seeing his chance, Hummer went for the gun he had hidden behind his back, but he was not fast enough. He watched in horror as Pacholuk almost casually aimed his gun and pulled the trigger. The terrible sound of the explosion was nearly drowned out by Hummer's howling of pain and shock when he saw the spray of crimson from Helen's exploding head. Her body kicked once and lay still, her white skin covered with red blotches; the carpet under her ruined head soaked up the blood jetting from the horrendous wound.

A terrible cold descended over Hummer's mind, freezing his emotions and feelings into a block of ice, cutting off any rational thought. His body went into overdrive, reacting automatically without any conscious thought. While Pacholuk moved his gun to point it in Hummer's direction, Hummer fell to one knee, his gun up. He heard the sound of it going off, registered the firing of Pacholuk's weapon.

Pacholuk stood motionless, an expression of surprise on his face. His left hand went up to his throat in an effort to stop the spurting red fountain. Then he folded; his body lay on the floor like a heap of dirty laundry waiting to be cleaned up.

The gun dropped from Hummer's hand, clattered to the tiled floor. He stayed in the kneeling position, hanging his head. He didn't want to look at the lifeless body of Helen. His mind was numb, his own body cold and without any feeling. He stayed like that for a long time, oblivious of his surroundings.

He was not aware of the changes happening in his mind.

The man he had hidden inside him for so many years, rose into his conscious being and made him stand up to survey the scene in front of him with a critical, emotionless eye.

Evan Pacholuk was dead, but he didn't feel any satisfaction. When he looked at Helen lying in her own blood, he suppressed any feelings of sadness and pity for himself. There would be enough time for that later when the arctic cold that had settled over his brain began to melt.

His gaze fell on Sarah, who sat in her chair, an expression of horror seemingly frozen on her features.

"Hold on, Sarah," he told her. His voice sounded hollow and foreign in his ears, the voice of a stranger but still so familiar. An old friend from long ago. "I'll get you out, but I can't do it alone. I need to call in some experts. Just hang in there a little while longer. Okay?"

She nodded, her face displaying the fear she felt louder than any words.

He took out his new cell-phone, searched for the note Mason gave him and dialed the agent's number.

"Hello, Frank. I didn't expect your call so soon."

"I need a bomb squad and a cleanup team at my home." Hummer said matter-of-factly, his voice emotionless.

"What happened, Frank?"

"Pacholuk was waiting for me in my house. There were casualties. I don't have to tell you to keep this quiet, Rick."

"I understand. I'll look after it."

After Mason hung up, Hummer sat down on the floor and waited.

The team came within the hour. Two cars. Hummer heard them pull up in front of the house, but he didn't get up to let them in.

Six agents came through the door, weapons drawn. When they saw Hummer sitting on the floor, one of them walked up to him and said,

"Are you Frank Hummer?"

Hummer nodded.

"Are you injured, sir?"

Hummer shook his head. "No, I'm fine."

"Can you stand up, please?"

Hummer complied. "You can put your weapons away," he said with a dead voice. "I shot the intruder."

The agent looked first at Sarah in the chair, then at Helen's and Pacholuk's blood-spattered bodies. "Is the male the intruder?"

Hummer nodded again.

"And the woman?"

"She was my houseguest. The intruder shot her before I killed him."

"What about the woman in the chair?"

"Her name is Sarah. She is my housekeeper. The box beside her chair will deliver ten thousand volts through her body if somebody interrupts the circuit. It is controlled by a laser circling her location. In addition, there is a bomb under her chair. I don't know if it is triggered by remote, her weight, or simply when the electric circuit to the box is cut off."

"All right. You seem to be in shock, sir. Please, accompany Agent Smithers outside and let us do our job. We'll get the young lady free, don't worry. You just look after yourself right now."

Hummer followed the agent outside. When he looked toward the two cars, he saw Special Agent Mason sitting in his wheelchair beside one of the cars. Hummer walked slowly in his direction, the turmoil inside his mind gradually settling, but the coldness didn't want to leave him.

Mason's eyes were somber as he watched Hummer coming toward him. "Frank," he said when Hummer stood before him.

"Thanks for coming." Hummer looked down at the agent.

"You all right?" Mason inquired.

"I'm fine." Hummer rubbed his hand over his eyes. "He shot her in cold blood," he said with a low voice. "There was nothing I could do."

"Who did he shoot?"

"Helen Middler. I never told you I loved her, Rick."

"Oh damn, Frank. I am so sorry."

Hummer looked back at the house, a sudden lump forming in his throat, but he suppressed it. He needed to be cold and merciless for what he knew must be done. "Congressman Gibson sent him."

Mason sat silent in his wheelchair. "There is only one way to get your revenge," he finally said.

* * * *

The next morning, he picked up Detective Schumann at eight-thirty, as promised.

"What the hell happened to you?" Schumann scrutinized Hummer with a mixture of pity and disapproval. "You look like you haven't slept for days."

"I guess the ordeal I went through is finally taking its toll," Hummer said, trying to shrug it off. He wanted to tell Schumann about the shooting, but it would have served no purpose. Mason's team had managed to free Sarah unharmed. He had sent her and her children away on a two-week holiday. She'd be accompanied by a female FBI agent to make sure she wasn't alone and to help her deal with what she had witnessed.

"Is the Congressman aware of our visit?" Schumann asked.

"No. I want to surprise him."

Fred Simmerman was already waiting for them. He nodded to Schumann when he slipped into the backseat of Hummer's car. "Nice to see you again, Detective. Any interesting arrests lately?"

Schumann threw a look at Hummer. "I've had some suspects in a case, but somehow that case turned sour for me. Lucky for the suspects." He smiled. "Actually, I'm glad it turned out that way."

Gibson's private golf course was about an hour's drive away. When they drove into the small parking lot and got out of the car, a couple of men wearing the uniform of a private protection agency stopped them. "This golf course is closed to the public," one of the guards said. "So, please leave without a fuss."

"We've been invited," Hummer said, giving the guards a cold grin.

"We know nothing about that," the first guard said. "I asked you politely. Now I'm telling you to beat it." His hand touched the gun on his hip.

Schumann flipped back his coat and showed him the badge clipped to his belt, at the same time exposing his own gun. "This says we're invited. Now you two be a couple of good boys and step aside before I arrest you for threatening an officer of the law with a weapon."

The guard swallowed and spread his arm away from his gun. "I never meant to draw it. Just wanted to intimidate you."

"You never indicated that to me. How was I supposed to know? You're lucky I'm not some gun-crazy cop who feels threatened every time he sees a civilian with a gun."

"I appreciate that, officer." The guard gave a strangled laugh. "I wouldn't want to antagonize a police officer. After all, I might someday be under your command."

"How's that?" Schumann narrowed his eyes and stared at the young man.

"I'm aiming to become a cop, maybe a detective some day," he said eagerly.

"Well, good luck. It's not as glamorous as it looks on TV and not as well paying as the private police force either."

"We'll be going in there now," Hummer interrupted the two. "I'd be grateful if you wouldn't let Congressman Gibson know about our presence. It is supposed to be a surprise." He winked. "By the way, I'm Mr. Gibson's future son-in-law."

Their eyes widened. "Are you dating his daughter Cheryl?" the other guard asked.

"I sure am. We're planning to get married soon."

"You're a lucky dog," the first one said and grinned. "I saw her only a couple of times, but she is quite some dish."

"Yeah, I'm some lucky dog." Hummer looked over at the row of golf carts. "I guess we'll be taking one of those carts."

They loaded up their clubs and took off. When they rounded a small crop of trees and topped a hill, they saw Gibson and a few other men not far away. Hummer changed direction and headed for the group of men.

At first, Hummer thought they might arrive before anyone noticed them, but then he saw three men jump onto all-terrain vehicles and come racing toward them. One blocked their way, while the other two flanked them. All three men carried automatic weapons, which they displayed freely.

"Where the hell do you think you're going?" the one who blocked them yelled.

"We've come to play a round of golf with the Congressman," Hummer yelled back.

"This is a private course. Didn't the guards at the gate tell you that?"

"They did, but we persuaded them to let us in."

The man drove his vehicle closer and waved his machine gun. "Well, this one persuades you to turn around and leave immediately."

"I'm Frank Hummer, the Congressman's future son-in-law," Hummer said calmly. "Your boss wouldn't be very happy if you didn't let me visit my soon-to-be father-in-law."

"I've never heard of you." The security man looked at the other two guards. "Have you?"

"Yeah, I've seen him. He was at the Congressman's last barbeque. I heard them arguing about something."

"That doesn't mean he and those other two clowns are invited. Go and tell Mr. Gibson."

The guard took off, the wheels of his machine spraying grass and dirt.

"Do you mind aiming that gun in another direction before you shoot someone accidentally?" Schumann said.

"If I shoot someone it will not be by accident."

"Let's not make this the first time. I get nervous staring into the muzzle of a gun and when I'm nervous my finger gets itchy, and that's not a good thing. It can turn out badly." Schumann spoke calmly but the threat in his voice was unmistaken. With a casual movement he flipped back his jacket, exposing his gun and badge.

"You're a cop?"

"Detective Schumann, remember that the next time you aim a gun at me. You may not be so lucky. Clowns like you make me sick." Schumann spat onto the ground. "Now, move out of the way so we can proceed!"

The man didn't move, but he lowered his machine gun. "Not until I get the okay sign."

At that moment the man who had gone to announce their presence came racing back. He stopped his vehicle beside the other security man. "The boss says it's okay. Let them through."

"Okay." He turned his machine around and drove off. The other two followed.

Simmerman, who hadn't said a word during the standoff, said, "Gibson seems to be a bit paranoid, having all these armed guards around."

"He has good reasons to be paranoid," Hummer said grimly. "Not everyone loves him." He pushed his foot down on the petal and headed for the small group of men who were watching them come closer.

Gibson didn't smile when he saw Hummer; neither did he show surprise to see him. His face was without expression.

He probably knows his henchman is dead. I feel like putting a bullet into his fucking brain right now.

"Good to see you again, Congressman," Hummer said with a tight smile.

Gibson's eyes were cold when he looked at Hummer. "It seems you've had an unfortunate encounter."

Hummer made a motion of dismissal with his hand. "It's nothing a few days of rest won't fix."

"Is there a reason for your visit?"

"What kind of question is that, Councilman? I came to play a round of golf with my girlfriend's father."

"Funny, when I talked to my daughter last night she was upset about something someone showed her. I think it was a video." Gibson actually chuckled. "Do you have an idea what that was about?"

"Not the faintest. By the way, this is Police Detective Schumann, a good friend of mine. And this is Fred Simmerman. I believe you've heard of him."

"I know of him. He's the CEO of Green Fuels Development, a company that will soon be out of business. I told you before, the future is oil not fuel made from corn or some other vegetable desperately needed to feed the people of our country." Gibson's eyes belied his calm demeanor. They seemed to burn with hatred as he stared at Hummer.

"I put my money in alternative fuels," Hummer said with the same calm voice. "That's where the future lies, and I know I'm going to have a great and prosperous future. How about you, Councilman?"

"My future looks bright. Why do you ask?"

"You told me the other day I'm running with the wrong crowd. I came today to tell you that it is you who is associated with the wrong people. By the way, you haven't introduced us to your companions. Do they belong to the same club as you, Councilman Gibson?"

"That would be none of your business, Hummer," Gibson said coldly. He pointed at the older man who was sporting a trim white beard. Hummer remembered seeing him at the barbeque. "This is Julian Sedanko, a good friend. He is the owner of Sedanko Oils." Gibson allowed himself a small chuckle. "He's almost as rich as I am. Almost."

"I suppose he is one of your brothers?" Hummer made a guess.

"I wouldn't tell you if he were. What exactly is it you want here, Mr. Hummer? As you see, we are trying to play golf."

"We brought our own equipment and we were hoping to be invited to play with you."

It was clear Gibson was not pleased with the situation, but he put on a show of good will in front of his guests. "You're welcome to use the course, but you're on your own. We've already started."

"That's okay. We'll find our way around. Where do we start?"

Gibson gave one of his security men a sign. "Go show them!"

They followed the man to the indicated place and started playing.

"This is a beautifully maintained golf course," Simmerman remarked as he watched Hummer teeing off. "And it's huge. It must have cost a fortune to build."

"I guess with money everything is possible," Schumann growled. "With my lousy government salary I could never afford to play a course like this. So, let's enjoy it."

As they played, Hummer took notice of the way the golf course was laid out, the hills, the ponds, the treed spots, but especially the wide open areas. It took them nearly four hours to complete the course. When they were finished, he had the whole place mapped out inside his head.

"That was great," Schumann remarked as they drove their buggy back to the entrance. "We should do this more often."

* * * *

Hummer didn't drive home. He was staying in a hotel for now, but he was going to rent a small furnished suite in a high-rise apartment building where he would stay until his house was cleaned up and new carpet installed in the living room. He wasn't sure if he ever wanted to move back into that house.

The hotel was clean but not fancy, which suited him just fine. All he needed was a bed and a closet to hang his clothing. There were plenty of restaurants nearby so he wouldn't starve.

When he arrived at the hotel, he called an old friend he knew in the military.

Sergeant Rutherfort. They had done business before.

"Larry. It's Hummer. I need a sniper rifle. What do you have?"

Rutherfort never asked questions that didn't concern him, which was why Hummer dealt with him. "You want a long distance rifle?"

"Yes."

"Then I would suggest the British-made L115A3 Long Range Sniper Rifle. We call it *The Long*. It is accurate for over a mile. They've been using it to take out the Taliban insurgents in Afghanistan quite successfully. When do you need it?"

"As soon as possible."

"I can have it for you tomorrow afternoon."

"Good. Call me when you have it. Here is my new number..."

Chapter Twenty-Two

It was the Fourth of July and one of those perfect beautiful days. The sun had not reached its southerly position yet in the bright blue sky and its reflection could be seen as a silvery streak in the small pond shimmering through the wall of tall trees. A light breeze ruffled the leaves in the tree under which the assassin in the camouflage outfit lay, waiting. He turned his head to look up when he heard the droning of a small plane overhead, but he knew the wide-reaching thick branches of the tree would hide him from being seen by anyone from above.

He had a good view across the length of the golf course from his location. His attention was focused on the hill nearly a mile away. When he saw a man appearing at the top of the hill, he looked through his scope to confirm it was his target, and then he took his time to carefully adjust the scope. Without hurrying, he put the crosshairs on the man's chest, waiting patiently for the perfect moment.

The man stood still for an instant, holding his golf club casually in both hands, getting ready for his next shot, when the assassin squeezed the trigger to deliver the bullet of revenge and death.

As his target fell to the ground, the assassin watched the two security men, who had been sitting on their machines, race toward his position. He had anticipated they may discover his location quickly. They were trained professionals and knew the golf course as well as he did and would know the most likely spot an assassin may choose. He tracked the first one, waited until he was within comfortable distance and shot him in the chest. The machine stopped abruptly as the dead man tumbled from the seat.

The second man swerved and aimed his machine toward a small bluff in an effort to escape the assassin's bullet, but before he reached the safety of the trees, the fatal bullet hit him in the head, killing him instantly.

The assassin lay silent for a minute and looked into the blue sky with a touch of regret. Not for what he had done, but for spoiling a perfect day with an act of vengeance. When he heard the twittering of a songbird in the tree above him, he smiled. It was after all going to be another beautiful day.

He picked up his weapon and rose to trot down the narrow path through the dense thicket toward the river. Jumping into the boat waiting for him in the protection of a clump of tall shrubs, he started the motor and maneuvered the boat out into the river. Before he opened the throttle fully to speed away, he threw the sniper rifle overboard.

He would have no more use for it.

The mighty waters of the Missouri River carried the weapon that had served as an instrument of justice and revenge further downstream, perhaps to be found by someone in the distant future, who may be wondering about the stories it could tell.

They would not be happy stories, only stories about death.

THE END

About the Author

Herbert lives near Winnipeg, Canada. He spends his free time spinning tales about imaginary worlds and the strange creatures inhabiting them. His first published story `The Anniversary Gift' appeared in `Sweet Revenge' published by Midnight Showcase. Even though he writes in other genres, his love is Science Fiction. He enjoys building alien worlds and societies. Most of his stories contain an element of Erotica. All of his books are available from Melange Books.

Website: http://www.hegro.shawwebspace.ca
Blog: http://hegro.blogspot.com
Email: hegro@shaw.ca

Books by Herbert Grosshans
Available from Melange Books, LLC

Science Fiction/Fantasy:
The Xandra, Book One, Daughter of the Dark
The Xandra, Book Two, Mother of Light
The Xandra, Book Three, Goddess of Life
The Xandra, Book Four, Lure of Seduction
The Xandra, Book Five, Escape from Paradise
The Xandra, Book Six, Iceworld
Seeds of Chaos, Book One, Eden's Gate
Seeds of Chaos, Book Two, Hell's Gate
Stardogs, Book One, Return to Redsky
Stardogs, Book Two, Redemption
Orion, Symbiont of Passion
Orolla, Warrior Priestess
Dual Visions (Cliffs of Time and Orion, the Hunt)
Stars in Chains, Book One, Slave
Stars in Chains, Book Two, Liberator
Outpost Epsilon
Lizard World, Book One, Epsilon
Lizard World, Book Two, Epsilon City
Lizard World, Book Three, Raptor's Tooth

Contemporary/Mystery:
Web of Conspiracy, Book One, Death of a Hero
Web of Conspiracy, Book Two, Traitors and Patriots
Web of Conspiracy, Book Three, Tainted Valor
Mark of the Cobra

Anthologies:
Tapestry of Dreams
Time Flares

www.ingramcontent.com/pod-product-compliance
Lightning Source LLC
Chambersburg PA
CBHW031000260626
47169CB00002B/628